Praise for

LAURIE BRETON

"Breton keeps the readers guessing from the first
page to the last...a great read."
—*Romantic Times BOOKclub* on *Final Exit*

"Gritty and realistic, *Mortal Sin* is a
powerfully written story...a truly
exceptional book on many levels."
—*Romantic Times BOOKclub*

"Breton's way with characters—and her
knack for giving her tales a twist—elevates
this story above most."
—*Romantic Times BOOKclub* on *Lethal Lies*

LAURIE BRETON

CRIMINAL INTENT

MIRA®

ISBN 0-7783-2280-7

CRIMINAL INTENT

Copyright © 2006 by Laurie Breton.

All rights reserved. Except for use in any review, the reproduction or
utilization of this work in whole or in part in any form by any electronic,
mechanical or other means, now known or hereafter invented, including
xerography, photocopying and recording, or in any information storage or
retrieval system, is forbidden without the written permission of the publisher,
MIRA Books, 225 Duncan Mill Road, Don Mills, Ontario, Canada M3B 3K9.

All characters in this book have no existence outside the imagination of the
author and have no relation whatsoever to anyone bearing the same name
or names. They are not even distantly inspired by any individual known or
unknown to the author, and all incidents are pure invention.

MIRA and the Star Colophon are trademarks used under license and registered
in Australia, New Zealand, Philippines, United States Patent and Trademark
Office and in other countries.

www.MIRABooks.com

Printed in U.S.A.

For my sister Jean,
for all the support and encouragement
you've given me over the years.
Thanks, Sis!

ACKNOWLEDGMENTS

Thanks, as always, to my agent, Ethan Ellenberg, and my editor, Valerie Gray. Thanks also to all the people at MIRA whose hard work and dedication help make each of my books the best it can be. You guys rock!

A special thank-you to all those English teachers who put up with me over the years while encouraging my love of the written word.

And as always, thanks to Paul for helping me maintain my sanity, for keeping me fed and for taking over birdcage duty during deadline madness. You are extraordinary.

Prologue

*H*urry, *hurry, hurry.*

The Friday-afternoon line of cars moved through the bank's drive-up window at the speed of a sloth. Outside the car, a drenching rain fell, blurring and bloodying the pavement behind a half-dozen sets of brake lights. Her wipers slapped across the windshield in a hypnotic rhythm that matched the thudding of her heart, echoing in her ears like the pounding of some primitive tribal drum.

Don't act nervous. Don't do anything out of the ordinary. It's just another day.

Beyond the sluggish line of cars, a police cruiser circled the parking lot. Her breath caught in her chest as the county cruiser slowed and the deputy inside craned his neck to look more closely at the line of cars. It was raining too hard to see who he was. Wade Pickett, maybe. Or Tommy Lee Gatcomb. Men she'd known all her life. Men she'd gone to grade school with. Was this a routine patrol, or was he following her?

There was no way of knowing who was or wasn't involved, no way of telling how many of Sheriff Luke Brogan's deputies had been poisoned by his particular brand of evil.

The cruiser continued out of the parking lot and onto the highway, and Robin exhaled a ragged breath. This couldn't be happening. This was like the script of a bad TV movie, or one of those suspense novels her mother used to be addicted to. In the real world, people's lives didn't spiral out of control overnight. In the real world, ordinary women like Robin Spinney, high school guidance counselor and soccer mom, weren't marked for murder.

The news had spread like wildfire through the high school after Katey Northrup had been abruptly removed from her French class just before lunch. Deputy Boyd Northrup, Katey's dad, was dead. Shot in the head. And the hideous, shocking word was whispered up and down the school corridors: *suicide…suicide…suicide.*

Gripping the steering wheel as she moved one car length ahead in line, Robin tried to wrap her mind around the concept that Boyd was dead, but the truth was impossible to comprehend. How could he be dead when she'd seen him, talked to him, less than twenty-four hours ago? Boyd Northrup had two kids and a pregnant wife. How was she supposed to explain to Peggy Northrup what had really happened to her husband? *It's all my fault that your unborn baby will never know its father.* How was she supposed to explain to a ten-year-old boy that his daddy really hadn't shoved the muzzle of his service revolver into his mouth and pulled the trigger? *Somebody else did it. The same somebody who killed your Uncle Mac.*

All because of a manila envelope. All because Robin's husband hadn't been able to leave well enough alone. Mac Spinney's obsession had cost him his life. Now, Boyd Northrup had paid the same ultimate price. He was dead because Robin had stumbled across something she was never intended to see, and hadn't been able to keep her mouth shut about it. Boyd, whose heart was bigger than his brain, must have confronted Brogan after she told him what she'd learned. And Brogan had taken care of him. Or, more likely, he'd had somebody else do his dirty work for him. Somebody who'd cleverly managed to make Boyd's death look like suicide. That was more Brogan's style. But she wasn't fooled. Boyd Northrup hadn't killed himself. Not that it really mattered at this point how it had happened. Dead was dead, and in the end, she was as responsible for Boyd's death as if she'd been the one who pulled the trigger.

Overnight, she'd become a liability. Eventually, Brogan would have to eradicate that liability. He'd already killed twice. Three times, if you went all the way back to the beginning, to Timmy Rivers, who'd been left to die on a deserted Mississippi highway. He wouldn't hesitate to kill again. This afternoon, while she counseled delinquent and apathetic teenagers, somebody had carefully and thoroughly searched her house. They hadn't found what they were looking for. She wasn't a fool. As long as she was the only person who knew where the envelope was, Brogan and his henchmen weren't likely to kill her.

But they could harass her. Squeeze her. Force her hand by threatening what she valued most in life—her daughter. If they laid a finger on Sophie, she would kill them barehanded. She couldn't take the chance. No matter how much she wanted to bring Brogan down, her daughter's safety had to come first. There was only one real way to ensure that safety: she and Sophie would have to disappear. Thoroughly, suddenly, and most likely, permanently.

Brogan's day would come. All this time—two goddamn years—she'd believed Mac's death was an accident. His patrol car had gone off the road and into a ravine, where it had rolled three or four times before bursting into flames. The accident investigation had been thorough, or so she'd been led to believe. The cause was eventually listed as driver inattention. That hadn't sounded like Mac, who'd been so meticulous about everything in his life, and she'd told Brogan so. But that particular stretch of highway, Brogan had reminded her, teemed with wildlife. If a deer had run out in front of her husband's car and he swerved to avoid a collision…well, that was all it would take.

She'd believed him. Why shouldn't she? There was no reason to think anybody might have meant Mac harm. Certainly not somebody he'd considered a friend. Luke Brogan might not be the most likable man she'd ever met, but he was a cop, and in her experience, cops told the truth. They were supposed to be the good guys, weren't they?

The silver Camry ahead of her inched forward. She was next in line. Robin took a deep breath to compose herself. This was just a routine transaction. Nothing out of the ordinary, a perfectly legitimate request. If the teller questioned her, she had a story already made up about an elderly aunt in Arkansas with a broken hip. It was what she'd told Marv Sampson, the high school principal, when she requested emergency leave. It amazed her how easily the lying came to her. She'd felt only a twinge of guilt as she spun a tale of her eighty-six-year-old aunt Emily, a spinster who had nobody but Robin to look after her during her convalescence. Marv had bought her lies without question, reassuring her that he could find somebody to fill in while she was gone. If her boss had accepted her story that easily, surely nobody else would question it.

The Camry pulled away from the window, and it was her turn. Robin pulled up in front of the speaker and lowered her window. Kelly Hardison, who'd grown up just down the street from Robin's split-level ranch, beamed from behind shatter-resistant glass. "Hi, Mrs. Spinney," the pretty brunette said. "Some weather we're having."

"If it rains any harder," Robin agreed, sliding her paycheck into the metal drawer, "I may have to start building an ark."

Kelly pulled in the drawer. "Cash your paycheck as usual?"

"Yes." With deliberate casualness, Robin added, "And I'd like to withdraw five thousand dollars from my savings."

"Oh, geez, Mrs. Spinney." Kelly's eyes widened in distress. "I'm sorry, but we have a five-hundred-dollar cash withdrawal limit at the drive-up. It's bank policy. If you want five thousand, you'll have to come inside the bank."

The clock on the wall behind Kelly's head read 4:57. Robin's left index finger, wrapped tightly around the steering wheel, began to twitch. "It's almost five now," she said, "and I'm running late to pick up Sophie. We're going away for a while…a family emergency…my great-aunt Emily broke her hip and I have to take care of her while she recuperates. To top it off, I've misplaced my debit card." Robin rolled her eyes as if unable to believe in her own stupidity. "I'm sure it's in my purse somewhere, but I don't dare to head for Arkansas without a substantial sum of cash. God knows how long we'll be gone, and I don't know if I can access Aunt Emily's bank account for her. I may need to use my own money to keep the household running until she's back on her feet." She hesitated before bestowing Kelly with an ingratiating smile. "I don't suppose you could make an exception for me?"

"I'm really not supposed to." Kelly glanced at the line of cars still waiting behind Robin, looked at her watch, and caved. "I suppose I could bend the rules, just this once. I mean, it's not like I don't know you." Sternly, she added, "But remember, it's a one-time thing. Because you're a regular customer, and I've known you like forever."

"Thanks, Kel. You're a lifesaver."

The girl's worried expression morphed into a wide grin. "Hang on," she said. "It'll take me a minute."

Robin waited an interminable time while rain drummed on the pavement and a plethora of nightmare scenarios raced through her head: Kelly had to get special permission from Hoyt Whitman, the bank president, to disburse that much cash; Hoyt was even now on the phone to the sheriff's office, asking them to send someone over to question why Robin Spinney was withdrawing such a large sum of money; the bank's computer was down, so they couldn't verify the balance in her savings account.

"Mrs. Spinney?"

The tinny voice coming from the speaker startled her. *Oh, God.* They weren't going to give her the money. "What?" she said in a Minnie Mouse squeak.

"You forgot to sign your paycheck."

"Oh." Her body went limp with relief as Kelly pushed the drawer back out. With trembling hand, Robin picked up the cheap ballpoint pen and scribbled her name on the back of the check.

Kelly quickly counted out Robin's biweekly pay. She tucked it into a white bank envelope along with the cash withdrawal and dropped it into the drawer. Sliding the drawer back out, she said, "Here you go. Have a safe trip. And if you haven't found that debit card by Monday, you should call us and have it cancelled."

"I will. Thanks, Kel." Robin took the time to tuck the envelope, thick with crisp, new bills, into her purse before she rolled her window back up and pulled away from the drive-through.

A drop of sweat trickled down her spine. She'd done it. She'd pulled it off. If she was careful, if she was frugal, the money would keep them afloat until she could figure out what to do next. Mac's life insurance had been kind to her. It had paid off the mortgage and the car, and had left her with a healthy nest egg. She had to believe it was his way of taking care of them from beyond the grave. But accessing that nest egg would leave a paper trail, and that was the last thing she wanted to do. Somehow, she would have to come up with another solution.

Oh, Mac. I'm so scared.

But she didn't have time to indulge her fear. It was five o'clock. Rush hour, or as close to rush hour as it ever got in Atchawalla, Mississippi. As she drove across town, Robin kept one eye on the rearview mirror, searching for some sign of Brogan or his men. But she saw nothing. They were probably waiting to catch her off guard. The joke was on them. By the time they came calling, Robin Spinney would be long gone.

At the middle school, Sophie waited at the entryway with a group of her friends. The girls called out farewells as Sophie dashed for the car, head down, leaping over puddles as she ran. She climbed into the car and tossed her backpack on the floor. Shoving a strand of wet hair away from her face, she said, "Is it true? What they're saying about Uncle Boyd? Everybody at school was talking about it. They said he killed himself."

Sophie's blue eyes, so like her father's, bored into Robin's face, and her mother's heart contracted at the vulnerability she saw there. Boyd Northrup, Mac's best friend and fellow deputy, had been a fixture in Sophie's life since birth. Losing him was like losing her father all over again.

"Well?" Sophie demanded when Robin said nothing. "Is it true?"

Robin put the car into gear and pulled away from the school. She wasn't ready to tell her daughter the truth. Not just yet. "I really don't believe he killed himself, sweetheart," she said. "It was probably just a terrible accident."

Sophie's eyes glistened with unshed tears. "That's what I kept telling people. Mom, he was at our house just last night. He was fine then."

"I know, honey."

"I just can't believe it. What will Katey and Matt do? And Aunt Peggy? She's due to have the baby any day. This is so awful."

And it was about to get worse. Poor Sophie. This was so unfair to her, tearing her away from her school, her friends, her home. She'd already been through hell when Mac died. If there was any other way…but there wasn't. If they stayed in Atchawalla, Brogan would find a way to kill them.

Downtown traffic was a nightmare, snarled in every direction. Wondering what the hold up was, Robin peered through the rain. Creeping along with the stop-and-go traffic, she was halfway down Main Street when she saw the blue lights ahead.

Fear sent adrenaline racing through her body. Her throat went dry, and her hands, grasping the wheel so tightly that her knuckles went white, trembled visibly. Brogan was after her. She wasn't going to make it out of town alive. In spite of her careful planning, she and Sophie were going to lose everything after all.

Stop it! she told herself. *You're acting paranoid. If you blow it now, Sophie could end up dead. You both could end up dead.*

She took a deep breath. After Mac died, she'd stopped going to church, but these were dire circumstances, and she needed all the help she could get. So she tacked on a silent prayer: *Please God, take care of us. If not for me, then for Sophie. She had nothing to do with any of this.*

At the intersection of Main Street and Gaskell, a deputy in a yellow slicker had blocked the road with his cruiser and was detouring traffic. Her heart thumping so loudly she feared he would hear it, Robin pulled up to him and rolled down her window. "What's going on?" she asked in a tone that she hoped projected casual curiosity.

The deputy leaned down to speak to her. He was young and clean-cut, blond-haired and blue-eyed—a stranger. "Road's closed ahead, ma'am," he said politely. "There's an accident on West Main Street."

She'd planned to take West Main out of town. Willing her hands to remain steady, Robin said, "Anybody hurt?"

"Nope. But it's one mother of a mess. Poultry truck hit a pickup head-on. Smashed the hell out of the pickup, and the poultry truck flipped over. Chickens running all over the highway. Those that aren't lying dead in the road, that is." His blue eyes warmed with humor. "Got the whole damn sheriff's department out there chasing after 'em in the rain. Me, I pulled traffic duty instead."

Her pulse thrumming rapidly, she offered up a silent thanks to God. With most of Brogan's deputies tied up chasing chickens west of town, she and Sophie might have a shot at heading east without being followed. "Thanks," she said, rolling up her window. With a quick little wave, she took a right turn onto Gaskell and began backtracking.

"Where are we going?" Sophie said.

"For a ride. If you're hungry, I stopped at Piggly Wiggly and picked up a couple of sandwiches. Tuna on whole wheat. Oh, and there's a big dill pickle in there somewhere, too."

Momentarily distracted from her grief, Sophie leaned over the back of the seat and rummaged through the bag. "Did you get me chocolate milk?"

Thank God for fourteen. At that age, food could always be depended on to distract. The fewer questions Sophie asked, the better. At least until they were out of Mississippi and had landed someplace safe. "I did," she said. "Bottom of the bag."

Ahead of her, a blue and red reflecting sign marked the I-20 entrance ramp. Above it, lettered in white on a green background, the names of distant places beckoned her. *Birmingham. Atlanta. Columbia.* Far from here, but were they far enough? Robin clicked her turn signal and slowed for the ramp. On this main thoroughfare that ran from Texas to South Carolina, Friday night traffic was steady. Heart thumping, she paused at the yield sign and watched a Wal-Mart truck zoom by. Behind it she spied an opening. With renewed determination, she accelerated onto the highway and smoothly merged with the flow of traffic headed elsewhere.

One

Six months later
Serenity, Maine

This was just a temporary gig.

Davy Hunter reminded himself of that fact for the umpteenth time as he met the cool blue eyes that gazed back at him from the rearview mirror of the police cruiser. It wasn't as though he'd made a lifetime commitment. This was just two months out of his life. Eight weeks. Sixty days. Not so very different from working as an office temp, the law enforcement world's equivalent of a Kelly Girl. If he got lucky, he'd coast through the entire two months. This was, after all, Serenity. His biggest challenge would be to avoid dying of boredom.

Fumbling for his travel mug, Davy raised it to his mouth and took a slug of black coffee. These early mornings would take some getting used to. He suspected they'd probably also curtail his customary late-night activities. A man approaching forty couldn't afford to burn the candle at both ends, not when he held the kind of responsibility that Ty Savage had just handed over to him.

He studied his mirrored reflection, still amazed by the stranger who looked back at him. He barely recognized himself. His eyes were clear, his hair neatly trimmed, his beard gone. He cleaned up pretty good for a guy who'd spent most of the last fourteen months buried in a bottle. If it hadn't been for Ty Savage, he'd probably still be there.

He'd tried to turn down this job, had tried to argue that his law enforcement days were over, that there were other people better suited to the position, that he preferred to work with wood instead of people. Wood was straightforward. It never lied to you, never played head games with you, never pretended to be anything but what it was. Wood never let you down. You could mold it to suit your own needs, and it wouldn't complain. If it broke, it was no big deal. You could just toss it out and start over again with another piece.

Fat lot of good arguing had done him. Ty had simply bulldozed over his every objection. *If you were good enough for the Feds, you're good enough for Serenity.* Davy'd expected the Board of Selectmen to roll on the floor in hysterical laughter when Ty presented him as his number-one choice for a temporary replacement. But damned if they hadn't been impressed by his credentials. It was amazing, the respect the word *Quantico* seemed to command among those who'd actually heard of the place. The board had approved him by unanimous vote. So here he sat in the parking lot of the police station, contemplating the clean-cut stranger in his mirror, dressed in a starchy blue uniform that scratched in the damnedest places, and scared shitless because he didn't know squat about running a police department.

Interim Police Chief. Cute title. One they'd strip him of quickly enough, once they discovered the unparalleled depths of his incompetence.

There was no sense in putting it off any longer. Feeling like a man about to face a firing squad, Davy drained his coffee mug, opened his door and stepped out of the cruiser. *Two months,* he reminded himself again as he climbed the steps to the police station. Two months, and he could go back to being invisible.

He heard the music the instant he opened the door, Jimmy Buffett and Alan Jackson revving up a live audience with the musical reminder that it was five o'clock somewhere. At a corner desk, Officer Pete Morin was engrossed in conversation, one beefy hand clamping the telephone receiver to his ear, the other hand scribbling furiously as he took notes. Behind the dispatch desk, Dixie Lessard sat filing her nails with an emery board and humming along with Alan and Jimmy. She glanced up, saw him standing there, and her eyes widened at the sight of him in his newly-pressed uniform. "Woohoo," she said. "You're looking good, Hunter."

Dixie was a friend, probably the only friend he'd have here in the hallowed halls of justice. There were people in this town who blamed him for what had happened to Chelsea, but Dixie Lessard wasn't one of them. "That's Interim Chief Hunter to you," he said with mock gruffness.

She grinned. "Hope that doesn't mean I have to kiss your ass every morning, *Interim Chief* Hunter."

He considered her suggestion. "I dunno. Did you kiss Ty's ass every morning?"

She rested her chin on her palm and said wistfully, "If only I'd been asked."

"Uh-uh, Dix. He's a married man these days."

"That doesn't mean I can't enjoy the scenery. Ready for your first scintillating day in law enforcement?"

He managed, just barely, to fend off a yawn. "I showed up, didn't I?"

"And just brimming with enthusiasm, I see."

"What are you talking about? This *is* enthusiasm. Not my fault if you don't recognize it."

Dixie's grin was wry. "Fine, then, have it your way. Make yourself at home. Coffee's in the corner behind my desk. Be forewarned, it'll grow hair on your chest if you don't already have it there. You empty the pot, you're expected to make the next one. Directions are taped to the wall. If you need secretarial assistance, come to me. I'm the department's jack-of-all-trades, so don't be shy about asking. I assume Ty already covered the important stuff in your meeting Friday, so—" She paused and dimpled. "Anything else you need to know?"

"Yeah." He crossed to the coffeepot, lifted the lid of his empty travel mug, and poured himself a refill. "I'd like to know why the hell I agreed to this insanity."

"That, my friend, is a secret known only to you." The phone rang, and Dixie swiveled in her chair and pushed a button, abruptly cutting off the offending object midring. Her voice dripping sweetness, she said, "Serenity Police Department. How may I direct your call?"

Pete was still tied up so, coffee in hand, Davy ambled off to Ty's office—his office, for the time being—and dropped into the chair behind the desk. He'd been in here a number of times, but he'd never really paid attention. It was simply a cop's office, with the standard ugly walls and third-rate equipment. From Alberta to Zimbabwe, police stations all looked pretty much the same.

But now that the office was his, at least temporarily, he took a good look around. Dust motes danced in a ray of sunshine in front of the single tall window. The shelves were loaded with books, all of them somehow relating to the criminal justice field. On the putty-colored wall above the bookcase, Ty's neatly framed college degree shared space with a bulletin board that held an assortment of memos. Everything was obnoxiously tidy. Even the walls, ugly as they were, looked as though they'd been recently painted.

On the corner of the desk sat a framed photo of Faith. Davy

picked it up and studied it. With her wild mop of dark curls and her vivid blue eyes, Ty's wife looked a decade younger than her thirty-seven years. She was laughing into the camera lens, those blue eyes devilish, as though she held a marvelous secret but didn't intend to tell a soul. A vast change from the somber, recently-widowed Faith who'd come here last year after her cousin died. Love appeared to agree with her. Or maybe it was pregnancy that had brought that dewy flush to her cheeks.

Either way, it was none of his business. His jaw clenched, Davy replaced the photo and slid open the desk drawer to inventory its contents. Ty Savage was relentlessly neat. There wasn't an item here that didn't belong. Pens and pencils, paper clips and staples, all arranged with obsessive orderliness.

Davy shoved the drawer closed. What the hell did he think he was doing, coming in here, trying to fill Ty's shoes? Even if he did know most of the town's criminal element on a first-name basis, his years as a federal agent hardly qualified him for this. He might know where all the local bodies were buried—both literally and figuratively—but what he knew about procedure in a small-town cop shop was laughable. Until he conquered that ignorance, he was doomed to stumble like a blind man.

He glared at the red-and-black DARE poster tacked to the wall. He should probably gather his people together, call a staff meeting. Make some kind of bullshit speech about how, in Ty's absence, they had to pull together and work as a team. But bullshit had never been his forte, and he'd never been much of a team player himself. It was probably wiser anyway, for the first few days at least, to tread lightly and observe heavily.

He wasn't a people person. Sure, he understood what made people tick. Understood humanity's baser motives—revenge, greed, the desire for power. Knew them intimately, understood how to work them to his advantage. Manipulation 101. It was one of the primary weapons in a federal agent's arsenal. But the people he'd associated with on a daily basis during the years he worked undercover weren't exactly the type a man was expected to make nice with. Hell, he wasn't sure he was even capable of making nice. How long would it take for the citizens of Serenity to figure it out? How long before they started complaining loudly to the town fathers about the surliness of their interim chief of police?

Back in the days when he wore a tie to work and rode a desk, his fellow agents had razzed him endlessly about his aloofness. He'd just shrugged it off, knowing it was all meant in fun. But during his undercover stint, he'd deliberately emphasized his taciturnity, made it an integral part of the persona he displayed to the world. Davy Hunter, silent and dangerous, a man who hung out with thieves and junkies and wouldn't hesitate to slit a man's throat if the guy was stupid enough to cross him.

He'd somehow managed to pull it off. Even people who'd known him all his life had bought his act. It was so over-the-top it was laughable. Sure, he was tough. You didn't get to be a federal agent without a solid core of toughness in there somewhere. But the image he'd portrayed had been little more than an exercise in thespian skill. Now that he'd left the DEA behind, he was finding the adjustment difficult. How was he supposed to make a smooth transition from rugged Neanderthal to a man who related to the world in a normal fashion?

The intercom on his desk buzzed. He stared at it for a moment, then fumbled with the button to answer it. "Yeah, Dix?"

"Got a call for you. I could've given it to Pete, but I thought maybe you'd want to get your feet wet right away."

He felt a little stir of adrenaline, the first he'd felt in a while.

Maybe playing rent-a-cop wouldn't be as painful as he'd anticipated. "What you got?"

"Shoplifter down at Grondin's Superette. He's giving them a hard time."

A shoplifter. Hell, it didn't get much more exciting than that. "Got it," he said. "Hey, is Pete still tied up?"

"Negative."

"Ask him if he wants to tag along."

Gilles Letourneau was royally pissed.

The wiry little drywall contractor charged toward him like a rampaging bull the instant Davy walked through the door of the office where Letourneau was being held. "Finally!" the contractor said. "Somebody who'll listen to my side of the story!"

Davy exchanged glances with Buzz Lathrop, the nineteen-year-old assistant store manager. The kid's relief at seeing two members of Serenity's finest walk through his door was palpable. Lathrop gulped and rolled his eyes in a gesture of helplessness and exasperation.

"I saw that!" Letourneau snapped. "Smart-ass young punk!"

"Mr. Letourneau," the kid said, not quite able to contain the quiver in his voice, "you have no reason to be calling me names. I'm just doing my job."

"Oh? So now it's your job to intimidate customers, eh? I'd like to see where that's written in your job description. I'll have you know, I'm calling my cousin Richard. He's a lawyer, and I'm gonna sue your scrawny ass off!"

From where Davy was standing, the only one who seemed to be doing any intimidating was Letourneau. The kid, who'd been a mere grocery clerk six months ago, was shaking in his shoes.

Davy braced his feet stiffly apart. "Gentlemen," he said, "I'm sure we can discuss this like civilized human beings."

"Yeah, right," Letourneau said. "What the hell are you doing here? Where the hell is Ty Savage? He'll put an end to this right now."

"He's taken a leave of absence, so you're stuck with me. I'd like to hear from each of you, one at a time, what happened here. Mr. Lathrop?"

The kid swallowed, his Adam's apple bobbing up and down. "This morning, Mr. Letourneau was observed removing a copy of the *River City Gazette* from the stand near the front door and exiting the store without paying for it. He was apprehended—" Lathrop paused to clear his throat "—he was apprehended in the vestibule by the front end manager and one of the baggers."

"Right there in front of everybody I know, these bastards strip me of my dignity. Right in the frigging vestibule!"

"Mr. Letourneau," Davy said, "you'll get your turn."

"This is ridiculous! It's a frigging newspaper, for Christ's sake!"

"Gilles." Davy fixed him with a hard, cool stare. "Shut up."

The little man abruptly clamped his mouth shut. "Thank you," Davy said, and turned back to Lathrop. "He was observed by whom?"

"By Natalie Fortin," Lathrop said. "One of our cashiers."

"And how much was this newspaper worth?"

It was a question to which they all knew the answer. Lathrop colored slightly. "Fifty cents. I know it's not much money, but the thing is—" He glanced at Letourneau and threw back his shoulders. "It's not the first time. He does it every morning."

Davy turned to look at Letourneau, who glared at him with bold defiance. Raising his eyebrows, he said, "That true, Gilles?"

"You know what?" Letourneau said. "Me and my family, we been shopping in this store for twenty years. Twenty years!

My four brothers and my sister. My cousin Richard and his wife. Me and Yvette. Between us, we got seventeen kids. That's a whole lotta milk, a whole lotta diapers. A whole lotta macaroni and cheese. You do the math. We could shop at Food City, you know? Or we could drive to Rumford and shop at the Hannaford store there. The prices are lower. But we'd rather shop here. My father went to school with Emile Grondin, and we've always taken care of each other. I scratch your back, you scratch mine, you know? We need groceries, we come to Grondin's. Emile needs a room redone, he calls me. Makes for better community relations, keeps everybody happy, and keeps the money where it belongs, right here in this town where my family's lived for three generations. Thousands of dollars I spend in this store every year. And this is how I'm repaid!" His righteous indignation was a sight to behold, his face so red he looked in danger of having a stroke. "I'm treated like a common criminal in front of half the town!"

His patriotic little speech might have been stirring, except that he still hadn't answered the question. Davy stifled the urge to sigh. Beside him, Officer Pete Morin stood, a hulking, silent presence. Probably enjoying the hell out of the show. Pete hadn't bothered to hide the fact that he wasn't thrilled about having to spend the next two months answering to Davy Hunter.

"Mr. Lathrop?" Davy said.

"Yes?"

"You say Mr. Letourneau does this every day?"

"Well, yeah. We've been watching him for months—"

"We?"

"The girls on the front end. Every weekday morning, they watch Letourneau come into the store. He goes to the coffee machine and pours himself a cup of coffee. Black, with two sugars. He pays for it at the checkout, then he picks up a copy of the *Gazette* on his way out the door."

"You have witnesses who'll swear to this in court?"

"Yes, sir. I mean, they've seen it happen, day after day. They told me about it. But I don't know if they'd be willing to go to court. I mean—it's only a newspaper."

Davy slowly turned cool, searching eyes on Letourneau. "Do you have anything to say to that, Gilles?"

"In the words of my persecutor," Letourneau snapped, "it's only a newspaper. What the hell is the problem? With all the money I spend in this store every year, I should be entitled to a free newspaper once in a while."

"So you're admitting that Mr. Lathrop's telling the truth."

"Holy mother of Mary, what difference does it make? The paper's right there beside the door. If they don't want me taking it, they should put it somewhere else."

Davy closed his eyes for an instant. When he reopened them, he said, "Tell me, Gilles. If you came out of the store this morning after picking up your coffee and newspaper, and saw Buzz here driving off in your pickup truck, what would you do?"

"What? What kind of question is that? How the hell am I supposed to answer that?"

"Would you figure it's okay, because the truck was parked right by the front door for anybody who wanted to drive it?"

"Of course not!" Letourneau snapped. "It's not his truck."

"Very good. That means you understand the concept of ownership. What does it say on the masthead of the *Gazette?* Does it say that the paper's free?"

Letourneau glared at him before spitting out a hard, mono-syllabic response. "No."

"Thank you. Mr. Lathrop, I believe that in exchange for your store not pressing charges, Mr. Letourneau would be willing to reimburse you for the cost of the newspapers he inadvertently borrowed over, say, the last six months. And, of course, he'd also agree that from now on, he'll pay for his morning *Gazette.* Am I correct, Gilles?"

"Do I have a choice? If I say no, you gonna haul me off in handcuffs and throw me in that little jail of yours? *Merde*." Davy didn't speak French, but he had a pretty good idea that the word wasn't complimentary. "I still say if they want me to pay for the damn thing, they shouldn't leave it by the front door."

"Buzz? That arrangement okay with you?"

Lathrop cleared his throat again and squared his slumped shoulders. "That would be acceptable to us, yes."

"Good. Six months times five days a week times fifty cents should come to—" He quickly did the math in his head. "Sixty dollars. Mr. Letourneau, I'm sure you'd be happy to write Mr. Lathrop a check right now for sixty dollars."

Muttering under his breath, Letourneau pulled out his checkbook, scribbled a check, and tore it off. "Here," he snarled, holding it out to Buzz Lathrop. To Davy he said, "Now can I go?"

"You can go," Davy said. "Have a nice day."

"Hah." Letourneau stalked to the door. Hand on the doorknob, he said, "Goddamn paper isn't worth fifty cents," and slammed the door behind him.

Annie Kendall pulled her ancient Volvo station wagon into the weed-choked parking lot of the Twilight Motel and Video Store and rolled to a stop next to a permanently darkened vacancy sign, its shattered neon tubing bearing mute testimony to the Twilight's quiet desperation. The motel's heyday had clearly passed, evidenced by the 1950s-era gas pumps sitting out front, and Annie couldn't help but wonder if the entire town wore the same bleak facade. All the better for her if it did. She wasn't expecting much anyway.

It was a good thing she wasn't. The drooping ridgepole gave the roofline the appearance of a swaybacked old nag. The building itself hadn't been painted in at least forty years.

What had once been white was now a dingy gray, and Annie realized it was entirely possible that even her meager expectations had been too high.

Nevertheless, the Twilight was all hers, from the saggy roof to the defunct vacancy sign to the crumbling parking lot. Every spiderweb, every mouse dropping, every water stain belonged to her, purchased sight unseen from an owner eager to dump the place and relocate to the sunbelt. Real estate values in this neck of the woods had tanked right along with the town's economy, and she'd bought the Twilight for a song. Now she just had to figure out what to do with it.

Rebirth. Or, as the French would say, *renaissance*. She liked the sound of the word, liked the feel of it, appreciated the symbolic link between her own life and that of the old motel that had been closed for more than a decade.

Hide in plain sight. That was the advice Uncle Bobby had given her. *Decide who you want to be and then become that person. Plant roots in the soil. That's how you build credibility.*

She'd done her research carefully before she left Robin Spinney dead and buried in a Dumpster on the outskirts of Detroit. It didn't get much more credible than this. Annie Kendall was planting roots in the soil, and this particular piece of property in this particular fading mill town seemed as good a place as any to start digging.

Annie turned off her ignition and was instantly enveloped in the familiar sounds of a rural summer day: the sweet fluid warble of a robin, the distant whine of an eighteen-wheeler, the rhythmic screek of a rusty Amoco sign swaying in the breeze above her head. The Twilight's dilapidated neglect reminded her of places she'd seen in the rural south as a kid, places that were little more than wide spots in the road where time had stood still. If she closed her eyes, she could still picture dented gas pumps, an old yellow dog sleeping in the dirt, an ancient soda cooler just outside the front door, filled with ice-cold bottles of Coca-Cola and grape Nehi.

But she didn't have time for daydreaming. She had too much to do, and her backside ached from sitting too long. Except for a single stop somewhere on the Maine Turnpike for a bathroom break and a snack, they'd been driving since dawn. Beside her, Sophie slept in the passenger seat, dog-tired after being dragged at an ungodly hour from her comfy bed in a Motel 6 outside Providence and driven to this place at the far end of the universe.

Annie still hadn't adjusted to the changes in her daughter. Sophie'd always been such a great kid, and the transformation had occurred pretty much overnight. A week before Soph's fifteenth birthday, Annie had come home one afternoon to discover that while she was gone, that sneaky bitch Adolescence, with all her angst, had swept in with hurricane-force winds, stealing away her sweet-natured daughter and leaving an irritable, bizarrely-dressed alien in her place. Sophie had hacked off the silky blond hair that had never been cut, and she'd dyed it jet-black. Now she wore it in a scruffy, shoulder-length style that hung like a dark cloud around her lovely face and turned her pale complexion ashen. She'd taken to dressing mostly in black, with a decided preference for Marilyn Manson T-shirts and black lipstick.

Although looking at her daughter made Annie's teeth ache, she'd bitten down hard on her tongue. Her mother had told her years ago that with kids, you had to choose your battles wisely. Annie had always found that to be sound advice, so she was saving her wrath for something bigger. And even though with her new look Sophie didn't exactly blend into the mainstream, still it was one hell of a disguise. Nobody who came looking for them would ever connect this belligerent Morticia Addams type with the outgoing, sweet blond teenager who'd played soccer and volunteered at the local animal shelter every Saturday. As hideous as Sophie's appearance was, it could conceivably save her life one day.

Hating to wake her sleeping daughter, Annie nevertheless touched her arm. "Soph," she said softly, "wake up. We're here."

Sophie stirred, stretched and blinked a couple of times before focusing on the ramshackle establishment they were parked in front of. "This is it?" she said in disbelief. "We drove all the way from Las Vegas for *this?*"

Trying to ignore the consternation in her daughter's voice, Annie said, "It'll be fun. An adventure."

"Right." Sophie wore contempt the way Annie's mother had worn Chanel No. 5. It rolled off her in waves. "Whatever you say."

The rest of her sentence was unspoken, but Annie heard the words anyway. *I've had enough adventure. I want to go home.* Over the past six months, her daughter had been forced, through no fault of her own, to give up everything. Her friends, her school, her home, her history. Even her family name. No wonder she'd rebelled.

But there was nothing Annie could do about it. She couldn't rewrite history. This was home now, and the past no longer existed. Pulling her keys from the ignition, she said with forced cheerfulness, "Come on. We might as well check it out and see what we've gotten ourselves into. Just think, Soph. All the videos you can watch, and no late fees."

Sophie rolled her eyes, but she got out of the car. At the center of the long building, a second-story overhang held aloft by rusty iron posts jutted out fifteen feet into the parking lot, ending above a concrete island where the aforementioned gas pumps sat. Beneath the overhang, above the door to the former motel office, a white wooden sign with black stenciled lettering read VIDEO RENTALS. Annie stepped into the shade beneath the overhang and approached the door.

She pulled out the shiny silver key she'd been handed by her attorney, but before she could slide it into the lock, the door swung open, and a noticeably pregnant young woman said, "Sorry. We don't open until noon."

For a moment, Annie was taken aback by the sight of the girl, whose dark hair was chopped off in an ultra-short cut spiked in forty different directions and lacquered with some kind of styling gel. She wore a pair of fuchsia slacks and an oversized white T-shirt emblazoned with the word *BABY* and a pink arrow pointing directly at the oversized mound of her belly.

Recovering, Annie said, "Hello. I'm Annie Kendall. And you would be…?"

"Oh, my God." The young woman's hands went to her mouth in a gesture of horror. "I'm so sorry! I thought you were a customer! I'm Estelle. Estelle Cloutier. And you're my new boss."

"It certainly looks that way. This is my daughter, Sophie. May we come in?"

Estelle winked at Sophie, who was staring at her open-mouthed, and stepped aside. "Welcome. *Mi casa es su casa.* Well, actually, it's *su casa* anyway, isn't it?" She let out a nervous giggle and covered her mouth with her hand to prevent any more giggles from escaping. The other hand came to rest on her expansive belly. "Take a look around."

The walls were paneled with the tongue-and-groove knotty pine that had been fashionable somewhere around 1959, but the shelves were newer, built by somebody who knew what he—or she—was doing. The room wasn't very big, but the walls were lined with movies, and a trio of long, freestanding shelving units created aisles where customers could browse through a fairly decent selection of videos. Blockbuster clearly wasn't in any danger from the competition, but for a small business in a small town, this place wasn't half bad.

"We're open from noon to eight, six days a week," Estelle said. "Sundays, we close at six. That's the way Mike always did it. Of course, it's your place now, so if you want to make any changes…" She drifted off, and Annie turned to look at her. The girl was leaning against the checkout counter, all wide, dark eyes, spiky hair, and bulging belly.

"You work here full-time?" Annie said.

"I'm the manager. I have a couple of high school kids who come in part time, but I'm the only full-time employee. Mike used to help out some of the time, but mostly he just let me run things. He said he trusted me, and besides, all he really wanted to do was retire and get the heck out of Dodge."

Annie considered her words. "And how much am I paying you?"

"Fifty cents over minimum wage."

Good Lord. Those were slave wages. Even in this neck of the woods, how did anyone survive on that kind of salary? Especially with a baby coming. Estelle wasn't wearing a wedding ring, but that didn't necessarily mean anything. Maybe she had a significant other somewhere who raked in the big bucks. Or maybe Annie needed to consider giving the girl a raise.

She glanced around again, wondering if the place did enough business to even support giving Estelle that fifty cents over minimum, and decided to play it by ear. "Once I get settled in, we'll have to sit down and go over everything. You can teach me the ropes."

"Cool."

"Meantime, where are the owner's quarters?"

"Oh, of course! You want to get settled. I didn't mean to babble on. It's a bad habit. Your apartment's upstairs. Right through the door over there. You have an outside entrance, too, around the corner by the pay phone."

"Thanks. Coming, Soph?"

Her daughter, who was browsing through the horror section, shrugged and set down the movie case she held in her hand. "They have all the *Friday The 13th* movies," she said.

"Well," Annie said. "There's something to really look forward to."

"I think that went well."

Officer Pete Morin, riding shotgun in the passenger seat, mumbled a monosyllabic response. Davy glanced over at him, but the red-haired giant, focused on the road ahead, remained silent as granite. He hadn't said two words since they left Grondin's. Hell, he hadn't said two words the entire time they were there. Davy wasn't exactly the Great Communicator himself, but Morin evidenced all the warmth of an iceberg.

It irked him. Pete Morin didn't have to like him. But as Interim Police Chief, he was Pete's direct supervisor. Like it or not, they were stuck with each other, and if Pete wasn't cooperative, it was going to make the next two months seem more like two years.

Taking a quick left onto the River Road, Davy drove past side street after side street lined with triple-decker tenements built as housing for mill workers during the latter part of the 19th century. Pete maintained his stony silence as they left civilization behind and hit the 45 mph speed zone along the lonely stretch of highway that followed the contours of the river. Hands placed neatly at ten and two on the wheel, Davy said, "You have something to say to me?"

"Be better if I kept my mouth shut."

"Maybe. Maybe not. I like to get things out in the open. Clear the air. If we have to work together, we need to be straight with each other. So I'll go first. You don't like me much, do you, Morin?"

"It's nothing personal."

"Is that so?"

"No. It's just—" Pete leaned his head back and sighed. "Ah, hell, who am I kidding? Of course it's personal."

"Let me guess. You think it should've been you who took Ty's place while he was gone."

"Damn right, I think that. But that's not all of it."

"Care to tell me the rest?"

"I've been a cop in this town for ten years," Pete said. "When Buck retired and Ty got his job, I kept my mouth shut, even though I'd been with the department longer. I figured what with nepotism and all, I didn't stand a chance of getting the job anyway. And there was a certain rightness to the chief's job being passed down from father to son. Besides, Ty had something I didn't have—a degree in criminology. So I figured the job was his by rights." Pete shifted his bulk, stretched his long legs and crossed one ankle over the other.

"That doesn't mean I was happy about it," he continued. "But I took it like a man. And after I'd worked for Ty for a while, I forgot I ever had a problem with him. He's a good cop, a good man, a good boss. Has his feet planted on the ground, right where they should be. He's steady and dependable. If he tells you the sky just turned green, you'd best be believing him. I'd trust him with my life. See, Hunter, that's the thing." The accusation in Pete's eyes was unmistakable. "I don't trust you. You royally screwed up. You got Chelsea killed, and you almost got Faith killed. How the hell am I supposed to trust you after that? How the hell am I supposed to believe that if I need you to cover my back, you won't be getting me killed?"

It was a valid question. Davy had botched a case, and the consequences had been tragic. How could he defend himself against Pete's accusation when it was the truth? He'd fucked up. People had died. In the end, he'd pissed off everybody, from the local citizens to the Serenity police to the freaking DEA. "I don't know, Pete," he said. "I honestly don't know." It wasn't much of a defense, but it was the truth.

Pete's response was a loud, undignified snort. Davy signaled for a right turn and wheeled the cruiser into the rest area along the riverbank, tires crunching in the hard-packed gravel. They sat for a while in silence, both of them looking at the river, both of them contemplating the fact that Chelsea had died here after her car plunged into the rain-swollen Androscoggin. "Look," Davy said, "we have to work together. It's only for a couple of months. Then you'll be rid of me."

"As far as I'm concerned, it can't come soon enough."

"Here's a big surprise. I'm no happier about it than you are."

Jaw set, Pete turned to look at him. "Yet you're the one sitting in the chief's office," he said, "in the chief's chair, staring at a framed eight-by-ten of the chief's wife. Just how, exactly, do you explain that?"

"It's not my fault. I tried to turn down the job. You know Ty. He doesn't like to take no for an answer. He completely ignored what I said and just went ahead with his plans anyway."

Pete muttered a curse under his breath. "What's done is done," he said. "I guess now we have to live with it."

"Exactly. So where do we stand? You and I?"

"I'm not taking you to the senior prom, if that's what you're asking. Look, I like my job, I have three kids to feed, and my wife likes to buy expensive things. I can't afford to mutiny. But I'll be watching you, Hunter. The first time you fuck up, I'll be calling the Board of Selectmen."

"Fair enough. So is this a truce?"

Pete sighed. "It looks that way." Scowling, he added, "For now, anyway. But I meant what I said, Hunter. Watch your step."

"So are we supposed to, like, pinky swear or something?"

Pete Morin didn't laugh at his pathetic attempt at a joke.

He just maintained that unflinchingly stony face. "You're an idiot," he said.

Davy put the cruiser into gear and pulled back out onto the highway. "Tell me something I don't already know."

Two

The second-story apartment was bare, but surprisingly cozy. Light poured in through the matching pair of large windows that faced the highway. Although the carpet was standard-issue beige and the room empty of furniture, the walls were papered with a pink-and-yellow rose pattern that gave the place a homey feel. The living room was big and square, opening onto a kitchen complete with a full-size range and refrigerator, and—could it be possible? A dishwasher! Annie's heart beat a little faster in appreciation. The appliances were outdated, but appeared to be in working order, and the homemade white wooden cabinets seemed adequate.

A note was tacked to the refrigerator door with a magnet. Annie crossed the room and took it down. *Thought you might be hungry,* it said. *There's a casserole in the fridge. Heat at 350 degrees for twenty minutes. Sorry we missed you. Cheers! Yvonne Boudreau.*

Yvonne Boudreau and her husband Mike were decent people, what her mother had always referred to as salt of the earth. They'd left for Florida yesterday, and although Annie had spoken on the telephone with both of them after they'd inked the deal for the Twilight, she'd never met them face-to-face. She had a feeling she would have liked them.

"They left us lunch," she said.

Sophie had already disappeared from view. Her voice floated through a door off the living room. "Who left us what?"

"The Boudreaus. They left us a casserole. Wasn't that nice of them?"

"Whatever." Annie could hear her daughter opening and closing doors. "Geez," Sophie said, "this bedroom gives new meaning to the word ugly." There was a pause, and then she said, "Um…Mom?"

"What?" Annie opened the refrigerator to check out the macaroni-and-beef casserole and the six-pack of Pepsi that Yvonne Boudreau had left for them. The fridge was immaculate, as was the rest of the living space.

"There's only one bedroom." Sophie emerged looking scandalized. "This whole place is just two rooms and a bath. Where the hell are we supposed to sleep?"

Annie closed the refrigerator door. "You, my dear, will sleep in the bedroom. I'll bunk on the couch. And watch your language."

"We don't have a couch." With a disparaging glance around the room, Sophie added, "Or a bed, for that matter."

"Oh, ye of little faith. We will. There's a secondhand furniture store in town. I bet if we're really nice to them, they'll deliver."

Her daughter didn't look convinced. Instead, she raised her chin and said, "Are we really staying this time?"

It was a valid question. They'd moved around so much. Every time Sophie had started to settle into a new home, started to make new friends, Annie had dragged her away yet again.

But you couldn't spend the rest of your life running.

Sooner or later, you had to stop. The odds against their being found in this out-of-the-way little town were astronomical. They had new names, new birth certificates, new social security numbers. Annie had a new driver's license, courtesy of the state of Nevada. Sophie had spent long enough in the Las Vegas school system to accumulate a brief academic history which Annie prayed would satisfy the Serenity school department. Neither of them had ever been to Maine before. They had no friends or relatives here, nothing to point a pursuer in this direction, and they were far enough from home so it was highly unlikely that anyone from Mississippi would accidentally stumble over them.

Annie had chosen Serenity because it was off the beaten path. There were no sites of historical significance in the area, no campgrounds, no ski areas or beaches. Nothing to draw tourists. Just a quiet, insular little town that had been built on a nineteenth-century economy and was now struggling to survive in a vastly different twenty-first century.

For the first time since she'd begun running, she felt almost safe. Almost. "We're really staying this time," she said.

Sophie stepped away from the bedroom doorway and into her mother's arms. They shared a hard, emotional embrace, made more poignant because these days, physical contact between them was a rarity. Fiercely, Annie said, "This is where we start a new life. We're safe here. You trust me, don't you, Soph?"

Her daughter avoided meeting her eyes. "I guess," she said.

She stroked Sophie's hair. It was still baby-soft, in spite of the dye job, and Annie was reminded of the two-year-old her daughter had once been. Time moved so quickly. In another couple of years, Sophie would start looking at colleges. Where had the time gone? It was all a blur of family vacations and PTA meetings, Saturday morning cartoons and soccer practice, and all the little day-to-day things that made life so precious. They'd had their squabbles, as all families do, but for the most part, Sophie had been a joy to raise. She'd been an easy baby and an easier child. At least she had until adolescence had reared its ugly head. Annie could only pray that once the current hormonal madness was over, Soph would turn back into a regular person, a bright, sweet young woman with a good head on her shoulders.

She planted a kiss on top of the aforementioned head. "Well, then, Miss Muffet—" Sophie groaned at the old family nickname "—what do you say we start unloading the car? Then we'll take a drive into town and see if we can find that furniture store."

"Okay, but if we're really staying this time, I want to get a job."

"Oh, Soph." Her heart took a sudden and unexpected plunge. "We've talked about this before."

"And every time we talk about it, you refuse to listen to me!"

"You're only fifteen years old. Right now, you should be concentrating on being a kid. Keeping your grades up, enjoying life, going to school dances and football games and parties. A job would interfere with that. You'll be in the working world soon enough." She brushed a wisp of hair away from her daughter's face. "Why rush it?"

"It would only be until school starts. Think about it, Mom. I'm stuck all summer in the puckerbrush in this dead little town where I don't know anybody. What am I supposed to do with myself all day if I don't have a job?" Sophie sent a disparaging glance around the empty room. "I'll go nuts if I have to sit around this place all the time."

Sophie was right. She hated to admit it, but her daughter had a point. Still she was afraid to give in. It wasn't just her reluctance to see Sophie growing up too quickly that concerned her. There was more to it than that. Ever since the day they'd fled their hometown with little more than the clothes on their backs, she'd been terrified to let her daughter out of her sight. Sending her to public school had been torture. Even though there was no way the school, or anybody else for that matter, could connect Sophie Kendall of Las Vegas with Sophie Spinney of Atchawalla, Mississippi, still Annie had lived in terror that they'd be found, that something unspeakable would happen to her daughter. A parent's worse nightmare.

She knew she was being paranoid. She knew that sooner or later she would have to relinquish her rock-solid maternal grasp. It wasn't good for Sophie. Wasn't good for either of them.

But not yet. Not when they hadn't even had time to unpack, let alone acquaint themselves with this place. "Maybe you could work for me," she said. "In the video store."

Sophie's look of horror would have been comical if she hadn't been so serious about it. "Yeah, right, Mom. Do you have any idea how lame that would be, working for my own mother? I don't think so. I want a real job, one that'll allow me to get out of this dump once in a while."

Annie sighed. "I'll think about it, Soph. But not until we've had time to get settled."

The police cruiser thumped down the rutted driveway hard enough to knock Davy Hunter's teeth together. He really ought to get the damn driveway taken care of. Fill in the potholes, spread some new gravel. Live a little less like some backwoods hillbilly. At one time, he'd planned to build a house here and have the trailer hauled off to its eternal rest. But after Chelsea died and he left the DEA, making improvements to the property had seemed pointless. Why bother to put money into something he didn't give a rat's ass about? Why bother when he had nobody to share it with? For most of the last fourteen months, he'd been so apathetic that his car could have disappeared completely into one of those pot-holes and he wouldn't have even noticed.

Maybe, now that Jessie was here, that would change.

Davy pulled up beside Jessie's car, parked in front of the ugly little green trailer he called home. The thought of her behind the wheel at sixteen was almost enough to give him a coronary. At least Ty had bought her a car that was a tank, and easy to maneuver on snowy back roads. The four-wheel-drive Jeep Cherokee might not be the most fashionable vehicle in the student parking lot at Serenity High, but it was one of the safest.

Having her here for the summer was worth whatever bull-shit he had to wade through as interim police chief. She could have gone with Ty and Faith to New York. Hell, she proba-bly should have. Broaden her horizons. Get out of this one-horse town where nothing ever happened. But her friends were here, and her job was here, and she'd opted to stay.

By some miracle, she'd opted to stay with him.

Buddy, Jessie's enthusiastic mixed-breed mutt, greeted him at the door, and Davy patted the dog on the head. Technically, Buddy was Faith's dog, but once he'd adopted Jessie as his human, there was no separating them. Taking him to New York for the summer hadn't even been an option. It had simply been understood, by all parties involved, that wherever Jessie went, her dog went, too. It was going to take some adjusting all around, especially for Davy's eight-year-old cat, Sir Lancelot, who'd been an only child until Buddy arrived on the scene. Even though Lance wasn't familiar with dogs, instinct had taken over when he was greeted by a curious wet nose and a lolling tongue. He'd arched his back and hissed, and as far as Davy could tell, he'd been hiding under the couch ever since. At night, while his evil adversary was asleep, Lance came out to eat and drink and use the litter box before scurrying back to his hiding place.

Jessie had tried to coax him out, first with soft words and later with an open can of cat food, but Lance had refused to budge. Davy was secretly proud of him for holding out even when temptation, in the form of a particularly aromatic can of mackerel, was waved right under his nose. Lance was no weenie. He was a tough guy, a man's man, a feline who'd rather starve than betray his principles.

His stepdaughter, dressed in a conservative white T-shirt and jeans, was moving about Davy's tiny kitchen, putting last-minute touches to dinner. At sixteen, Jessie was so cool, so self-assured, it was scary. He sure as hell hadn't been that way at her age. As he recalled, at sixteen he'd been an unruly mess of stringy hair and raging hormones and as-yet-unrequited love for her mother. Dish towel in hand, Jessie bent to open the oven and check on the main dish. Whatever was in there smelled heavenly. "Hi," she said. "How did your day go?"

"Peachy. A laugh a minute. Listen, Skeets, I don't expect you to cook for me."

"Are you kidding? I love to cook." She left the oven door open a couple of inches, stretched to turn off the heat, then picked up a big spoon and stirred whatever was boiling on the back burner. Turning, she gave him a killer smile that nearly stopped his heart. "I'll have you know that I'm a world-class cook. You just happen to be the lucky recipient of my talents."

Jessie had come a long way from the shy, mousy little girl she'd been when her mother died. She and Chelsea had been closer than Siamese twins, and he'd been fearful about how her mother's death would affect Jess. But she'd gotten through it far better than he'd expected. Far better than he'd gotten through it himself. Over the course of the past year, Jessie had come out of her shell, had blossomed and thrived.

The credit for that belonged exclusively to Ty and Faith. It couldn't have been easy for them, starting out married life with a teenage foster daughter. Especially when neither of them had a clue about raising kids. But they'd taken Jessie Logan to their collective bosom as though she'd been their own. Exposed to their special brand of love and discipline and nurturing, Jessie had flowered, and for that, he would be eternally grateful.

Not that he had any right to be grateful. He had no rights to Jessie at all. Chelsea had made that abundantly clear, had reminded him as often as possible that he wasn't the man who'd fathered her daughter. It had been the biggest bone of contention between them. With her customary tunnel vision, Chels had failed to see how much it hurt him to be reminded that another man had sired Jessie. Or maybe she'd seen, and simply hadn't cared. Chelsea Logan had been a self-centered woman. He'd loved her in spite of it.

But biology be damned. In every way that mattered, Jessie was his kid. Over the course of the past sixteen years, he hadn't yet noticed any other guy stepping forward to take responsibility for her existence on this planet. After Chelsea died, he would have taken Jessie, kept her with him, if Chels hadn't made her wishes known long before the will was even written. If anything ever happened to her, she'd told him time and again, she wanted Faith to have Jessie. End of discussion.

"Did you have to deal with a lot of idiots today?" Jessie said now.

It took him a minute to regroup. "Idiots?"

She stood there in his kitchen, her long, dark hair flying every which way, and studied him with an indulgent little smile that was more adult than adolescent. "Ty's always complaining about the idiots he has to deal with."

"Oh. Those idiots. Yeah, I saw a lot of those today." Darkly, he added, "Several of 'em right in my own department."

Jessie's eyes widened, and then she giggled, a sound that reduced her instantly to the barefoot ten-year-old she'd been just a day or two ago. "That I want to hear about. Supper will be ready in ten minutes. I just need to set the table. You have time to change if you want to. Then you can tell me about the idiots."

Supper was a low-key affair. He entertained her with stories about his day—the ones he could repeat to her—and she talked about her summer job renting videos at the Twilight. "I talked to Faith today," she said.

He paused, fork held aloft. "She doing okay?"

"She's already going stir-crazy. She said, and I quote, daytime TV is a garbage receptacle catering to nonproductive, nonthinking invertebrates. End of quote."

He grinned. He could imagine Faith saying something like that. What he couldn't imagine was her spending the next six weeks flat on her back. "I take it she's already made the acquaintance of Jerry Springer and Judge Judy."

"She says she's overdosing on reruns of *Unsolved Mysteries*. But she's following doctor's orders and staying off her feet. She knows Ty will strangle her if she doesn't."

He helped himself to a second slice of roast beef. "Everything okay with the babies?"

"According to her obstetrician, everything's fine. He just wants to play it safe."

After supper, Jessie cleared away the dishes, gave him a peck on the cheek, and left. It was her night off, and she and her best friend, Becca McLaughlin, were taking in the latest *Harry Potter* movie. Jessie was an amazing kid, a good kid. The best. She'd only been gone for ten minutes, but already the place felt cold and empty without her vibrancy to warm it. Even Buddy felt the loss. The dog lay in front of the couch, his head on his paws, sad brown eyes watching Davy's every move.

"She'll be back in a few hours," he told the dog. "I miss her already, too." He felt foolish for talking to the damn-fool creature as though it were human, but Buddy acted as though he understood every word that was said to him. Davy knelt and chucked the dog under the chin. Buddy raised his head and swished his tail back and forth on the rug, and Davy got back up, poured himself a cup of coffee from the pot that was sitting on the sideboard, and headed out to his workshop.

He took a long swig of black coffee and set his cup down on his work table. Out here, the scents of summer mingled with the pungent aroma of sawdust. He opened a can of honey-colored stain, found a clean rag, and turned on the CD player. Kneeling, he began applying the stain to the drop-leaf table he'd just finished making.

The work was familiar, comforting, and as he worked, the sweet simplicity of Keith Urban's music began working some of the day's tensions out of his shoulders. Davy Hunter loved working with his hands. Loved working with wood. Loved its fresh scent, its smooth, silken texture, loved the way the stain worked with the grain of the wood to create wonderful geometric patterns that couldn't be duplicated by man. Like fingerprints, no two pieces of wood were alike, and every work he created was unique.

He took another sip of coffee. It would never be his beverage of choice, but it was all he allowed himself these days. No more twelve-pack pity parties. No more three-day benders. He held a responsible position within the community, and he had Jessie to think about. She might look as though she had it all together, but she was still just sixteen. She was depending on him to take care of her for the next two months.

Davy suspected that was a big part of the reason Ty had wanted him for the job. It kept him out of trouble, gave him something better to do than sit around drinking beer and feeling sorry for himself. The fact that Ty had entrusted the safety of the town of Serenity—not to mention Jessie—to him said something about their friendship. Like any long-term relationship, it had gone through some rocky times, but in the end it had held strong. This was Ty's way of letting him know that, in spite of the fact that he'd fucked up royally where Chelsea was concerned, his old friend hadn't lost trust in him. Ty had given him a chance to redeem himself.

And he would, damn it. This time he'd get it right. This time, nobody would die. For the next sixty days, he'd simply place one foot in front of the other and walk a straight and narrow line. Without wavering, without stumbling, without falling on his ugly mug. He'd prove to all of his detractors that Davy Hunter was a capable, competent human being, and not the worthless piece of garbage that so many people seemed to believe he was.

When the phone rang, he wiped his hands on a clean rag and went to answer it. "David?" said a voice as wispy and insubstantial as a Kleenex tissue. "You have to come over. It's an emergency."

"Gram," he said, his hands tightening on the rag. "What's wrong?"

"Koko got out, and I can't find her. She's not supposed to be outdoors. Somebody will steal her. Or she'll get run over."

As gently as possible, he said, "I'm sort of in the middle of something." He really wanted to get the staining done tonight. Now that he was gainfully employed, he didn't have much free time to devote to his woodworking projects. Holding back a sigh, he said, "I don't suppose there's any way this can wait an hour or two?"

"By then, it'll be too late. She'll be gone." Her voice climbed into a higher register, a step closer to hysteria. "I don't know what to do."

Davy glanced at the table he was working on and gave in. What choice did he have? Gram's emergencies always took priority over everything else.

"Give me ten minutes to clean up," he said. "I'll come over and find your cat."

He'd tried several times over the past year to convince Gram to sell her house and move into Spruce Run, one of those assisted-living facilities where elderly people could maintain their independence but still receive 24-hour assistance. He'd even brought over a brochure or two and read all the scintillating details to her. Gram, of course, had thought the idea absurd. "Why do I need a stranger on call," she'd said, "when I already have you?"

That was the problem. She already had him. Perhaps because of her blindness—or maybe it was just orneriness—Gram had no concept of time, no clue that other people had lives they needed to attend to. No matter what time of day or night an emergency arose, she had only to hit speed dial 1 and he'd be there within minutes. The problem was that her definition of emergency and his seldom matched. So far he'd been called out to change the lightbulb in her refrigerator, to chase a raccoon off her front porch, to sniff the milk and make sure it hadn't soured. And now, to find her missing cat.

When Gram had reached her mideighties and her health had begun to fail, he'd been unanimously elected her caregiver. He got the job by default. Who else was going to do it, if not him? Sure as hell not his sister, Dee, who had six kids and a useless husband and a pinched look about her mouth that suggested she had been sorely disappointed by life. The last time Davy'd had the audacity to suggest that she might consider helping out with Gram once in a while, his sister had gone ballistic. She'd sputtered about how busy her life was, chasing after a half-dozen kids and trying to keep the floors scrubbed and the laundry done, not to mention working to support the family. How dare he, who hung out with riffraff and had nothing but spare time, criticize her for failing to take on yet another responsibility in the form of the octogenarian who'd raised them?

Nope, Dee wouldn't be picking up the slack any time soon. Nor would Brian, his kid brother, who'd seen the writing on the wall and blown this town before the ink was dry on his high school diploma. Not that Davy blamed him for leaving, all things considered. They never talked about Brian; he and Dee and Gram, never even mentioned his name. It was as though his brother had died, and the pain was so great that the only way the family could survive was to perpetrate this elaborate ruse that he'd never existed in the first place. No, Brian wasn't about to come home and take care of his ailing grandmother. The last time Davy'd heard from his brother was six or seven years ago, when Brian had called from New Mexico. He was living in Taos, where he'd made scores of friends. Life was good. He'd met someone. It was looking serious; they'd just bought a small house together. Alec was a chef by trade, and they'd decided that with his culinary talents and Brian's head for business, they should open a restaurant. But start-up costs were killer, and they were short on capital. Maybe big bro would be interested in investing in their little venture?

Davy had sent his brother a check for five thousand dollars. Guilt money. Guilt because he hadn't been good enough at protecting his doe-eyed, sensitive little brother from schoolyard taunts, from Dee's sanctimonious determination to pretend she'd never even had a baby brother, from Gram's well-meaning but misplaced attempts to fix the part of Brian that she deemed defective. He hadn't been able to protect Brian from being unloved, so he'd tried to make up for it with money.

He'd never heard from Brian again. The check had been cashed almost immediately, but Brian hadn't acknowledged his generosity with so much as a phone call. Davy hadn't been surprised. Disappointed, maybe, but not surprised. They were one fucked-up bunch, the Hunter clan. He and Brian and Dee were poster children for dysfunctional. Then again, did anybody really come from a functional family? Had anybody ever seen one? Did anybody even know what one was supposed to look like?

When he pulled into Gram's driveway, he took a good long look at the house where he'd grown up. At nearly forty years of age, he couldn't remember a time when the siding had been any color other than a silvery gray. Rot had begun to eat away at the windowsills and the eaves, and the place needed a new roof. He'd offered to spend some money on the house, fix up the worst of the damage inflicted by time and neglect, but Gram had adamantly refused his help. The house, she'd told him, was adequate for her needs. Once she was gone, it would be up to him to decide its fate. For now, she didn't intend to make any changes.

A cluster of homemade bird feeders hung haphazardly from a spruce tree near the kitchen door where Gram waited anxiously. Dressed in a tangerine-colored housecoat, a green cardigan, and pink fuzzy slippers, she bore an uncanny resemblance to a carton of rainbow sherbet. She peered out through the screen as he climbed out of his car.

"Gram," he said, "you need to keep your door locked. Remember, we talked about that?"

"It's locked," she said cheerfully. "See?" She lifted the ineffectual silver hook from its equally ineffectual silver eye and beamed at him. Granted, this was a small town, but even in small towns, things happened. He should know. He'd worked DEA long enough. A couple of coked-up teenagers looking for something to pawn to support their habit could do a lot of damage to a little old lady who was legally blind, a little senile, and far too trusting for her own good.

"You stay inside," he told her. "I'll look for Koko."

He got down on his hands and knees and shone his flashlight under the saggy wooden steps. No cat in sight. With his eyes trained on the house's crumbling foundation, where a cat might seek cool shelter on a warm summer evening, he worked his way around to the back. Out here, the ground was crooked as hell, and the grass hadn't been mowed in a decade or two. If he was a cat, this was where he'd hide. He traipsed the grounds, flashlight playing in a wide arc, grateful for once that Gram didn't have any close neighbors to wonder what the hell he was doing out here, walking around in circles like a crazy man. "Here, kitty-kitty-kitty," he said.

No response. "Come on, Koko," he muttered. "You may have time for fun and games, but I still have a couple hours of work left tonight, and I have to be up at five. You're not helping much."

The evening was silent, save for the soft rustle of grass blowing in the breeze. He made his way to the old horse barn and gingerly tested the floor with a foot to make sure he wouldn't fall through. He'd be willing to bet that nobody'd been out here since he and his siblings were kids. The old floorboards creaked under his weight, but they held up. He checked every corner, every place a small gray tabby could possibly hide, but the only signs of life he saw were a couple of fat spiders hanging overhead.

Great. He might as well kiss tonight's work goodbye. He'd never get away from here if he didn't miraculously produce the AWOL feline. Gram might be soft-spoken, but that quaking voice disguised the true hard-ass who lurked behind the facade of serene gentility. Lorena Hunter was the queen of manipulation.

With heavy heart and heavier tread, he trudged back around to the front of the house. Gram was still waiting anxiously behind the screen door. "Did you find her?" she said. "Did you find Koko?"

"Not yet. Let's give it a few minutes and try—" His attention was snagged by a movement in the kitchen behind her, a shadow that morphed, right in front of his eyes, into a small, gray tabby. "What's that?" he said.

"What's what?"

The cat sat down three feet behind his grandmother and began delicately washing one of her tiny front paws. Pausing for an instant, the dainty creature met his glance, and he would have sworn it was smugness he saw in those narrowed yellow eyes. "That," he said. "Right behind you. If she got out, what's she doing inside the house?"

Gram turned away from the screen door. "Koko?" she said feebly. "Is that you?"

The cat abandoned its toilette, stood up and furled itself around his grandmother's legs. "Shame on you," Gram said with a delight he found totally unwarranted. "Shame on you for scaring me like that." She knelt to pat the cat, who rubbed affectionately at her hand. "Naughty, naughty kitty."

Davy could have come up with a few other choice names for the errant feline, but he held his tongue. At least now he could get back to work.

"I could have sworn she got out," Gram said with utter ingenuousness. "Oh, well, as long as you're here, you might as well come in. I have fresh-baked chocolate chip cookies. I just made them. I know how much you like chocolate chip."

He opened his mouth to tell her he didn't have time for a visit, then decided it would be easier to just roll with it. He'd get away much more quickly if he simply let her have her way. Gram rose back up from her kneeling position with the ease of a twenty-year-old and pushed the screen door open for him. "Sit down at the table," she said. "I'll pour you a glass of milk."

The cookies were heavenly, and still warm. He shot her a speculative glance while she sat across the table from him, beaming as bright as the sun at high noon. It seemed convenient that she'd just happened to be baking cookies when her cat just happened to escape out the kitchen door. Especially considering that the missing kitty had been here in the house all the time. Was her befuddlement genuine, or had he been royally bamboozled?

"So," she said, still beaming, "how's the new job going?"

Not so good, he wanted to tell her. *Pete Morin's gunning for my ass, and if he has his way, I'll probably get canned.* But he didn't say it. "Fine," he said instead.

"There's something I've been worried about," she said. "I thought you might know what I should do about it."

"Sure, Gram." He raised his glass of milk to his mouth. "What is it?"

"Alien abductions."

He almost choked on the milk. Coughing, he set down the glass and reached for a napkin from the plastic holder in the center of the table. "Alien abductions?" he said, blotting his mouth. "Where the hell did you hear something like that?"

"From Elsa," she said ingenuously. "She read me a story about it from the *National Enquirer,* about people living in rural areas being abducted at night by aliens. They take you up into their mother ship and run all kinds of oddball medical tests before they let you go. I live all by myself out here, and to tell you the truth, it scares me to death. I thought since you're a cop, you could tell me how to protect myself."

Elsa Donegan was the young woman he'd hired to come in three times a week. She did light cleaning and grocery shopping, made sure Gram's medications were in order, kept her company and read to her, since Gram's diabetes had left her blind in both eyes. He'd have to have a chat with Elsa about her choice of reading material. "You shouldn't let her read that crap to you," he said. "You know it's all made up."

"What do you expect her to read, Tolstoy? Good God, David, I'm eighty-six years old. That's enough reason to be depressed without reading about people throwing themselves under trains. I want a little entertainment. There isn't a thing worth watching on TV since they took *Friends* off the air. All they have on nowadays is cheap sex and reality shows. Paris Hilton and Donald Trump and a bunch of people nobody knows. I don't get it. But Ross and Rachel, now that was entertainment."

He had a headache coming on. He could feel it starting to pound, just behind his left eye. "Gram," he said patiently, "don't be losing any sleep worrying about aliens. You have a better chance of winning the Megabucks. By the way, these cookies are terrific."

She beamed. "It's my secret ingredient," she said, aliens, Paris Hilton, and *Friends* already forgotten. "Ever since I've been using it, my friends all say my cookies are better than theirs."

The cat padded in from the living room, made a soft *chirrup* and leaped into his lap. He could have easily strangled the creature, but it wouldn't have earned him any brownie points. Instead, he rubbed behind its ears. The cat dropped and rolled onto its back, purring loudly.

"Gram," he said, "I really have to go now. I'm right in the middle of a woodworking project. And I have to work in the morning."

"Of course," she said, her voice trembling slightly. "I should never have called you out here over something so trivial as a lost cat. You have much more important things to do than humor an old lady."

His headache got worse. The cat sat up on his lap and favored him with a baleful stare, then haughtily dropped to the floor and stalked out of the room. "Come on, Gram, that's not fair," he said. "You know I don't mind coming over if you have a problem. I just can't stay and chitchat right now. We can visit some other time."

"That's what your sister says every time I call her. I don't suppose you've talked to her lately? It's been so long since she's visited." Her lower lip wobbled ever so slightly. "The kids are growing so fast. Little Abby's just a baby. I'm afraid she won't even remember me the next time she sees me."

Goddamn Dee. Maybe he should strangle her instead of Gram's cat. He was tired of making excuses for his sister, especially when his grandmother could see right through them. He did it again anyway. "You know how busy she is, Gram. The kids keep her running, and when she's not chasing after them, she's at work. I'm sure she doesn't mean to neglect you."

"If that good-for-nothing husband of hers would get off his duff and get a decent job, maybe she wouldn't have to work so much. All he does is sit around all day drinking beer and playing video games."

Despite the fact that his opinion on this particular subject happened to coincide with hers, he kept his mouth shut. Gram had never been known for her discretion. Anything he said was likely to get back to Dee. His relationship with his sister was already rocky enough. He didn't need to give her any more ammunition. "I'll talk to her," he said. "I promise."

"Would you, David? That would be wonderful! Now, you run along and get back to your work. Koko and I will be just fine. Elsa's coming in the morning, and we're going for a drive. But I'll be home all day Wednesday. You make sure and tell Dee that when you talk to her."

Davy kissed her dry, papery-thin cheek and climbed into his car, sitting there for a minute before he started the engine. The old girl was clever, he had to give her credit for that. She'd worked him over so smoothly, he hadn't realized what was happening until she was done.

The wooden kitchen table was so beat up that the guy at the secondhand store had thrown it in for free. The scarred oak looked as though it had been regularly battered with a sledgehammer. At some point in time, an enterprising lover had carved his or her romantic sentiments into one corner of the tabletop. *TJ and LS 4-ever.* Annie wondered if TJ and LS had gotten their happy ending. Probably not. There weren't very many happy endings any more. Maybe there never had been.

She'd paid five bucks apiece for the mismatched wooden chairs. Two of them, one for her and one for Sophie. Annie sat in one of them now, sipping cheap supermarket wine from a green-stemmed goblet while she squinted at the screen of her Gateway notebook computer. Above her head, the kitchen light, one of those circular fluorescent things that dated back to the 1950s, flickered and hummed. Sophie had finally fallen asleep an hour ago in the saggy twin bed they'd bought this afternoon. The poor kid was exhausted, wiped out, totally fried.

She wasn't the only one. It was past eleven, and Annie was going on twenty hours without sleep. It was time to shut down the computer and crawl beneath the blankets on the lumpy couch that was the best Trader Moe's Used Stuff had to offer. But she was wired, restless, not yet ready to sleep. She'd opened the bottle of wine in the hope that it would relax her enough so she could shut down for a few hours. So far, it had failed in its mission.

A soft breeze fluttered the curtain at the window, and she sat up straight and scraped the damp hair back from her forehead. The air felt so good. Leaning back, Annie closed her eyes, the wineglass dangling loosely from her fingers. She liked it here, liked the small-town feel of it already. It would be a good place to raise her daughter. Better than Detroit, better than Las Vegas. Cities made her feel stifled, anxious. Too many people, too much noise, too much traffic. Just plain *too much.* But the state of Maine, with its miles of pine forests, sprinkled here and there with small towns, felt like home.

Roots, Annie thought. *You have to put down roots. Build credibility.*

On the computer screen in front of her the online version of the *Atchawalla Journal-Constitution* sat open. It was a presumptuous name for a small daily newspaper in an even smaller town. Still, Annie read it daily, obsessively, every word of it. In search of…what? She wasn't sure. But if she missed a day, surely she'd miss something of consequence.

Tonight, she'd hit pay dirt. The headline, hidden away in the local news section, had grabbed her attention immediately. *District Attorney Tapped for Bench. Feldman Likely Successor.*

Wineglass in hand, Annie hunched over the laptop and clicked on the link. The story about Luke Brogan's brother was brief. Just a handful of sentences, but she read them carefully, read them twice, then a third time, just to be certain that what she saw was real.

ATCHAWALLA, MS—It was announced yesterday that Atchawalla County District Attorney Marcus Brogan has been appointed to a seat on the Superior Court bench left vacant by the sudden and untimely passing last week of the Honorable Judge Abner Mellen. Brogan, a lifelong resident of Atchawalla, received his law degree from Mississippi State University and practiced family law for fifteen years before taking a position in the County Prosecutor's Office, where he rose in the ranks to his current position of District Attorney, which he has held for seventeen years. Although the Prosecutor's Office declined to confirm or deny the rumor, the *Journal-Constitution* has heard from a reliable source that, possibly as early as next week, Assistant District Attorney Rachel Feldman will assume Brogan's duties pending a November election.

Rachel Feldman. How interesting. Annie'd never met the woman, but she knew of her. Knew her story, knew that Mac had liked and respected her. A graduate of Columbia Law School, Rachel Feldman was young and eager and smart. Smart enough, Mac had said, to keep her mouth shut and her eyes open, smart enough to know that she'd been hired to appease the gods of Equal Opportunity. As both a woman and a Jew, Feldman had managed to fulfill two criteria at once. The good old boys must have been dancing a jig the day her application arrived in the mail. There was just one thing they hadn't counted on when they hired her: Rachel Feldman turned out to be one crackerjack attorney.

A tenuous flicker of hope sprang to life inside her, and Annie struggled to tamp it down. It was too soon, too premature, for anything as tangible as hope. But for the first time, there was possibility. The possibility that, with Marcus Brogan out of the way and Rachel Feldman sitting in the D.A.'s office, this nightmare might actually see an end. Justice might be done. Luke Brogan might end up where he belonged—behind bars—and Annie might be able to reclaim the life he'd stolen from her.

For Sophie's sake, she had to find a way out of this mess. She didn't worry so much about herself. No matter what happened, she would never return to Mississippi. She'd made that decision the day she left. She had chosen to live in Serenity and she was putting down roots. No matter what the future brought, she had every intention of staying here.

But it was different for Sophie. A young girl her age needed a future that was wide open. It wasn't fair to hobble her to a muddied past and a fictitious present. Certainly staying alive, staying ahead of Brogan, was their main priority. But for Sophie, it wasn't enough. There had to be more. And there was only one way Annie could ensure her daughter's future happiness. She had to bring Luke Brogan down. Maybe, somehow, Rachel Feldman could help.

Her cell phone, a gift from Uncle Bobby, rang. Annie hesitated for a moment before she answered it. There was only one person who had the number, and if he was calling her this late at night, it wasn't with good news.

"Did I wake you?" Bobby asked.

"No. I'm just sitting here, trying to wind down. It's been quite a day." While he listened with interest, she proceeded to fill him in on the day's events. It was her way of stalling, her way of avoiding hearing what he had to say until she could avoid it no longer.

Finally, she ran out of things to say. "I'm calling," he said, "because I thought you'd want to know about the rumors I've been hearing."

She clutched the phone more tightly. "What rumors?"

"Some private investigator's been sniffing around, asking questions about Robin Spinney."

Oh, shit. Annie squeezed her eyes closed against the sudden dizziness that overtook her.

"Annie? You all right?"

She took a deep breath. "I'm all right. I'd hoped…well, you know what I'd hoped."

"That he wouldn't come looking. Yeah, I know. But you knew he would. We expected this. It doesn't mean a damn thing except that we read him right. He can't find you. You did a fine job of covering your tracks."

Such a fine job that even Bobby didn't know where she was. All he had was a cell phone number and the nebulous knowledge that she'd bought an old motel in a small town somewhere in the Northeast. It was better that way, for both of them. "I hope you're right," she said.

"So tell me about the video store."

"It's nothing to write home about. I have a couple of

part-time high school kids and one very pregnant full-time employee who looks like a flake but seems to be able to run the place with one hand tied behind her back. It's hard to say how much revenue it's bringing in. Mike Boudreau gave me some figures, but I suspect he may have inflated them. We'll see."

"What about the motel? You got any ideas yet about what you want to do with that?"

She toyed with the stem of her wineglass. "It's in pretty rough shape. I haven't had time yet to look at the guest rooms. But if it's feasible, I'm considering converting it into apartments. No matter where you live, there's always a need for housing. If I could convert the place into three or four apartments, it would give Sophie and me a regular income aside from whatever piddly amount the video rental brings in."

"Not a bad idea."

"And it would be a good way to settle into the community. Put down those roots you talked about."

"Remember what I told you. Don't act like you have anything to hide. People will see it if you do. Make nice with the neighbors, get to know your friendly checkout clerk at the local supermarket. You're just an average, middle-class, thirty-something single mother starting out fresh in a new place. It's ninety percent attitude. You believe you're who you say you are, they'll believe it, too."

"I'm scared, Uncle Bobby. What if I can't pull this off?"

"'Course you are. You're also strong and resourceful. You'll do fine. Just remember why you're doing it. Listen, you got enough money to get by?"

"I do. I'm very frugal." He'd already done so much for her—in terms of financial and emotional support—that it was staggering to think about. She owed him so much, she'd probably never be able to repay him. She had to take it from here without his help.

"You let me know if you need anything. How's the little one doing?"

"Sophie's fine. A little miffed, maybe, at being dragged clear across the country. But she's a trouper."

"Just like her mother. You get some sleep, now, you hear?"

She hung up the phone, not sure whether she felt better or worse. She'd prayed that Brogan would just give up, let her go. Out of sight, out of mind. She realized now that it was a foolish, naive hope. The information in that manila envelope could destroy his life. A man like Luke Brogan wouldn't let that happen. He was tough, he was hard, he was relentless. And he would mow down anybody who stood in his way.

Remember why you're doing it. Uncle Bobby was right. She had to focus, had to keep reminding herself that she was doing this for her daughter. She'd forced herself to walk away from the life she and Mac had built together, forced herself to become a stranger in order to keep herself and her daughter alive.

It had taken some getting used to, but she hardly ever slipped up any more. She hardly ever reacted when she heard the name *Robin* spoken in a crowd. She'd come to think of herself as Annie, had spent hour after hour practicing writing her new name, until it became second nature to her. Repetition was the key. Train the hand as well as the mind. It was like remembering to write the new year on every check you wrote after December 31. After enough times, you didn't have to stop and think about it anymore. It just came naturally.

She closed down the laptop, walked barefoot to the bedroom door and opened it silently. Sophie lay in a slender thread of moonlight, bedding bunched up at the foot of the bed, her lanky limbs flung out wildly in every direction. It was true, what she'd told Uncle Bobby. Her daughter was a trouper. When she'd decided that it was time for Sophie to know the truth about why they'd run away and just how precarious their situation was, her daughter had tried hard to understand.

"Try to think of it like this," Annie had told her. "Haven't you ever had a secret fantasy about becoming somebody different? Living somebody else's life? Changing everything about yourself and starting over again?"

Her daughter had shrugged. "I suppose. Everybody feels that way sometimes."

"Well, here's your chance."

Sophie had considered her words for a very long time. "But if we become different people, will that mean Dad isn't my father any more?"

Annie's heart had ached for her almost-fifteen-year-old daughter. "Of course not! No matter what you call yourself, it doesn't change who you really are inside. Daddy will always be your father."

"But won't he be mad at us if we change our name? Spinney was his dad's name, and his dad's before that."

"Absolutely not." Annie had threaded fingers with her daughter, clasping hands tightly. "Right now, your dad is so proud of what we're doing that he's watching over us, every step of the way."

"You mean like a guardian angel?"

"Exactly."

Sophie had pondered the situation a little longer. "Can I still be Sophie?"

"Absolutely. You'll just be Sophie Kendall instead of Sophie Spinney."

"Fine," she'd said. And that had been that.

Now, with a wobbly smile, Annie blew her daughter a kiss and silently closed the bedroom door.

The couch she'd bought from Trader Moe was every bit as lumpy as she'd expected. Wrapping herself in a soft blanket, she punched her pillow into a tight ball and closed her eyes. They'd made it this far because they were strong and smart. A great deal of time and planning had gone into shedding their old identities and building new ones that would hold up when examined in the harsh light of day. She'd used her savings to purchase the little tract house in Dearborn from one of Uncle Bobby's companies, then secretly signed it back over to him and pocketed the cash. She suspected that what she'd done wasn't strictly legal, but she hadn't bothered to question it. It didn't take a genius to figure out that not all of Uncle Bobby's business dealings operated on the right side of the law.

But she and Sophie were safe. That was the bottom line. And tomorrow they would begin, brick by brick, to build their new life.

Three

It took three cups of morning coffee to work up her courage.

The day was going to be a hot one; already the thermometer registered eighty in the shade. She didn't want to do this, but she'd promised, and the longer she put it off, the more difficult it would be. She might as well get it over with. Maybe it wouldn't be so bad. Like swallowing awful-tasting medicine, sometimes the anticipation was worse than the reality.

The phone rang four times before Bill Wyatt answered. "Daddy?" Annie said. "I just wanted to let you know that we got here in one piece."

In the background, she could hear the murmur of voices. "Just a minute," he said, setting down the phone with a dull thud. After a moment or two, he picked it back up. "Damn TV," he said. "Why haven't you called? I was starting to think something happened to you."

Why was it that every word out of his mouth always sounded like criticism? Maybe she was just being too sensitive. As a child, she'd been constantly reminded that she was too much like her mother, the drama queen of Atchawalla. "I told you it might be a couple of days," she said.

"And I'm not supposed to worry? I don't know how to get

in touch with you. You're not even using your own name. Something could happen to you, and they'd never find me to notify me. Do you have any idea how that makes me feel?"

Powerless, she imagined. And if there was one thing Bill Wyatt didn't like, it was to feel powerless. *Relax,* she told herself. *Don't let him get to you.*

But somehow, he always got to her. "I'm sorry, Dad," she said. "It's just been so hectic. When we got here, we didn't even have a bed to sleep in. I had to go out and buy furniture."

"Can you afford that?"

She wondered why he was asking, since she doubted he was about to offer financial assistance. Not that she would have accepted it if he had. "I bought secondhand," she said. Then, with forced enthusiasm, she added, "How's Lottie?"

Lottie Trent was a perky blond widow he'd met at a bingo game at the VFW hall eight months earlier. Annie couldn't imagine her father, with his ramrod-straight posture and steel-gray military haircut, playing bingo. But he swore that was where he and Lottie had met. A handsome if slightly intimidating man at seventy-one, Bill Wyatt maintained a trim figure and was still in possession of both the hair and the teeth that nature had bestowed upon him. That made the ex-marine a highly coveted commodity among the senior set, where single women outnumbered single men two to one. To Annie's amusement and his chagrin, her dad was the darling of all the twittering, gray-haired widows in his retirement complex.

"Lottie's fine. She went to Tallahassee for a few days to visit her daughter. She's flying back tonight. Monday, we're leaving on a Caribbean cruise."

"Wow." His romance with Lottie must be serious. None of Dad's previous lady friends had managed to convince him to set foot on the deck of a cruise ship. She tried to picture him in a Hawaiian shirt and shorts, but the image her mind conjured up was unthinkable. For as long as she could remember, Bill Wyatt had worn pressed khakis and dress shirts, seven days a week, fifty-two weeks a year.

"Lottie and her husband used to go all the time," he grumbled. "She claims I'll love it. Seven days of sun and fun. San Juan, St. Thomas, Barbados, Aruba. Everything for one price. Meals, tips, the whole enchilada." He snorted. "I'll probably go stir-crazy after the first day."

"Come on, Dad, it sounds great."

"We'll see. So you still don't intend to tell me where you are." He paused meaningfully. "Or who you are."

Her gut twisted at the disapproval she heard in his voice. "I can't, Dad. You know why. I don't want to put you in danger."

"That's the most ridiculous thing I ever heard! I don't understand any of this! If you didn't do anything wrong, why did you uproot yourself and Sophie and go into hiding? You're living like fugitives, for Christ's sake!"

In Bill Wyatt's book, running away from trouble was the coward's way out. He believed in facing it, no matter what the outcome. In his opinion, which he voiced with maddening frequency, she should have stayed and held her ground against any and all enemies.

"We've been over this before," she said with rapidly waning patience. "I had good reason for leaving Mississippi the way I did. Do you really think I'd live this way if I had any choice? Looking over my shoulder at every turn?"

"There's always a choice. You could have gone to the authorities if you really believed you were in danger."

Did she hear just the slightest emphasis on the word *believed?* Did her own father think she was nothing more than some hysterical housewife who'd imagined this whole scenario? Aghast, she reminded herself that he didn't know any of the details. He didn't know the truth about what had happened to Mac. He didn't know about Luke Brogan or his older brother Marcus, the most powerful man in Atchawalla County. Her father only knew that she'd somehow gotten into trouble and had run for her life. She tried to tell herself that it wasn't his fault, that his values weren't the same as hers, that his military training was to blame for his unyielding attitude.

But in the end, it all boiled down to one simple truth. In his eyes, she was a failure, and no matter what she did, she would never win his approval.

Wearily, she said, "Dad, I have to go now. I have a million things to do. I'll call you soon."

"Damn it, Robin, I'm telling you this for your own good. Running's not the answer. No matter what you're running from, sooner or later it'll catch up to you."

"I'll try to remember that, Dad. Enjoy your cruise. Give my love to Lottie."

She hung up the phone, her body trembling with a familiar mixture of pain and anger. How many years had she spent trying to win her father's love? As a child, she'd worshiped him, but he'd never noticed, never acknowledged his little girl's need to be loved. His treatment of her had been cold, hypercritical, dismissive. Bill Wyatt had wanted a son, and he'd made no bones about the fact. He'd never forgiven her for being a girl, had never forgiven her mother for being unable to have more children. As an adult, Annie had vowed to move forward with her life, to bury the ache she carried inside her and to stop looking back. But she'd never quite been able to. In spite of the strain between them, he was still her dad, and some deeply buried part of her still held onto the fantasy that with her mother gone, the two of them would become each other's mainstay.

It was a silly, childish dream, one better discarded than nurtured. Bill Wyatt was who he was, and he was too old and too stubborn to change.

She worked off some of her frustration unpacking. Because they'd moved so frequently, she and Sophie had learned to travel light. Even so, they owned as much junk as they could possibly squeeze into her Volvo wagon. They'd put away the clothes last night, but the living room was still piled with boxes. Annie picked one at random and began emptying it. The silverware, stored in its protective case, went directly into the kitchen drawer. But the glassware—plates, cups, bowls—all had to be washed before she could put them away. She carefully unwrapped each piece, discarded the crumpled newspaper, then loaded them into the dishwasher.

The job kept her busy until ten-thirty, when she switched on the dishwasher, poured a cup of hazelnut coffee into a ceramic mug, and went downstairs. Estelle was just climbing out of a blue-and-white Ford 4x4 pickup. The man behind the steering wheel eyed Annie through mirrored sunglasses, revved his engine a bit, and leaned to kiss Estelle goodbye. Then he wheeled the truck around, and with a roar of his engine and a squeal of his tires, he pulled out onto the highway and left her standing on the Twilight's crumbling pavement.

"My boyfriend, Boomer," Estelle explained with a roll of her eyes. "He'd sleep with that freaking truck if he could figure out how to fit it into the bedroom."

What kind of mother, Annie wondered, would christen her child with a name like Boomer?

When Estelle went on to explain, "His real name's Maurice," giving the word the proper French pronunciation, she wondered for an instant if she'd spoken the thought out loud. "His dad started calling him Boomer when he was a baby," Estelle said, "always falling down and bumping himself on the furniture. It just sort of stuck. And with a name like Maurice, Boomer seemed the lesser of two evils."

Maurice Chevalier notwithstanding, Annie was with her all

the way. "Thanks for coming in early," she said. "I know it makes a long day for you."

"No prob. I'm past the tired stage. I have so much energy these days that sometimes I forget I'm pregnant."

They spent the next ninety minutes going over details of the video rental operation. Annie familiarized herself with the day-to-day operations and took a quick look at the books, which she intended to go over in more detail later. Estelle seemed smart and capable, and Annie decided she definitely needed to give the girl a raise. Estelle was basically running the entire operation, with a minimum of part-time help, for a wage so low it was embarrassing.

At noon, Estelle opened the shop for business, and Annie went back upstairs. When she walked into the apartment, Sophie was standing at the refrigerator, her hair uncombed, dressed in the ubiquitous black T-shirt over navy running shorts. Staring balefully at all that gleaming white emptiness, Sophie announced, "I'm starving, and there's nothing to eat."

"We can fix that," Annie said. "Go comb your hair and put on a pair of shoes. We're going shopping."

Fifteen hundred miles away, Sheriff Luke Brogan sat on a hard wooden bench in a small riverside park and watched his granddaughter, Annabel, chase a female mallard across the lawn. It had been a dry summer so far, and the blistering sun had done significant damage to any greenery that wasn't protected by a sprinkler system. The duck waddled comically across the withered grass, and Annabel's delighted laughter floated back to him. Behind the little girl, past the small pleasure craft that crowded the bank, a massive oil barge slowly worked its way upriver. "You stay away from the riverbank, you hear?" he shouted to Annabel.

She paused, turned that exquisite little blond head of hers, and gave him a heart-melting smile. "I will, Grampa."

Beside him on the bench, Louis Farley popped open the briefcase that rested on his lap and took out a slender blue binder. "Here's your report."

Brogan took the binder without comment. Farley had come highly recommended. But with his manicured nails, his prissy suit and his rimless glasses, Louis Farley looked more like some pansy-ass attorney than a private investigator. Still, Brogan knew that the tough-guy P.I. image made famous by Hollywood was little more than a fictional invention. Nowadays, most investigative work was done by computer. A fifteen-year-old could do the job. In spite of Farley's sissified ways, Brogan had been assured that if a missing person could be located, he was the man to do it.

"I'm afraid there isn't much to report so far," Farley said.

Weighing the slim document in his hand, Brogan said, "How about you give me the fifty-cent version?"

"Of course. I was able to trace Robin Spinney as far as Detroit. Not surprising, since she was born there."

Brogan's stomach muscles contracted. "And?"

"After that, I lost her." Farley closed the briefcase with a snap and set it on the ground beside his feet. "Shortly after she left town, she withdrew her savings from Atchawalla First Federal and purchased a house in the Detroit area. A two-bedroom ranch in Dearborn, about ten miles outside the city. She paid cash for it. But she never lived there."

An insect buzzed past Brogan's head, and he swatted at it. "Who does live there?"

"Nobody. The house is sitting vacant. She purchased it and then disappeared."

Annabel was still chasing the mallard, both of them making erratic circles in the grass. "She must've sold it," Brogan said. "Liquefied her assets."

"If she did, there's no record of it. Her name is still on the deed. It's a matter of public record. Unfortunately, that's where the trail ends. Since she bought the house, none of her bank accounts or her credit cards have seen any activity. She hasn't been employed anywhere, at least not under her own social security number. She hasn't registered an automobile, and her daughter hasn't been enrolled in any Detroit-area schools. I checked every high school within a thirty-mile radius and showed the girl's picture around. Nobody knew her. Robin Spinney simply bought that little tract house in Michigan and then vanished."

Which meant that she'd gone into deep hiding. She knew he was after her. "What about her family? They still in Detroit?"

"Her mother's dead. Cancer, four years ago. Her father's still alive. He lives in one of those retirement communities in Florida."

"You check him out?"

"I spent a week down there, shadowing his moves, surveilling his condo. No sign of Spinney, and no suspicious moves on the part of Wyatt." Farley pursed his mouth in a brief gesture of distaste. "Not unless you count bingo as suspicious."

"Somebody's helping her," he said thoughtfully. "Maybe not her father, but somebody."

"It looks that way."

"I want you to keep looking. Dig a little deeper on her old man. Find out who she still has in the Detroit area. When you find out who's helping her, you'll find her."

"You do realize," Farley said amiably, "that she could be anywhere? It's a big country. She could have headed to Canada or Mexico. Most likely, she's living under an assumed name. She could even be dead."

"She's not dead. Keep looking."

Farley shrugged and leaned to pick up his briefcase. "It's your nickel."

"That's right. It's my nickel. Two people don't just vanish

into thin air. Keep on looking until either you find her or I tell you to stop."

After Farley had gone, Brogan sat there for a long time, watching Annabel, watching the river traffic, wondering how it was that a single instant, a single mistake, could forever alter a man's life and start him on a steady descent into his own personal hell.

Just two more years, he reminded himself. If he could hold on for just two more years, he'd have his thirty years in, and he could retire with full benefits while he was still young enough to enjoy it. Buy himself a little houseboat down on the Gulf and spend his golden years fishing. If Robin Spinney didn't fuck it up for him.

A cloud crossed the face of the sun, momentarily turning the surface of the river a steely gray. So much blood on his hands. So many lives disrupted, destroyed, in a ripple effect that Luke Brogan could never have imagined if he hadn't seen it played out right in front of his own eyes. Even if he wanted to stop it now, it was too late to act on any regrets he might have. Once set in motion, the ripple was irreversible. There was only one possible conclusion to this scenario: when he found Robin Spinney and her daughter, he would kill them. Maybe once they were dead he could stop looking over his shoulder and start sleeping again.

The oil barge was far upriver now, headed for Memphis or St. Louis or wherever the hell it was going. From her perch atop the Civil War cannon that graced the small park, Annabel waved to him. He waved back. She hopped down, and with another of those billion-dollar smiles, she came loping across the grass with all the grace of a three-legged hippopotamus. Flinging herself onto his lap, she said, "Can we get an ice cream, Gramps?"

"Well, now, I don't know," Brogan said, settling her on his knee. "Your mama will likely skin my hide if I let you spoil your lunch."

She wiggled her bony little rump, trying to find a comfortable spot on his leg. "Mama doesn't have to know."

"I suspect she'll notice if you don't eat your meat and potatoes."

She wrinkled her nose. "I don't like meat and potatoes. I like ice cream."

"Tell you what. How about we share an ice cream? I'll help you eat it. That way, you can leave room for lunch."

The little girl studied him with solemn brown eyes. "Peppermint stick?" she said hopefully.

He didn't much care for peppermint stick, but he knew Annabel loved it, and he hadn't yet figured out how to say no to her. "My favorite," he said. "Let's go, sugarplum."

She slid down off his knee. He folded the investigator's report and pocketed it. Hand in hand, they headed off across the park in search of peppermint stick ice cream.

The floor at Grondin's Superette tilted like a ship's deck in a gale-force wind. Her shopping cart kept listing to the left, and Annie had to struggle to keep it moving in a straight line down the center of the produce aisle. Stopping beneath a sign that advertised FRESH PRODUCE, she picked up a head of lettuce. The outer leaves were wilted and had started to turn brown around the edges. Annie put it back and began searching for something a little fresher. Sophie careened around the corner, arms loaded, almost bumping into a young mother with two toddlers in tow. "Sorry," she breathed before dropping her plunder into the cart. Annie eyed the bag of potato chips, the jar of sweet pickles and the twin boxes of Frosted Flakes and said, "I see you're on a health food kick."

"Be right back. Geez, this place smells like rotten bananas."

Annie watched her daughter disappear again. With a sigh, she tossed a marginally acceptable head of lettuce into the cart. Sophie was a picky eater who had a habit of getting onto these food binges when she'd eat the same bizarre item day after day after day. For the longest time it had been Marshmallow Fluff on Ritz Crackers. Annie had tried everything she could think of—threats, coercion, pleading—to get her daughter to eat something else. But nothing had worked. Then one day, seemingly out of the blue, Sophie had abandoned the Ritz Crackers and Fluff for canned peas and tuna fish. At least the tuna had protein.

By the time they reached the checkout, Annie had bought enough food to feed an army. When the cashier rang up the total, she gulped. But it couldn't be helped. Setting up housekeeping in a new place was expensive. She'd had to buy staples, had to stock up on milk and butter and toilet paper. Next time around, she'd spend a more reasonable amount.

They loaded the groceries into the back of the Volvo, and Sophie returned the cart to its corral. Annie started the engine and they quickly cranked down their respective windows. Not for the first time, she thought wistfully of the new SUV she'd sold in Detroit for half of its Blue Book value. The vehicle had been loaded: four-wheel-drive, CD player, air-conditioning, pushbutton everything. But beggars couldn't be choosers. The Volvo was sturdy and dependable, in spite of the 200,000 miles on its odometer. The FM radio played just fine, and she and Sophie were fully capable of rolling their own windows up and down. So what if her T-shirt was sticking to a giant wet spot between her shoulder blades? So what if her hair felt limp and frizzy and totally unmanageable? The Volvo had gotten her all the way here from Las Vegas, and in the greater scheme of things, its lack of air-conditioning was nothing but a minor irritant.

She was halfway home, on a deserted stretch of road that ran alongside the river, when without warning, steam began to pour out from beneath the hood. Annie silently cursed the idiot lights that should have warned her there was a problem, lights that had probably stopped working some fifty thousand miles ago. She steered the car onto the shoulder and rolled to a stop. "What's wrong?" Sophie said.

"I don't know. The car's overheating." Annie turned the key and pumped the gas. The engine cranked, but the car didn't start. It was probably her fault for mentally praising the Volvo's dependability. She'd probably jinxed it. "Come on," she muttered, cranking it again. But the battery was old, and with each successive attempt, it grew weaker and weaker.

She thought about the gallon of milk in the back, about Sophie's Popsicles and the small piece of sirloin she'd picked up for dinner tonight. She calculated the distance home, recalculated it in terms of distance divided by walking speed, then factored in the temperature and the weight of the groceries they'd bought. It wasn't even remotely feasible. Even if they only carried the perishables, it was at least a mile in ninety-degree heat. Then they'd have to find a way to get back to pick up the rest of the stuff. It wasn't going to happen, not in this lifetime.

"Well, shit," she said.

Four

It had been one hell of a morning.

He'd been dragged out of bed at the crack of dawn after Andy Kavanaugh's kid missed a curve on his way to work and wrapped his car around a tree. Miraculously, the kid had survived the accident with only a few broken bones. He'd been LifeFlighted to Central Maine Medical Center in Lewiston because the local hospital was woefully inadequate, and Davy could only hope he'd learned that when the speed limit sign said forty-five, it didn't mean sixty-five. Not on Maine's bumpy, winding back-country roads. The Kavanaugh kid had been lucky. It could have been a lot worse.

Cleanup had taken a big chunk out of his morning. When he got to the office, he found a three-inch stack of paperwork sitting on his desk, waiting to be read, signed, and approved. He spent a good hour working his way through that, ending with the report that Officer René Bellevance had filed on a domestic dispute he'd handled last night out at Aube's Trailer Park. Danny Veilleux had downed a few too many Budweisers while watching the Red Sox game. When his wife Patricia, who'd had more than a few herself, had the audacity to turn off the TV so he'd pay attention to her instead of the game, all hell had broken loose. Danny had thrown the remote control at her, hitting her on the temple, and she'd gone after him with her great-grandmother's cast-iron skillet.

Fortunately, the neighbors had dialed 911 before they could kill each other. Patricia had come out of it with a black eye from the remote and a sprained pinky from clobbering Danny with the frying pan. She'd slept it off in lock-up. Her husband hadn't been so lucky. He'd received a concussion and ten stitches, and he'd spent the night in the hospital. They were both due in district court tomorrow morning to answer charges of D&D and assault.

He'd just finished initialing René's report when he got called out to Roy Kimball's place, where he spent forty-five minutes talking Roy out of pressing charges against the Henderson kids for trampling his prize begonias. Again. Apparently there'd been a long-running feud going on between Kimball and the Hendersons ever since the young couple moved in next door with their three rambunctious boys. The kids didn't mean any harm. They were just boys, doing what boys do. Roy, the stubborn old coot, refused to put up a fence to keep them out. And Davy was caught in the middle. What was he supposed to do, arrest the three boys, ranging in age from five to eight, for trespassing? It had taken some doing, but he'd finally managed to calm Roy down, smooth things over, avert disaster. At least until the next time.

And he had no doubt there'd be a next time.

Squabbling neighbors, domestic disputes, lead-footed drivers with no concept of the term *speed limit*. He wondered how Ty did this, day in and day out, year after year, without going absolutely apeshit. If he had to put up with two months of this crap, he'd probably end up in a rubber room somewhere. It didn't help that he'd stayed up too late last night, staining the damn table. He was overtired and cranky, it was past his lunchtime, and he'd skipped breakfast. At this time of day, Lenny's Café would be filled to overflowing. There wouldn't be a free booth in the place. His best bet was probably the McDonald's across the river. It was three miles out on the state highway, but their drive-through was usually pretty quick. He could pick up a Big Mac and a Coke, and eat right there in the car.

Davy reversed direction, crossed the old iron bridge, and headed north along the river. He passed the cutoff to Gram's house, passed Aube's Trailer Park, where his sister lived. Passed the old one-room schoolhouse his parents had attended back in the 1950s. It was deserted now, a ghost of its former self, weeds growing around the foundation, all the windows long since broken out, graffiti spray-painted on the doors. A haven, he imagined, for squirrels and woodchucks and God only knew what else.

He was on the lonely stretch of highway three-quarters of a mile out when he saw her standing by the side of the road, a little bit of a thing in jeans and Hard Rock T-shirt, gazing balefully at the plume of steam rising from beneath the raised hood of an ancient blue Volvo. Nearby, a bored-looking teenage girl sat in the grass with her arms folded around upraised knees. The kid was dressed all in black, with shoulder-length black hair that could stand a good combing, black lipstick, and a matching pair of oversized safety pins in her earlobes.

He knew who the woman was. Everybody in town knew who she was. Annie Kendall was new in town, and he had it on good authority that she'd just bought Mike Boudreau's run-down motel and video store. What the hell she could possibly want with that sorry-assed piece of real estate, he couldn't imagine. But he'd heard it from the horse's mouth down at Lenny's. Mikey had sold the Twilight to her lock, stock, and videos, and he and the missus had loaded everything they owned into their RV and retired to Florida, where a man didn't have to shovel snow or wear long johns nine months out of the year.

His stomach growled, and Davy silently told it to chill out. With a sigh, he glanced into his rearview mirror, signaled, and pulled onto the shoulder. He wheeled the cruiser around in a tight U-turn, back in the direction from which he'd come, and pulled to a stop behind the broken-down Volvo. Activating his blue flashers so some dumb-ass wouldn't plough into him— not that flashing blue lights would necessarily prevent that— he unfastened his seat belt.

It looked like the Big Mac would have to wait.

"Um…Mom?"

Annie glanced up, and her daughter pointed a slender, black-clad shoulder toward the rear of the Volvo. Stepping out from beneath the hood, Annie peered down the side of the car. Parked directly behind her was a white Crown Victoria with blue lights flashing. She'd never even heard it pull up; the hiss from the escaping steam had drowned out the sound of the cruiser's engine. This was great. Really great. All she wanted was to blend in and be invisible. Instead, twenty-six hours after she hit town, she'd already attracted the attention of the local cops.

Good going, Kendall.

She wiped her hands on her jeans and stood her ground as he opened his door and emerged from the patrol car. *God,* she prayed, *please don't let him be one of those small-town Nazi types.* As a cop's wife, she'd seen more than her share of men who let the badge go to their heads. The last thing she needed was some redneck bully giving her a hard time.

He had long legs. They didn't move quickly, but with each step they covered a lot of ground. The rest of him was tall and rangy, with dark blond hair that fell neatly to a spot just above his collar. As he drew nearer, she guessed that he was somewhere near forty. His eyes hidden behind polarized lenses, he wore the starchy, spit-shined look and the smooth confidence of every cop she'd ever known.

"Ma'am," he said. "Mind if I take a look?"

Annie tucked her hands into her pockets so he wouldn't see that they were trembling. "Officer," she said. "By all means."

He moved past her, leaned over the engine, and poked around. Checking belts, hoses, all the things she'd already checked. The back of his neck was several shades paler than the rest of him. Either he always wore a collar, or his haircut was very recent.

A trickle of sweat ran down her spine.

It didn't take him long. "Looks like your radiator's shot," he said, rubbing his hands together and emerging from beneath the hood. It was the same conclusion she'd already reached; it didn't take an Einstein to figure it out. "You have AAA?"

It had been one of the first things she'd done, even before she bought the car. One more legitimately acquired piece of ID, one step closer to cementing her new identity. Who would question the validity of an AAA card? "Yes," she said.

"If you'd like, I can give Sonny's Towing a call. He'll haul her in and have her fixed up in no time."

"That won't be necessary, Officer. I can call AAA myself."

He adjusted his sunglasses. "Yeah," he said, "you probably can. But I can save you time if I call Sonny directly. We went to high school together."

Ah, yes. The insidious old boys network. A hard nugget of resentment sprang to life inside her. She opened her mouth to argue, then realized it wasn't worth the effort. "Thank you," she said stiffly. "Let me get my card."

He followed her, stood waiting by the driver's door while she fumbled clumsily for her wallet. He took the AAA card without speaking, walked back to his patrol car, and got in.

"Mom?" Sophie whined from her perch by the roadside. "What about my Popsicles? They'll melt if they don't get home pretty soon."

"If they melt, I'll buy new ones."

The cop climbed back out of his patrol car and returned to where she stood with her arms folded across her chest. Handing her the AAA card, he said, "Sonny'll be along in about a half hour. Meantime, you should probably get those groceries home. You help me load 'em in the cruiser and I'll give you a ride."

"There's no need for you to do that, Officer—" she focused on his name tag "—Hunter. There must be taxi service in Serenity."

"I can't let you do that, ma'am."

"I—why, for God's sake?"

"There's only one taxi in Serenity, and you'd be taking your life in your hands. Believe me, you're better off riding with me."

Was this his attempt at being charming? She couldn't see his eyes behind those dark glasses, and it increased her irritation, because she had no way of gauging his sincerity. Or lack thereof.

"You don't even know where I live," she said. "For all you know, I could be just passing through."

"I know where you live."

Her pulse began a slow, steady thrum. "How, exactly, is that possible?"

His face, chiseled from hard stone, relaxed into a semblance of a smile. It erased ten years from his age. "Serenity's a small town," he said. "When an attractive blonde driving a blue Volvo with Nevada plates buys a run-down motel and video rental store, everybody in town hears about it."

So much for blending in and being invisible.

Sophie and the groceries took up the back seat, so Annie rode up front with Hunter. He wasn't the type to make small talk. Instead, he sat silent and aloof, both hands on the wheel, eyes steady on the road ahead, all business. Annie took the opportunity to study him from the corner of her eye. His profile was chiseled to stone-cold perfection, his chin firm and unyielding, his nose long and straight. She suspected he didn't smile often. Above the blue collar, his Adam's apple was clearly visible.

She'd always drummed it into Sophie's head that policemen were her friends. After all, Sophie's father had been a cop. Annie had always trusted them implicitly until she'd been given a reason not to. What a bizarre turn her life had taken. She'd been married to a cop for a dozen years. Yet now, sitting beside this cop in the front seat of his patrol car, her palms were sweaty, her heartbeat irregular. Fear did the damnedest things to a person.

She wondered what color Hunter's eyes were, hidden away behind those dark glasses. Blue? Brown? There was an aura of mystery to him that piqued her interest. The glasses provided excellent camouflage. Did the uniform do the same? What other secrets might he be hiding?

Estelle was standing in the doorway of the shop when they pulled up. "Davy," she said to the cop, and he acknowledged her with a silent nod of his head. "What happened?" she asked Annie.

"Busted radiator," Annie said, scrambling to follow Hunter's long legs up the outside staircase to her apartment. He stepped aside and she squeezed past him on the narrow landing, fumbling to get the key in the lock. They set the groceries on the kitchen counter and went back for a second load. Estelle, looking cool and bright in a lime-colored blouse and yellow plaid pants, leaned against the door frame and watched them.

"I'd help," she said, "but…"

"You're pregnant," Annie said. "You shouldn't be carrying heavy things."

"Can I get that in writing so I can shove it in Boomer's face?"

While Annie waited, Hunter leaned into the back seat of the cruiser. He gathered up a couple of bags, turned and loaded them into her arms without speaking. The next two bags were Sophie's. She groaned when they came her way. "This living on the second floor," Soph said, "is really going to suck."

Annie shot her a lethal look. Her daughter scowled, but she knew when it was time to shut up. Sophie hoisted the bags high and headed back up the stairs.

Hunter closed the door of the police car and followed Annie up the stairs. They set the last of the groceries on the kitchen counter and stood there in an awkward silence. "Before I forget," he said, "you'd probably like Sonny's phone number."

"Oh. Yes. Of course." Annie dug in her shoulder bag, came up with a pen and a scrap of paper, scribbled the number he gave her and then read it back to him to make sure she'd copied it down correctly. He reached up to adjust the glasses, and for an instant, she thought he was going to take them off. She waited, her breath held at bay. But he lowered his hand.

"Don't let Sonny take advantage of you," he said. "If his price doesn't sound reasonable, insist on seeing a written estimate. You're a woman, and you know how that can go."

Capping the pen, she said briskly, "Thank you. For everything."

"Just doing my job," he said. "Have a nice day." And he nodded politely in Sophie's direction.

Annie followed him to the door and watched him walk back down the stairs and fold his lanky frame into the police cruiser. The Crown Victoria started with a powerful roar. He adjusted his seat belt, tugged on it to make sure it was secure, then glanced up at her, still standing in the open doorway.

Their gazes met, and he stared straight at her through those opaque glasses that revealed nothing. Then, turning his attention elsewhere, he spoke into his two-way radio, wheeled the car around, and pulled out onto the highway.

"Mom? Stuff's melting all over the counter."

Ah, to be fifteen again, and totally helpless. Dragged back to reality by her daughter's voice, Annie realized she was still clutching the phone number to Sonny's Towing. Folding the piece of paper, she tucked it into the pocket of her jeans, closed the door, and headed back to the kitchen to salvage what was left of her perishables.

An hour later, groceries tucked away and Sophie mollified with a can of Franco-American and a watery blue Popsicle, Annie picked up the phone and called Sonny Gaudette.

"Ayuh," he said. "I checked her out and she definitely needs a new radiator."

"How much will that cost?"

"Depends on how hard it is to find one."

"Find one?" She didn't like the ominous sound of his words. "Are you telling me you don't have one in stock?"

"Don't see too many Volvos around here. I'll have to call around. Thing is, they never die. Just like that little pink rabbit with the drum, they just keep going, and going, and—"

"So you have no idea when I can get my car back?"

"Once I find one, it won't take any time at all to put it in. I'll start calling Friday morning, and—"

"Friday? But that's three days away!"

"Yup. I got a ring job that'll take all day tomorrow and most of Thursday. I'm closed on the weekend, but if I can find a radiator sometime Friday, you should have your car back by Tuesday. Wednesday at the latest."

Tuesday or Wednesday. A whole week away. How was she supposed to get around in the meantime? "You're kidding," she said. "I don't suppose you have a loaner available until then?"

He chuckled, as though what she'd said was somehow humorous. "'Fraid not. You could probably rent a car in Lewiston." Cheerfully, he added, "'Course, you'd have to get there first."

She knew she wasn't going to like the answer, but she had to ask the question anyway. "Where's Lewiston?"

"About forty miles downriver. Give me a call on Monday. I should know more by then."

Florida was a shithole.

The instant he left the air-conditioned comfort of Miami International Airport, the steaming, smothering wall of heat smacked Louis Farley directly in the face. His lungs struggled to draw in the soupy thickness. Ten seconds in the Florida heat, and already he needed a shower. The single carry-on bag he'd packed felt like it weighed eighty pounds. No wonder they called this place God's waiting room. If old age didn't get you, the climate would. Why the hell anybody would choose to live in this earthbound version of hell, he couldn't imagine. It was like traveling to a foreign country. He hadn't dealt with a single person for whom English was a native language since he stepped off the plane. With all those Julios and Miguels and Jorges running around, he might easily have landed in Havana. Louis reached into his jacket pocket, withdrew a clean white handkerchief, and mopped his face. The next time he had to travel to southern Florida on a job, he was asking for more money.

He found the rental car easily, a plain white compact sedan as he'd requested. Unobtrusive, and less susceptible to the oppressive heat. Louis unlocked the door, set his bags on the passenger seat, then took off his jacket and hung it carefully from the hook over the back door. The interior was spotless, also as requested. He slid into the driver's seat, started the engine, and cranked the air-conditioning.

As the A/C began to drive the unbearable humidity from the car, he pulled out the street map he'd brought with him and studied the route that he'd marked with a yellow highlighter. He'd been here before, just a couple of weeks ago, but with Miami traffic being what it was, it couldn't hurt to refresh his memory. When he was satisfied that he knew where he was going, Louis maneuvered the little car out of airport parking and into a sea of slow-moving traffic. He still hadn't gotten used to how flat Florida was. He'd grown up in the mountains of Vermont, and all this flatness seemed foreign to him. Not to mention the congestion, block after block of small, flat-roofed houses on tiny lots crammed hip to hip to allow room for more and more snowbirds to land.

Ahead of him, a white-haired granny in a 1970s-era Oldsmobile Toronado drove like death had already come and claimed her. She stopped for a red light, and Louis tapped his fingertips impatiently against the steering wheel. The light took forever. When it turned green, he raced the engine of the little rental car, hoping that Granny would take the hint. But she pulled away from the intersection with all the haste of a hearse at the head of a funeral procession.

Louis loosened his tie and opened the top button of his shirt. Impatience would get him nowhere. He had to keep a cool head. Haste would only lead to mistakes, and he couldn't afford a mistake. He was a professional, and Brogan was expecting him to act like one.

It was just this damn heat. It was enough to drive a man crazy.

After a series of red lights, he finally lost Granny and her Toronado. A few blocks later, he saw the motel ahead, the same place he'd stayed the first time he'd come down here. Inexpensive, but clean. No cockroaches hiding in the bathroom, no recent knifings in the parking lot. Long and low, the two-story building was fashioned of white stucco, with a small pool encircled by a chain-link fence sitting out front, next to a narrow strip of lawn decorated with pink flamingos. Southern Florida at its tacky best.

The desk clerk's name was Rosalita. Louis paid for two nights and carried his bag to a room on the second floor. Outside the door, an orange plastic deck chair perched on the balcony, giving him a bird's-eye view of the pool area, just in case he wanted to ogle the sweet young things in their bikinis. Except that there weren't any sweet young things to ogle. Right now, the only bodies he saw around the pool were a five-year-old kid playing with a pair of blow-up water wings and a pudgy middle-aged woman—probably the kid's grandmother—who'd tried unsuccessfully to hide her crepey thighs beneath the ruffled skirt of her flowered one-piece bathing suit.

Like everything else in southern Florida, the motel room was air-conditioned. Louis stripped out of his limp traveling clothes, took a tepid shower, and changed into the tan Bermudas and tropical-print shirt he'd bought in the airport gift shop. Flip-flops, a white cotton sun hat, and mirrored sunglasses completed the ensemble. Louis studied his reflection in the bathroom mirror and decided he looked like an idiot. But Florida was overrun with idiots dressed just like him. Nobody would give him a second look.

When he went back out, the woman and the kid were gone. Nobody stayed out in this kind of heat for long, not if they had a choice about it. He got back into the rental car and drove to the condominium complex that Bill Wyatt called home. It looked just like every other senior-citizen complex he'd seen down here. The damn things were everywhere. This one was painted a soft shade of pink. Why did it seem as though everything in Miami that wasn't white was pink? It was one of life's little mysteries, one he'd probably never solve.

Louis squeezed the rental car into a tiny slot across the

street from the complex, pulled out his cell phone and a clipboard filled with papers, and pretended to be conducting business. Just a regular guy on vacation who'd brought work from the office—poor sucker—and didn't want to endanger anyone by using his cell and driving at the same time.

At precisely 3:21 p.m., Bill Wyatt drove into the complex. He parked in his usual spot and got out of the car, dressed in tennis whites and carrying a racket. Right on time. It never ceased to amaze Louis what creatures of habit humans were. Every weekday at two o'clock, Bill Wyatt took tennis lessons at the nearby Dade Highlands Country Club. Wyatt stopped to talk to a neighbor who was out walking his shih tzu, then he disappeared into the complex. Building C, first floor, unit 1.

Twenty minutes later, right on schedule, Wyatt reappeared, dressed for his nightly dinner date with Lottie Trent. He would pick up his lady friend and they'd go to dinner at Clem's Clams. It would take them approximately ninety minutes from appetizer to dessert. After dinner, they'd return to her condo a few blocks away, where they'd draw the curtains and spend another forty minutes doing God only knew what. Louis didn't even want to go there.

He had Wyatt's schedule down pat. During the week he'd spent surveilling Bill Wyatt during his last trip to Miami, the man had never deviated from his routine. Wyatt was as predictable as the tides. So tonight, while Bill Wyatt was eating dinner and probably getting his pipes cleaned, Louis Farley would be searching his condo in pursuit of something, anything, that might lead him to Wyatt's daughter.

The water damage to her number-three guest room started just above the bathroom door and stretched halfway across the room. The discolored ceiling tiles sagged like an old woman's breasts, and the mildew smell was so strong that Sophie had stuck her head in, looked around, and immediately remembered somewhere else she needed to be.

Annie was standing in the middle of the room, studying the damage, when a voice from the open doorway behind her drawled, "Honey, you have got your work cut out for you."

With a startled gasp, Annie spun around. The woman who stood in the doorway was in her late thirties, with a pretty face, a devilish twinkle in her eye, and a head of dark, wavy hair that tumbled around her shoulders. "Sorry," she said. "I didn't mean to startle you. I'm Jolene Crowley. Jo for short. Jackson and I live across the street."

Breathing hard, Annie rested a hand over her heart. "You scared the stuffing right out of me."

Wryly, Jo said, "I do that to a lot of people, I'm afraid."

"It's all right. I just didn't realize anyone was there." Recovering, she stepped forward and offered her hand. "Annie Kendall," she said. "I'm the proud owner of this lovely establishment."

Jo's handshake was firm and brisk. "So I've heard." Her gaze made a sweeping assessment of the room. "People are already laying odds on how soon you'll run away screaming."

"Are they now? What was your bet?"

"My money's on you, hon. You look tough as nails to me. Although I can't imagine why anybody would want to move here if they didn't have to."

Annie turned her attention back to the ceiling. "I'm just a single mother," she said, parroting Uncle Bobby's words, "starting out someplace new."

Jo came to stand beside her. Folding her arms across her chest, she studied the huge water stain overhead. "Well, you sure picked a lulu of a place to start out. Hard to believe something as innocuous as a little water could do that much damage."

"Do you suppose the roof's gone, or can it be patched?"

"Damned if I can tell. It's one hell of a mess, that's for sure. But the place has sat empty for a dozen years at least. In that amount of time, even a small leak could do some pretty substantial damage."

"Especially in this climate," Annie agreed.

"I could ask Jack to come over, climb up on the roof and check it out. He's used to heights. He works as a lineman for CMP."

"CMP?"

"The electric company. He spends half his life up in the air. Good God, this place is a mess."

They turned in unison and critically examined the ruined mattress, the moldy carpet, the limp curtains of a hideous faded yellow that hung in the windows. "If I was Catholic," Jo said with cheerful repugnance, "I'd cross myself."

"Maybe I should consider renovating with a lit torch."

"Oh, I wouldn't give up on it just yet. You'd be surprised what a carpenter could do with the place. If you're willing to put the money into it, of course. Which reminds me, I see you've met Davy."

Annie glanced over at her. "Davy?"

"Hunter. Police chief. I saw him drop you off earlier. You having car trouble?"

"A broken radiator. So Hunter's the chief of police?"

"Interim chief, actually. Among other things." Jolene wandered around the room, drew a slender forefinger through the thick layer of dust that covered the bed stand, and made a face. "My brother Ty is the police chief, but he's on a leave of absence. His wife's carrying twins. High-risk pregnancy. Her obstetrician's in New York and he wants her off her feet for the next little while, so they're staying at her town house in Manhattan until the babies are born. Davy's filling in here until Ty gets back."

"He seems a little…grim, for lack of a better word."

"That's just Davy. He keeps to himself. Doesn't have a lot to say to anyone. But he's an okay guy. I've known him all my life. And just for the record, he's not married."

"I don't remember asking."

"But you were wondering," Jolene said. "Anyway, that's not why I came over. You have a teenage daughter?"

"Sophie."

"I have to teach summer school. Starting next Tuesday. Four days a week, six hours a day, for four weeks, I'm going to be shoehorned into a classroom bursting at the seams with obnoxious little heathens. The girl who usually babysits for me got a real job this summer. Wouldn't you know it? I thought maybe your daughter would be interested."

It would be the ideal solution to Annie's dilemma. Sophie would stop whining about being bored, and she'd be working right across the street, where Annie could keep an eye on her. Soph would make a little money to pay for school clothes, and wouldn't have to wander far from home to do it. It was a win-win situation, one that included payoffs for both of them.

"She'd probably be very interested," Annie said. "She's already hounding me about getting a job. How old are your kids?"

"Nine-year-old twins. Sam and Jake. They're good kids. A little rambunctious. You know how boys can be. But they're good kids."

Annie beamed at Jolene Crowley, who might just be her new best friend. "I don't know about you," she told Jo, "but I've had enough of breathing mold spores. Sophie's probably in the shop with Estelle, comparing favorite horror movies. We might as well go talk to her about it." She hesitated. "There is one thing I have to warn you about. You know how Picasso had a blue period?"

"Sure. Why?"

"Well—" Annie scraped back a fistful of hair from her face "—Sophie's currently going through a Marilyn Manson period. She looks a little like a corpse in its funeral shroud, but she's really nowhere near as scary as she seems."

"Honey," Jolene said, patting her on the shoulder, "I teach high school. When it comes to teenagers, I have no fear."

He usually made a point of avoiding the Big Apple when Dee's copper-colored '78 Cougar was parked in one of the employee parking spots, but tonight, Davy wheeled the Crown Victoria into the empty space next to hers and turned off the engine. It had been a terrible day, and he was wiped out, but he'd made a promise to Gram, and he was obligated to keep it. Family obligations had never been his strong suit, and some days, he wondered why he stayed here in this god-forsaken place. Wondered why he didn't just pack his bags and head back down to D.C. He'd left the agency on shaky terms after Chelsea died, but if he came crawling back on his knees and groveled, he probably had a pretty good shot at convincing Covington to give him his old job back. Or at least a reasonable facsimile of his old job. After the way he blew that last case, they'd probably never send him back into the field, but right about now, a desk job in D.C. looked pretty damn good.

He got out of the car, went inside, and headed down the narrow aisle toward the soda cooler. His sister was alone behind the cash register, a short line of customers in front of her. After chasing kids all day, Dee worked the four-to-twelve shift at the Big Apple to put food on the table and shoes on their feet. His brother-in-law, Ray, had never held a job for longer than a few months. Every so often, mostly to get out of the house and away from a bunch of screaming kids—not to mention Dee's mouth—Ray would sweet-talk somebody into hiring him. Highly skilled jobs like washing dishes at

Lenny's or pulling auto parts for Sonny Gaudette. But the jobs never lasted long, and for the most part, Ray sat on his rapidly expanding ass in front of the TV and let Dee support the family.

If she had half a brain, she would have ditched Raymond Arsenault years ago. But something kept her with him. Maybe it was fear of the unknown. He tried to imagine what it would be like to face life as a single mother of six kids under the age of twelve, but it was unimaginable. Still, Davy would have been willing to help her, if only for the sake of the kids. His sister might be difficult, but she was still his sister.

Davy took his place in line. Behind the counter, Dee made change routinely, joylessly. At thirty-five, her lackluster brown hair was already streaked with gray, and she still carried the thirty extra pounds she'd put on three or four pregnancies ago. When the customer ahead of him left, Davy plunked a six-pack of Pepsi down on the counter. "Dee," he said.

"Davy." She checked the price of the soda and rang it up. "How goes the crime-fighting battle?"

"Not much crime to fight." He pulled out his wallet, handed her a ten.

"That's what I hear." She fumbled in the drawer for change, counted it out. "I also hear you've taken to rescuing damsels in distress."

Annie Kendall. Christ, a man couldn't pass gas in this town without everybody knowing about it. "Where'd you hear that?"

"You know Serenity. Word gets around."

"I'll say." He pocketed his change, tucked his wallet away. "How're the kids?" He deliberately didn't ask about her husband. He'd never had much use for Ray Arsenault, and he never would. His feelings toward Ray were responsible for at least a portion of the tension between his sister and him. Not all of it. But a portion.

Bagging the Pepsi, she said, "They're growing too damn fast. I had to take Jill to Wal-Mart this morning because she didn't have anything to wear. She's outgrown every pair of pants she owns. I swear to God, that kid's shot up a good six inches in the last three months."

Was it his imagination, or was there a hint of accusation in her words? If so, he couldn't imagine why. It wasn't his fault she'd chosen to marry a man who wasn't willing to support her or the children they'd spawned. Clearing his throat, he said, "I saw Gram last night."

His sister stiffened and crossed her arms over her ample bosom, which strained against the material of her flowered knit top. "Oh?" she said coolly.

"She called me over. Another of her emergencies."

Dee rolled her eyes. "I just bet. What was it this time?"

"The cat got out. I had to go hunting for the damn thing. Except that after I spent twenty minutes running around the yard calling *kitty-kitty-kitty,* it turns out the cat was in the house all the time."

Dee propped herself against the cash register. "There's a surprise. I've told you and told you not to run every time she calls. Your life isn't your own because of her. Why the hell do you think I stay away? I'd be over there three times a day if I let her get away with the stuff she pulls on you."

He felt a headache coming on, the same headache that had teased him at Gram's last night. "That's just the thing," he said. "It was a ploy."

"What'd I tell you?"

"But I wasn't the target."

"Oh?"

"No. You were. She wants you to visit. She says she hasn't seen you in months."

"Oh, Jesus. Here we go again."

"Look, Dee," he said, wading in when all his instincts told

him to stay out of it, "nobody's asking you to take responsibility for the woman. Just stop by for an hour. Bring the kids. It would mean the world to her."

"No."

"Why, for Christ's sake?"

Dee rested both palms on the counter. Leaning forward, she said, "Every time I go over there, she tries to get her hooks into me. I don't have time to run her errands. I don't have time to chase her goddamn cat. I don't have time to deal with her fabricated emergencies. I have six kids. I have this lousy job and a car that's being held together with rust and duct tape. I'm tired, Davy. Don't you get it? My plate's already full. When am I supposed to visit, at three o'clock in the morning? Let me check my date book. Maybe I'm available next Thursday."

It might have been a tear he saw glistening in her eye. Or maybe it was just a trick of the light. "Damn it, Dee," he said, "the woman raised us. She didn't have to. She could've just said to hell with us and let us go into foster care while Mom played ring-around-the-rosy with the state's penal system. Instead, she gave up her own life to raise three kids who weren't her responsibility. Don't you think we owe her something?"

"Owe her something? She didn't do us any frigging favors! She should've left well enough alone. Maybe I would've gotten out of this town if Gram hadn't kept us here."

He stared at his sister, disbelief and disappointment grinding away at his gut. She wasn't going to let it go. No matter how old she got, Dee simply couldn't let go of the fact that they'd grown up poor.

Oh, they'd always had clothes to wear, and they'd never gone hungry. Gram had made sure they always had enough to eat. Looking back, he wondered how, even with the help of that monthly DHS check, she'd managed to raise three kids on her woefully inadequate fixed income. There she'd been, a woman in her sixties who should have been enjoying her golden years. Instead, she'd spent two decades and most of her retirement income raising three wild-eyed, ungrateful hellions. It was a miracle she'd survived.

Somehow, being poor hadn't affected him or Brian, not like it had Dee. They'd been too busy being guys, doing guy things, to take much notice. That seemed to be a major difference between boys and girls. Give a boy a tattered sweatshirt, a pair of smelly sneakers, and a basketball, and he'd be in hog heaven. Girls were different. They needed to be surrounded by pretty things in order to feel good about themselves. Where he and Brian had accepted being poor without giving it much thought, it had eaten away at Dee like a cancerous growth. She had carted the mantle of poverty around on her back, a burdensome wooden cross that had crippled her. He couldn't remember a time when his sister had been happy. She hadn't always been the shrew she was now, but growing up in Gram's household had warped her somehow. The end result was what he saw standing in front of him now.

But damn it, a lot of people grew up poor. A lot of people grew up far worse off than he and Dee and Bri, and they managed to survive their unhappy childhoods. But Dee was stuck somewhere in adolescence, buried beneath the weight of that cross she bore, and thoroughly convinced that she was the only one who'd ever had something bad happen to her. Sometimes he wanted to scream, "Get over it!" but he knew it wouldn't help. In her eyes, his hostility would simply be further proof that her life was shit and it wasn't her fault. Dee was looking for somebody to blame, some scapegoat, something she could point to and say, "There, that's it! That's the reason my life sucks so bad!"

God help her. She wasn't going to find it.

A customer came into the store, walked to the soda cooler and took out a two-liter bottle of Coke, then got in line behind Davy. His sister looked at him pointedly, clearly waiting for him to leave so she could get back to work.

Davy took the hint. Tucking the six-pack under his arm, he said, "I'll see you around." And left without looking back.

Louis waited twenty minutes after Wyatt left, just to make sure the old man didn't return for some forgotten item. Then he got out of the car and walked right up to the front door of Building C as though he had every right to be there. Dressed the way he was, nobody would take him for a B&E man. Nobody would look twice. He looked like every other yahoo in south Florida.

Security in this place was a joke. Louis looked around for cameras, hidden or otherwise, but there were none. He pulled on a pair of latex gloves and went to work on the door lock. It took him about fifteen seconds to bypass the lock and let himself into Wyatt's condo. He did it neatly, without damaging anything. He always did everything neatly, never left any evidence behind. Once he was inside, he locked the door behind him, took off his sunglasses and tucked them into his shirt pocket. He made a quick survey of the layout, checking entrances and exits and closing blinds so he wouldn't be on display to the other residents of the complex.

In Wyatt's bedroom, next to the antique dresser, he found a large green-and-yellow parrot in a cage. The creature watched him with bright-eyed curiosity tempered by caution. Louis wondered if the bird could talk. When he was a kid, he'd always wanted a pet bird, but his mother had been allergic, so he'd had to content himself with looking at the colorful pictures in books and magazines instead. "Hello," he said to it. "Pretty birdie."

But the bird just stared silently, creeping him out with those beady little eyes. Was it his imagination, or did he really see malice in those inky depths? "Same to you, buddy," he said, and ambled off to the living room.

The condo had that whitewashed, generic look that he hated. White walls, white carpet, white appliances. Beige vertical blinds hanging in front of sliding glass doors that led to a three-foot by three-foot patio. Except for the bird, it was bland, colorless, and boring. But tidy. Either Wyatt had a housekeeper, or he was exceptionally neat. Not an item was out of place; the houseplants all looked lush and healthy, and he couldn't find a speck of dust anywhere.

On an end table sat a framed photo of Robin Wyatt Spinney with a big, broad-shouldered, handsome man who must have been her husband. She looked younger than she did in the photo Brogan had given him. She was wearing a floppy straw hat, and the man had his arms around her. They both wore wide grins. It was obvious that they'd been happy together.

Looking around, he spied a second photo, this one of Spinney and her daughter. Both of them stared boldly into the camera, both young and blond and beautiful, both of them knowing that the camera lens would be nothing less than kind to them. But he could see a difference between this photo and the other one; although they were both smiling, something was missing from this photo. The joy had disappeared from Robin Spinney's eyes. This one had been taken after Mac Spinney died.

A man who kept photos of his daughter where he could look at them every day had to be in some form of regular contact with her. Letters, phone calls, e-mail. Somewhere here, there had to be something that would point him in the right direction.

He started with the desk in the den, because it was the most likely place. He found Wyatt's bills, neatly organized in alphabetical order, in the top drawer. He was beginning to like this guy. If nothing else, Bill Wyatt was making his job easier. It took him just a few minutes to rifle through six months' worth of paid bills. He found nothing unusual, nothing that sent up a red flag. Electric bill, telephone bill, car payment coupons, a single credit card, seldom used and nowhere near the credit limit. Not a single long-distance phone bill.

Louis moved on to the Rolodex, thumbed through it. Not much here. Wyatt wasn't exactly a social butterfly. Most of the numbers here were pretty standard fare. Dry cleaner, country club, Domino's Pizza. Nothing that jumped out at him, so he moved on to the computer.

It was a Dell, last year's basic model without much in the way of bells and whistles. Wyatt obviously wasn't a computer geek. Louis booted it up, sifted through the hard drive contents and found nothing. He pulled up AOL. Wyatt had a single screen name, and—would you look at that! His password was saved. Trusting guy, especially for a former military man. But of course, for a man who lived alone, privacy wouldn't be an issue.

Judging by the contents of his e-mail, Bill Wyatt was really into parrots, and most of his mail came from his parrot-loving friends. They spoke in some kind of birdie lingo that Louis found hilarious. They referred to their feathered children as fids and to themselves as parronts, and bragged about the accomplishments of those fids as though they were human.

Nut cases, Louis thought. They were all nut cases. He checked the AOL file cabinet and found more of the same. Total dead end. The IE history folder revealed that Wyatt went to parrot forums a couple times a week, did his monthly banking online, and apparently had a weakness for naked, big-breasted women with names like Honey and Ginger. He wondered if Lottie Trent knew that her boyfriend was into more than just parrots online. Of course, these were modern times. For all he knew, Trent and Wyatt visited those XXX-rated sites together. They could be on their way to Trent's condo even now to view their recommended daily allowance of porn. Maybe that's what they did during those post-dinner rendezvous.

Having gotten more of an education than he wanted, Louis shut down the computer, still no closer to finding Robin Spinney than he'd been when he started. He looked through the rest of the desk drawers, but found nothing there. No phone number scribbled on a sticky note, no address written in the margin of the telephone book. Zilch. Nada. A big zero.

He was beginning to think this was a dead end, and he imagined the look of displeasure on Luke Brogan's face when he told the sheriff that he'd been unsuccessful at locating Robin Spinney. Brogan's displeasure wasn't something he wanted to experience in person. The sheriff could be a mean son of a bitch when he wanted to. No, there had to be a way, and Louis was going to find it.

He was in the kitchen, thumbing through the pages of the wall calendar—parrots, wouldn't you know it—when he heard the sound of a key in the lock. Louis froze as the front door opened. What the hell? Wyatt wasn't due home for another—he glanced at the wall clock—forty-three minutes. Panicked, he looked around for an escape route, but the kitchen, which connected directly to the condo's living room, had only one tiny window over the sink, and there was no way he was going to squeeze through it. That left only one means of escape: directly through the living room that Bill Wyatt had just entered.

He glanced around for a weapon. On the counter, resting in a wooden rack, he found an old-fashioned marble rolling pin. He snatched it up, hefted it, impressed by its weight. Louis found the idea of violence distasteful but in a situation like this, a man had to save his own hide any way he could. Breathing hard, he stood to the left of the refrigerator in the pint-size kitchen, rolling pin in hand.

Wyatt walked into the room, carrying a white takeout bag with the Clem's Clams logo. Bill Wyatt was a big man, but Louis had a couple of advantages. He might not be a kid any longer, but Wyatt had at least thirty years on him. And Wyatt didn't have a clue that Louis was standing in his kitchen.

Wyatt glanced up and saw him. The bag fell from his hand and landed with a plop on the kitchen floor. "What the hell?" he said. "Who the hell are—"

He never got to finish his question. Louis swung the rolling pin. With a sharp, sickening crack, it connected with Bill Wyatt's skull, and the big man went down like a fallen oak. He lay on the floor, silent and unmoving. Louis dropped the rolling pin. It landed on the floor next to Wyatt with a loud thud. Sweat trickled down his sides as he stood over the body on the floor, breathing hard and wondering how things had spiraled so far out of control. How could his plan have gone so wrong so quickly?

There was only one thing he could do. His heart thudding like a locomotive, Louis left Wyatt lying there and ran like a frightened jackrabbit for the door. He didn't even bother to see whether or not he'd killed the man.

He just got the hell out.

Five

Annie was downstairs in the tiny office behind the store, going over the books with a fine-tooth comb, when she heard a dull thud coming from somewhere above her. Startled, she glanced ceilingward, puzzled because the apartment was both empty and locked. An instant later, there was a second thud, and she realized the sound wasn't coming from her apartment. Through the open window, she was hearing the unmistakable sound of footsteps, walking around on her roof.

Prickly fingers of anxiety danced up and down her spine. She was alone here, utterly alone, for the first time since she'd arrived. Estelle wasn't due in for another two hours, and Sophie, already bored to death with sitting around the Twilight and anxious for next week to roll around so she could start her new babysitting job, had wheedled and cajoled until finally Annie caved and allowed her to ride her ten-speed down the treacherous state highway and into town. It had been a tough decision. The rational woman in her had argued that Sophie was fifteen and fully capable of riding her bike a couple of miles into town. The irrational mother who was the rational woman's evil twin didn't bother with argument. She simply constructed a grisly and effective mental image of her precious daughter crushed beneath the wheels of a pulp truck. Dead on the shoulder of the highway, like Timmy Rivers.

But Sophie wasn't Timmy Rivers, and this wasn't Atchawalla. It was broad daylight on a summer morning, and Sophie wasn't the kind of kid to take chances. She was a careful biker who obeyed traffic laws, always wore her helmet, and paid close attention to approaching vehicles. So the rational woman had won the battle, but it had been a hard sell. Now, as a result of having taken a giant leap toward cutting Sophie loose from her own obsessive mothering, Annie was left alone to deal with whoever—or whatever—was up on the rooftop.

Somehow, she doubted that it was old Saint Nick.

She glanced around the office in search of a weapon. All she could find was a pair of scissors. At close range, they would undoubtedly be quite effective, but Annie wasn't sure she wanted to get that close to somebody bent on doing her harm. If she were lurking outside somebody's home, those shiny blades, gleaming in the sunshine, would certainly give her pause. She could only hope they would have the same effect on whoever was out there.

Scissors in hand, she let herself out the front door and walked around the corner of the building. At the Crowley house across the highway, a pair of young boys took turns tossing a basketball through a rusty hoop hung over the garage door, their excited voices carrying over the buzz of a lawn mower from two houses down. Beside the door to her number-three guest room, directly above a cluster of milkweed that had shoved its persistent little head right up through the pavement, a battered aluminum extension ladder leaned against the side of the building. Shading her eyes, she followed its length, up past the door frame, past the roof overhang, and directly to the man who stood on her roof...testing the boards.

The breath exited her body in a giant whoosh, leaving her feeling like an idiot, standing there brandishing a pair of lethal-looking scissors like some would-be Edwina Scissorhands. Dressed in tan Dickies and a tattered navy sweatshirt, the man gingerly poked his foot, clad in a retro-look red-and-white high-top canvas sneaker, at what appeared to be a spongy spot beneath the shingles.

"Hello?" she said. "Can I help you?"

The stranger glanced down at her, then moved closer to the edge. Annie got a snapshot impression of shaggy brown hair that could have benefited from a good combing. A broad, pleasant face. Nice eyes. And a smile that must have felled more than a few females in his time.

"Jack Crowley," he said. "Jo told me you have a leak."

The light bulb went on over her head. "Jolene's husband," she said, tucking the scissors behind her back. "The CMP lineman."

"That'd be me. Hope you weren't planning on using those scissors on me."

Score one for rampant paranoia. She hoped the sunlight was bright enough to camouflage her flush. "Only if you pulled a weapon first. Thanks so much for coming over."

"Not a problem. Jo always makes me a list of things to do, and I just fall in line like a good little soldier." Coming from another man, his words might have sounded resigned, even bitter. But uttered by Jack Crowley, they seemed matter-of-fact, almost cheerful.

Shading her eyes again to see him better, she said, "So what's the verdict?"

"Well…" He drew the word out into several syllables. "I'm no roofing contractor, just a backyard handyman, but it looks to me like your roof's in pretty good shape." He hunkered down, balancing himself with one hand pressed against the shingles. "You check the rest of the rooms?"

"Yes. This seems to be the only area that's leaking."

"I'd imagine this could be fixed pretty easily. A four-by-eight sheet of plywood, a roll of tar paper, and some roofing shingles ought to do it."

"How hard would it be? The work?"

"That depends. You thinking of doing it yourself?"

Mindful of her rapidly dwindling bank account, Annie said, "Yes."

With a wicked grin, he said, "You're not afraid of heights, are you? From the ground, this doesn't look very far up. But once you get up here, your perspective changes. Suddenly it's one hell of a long way down."

"Heights don't bother me." Her fears ran more to random traffic accidents and homicidal sheriffs, but he didn't need to know that.

"Come on up if you want. I'll show you."

She set the scissors down on the pavement, then grabbed the ladder and hoisted herself up onto the first rung. It wasn't the first time she'd climbed one of these things, but it had been a while. When she reached the top, she paused, hands braced against the shingles. "Nice view," she said.

And it was a nice view. From here, she could see right over the roof's shallow peak and down a wide sweep of river, its lush green banks lined with willow and birch and wild fern.

"This place is beautiful," she said. "I'm surprised the town doesn't attract more tourists."

"Economy went down the toilet when the cotton mill closed. There's nothing to come here for. Don't know if you've been downtown yet, but there's probably a half-dozen empty storefronts. The President keeps telling us the economy's in recovery. Guess he hasn't been to Serenity lately."

"Yet people stay here."

He shrugged, glanced across the road, to the tidy white frame house and the two boys trading good-natured insults in the driveway. "Jo and I, we've lived here all our lives. We're a lot luckier than some. No matter how poor a town is, people still need electricity. And they still have to educate their kids. That equals job security for us. Serenity's not such a bad place to live."

"That's good to know, especially since I just bought property here."

"Speaking of which." He returned his attention to the roof. "See this spot here? It's soft. Real soft." He demonstrated, pressing against it with the toe of his sneaker. The spongy wood flexed beneath the pressure, and when he removed his foot, the indentation made by his toe was still clearly visible. "But the rest of her's solid as a brick. You tear off the shingles, replace this sheet of plywood with a clean one, lay down a strip of tar paper and reshingle her, she'll be good as new."

It looked almost possible. "What's the best way to anchor the shingles?"

"I'd use a staple gun. It's fast, it's clean, and you won't hammer your thumb. You start at the bottom edge and work your way up. That way, they overlap, and since water runs downhill, there's no way it can creep up underneath and get to your plywood."

"Mr. Crowley, you're a font of wisdom. Thank you so much."

"Just being neighborly. And it's Jack."

"Jack."

"You're welcome to use my ladder. I'll leave it here. You can bring it back when the job's finished. Jo's been after me to clean out the gutters." He flashed her another of those heart-stopping grins. "This'll give me an excuse to put it off for a while longer."

Wryly, she said, "So glad I could be of service."

"If you need transportation to the lumber store, I have an old pickup truck I use for that kind of thing. Feel free to take it. Just ask Jo for the keys. If you wait for Sonny to get your car fixed, it could be October before your roof gets repaired."

He followed her back down the ladder and hopped to the ground. "Oh, before I forget—we're having a little get-together Friday night. Just a few friends. Jo and I would love for you and your daughter to come. Around six would be good. That'll give us a couple of hours before we're forced to go indoors to avoid becoming human pincushions. Those damn mosquitoes'll eat you alive if you let 'em."

"A dinner party," she said. "I don't think—"

"Whoa," he said, and held up a hand. "Nothing that fancy. This is Serenity. Our idea of a party is a six-pack of Old Milwaukee and a bag of Doritos."

She couldn't help smiling. "Sounds like my kind of party."

"It's all real casual. We'll barbecue some burgers, sit around swilling beer and telling tall tales, take a dip in the pool if we feel like it."

"It sounds like fun," she said, "but I just got here, and—"

"All the more reason you should come. It looks to me—" he craned his neck to study the derelict building in front of them "—like you're planning to stay for a while."

"Well, yes, but—"

"Then you might as well get to know the neighbors. We'll see you Friday around six."

The hospital room was unnaturally silent, the only sound the soft beeping of the monitor beside the bed. Bill Wyatt lay so still and pale against crisp white sheets that Lottie would have thought he was dead if not for the gentle rise and fall of his chest and the indecipherable squiggles that ran across the monitor.

She'd talked to the police earlier, trying to make sense of this, trying to understand why anybody would have broken into Bill's condo and attacked him. The cops had said robbery was probably the motive, but what did Bill have that was of any value? He lived on a fixed income, owned no jewelry or coins, no stocks or bonds or valuable antiques. Probably the most valuable thing he owned was Romeo, the yellow-fronted amazon parrot, but they hadn't touched Romeo. Thank God, because it had been his screeching and squawking that had brought Everett Freeman across the hall to see what all the ruckus was about. If Romeo had been quieter, or if Everett had stayed over at Eleanor Tolley's place like he did sometimes, Bill probably would have been dead by the time anybody found him. Lottie had never much cared for Romeo, but now, the parrot had been elevated to hero status.

She'd returned from Tallahassee energized, almost giddy in her excitement over the upcoming cruise, and this unexpected turn of events had left her stunned. She'd been a little shell-shocked when the doctor came in, and although she'd listened carefully to everything the doctor had had to say, she hadn't taken it all in. Dr. Herrera, a young woman about the age of her granddaughter, had been kind. Gently, and with great patience, she'd attempted to translate all that medical gibberish into layman's terms that Lottie could understand. But all Lottie wanted was the bottom line. Was Bill going to make it or not?

That, Dr. Herrera had said briskly, was out of her hands. She was doing everything in her power to make Bill well. The rest was up to God. And, she'd added, almost as an afterthought, to Bill himself.

The stubborn old fool. How many times had Lottie told him that he needed to install a decent security system? She'd lived in southern Florida longer than he had. The region might be a tropical paradise, but it had its flaws, one of them being a skyrocketing crime rate. Lottie had friends who'd been victimized, and she'd learned from their mistakes. But Bill, who always had an answer for everything and who was quite possibly the most stubborn, infuriating man on the planet, had ignored her words of warning.

Damn him. What was she going to do if she lost him?

He wasn't showing signs of improvement. Lottie might not be a doctor, or even a nurse, but she wasn't an idiot. She knew that the longer he remained in a coma, the poorer his chances of recovery. She needed to contact his daughter. Even if the worst didn't come to pass, Robin needed to know that her dad was in the hospital and in a bad way. Bill would probably strangle her if he found out, but this time, he wasn't getting the final say. Lottie didn't know the exact nature of the rift between Bill and Robin, just knew they'd had some kind of falling-out. Bill didn't even know where his daughter lived. She called him regularly, always the dutiful daughter, but she stubbornly refused to give him an address or phone number.

Robin had gotten into some kind of trouble. Lottie had inadvertently heard them arguing about it on the telephone one day. Or at least she'd heard Bill's end of the conversation. She hadn't meant to eavesdrop, but she'd been brewing tea in the kitchen and Bill hadn't exactly been quiet. He'd been ragging Robin about somebody named Bobby Sarnacki, somebody she'd apparently run to for help instead of coming to her own father. Bill had made it crystal clear exactly how he felt about this Sarnacki character, who apparently had a less-than-stellar reputation with the Detroit police. The argument had ended in a stalemate, as Lottie suspected most of their arguments did. Bill had spent the rest of that afternoon in a surly sulk. She would have kicked his scrawny hindside from here to the moon if she'd thought his sour mood was a result of pure orneriness. But there was more to it than that. Bill was hurting. Despite their differences, he thought his daughter had hung the moon, and the discord between them was killing him.

It was time for Bill and Robin to heal that rift. Glancing

at the pale, still man lying in the hospital bed, she prayed it wasn't too late for them. Bobby Sarnacki must know how to reach Robin. All Lottie had to do was call him. She knew Bill wouldn't approve, but that was just too bad. She had to do something besides sit here by his hospital bed, hour after hour, her heart in her throat as she watched the man she loved inhale and exhale, terrified that each breath would be his last. If she could track Robin down, at least she'd feel as though she was doing something useful.

Lottie leaned over the bed, pressed a gentle kiss to Bill's temple. Then she picked up the phone, pressed 9 for an outside line, and dialed information. "Detroit, Michigan," she said resolutely. "Robert Sarnacki."

It had been years since Annie had driven a standard shift, and Jack Crowley's ancient Chevy pickup had the stiffest clutch she'd ever encountered. The truck coughed and rattled and shook all the way into town. When she'd come knocking on the Crowleys' kitchen door, Jo had tossed her the keys and told her to keep the truck for as long as she needed it. "It may be a while before you get your car back," she'd said. "You'll need transportation in the meantime. Jack never uses the damn thing anyway. Besides, if we need it for something, we know where you live."

She'd tried to talk Sophie into going with her, but Soph had already checked out Serenity's shopping district this morning, and she wasn't impressed. There was no record store, which in Sophie's mind was akin to treason. Nor were there any trendy clothing stores. No Hot Topic, no PacSun. According to Estelle, the nearest mall of any significance was in South Portland, which to a fifteen-year-old might as well have been the face of the moon. The world was undoubtedly about to come to an end. In a deep blue funk, Sophie had opted to go downstairs and hang out with Estelle. She was quite taken with the young woman, for reasons Annie hadn't quite figured out. Of course, it didn't hurt that the shop was furnished with a color television and VCR. During slow periods, Estelle usually caught up on her movie watching.

Annie's first stop was the bank, where she opened a new checking account and arranged for money to be transferred from her old account in Las Vegas. Afterward, she swung by the local hardware store to pick up the basic tools she'd need for the job. A hammer and crowbar. Nails. Heavy-duty staple gun and staples. Work gloves. Her last stop was Serenity Building Supply, where she purchased lumber, tar paper and roofing shingles, which a burly teenager hefted into the bed of the pickup for her. Somehow, she would have to get them out of the truck on her own. Somehow, she would have to carry all those heavy materials up onto the motel roof. Maybe she could bribe Sophie into helping. As a mother, Annie'd never been afraid of using any tool that was in her psychological arsenal, and bribery had proven effective on more than one occasion.

It was early afternoon when she returned to find Estelle and Sophie perched on the front steps, sharing a pepperoni pizza and a two-liter bottle of Coke. No matter what kind of food kick Sophie was on, she never turned down pizza. "I paid for it from the cash drawer," Estelle explained. "We were both starving, and every Wednesday, Clyde's has a special. A large one-topping and a bottle of Coke for $5.99. Plus free delivery. You can't beat a deal like that. And it's the best pizza in town."

Sophie was too busy cramming food into her face to add her two cents' worth, but if body language was any indication, she was in total agreement that it was, indeed, the best pizza in town. Annie leaned over and snagged a slice. She bit into it and closed her eyes in appreciation.

"Yum," she mumbled through a mouthful of culinary heaven.

Brushing crumbs from her hands, Estelle said, "Did you get everything you needed for the roof?"

Annie swallowed. "I think so. The weather forecast is looking good for the next couple of days, so I'm going to start ripping off shingles this afternoon."

"Heights don't bother you?"

"No. I'm more concerned about falling through the roof than off it."

"Well, if you do fall through, just make sure you land on the bed instead of the floor."

Annie finished her pizza on the way upstairs. She changed into jeans and a T-shirt, then dug in the bottom of the bedroom closet until she found the Atlanta Braves baseball cap that Sophie no longer wore. She pulled her hair back into a ponytail and tucked it through the hole in the back of the hat. Then she went back downstairs and gathered up the tools she'd bought. She wasn't sure exactly what she'd need, but if she took them all with her, she wouldn't have to keep climbing up and down the ladder.

It was backbreaking work. Jack Crowley had forgotten to mention that fact. The hat gave her little protection from the blistering afternoon sun. The gloves were hot and unwieldy, and after a short time, she yanked them off and tossed them to the ground. The shingles were mule-stubborn. They'd been here for close to thirty years, and they evidently had no desire to leave. And they were aged just enough so that they had a tendency to disintegrate when she tugged on them. She must have been nuts when she decided to do this job herself.

Still, she persevered. Annie Kendall might be many things, but she was no quitter. While she tugged and prodded and peeled shingles, she observed video rental customers coming and going. Business wasn't bad for a weekday afternoon, and as she performed the mindless task, her mind churned with ideas for increasing that business.

Around three o'clock, she took a break to run cold water over her sweaty, dirt-smudged face and drink half a bottle of Poland Spring water. She found sunscreen in the bathroom. Smearing it generously on her arms, her face, the back of her neck, she wished she'd thought of it sooner; she could already feel herself burning. But it was too late for should-haves. The damage was already done. At this point, all she could do was prevent it from getting any worse.

It was nearly suppertime when she pulled the last shingle from the four-by-eight sheet of punky plywood and decided she'd done enough for today. Annie slid to the roof's edge and found solid footing on the ladder. She tossed the hammer and crowbar to the ground, littered with crumbling shingles and old roofing nails. Tomorrow morning, she'd replace the plywood and start putting it all back together. Right now, all she wanted was a long, hot shower and something to eat. After supper, if Sophie was game, they'd find a good movie downstairs and spend a quiet mother-daughter evening watching it.

It could've been worse, Louis decided. He could have sent the old man to the morgue instead of Jackson Memorial Hospital.

He hadn't intended to resort to violence. That wasn't his style. But he'd panicked. If he got caught breaking and entering, he'd lose his P.I. license, and where would that leave him? He'd managed to escape without being caught, but the whole mess still had him rattled. Nothing like this had ever happened to him before. He was always coolheaded, always tidy. Always went in clean, came out clean. Never, in all his years as a P.I., had he deliberately hurt another human being. This time, he'd screwed up in a major way.

He had a really bad feeling about this case. It had trouble written all over it. He didn't know what Robin Spinney had done to incur Luke Brogan's wrath, but somehow he doubted the good sheriff was tracking her down with the intent of handing her some inheritance from a long-lost aunt. More likely, she had something on Brogan. There was a certain desperation to the man's grim determination that told him Brogan found locating her to be of paramount importance.

Nevertheless, Louis had always believed in giving the customer top-notch service for the money he was paid, service that was discreet, confidential, and efficient. He took pride in his work. In this life, you got what you paid for, and Louis Farley didn't come cheap. But he was worth every penny he charged. It wasn't his job to question why Brogan wanted to find Spinney. It was his job to locate her. Nothing more, nothing less. What Brogan chose to do with her—and her daughter—after he found them was somebody else's problem.

So why the sour taste in his mouth? Why was he popping antacids every time he looked at that grainy black-and-white photo Brogan had given him of fifteen-year-old Sophie Spinney? He never became emotionally involved in any of his cases. Becoming emotionally involved was suicide, and Louis Farley didn't have a suicidal bone in his body. But something about this case spooked him, and the deeper he dug, the spookier it got.

He wanted out of Florida. Wanted out in a big way. The heat, the humidity, the bugs were more than a man could take. But it was too soon to leave town. With Wyatt lying in a hospital bed, sooner or later his daughter was likely to show up to check on Daddy's welfare. Even if she didn't, Lottie Trent was sure to be hovering. Which meant that Louis needed to stick around, just in case.

In the hospital gift shop, he bought a half-dozen oranges, a small get-well-soon bouquet of pink tulips in a mug shaped like a smiling bunny rabbit, and the new Nora Roberts paperback. People could scoff at romances all they wanted to, but with a romance, you were always guaranteed a happy ending, and in his line of work, Louis could use all the happy endings he could get. And that Nora was one heck of a storyteller. Besides, the book would make an outstanding icebreaker. Any man who sat alone in a hospital waiting room, reading Nora Roberts, was bound to be approached by nearly every woman who happened by. There was one particular woman whose approach he was very interested in. If he sat there long enough, eventually she was bound to happen by.

It was a long afternoon. He fended off the attentions of three middle-aged women and one male nurse, and was on chapter five and his third orange when Lottie Trent walked in, rubbing her wrist as though she were in pain. Louis glanced up casually from his book. Lottie had dark circles under her eyes, her complexion was pasty, and her hair looked like it hadn't been combed in days. While he watched, Lottie walked to the vending machine across the room, dropped in a couple of coins, and pushed the button. Nothing happened. Lottie pushed the button again, jiggled the machine a little, and uttered a soft sound of frustration.

Louis set down Nora, being careful not to lose his place, and said, "Can I help you with that?"

Lottie glanced up, looking a little dazed. Her focus sharpened, and she offered a weak smile. "Thank you," she said. "It doesn't seem to want to let go of my Reese's."

He got up and crossed the room. "These foolish machines," he said, "they're not good for much, are they?" He grabbed the machine in both hands and rocked it back and forth until Lottie's peanut butter cup fell. "There," he said, wiping his hands on his khakis. "All better."

While Lottie peeled open the crinkly paper wrapping, Louis returned to his seat and picked the book back up. He read another page, glanced again at Lottie, who was standing by the window, chewing on chocolate and staring into space. "My wife's having surgery," he said.

She turned her head, regarded him blankly, before comprehension struck. "Oh," she said. "What for?"

"She's having a hysterectomy. Poor Ruthie was having these terrible female complaints for months and months. The doctors just kept ignoring her. You know how they are. If a woman has chronic complaints, the doctors act like she's just some hysterical housewife. A hypochondriac. You know what I mean?"

"Absolutely. I've had that very thing happen to me."

"I have half a mind to sue the bas—I mean, the jerks, for malpractice. But she finally found Dr. Miller. Dr. Jennifer Miller. Poor Ruthie should have gone to a woman in the first place. She's the best gynecologist in southern Florida. Maybe you've heard of her?"

Lottie wrinkled her brow and gave it some thought. "I don't think so," she said.

"Dr. Miller did a thorough exam and found out Ruthie was just loaded with fibroids. So of course she recommended a full hysterectomy. Ruth was a little worried about losing her femininity. I mean, she's young for something so radical— only forty-three—but I told her it didn't matter. It's not like we're going to have any more kids anyway, and she's just as beautiful to me now as she was the day I married her, twenty-five years ago."

"That's so sweet. Not many husbands these days dote on their wives like that."

"Are you kidding? She's the best part of me. Without Ruthie, I'd be nothing." He studied her with avid curiosity. "Are you married?"

"I'm a widow. My husband died three years ago of coronary artery disease. It was very sudden. We'd been married for almost forty years."

"Geez, I'm sorry to hear that. It must've been hard. I don't know what I'd do if anything happened to Ruthie. To tell you the truth—" he paused, shrugged sheepishly "—I'm a little embarrassed to admit this. Guys are supposed to be tough. But I'm pretty nervous about this surgery. The doctor keeps saying it's a routine operation, that thousands of women have hysterectomies every year. And I know it's true, but none of those women is my Ruthie. If something went wrong—" He broke off abruptly and shook his head. "I just don't know what I'd do."

"She'll be fine," Lottie said. "Your doctor's right. My daughter had a hysterectomy just last year. She was back at work six weeks later, healthy as a horse."

"That makes me feel a little better. Knowing somebody who's been through it. I mean, I don't know your daughter, but I'm here talking to you, and that makes her more real to me than those thousands of anonymous women the doctor referred to. You know what I mean?"

"Of course. Trust me, Ruthie will be fine. She'll be playing tennis in a few weeks."

"That's amazing," he said, "considering she's never played tennis before." They both chuckled at his stupid joke, and he allowed the silence to build between them before he said, "So why are you here?"

Lottie's face grew somber, as if she'd been momentarily distracted from her problems but had now remembered why she was sitting in a hospital waiting room. "My boyfriend, Bill," she said. "He has a severe head injury. I'm so worried."

Louis tsk-tsked in sympathy. "I can imagine you would be. Car accident?"

"No." Lottie crossed the room and sat down in the ugly green vinyl chair next to his. "Somebody broke into his condo and attacked him with a marble rolling pin from his own kitchen. They left him for dead. If his neighbor hadn't stopped by—" A tear fell from the corner of her eye, and she rubbed at it with her fist.

"My God," he said, "that's terrible. Why on earth would anybody do something like that?"

"I don't know." Lottie raised her shoulders in a shrug, then let them fall in resignation. "The police think it was a robber, but as far as I could tell, nothing was taken."

"Maybe your boyfriend—Bill, was it? Maybe Bill surprised him before he could take anything."

"Maybe."

"So does Bill have any family, or are you it? I've read that sometimes, having loving family members around can make the difference between life and death in a case like this."

She paled at the word death, but nodded somberly. "I've heard the same thing. He has a daughter. Robin. And a granddaughter, Sophie. Such a pretty little thing." She smiled ruefully. "Well, not so little. She must be fourteen or fifteen. Cute as a bug. I've tried to reach them, but I can't seem to track them down, and it's making me crazy."

He raised both eyebrows. "You can't track them down?" he said. "You mean, they're not home?"

"Worse than that, I'm afraid." She looked sheepish, as if embarrassed at having to admit the depth of her own ignorance. "I don't know where they live. Even Bill doesn't know." At his quizzical look, she rushed to explain. "They had a falling-out sometime back. Apparently Robin's moved around a bit in the last few months, and she hasn't told her father where she is."

"Gee, that's awful. And nobody else knows where she is?"

"There's one person who might know. A relative of theirs. He lives somewhere in the Detroit area, and I'm pretty sure that if I could locate him, I could find Robin. But apparently he has an unlisted phone. I've tried, but I can't seem to track him down. Directory assistance didn't have a listing for him."

"Hey, talk about coincidences! I used to live in Detroit! Maybe I know him."

Lottie's blue eyes widened. "You're kidding," she said.

Louis grinned and held up two fingers in a mock salute. "Scout's honor. What's his name?"

"Bobby. Robert Sarnacki."

Louis crinkled his forehead. "Hmm…Sarnacki, Sarnacki. Nope. Don't know any Sarnackis. Darn. I was really hoping I could help you out."

Lottie sighed in resignation. "So was I."

He glanced at his watch and frowned. "Ruthie should be out of surgery by now. They said they'd let me know, but you know how they are in these places. I could sit here all day and nobody'd bother to come by. Do you suppose you could watch my stuff while I run down to the nurses' station and see if I can find out what's going on?"

"Of course." Lottie's smile was warm and genuine. "It's the least I can do for you after everything you've done for me."

"I haven't really done all that much," he said modestly.

"You would have if you could. If only you knew Bobby Sarnacki. And don't forget that Reese's peanut butter cup. If you weren't here, it would still be hanging there, waiting for the next sucker to come along."

He chuckled. "I guess you're right," he said. "Hey, help yourself to an orange. They're really great. There's nothing quite like a fresh Florida orange."

Louis left the waiting room and walked down the hospital corridor, hands in his pockets, a spring in his step. Just another visitor. Here today, gone tomorrow. He flashed a bland, unremarkable smile at a cute brunette R.N. as he passed the nurses' station and kept on going, directly to the bank of elevators at the end of the corridor.

Robert Sarnacki. Detroit.

Louis Farley whistled as the elevator took him downstairs to the lobby. He was still whistling when he walked out the front door of the hospital.

Six

There wasn't an inch of her body that didn't ache: back, shoulders, neck, thighs. Annie's face and arms, sunburned to within an inch of their lives, felt white-hot and tight, as though she'd grown overnight and her skin had yet to catch up. It must be true that no good deed went unpunished. Today, she had to finish the damn roof. A benevolent God would at least have given her an overcast day to work with. But it was another sunny, humid day—proving once and for all that God was a man—and Annie just couldn't wait to spend it twelve feet in the air, stapling shingles to splintery plywood.

She took a cool shower, gradually adding warm water until at last it was steaming-hot against her overworked back muscles. The benefits were minimal, but at least when she stepped out of the shower, her stiff muscles were flexible again. She dried off gently because of the sunburn, pulled her wet hair back in an elastic she found lying around, and dressed in the only white jeans she owned. In the closet, she found a pale blue cotton long-sleeved shirt. She rolled the cuffs up to just below the elbow, then liberally applied sunscreen to every inch of exposed skin.

Breakfast was a bowl of Frosted Flakes and a slice of toast

with peanut butter. To hell with worrying about the size of her thighs. If pounding nails and hauling roof shingles didn't work off the calories from her morning repast, she might as well just give up right now and begin that slow slide into middle age.

When she finished her breakfast, Annie put her empty cereal bowl in the dishwasher. "What are you planning to do today?" she asked Sophie.

"I don't know. Maybe hang around downstairs with Estelle." Sophie glanced up from the breakfast table, shoved a stray wisp of raven-dark hair away from her face in a gesture that reminded Annie of herself. "There isn't much else to do in this one-horse town."

"Hey, if you can survive until I get my car back, we'll drive down to Portland and do the mall. We can shop at Claire's and eat tacos at the food court."

"Geez, Mom, you're way behind the times. I haven't shopped at Claire's in ages. That's for, like, girly girls."

"Girly like you used to be, you mean? Forgive me. I guess that would be pretty lame."

Sophie rolled her eyes. "You sound like such a dork when you're trying to talk like a kid. You're too old, Mom. Give it up." Brightening considerably, she added, "But I wouldn't mind doing the Portland mall. Estelle says it has Hot Topic. Their stuff is way cool."

"Well, then." Annie took a bottle of water from the fridge. "We'll have to shop at Hot Topic instead."

She had stored her tools in the small closet beneath the staircase that led to the shop. Annie descended the creaky stairs, opened the closet door and took out the hammer, the crowbar, the hated gloves. Wishing she'd thought to buy a tool belt, she swung around to take the most direct route to the front door.

She took a single step into the shop and stopped dead in

her tracks. The front door hung wide open, swinging in the breeze, and the shop itself looked as though a tornado had blown through. The shelves had been swept bare, movies scattered everywhere. One of the freestanding shelving units had been upended, its contents dumped haphazardly on the floor. Dozens of movie cases had been opened, and yards of VHS tape lay unspooled, tangled and hacked to pieces amid the rubble. The cash register had been tossed onto the floor, the computer screen smashed. Whoever did this had topped off his handiwork with neon-pink spray paint, applied everywhere in crooked stripes and circles. She could still smell the paint. On the far wall they'd painted a single word on the knotty pine, obscene and condemning. Aimed at her?

BITCH.

"Mother of God," she said. She took another step into the room, felt the anger begin. She'd come here for refuge, not for this. Who would have done a thing like this? Who would have criss-crossed hot-pink spray paint like a psychedelic spiderweb over her tidy white wooden counter? Who would have kicked in her front door and torn open bags of popcorn, strewing corn kernels everywhere? Who would have unwound movie after movie and sliced the tape to ribbons, probably with the very scissors she'd used to defend herself with just twenty-four hours ago? What kind of animal would be this destructive, this angry at the world? And why her, when all she wanted was to be left alone?

With a deep sigh, she went back upstairs to call the police.

His eyes were blue.

Not a nice, safe blue, Annie decided, not the warm blue of a summer sky. No, Davy Hunter's eyes were a dark, chaotic blue, like the sea during a hurricane. Dangerous eyes. At once hot and cold, unsettled, so turbulent they had her instantly revising her initial impression of him. The aloofness was a façade. Somewhere inside those impenetrable depths lurked a man whose emotions roiled as furiously as the ocean they resembled. It was only on the outside that he resembled a chunk of stone.

"I don't understand this," she told him as he silently surveyed the disaster that had been her video shop. "Who would target a place like this, and why?"

"I don't know." He reached for the two-way radio on his hip and spoke into it. "Hey, Dix, is René hanging around the station?"

"He is," said a scratchy voice at the other end. "You need him for something?"

"Send him out to the Twilight. Tell him to bring a fingerprint kit. And a camera. And make sure there's film in it."

"Something big going on out there?" the dispatcher said.

"Break-in at the video store. Whoever did it vandalized the place pretty good."

"Damn troublemakers. Okeydoke, I'll send René right over."

He hung the radio back on his hip and cautiously waded into the debris. From the doorway that led to the back staircase, Sophie silently watched him, wide-eyed with a combination of horror and excitement. She'd never witnessed anything like this before, and Annie knew that for a teenager like Soph, something as novel as this catastrophe was bound to produce some measure of forbidden thrill. It was like watching those horror movies she was so fond of. She might be revolted by the grisly scenes, but at the same time, she was human, and possessed of that innate human curiosity which made the abhorrent fascinating.

As long as it was happening to somebody else.

"I'd ask if anything was missing," Hunter said dryly, "but how would you tell?"

"What would they take in a place like this? *Harold and Kumar go to White Castle?*"

He glanced over his shoulder, her sarcastic zinger seeming to miss him completely. "Did you keep money in the cash register?"

"No. Estelle deposits it at the bank every night after closing."

Squatting, he picked up a length of loose video tape, let it slide through his fingers. "Have you talked to Estelle yet this morning?"

"I called her right after I called you. She should be here any minute."

He straightened back up, turned and focused those blue eyes on her. "I'll need to talk to both of you. Who else was working last night?"

"How the hell should I know? Some teenage boy. Kenny somebody-or-other. You'll have to ask Estelle. I haven't been introduced yet."

His gaze grew contemplative. "You seem pretty pissed off."

"Really? What was your first clue?"

"Care to tell me why you're so angry?"

She gaped at him in disbelief. "Wouldn't you be? I feel violated. I may not have been here long, but this is my property. Nobody has a right to do this to me."

"You're sure that's all there is to it?"

"What the hell is that supposed to mean? Are you asking me if I have some kind of feud going on with somebody in this town? Like the Montagues and the Capulets? In case you've forgotten, I just got here three days ago. I'm sure if I live in this town long enough, I can find somebody to feud with. But three days is a little soon, wouldn't you say?"

He didn't answer her. They faced each other boldly, a charged silence between them. Outside the open door, a vehicle pulled into the yard, its racing engine telling her it could only be Boomer's truck. "Estelle's here," Sophie said quietly.

Was that relief Annie heard in her daughter's voice? Poor Soph. She was probably wondering what alien force had taken over her mother's body. Especially since Annie was wondering the same thing herself.

She deliberately turned her back on Hunter as Estelle stepped through the open door, looking downright pallid, right from her ashen face to the conservative blue maternity top decorated with pink and blue teddy bears. Estelle took a long look around the room and said, "Those bastards."

With slow deliberation, Hunter said, "You know somebody who might do something like this, Estelle?"

"Hey, Davy. No, I was using the term generically. I don't have a clue who might've done this. If I did, I'd probably take the law into my own hands and throttle the shitheads myself." She paused to look around. "Damn them. All those movies destroyed." Her gaze landed on Annie's face. "Hey," she said gently. "Annie, Soph. What a way to start the day."

"Tell me about it," Annie muttered.

A second police cruiser pulled into the yard. "Stick around," Davy Hunter said. "I'll want to talk to both of you in a few minutes." Glancing at Sophie, he added, "All three of you."

The second cop looked barely older than Sophie. Cute as a button and of moderate height, he was a little stocky, with peach fuzz lining his upper lip. While Hunter stood outside conferring with him, Estelle picked her way through the rubble to Annie. "Hey," she said, threading her arm through Annie's. "I've worked here for four years. This place is as much mine as it is yours."

"Probably more," Annie admitted.

"They better catch the rat bastards who did this. They better catch 'em and string 'em up."

"They will," Annie said. "I guarantee they will, because I

intend to make Hunter's life miserable until they do." She gave Estelle's arm a squeeze. "Come on, let's go get a cup of coffee. When Hunter needs us, he'll know where to look."

While Hunter and his assistant—René Bellevance who, according to Estelle, had a wife and three kids and was older than he looked—took pictures and dusted for fingerprints, the three of them sat upstairs and drank coffee, Annie and Estelle at the kitchen table and Sophie perched on the counter. It was too hot for coffee, but Annie didn't know what else to do with herself. Normally she didn't allow Sophie to drink the stuff, but today wasn't an ordinary day, and she suspected that in spite of Sophie's eager curiosity, the abhorrent had struck a little too close to home.

"I have insurance," she said to nobody in particular. "Cleaning up will be a bitch, but I have insurance. It'll pay to replace what we've lost."

One more headache. Once the police were done processing the crime scene, her next call would have to be to the insurance company. They'd probably want to send out a rep to look over the damage, and God only knew how long it would be before she could start cleaning up the mess and putting some kind of dollar amount on the loss.

And somewhere along the way, she realized, she still had to shingle the roof.

She thought briefly about calling Uncle Bobby. This thing had spooked her pretty bad. But it didn't have anything to do with Brogan. It couldn't. Even if it did, she was determined to stand on her own two feet. She had to stop depending on her uncle's strength and generosity. She was a grown woman. It was time she started acting like one.

Estelle stirred sugar into her second cup of coffee, and Annie's motherly instincts kicked in. "Should you be drinking that while you're pregnant?" she said. "All that caffeine can't be good for the baby."

"Hey, I gave up cigarettes and booze. A girl has to hang on to one or two of her vices."

Annie couldn't argue with that. "So," Sophie said, studying her mother over the rim of the coffee mug she held in both hands, "why do you guys think somebody did this to us? I mean, us in particular."

Annie didn't have an answer for her, unless this was connected somehow to Luke Brogan. Could it be possible that he'd found them? But this didn't seem his style. Brogan was much more subtle than this. Whoever'd committed this travesty possessed all the subtlety of al Qaeda. "I don't know, Soph," she said. "It probably wasn't aimed at us. Somebody saw an opportunity and took advantage of it."

Sophie, perched on the counter, kicked a leg absently against a cupboard door. "But why would anybody vandalize a video store? Because they hate movies? I mean, it doesn't make sense."

"There are people out there," Estelle said grimly, "who don't give a rat's ass about other people or respect their property. They do what they want, when they want, just because they can."

"Well, it makes me just want to hurt them right back!"

"I understand that, Soph," Annie said. "But you can't. If you do, then they've brought you down to their level."

"Yeah?" Sophie said indignantly. "Well, what right do they have to screw with my life, just because they can?"

Annie realized they were no longer talking about last night's vandals. Sophie's resentment ran deep. Luke Brogan had stolen away her father, her home, the very life she'd always known, just because he could. It was a terribly unfair lesson to learn at such a tender age, and Annie wondered, not for the first time, if her daughter might benefit from counseling. But under the circumstances, she didn't dare to send her. Doctor-patient confidentiality be damned. Annie couldn't risk allowing anybody to know the truth. Not while Luke Brogan was still walking around out there, a free man.

She heard footsteps climbing the stairs, and then a sharp rap on the door. Annie got up from the table and let Hunter in. "Coffee?" she said.

"Thanks." He leaned against the counter, those lanky legs crossed at the ankles. "Black's fine."

She poured it, handed it to him, waited while he took his first sip. "Well?" she said.

He shifted position, angled narrow hips more comfortably against the edge of the Formica countertop. "I had René look around, check to make sure they didn't touch anything else. All the guest rooms are locked, and he didn't see anything that looked out of place. It seems all they were interested in was the shop."

"I have to call my insurance company. They'll probably want to send somebody out to look at it."

"We're done processing the scene. There is something I'll need the three of you to do. You, and everybody who works for you. I'd like you to stop by the station to be fingerprinted."

Her heart began a slow thudding. "Why?"

"You've all spent time in the shop. We need to eliminate your prints from whatever we got today."

It made sense in more ways than one. The fact that it terrified her didn't negate that. Not only would it move the investigation along more quickly, but it was best for her and Sophie if she gave the police their prints up front, removing them immediately from the list of possible suspects. Her prints and Sophie's both existed in some database somewhere. But the names attached to those prints didn't match the names they were using now. Giving their prints to Hunter was risky, but less so than allowing him to run them along with any others he might have found. "Sophie and I can stop by sometime today," she said. "What about you, Estelle?"

"I might as well come with you. What else do I have to do? It doesn't look like I'll be renting out videos anytime soon."

While Annie listened, Davy Hunter walked Estelle through last night's closing routine. Everything had gone as usual. She'd closed down at eight, waited for Kenny Moreau's older brother to pick him up, then locked up as she always did. Cashed up, emptied the register, put the receipts into an envelope and the money into a zippered canvas bag. She'd spent a few minutes tidying up. Boomer had picked her up around eight-thirty, and on the way home, they'd swung through the Key Bank drive-through, where she'd deposited the money bag in the night deposit slot. Then she'd gone home. She and Boomer had watched some television and gone to bed around ten.

Annie's evening had been equally uneventful. She and Sophie had popped a bag of popcorn and watched a couple of videos. They'd gone to bed around midnight. Both of them were sound sleepers. Neither of them had heard a thing during the night. Neither of them had any idea that anything was amiss until Annie had gone downstairs and discovered the wreck that had once been her video store.

"Even for a sound sleeper," Hunter said, "it's hard to believe you didn't hear anything. Whoever did this must've made a fair amount of noise."

"Yes," Annie said, "but you have to realize that the store's directly under the kitchen. I sleep in the living room. It's in the overhang, so I might not hear what's going on downstairs. And Sophie's fifteen. She could sleep through a nuclear explosion."

His blue eyes zeroed in on her as though he wasn't quite sure he believed her. "And you're certain," he said, "absolutely certain that you don't have any enemies who might've done this out of spite?"

"I already told you, I don't even know anybody in this

town. I've met a handful of people, in the most superficial of ways. The Crowleys across the street, Mr. Gilbert at the bank. I've patronized the hardware store and the lumber company. Grondin's Superette. Sonny Gaudette, although I have yet to meet him in person. That's pretty much it."

"And there's nobody you know from before you came here, somebody with a grudge, who might have followed you to Serenity?"

Thinking of Luke Brogan, she considered the possibility and dismissed it. "No," she said. "Unfortunately."

"Sophie? What about you?"

"I rode my bike downtown yesterday morning. I went into a couple of the stores on Water Street, but I didn't talk to anyone. Oh—I did stop at the library to get a library card. I talked to the librarian for a few minutes. Mrs. Atwater? The only other person I've met here is Mrs. Crowley. And her twins. I'm going to babysit for her starting next week."

"Okay. Now I'm asking you the same question I asked your mom. I want you to really think about it. Do you have any old enemies who might have thought this was a funny thing to do? Anybody who might've wanted to get back at you for some reason?"

"Mr. Hunter," Annie interjected, "this is ridiculous. We just moved here from Nevada. I hardly think any of Sophie's fifteen-year-old acquaintances would travel that far just to vandalize my video store."

"Neither do I, Ms. Kendall," he said, "but I have to ask. No old boyfriends, Sophie? Any guys you've turned down for a date? Maybe somebody who wanted to get a little friendlier than you thought was appropriate?"

"No," Sophie said solemnly. "I don't date."

"All right. What about you, Ms. Kendall? You're an attractive woman." Those blue eyes took her in, head to foot. Appraising her worth, the way another man might estimate the value of a used car. "You must have a few gentleman friends in your past. Anybody who has a reason to harass you?"

"My husband died two years ago, Mr. Hunter. There's been nobody since then."

"Nobody," he echoed, as if he found it difficult to believe.

"That's right," she said defiantly, thinking he was getting just a little too personal here. "Nobody."

"Look," he said, "I really don't mean to pry. It's just that sometimes a victim will remember something when their memory's jogged, something they wouldn't have thought of on their own." He set down his coffee mug on the counter behind him. "Sometimes, something that seems trivial turns out to be important."

He was right. Annie let out a hard breath and willed herself to relax. "I'm sorry," she said. "I don't mean to be difficult. This thing has me more spooked than I'd like to admit."

"That's understandable. Estelle? We haven't heard from you yet."

Estelle shrugged. "I already told you, I don't have a clue who might've done this. I certainly don't have any enemies."

"Boomer have a run-in with anybody lately?"

"Not that he's mentioned. And isn't that reaching a bit? I can't imagine somebody tearing this place apart because they were pissed off at Boomer."

"It's pretty far-fetched, I'll admit. But I have to cover all the bases. Have you had any bad experiences at work lately? Any disgruntled customers who thought they were above having to pay a late fee?"

Estelle started to shake her head, then paused. Thoughtfully, she said, "There was this one incident that happened a couple of weeks ago. This guy came in the shop, and he was feeling no pain, if you get my drift. Three-thirty on a Sunday afternoon, and he was so drunk he was staggering. He started hassling me—"

"Over what?"

"He wanted some movie that wasn't in. Somebody else had already rented it out. That didn't set too well with him, so he took it out on me."

"What happened?"

"He started getting physical. Grabbed me by the arm. I got scared." Her hand went to her belly in a protective gesture that was probably unconscious. "I reached for the phone to call the cops, but his buddy apologized and dragged him out of the store."

"And you never reported the incident?"

"No. I mean, he was gone. I guess I could've filed a complaint, but it was over and done with. Why stir up trouble if you don't have to?"

"I don't suppose you know his name?"

"Oh, yeah," Estelle said darkly. "I know his name, all right. I went to high school with him. Jeffrey Traynor. He was a shithead in high school, and he's a shithead now. Some things never change."

Annie walked Davy Hunter to his car. At close range, she could see the tiny wrinkles that fanned out from the corners of his eyes. There was something about those wrinkles, some vulnerability they exposed, that reached inside her and tugged at some half-forgotten emotion.

She cleared her throat. "Do you think anything will come of this Jeffrey Traynor?"

Sunglasses in hand, he leaned against the driver's door, his arms folded across his chest. Even leaning, he was tall enough that she had to lean back to look up at him. "I wouldn't get my hopes up too high," he said. "Traynor was drunk when he came into the shop and hassled Estelle. He probably woke up next morning with a wicked hangover and a boatload of ver what he'd done the night before. Once people sober up, they usually regret the things they did while they were under the influence. He probably won't dare to come near this place ever again."

He sounded as though he was talking from personal experience, but she didn't know him well enough to comment. "What next?" she said instead.

"Next," he said, "you come down and give us your prints so we can eliminate them. Then we run the ones that don't match any of yours, and hope something pops. I'll be talking with Jeff Traynor, see if I can prod anything out of him. And with Kenny Moreau. Kids his age, sometimes they get involved in feuds. We don't have any gangs per se here in Serenity, but still there are cliques. Rivalries between different groups. Sometimes, resentment over some real or imagined slight gets carried a little too far. Plus, we'll keep our eyes and ears open. With this kind of thing, people have a tendency to brag. That's how most of 'em get caught. I'd like to say it's good police work that nets these guys, but the truth is, they usually trip themselves up because they can't keep their mouths shut." He kicked absently at a chunk of broken pavement. "You have this place insured?"

"Yes, thank God. I need to get it back up and running as soon as I can. I'm not so worried about losing revenue. To tell you the truth, I'm not sure how much profit the store's making anyway." She dragged a hand through her hair. "I've gone over the books, but not in depth. Not yet. So I still don't have a complete picture. Mike Boudreau was in one hell of a hurry to dump this place. Maybe there's a reason for that." She paused, a little embarrassed at revealing her own softheartedness. "My big concern is Estelle. I have a feeling she really needs this job."

He fiddled with the bows to his sunglasses. "To tell you the truth, I'm more concerned about you. This happened downstairs while you and your daughter were asleep upstairs."

Sophie. She'd been so wrapped up in her anger that she hadn't even considered their safety. Concerned, she said, "You think whoever did this might come back?"

"Probably not. Still, you ought to think about getting some kind of security system. At least install some decent locks. I'd replace the front door while I was at it. They kicked it in like it was made of cardboard. Get yourself a steel door and have it professionally installed. They're not infallible, but anything you can find that'll put some distance between you and them is an improvement over what you have now. What about smoke alarms? I assume you have them, and they're in working order."

"Yes. Of course. But—" Her heart clutched in her chest. "You don't really think somebody would—"

"No. But it pays to be cautious." He stepped away from the side of the car and opened the driver's door. "I'll be in touch. Thanks for the coffee."

He slid into the driver's seat, locked his seat belt. While she watched, he turned the key in the ignition and started the engine. With the push of a button, the driver's window slid down soundlessly.

"Watch yourself," he said. And drove away without looking back.

Seven

This was supposed to be a place of peace, a place of tranquility, but all he felt in his gut was turmoil. Over in the back corner, a groundskeeper was working around the grave markers, raking the grass, pulling up wilted flower arrangements and tossing them in a wheelbarrow. Overhead, birds twittered in the trees. It was hotter than a son of a bitch, but Davy's hands and feet had turned to ice the instant he climbed out of the patrol car. A barn swallow darted and swooped above his head as he picked his way across a carpet of lush green to the reality he'd been avoiding for what felt like his entire life. Five rows down and three across. Just like a crossword puzzle. After thirty-five years of squabbling with her father, Chelsea's destiny was to spend eternity at Cyrus Logan's side. She was probably still laughing at the irony of it.

Funny, he drove past the cemetery a half-dozen times a day and seldom gave it a thought. It was easier that way, easier to remain in denial, easier to wall himself off from the pain than it was to face it. Since the day they put Chelsea in the ground, he hadn't set foot in this place. He'd seen her after they pulled her out of the river, before Keith Gagnon got a chance to pretty her up with embalming fluid and cosmetics. Ty ha tried to convince him that he didn't want to see her like that, that he wouldn't want to remember her that way. But what the hell difference did it make how he remembered her? Whether his memories were of Chels laughing and vibrant, or heaving a mug of hot coffee at him and screaming like a fishwife, it wouldn't make a damn bit of difference. Dead was dead, and all the wishing in the world wouldn't change it.

He hadn't attended the funeral. People thought it was strange, but he simply hadn't had it in him. He'd made all the arrangements and paid for it out of his own pocket. Paid for everything, from the casket with its satin lining—and who the hell needed satin when they were dead?—to the headstone that marked her grave. It was time, he supposed, to find out just what he'd gotten for his money.

Davy located her grave and squatted down on his haunches to get a better look. The stone he'd bought was a simple rectangle of gray granite. He wasn't the kind of man who believed in sentiment. There were no little cherubs, no hearts or flowers, no *beloved mother* or *beloved wife* or even just plain *beloved*. The stone was simple, straightforward, to the point. Chelsea Logan, born in this year and died in that one. Chelsea Logan who, by dying, had acquired the same status as everyone else here. Death, the great equalizer, had finally put her on an even footing with her neighbors.

He wasn't sure why he'd picked this particular hot summer morning to come here and lay himself bare, to scrape at the scab without mercy until he revealed the raw wound beneath. Something inside him, some internal clock, had told him it was time. He hadn't bothered to bring flowers. He'd never brought her flowers when she was alive. It would be hypocritical to start now.

She'd been sweet and spiteful, tender and twisted. From 'ime she'd been old enough to know the difference be- 'nale and female, Chelsea Logan had exploited that difference. When she walked into a room, all heads turned and all other women became invisible. It was just her way. She was the golden girl, adored by many, hated by an equal number. She played on her strengths and struggled to overcome her weaknesses, both real and imagined. Chelsea might have been beautiful, but she was far from perfect. She had her faults, some of them blatant, screaming faults that even he hadn't been able to overlook. He'd loved her anyway. What that said about him, he wasn't sure he wanted to know.

They'd been a family once upon a time, he and Chels and Jessie, so far back in history that Jessie had been small enough for him to carry around on his shoulders. It had been the happiest time of his life. But the marriage had ultimately failed. Tying Chelsea down was like caging a wild bird. She'd been miserable. Because misery loves company, he'd eventually been miserable right along with her, and what was the sense in even bothering to try once that happened? So they'd split up.

In retrospect, divorce had worked out a lot better for them than marriage ever had. As long as he was willing to overlook her numerous liaisons with other men, they'd gotten along just fine. For the better part of a dozen years after the divorce, they'd maintained an on-again, off-again relationship. Chelsea would get bored with whatever or whoever she was doing, and she'd crook her finger, and he'd come running. He'd known the relationship was toxic. He just hadn't been able to break his addiction to Chelsea's slow-acting poison. Having a piece of her, however small and insignificant, had always seemed preferable to having none of her.

Now that he actually had none of her, he was finding that it wasn't really so very different after all. As long as he stayed away from this place, he could pretend their relationship was on yet another hiatus, that he and Chelsea had once again wandered to opposite ends of the earth and would eventually rendezvous back here in Serenity again.

But it was nothing more than a fantasy. The proof was here in front of him, etched indelibly in cold granite. *Chelsea Logan. 1969-2005*. The end of the fairy tale.

He wanted a drink. Right here in the cemetery, a hundred yards from the sanctity of the First Methodist Church and two hours before noon, when the official drinking day got started, he wanted a cold beer or two or twelve. The real thing, not that near-beer that was a pale imitation of what it was designed to take the place of. If he had a twelve-pack in his car right now, he'd spend the rest of the day sitting here in this cemetery, in the midst of all these dead people, and drink himself into a stupor.

But Davy Hunter was nothing if not a practical man. He didn't have any beer, and if he didn't show up back at the station pretty soon, Dixie would send Pete out looking for him. And though it might be the worst kind of cliché, it was true that there was no sense in crying over spilt milk. Life went on, even when you didn't want it to. If there was one thing he'd learned from the last fourteen months, it was that.

Out of nowhere, his mind conjured up a picture of Annie Kendall, all soft blond hair and outraged blue eyes and righteous indignation. How much did she have to do with the reason he'd come here today? He didn't dare even attempt to answer that question. It wasn't a place he was ready to go. But he was too honest to lie to himself. Something about the woman had reached inside him and touched that wall of stone he'd built up as a defense mechanism. That was as much as he was willing to admit at this point. Something inside her spoke to something inside him. It was too soon to read anything into it, enough simply to acknowledge its existence. That acknowledgment was a single, tentative first step back toward the land of the living.

That and his visit here today.

Davy stood up and stretched his cramped muscles. He had

things to take care of. People to talk to. An investigation to run. Now that he'd finally come here, he knew he'd be back again. So did Chelsea. When she was alive, Chels had always been able to see what was inside him. There was no reason to think death had changed that. No need for goodbyes. Chelsea wasn't going anywhere. Neither was he, not for a while, anyway.

As he walked back across the springy grass to the police cruiser he'd left parked at the gate, Davy realized for the first time that maybe he was going to survive this tragedy after all. Maybe having something to focus on would be good for what ailed him. Maybe, he reluctantly admitted, Ty Savage had known what he was doing all along.

He fired up the Crown Vic, radioed in to Dixie so she wouldn't think he'd driven off a cliff somewhere, and headed across town to question Jeff Traynor.

Tracking down Robert Sarnacki was a piece of cake. All Louis had to do was run a credit check on the man, and *voilà!* He had Sarnacki's address and phone number right in front of him. Judging from his credit report, Sarnacki could easily have owned the goose that laid the golden egg. He had a mortgage that would have bankrupted most normal working people, auto loan payments totaling more than Louis's monthly rent, and various types of business expenses, although it was difficult to tell from the credit report just what business Sarnacki was in. The man had all his little duckies lined up in a row, and one of the cleanest credit records Louis had ever seen. There wasn't a blur on his record, not even so much as a late payment on his wife's Marshall Field's card.

He had to dig a little deeper to find out how Sarnacki and Spinney were related. Turned out Sarnacki was her mother's second cousin, which explained why Louis had missed him completely on the first go-round. Usually by the time blood got diluted that far, there was little to no contact between relatives. But apparently Spinney and Sarnacki were close, to the consternation of her father, who obviously didn't approve of the man.

When he ran a Google search, he hit pay dirt. Robert Sarnacki was in construction, although he had his finger in a number of other pies, and there were rumored ties to the Mob. Those rumors had yet to be substantiated, but they were enough to justify Bill Wyatt's dislike of the man. Sarnacki was Loaded, with a capital *L,* which explained the exorbitant mortgage and the expensive cars.

It didn't take an Einstein to fit it all together. Sarnacki and Spinney were thick as thieves. The man lived in Detroit, he owned property all over the greater Detroit area, and he was filthy rich. Robert Sarnacki not only knew where Robin Spinney was, he'd probably financed her disappearance himself. Louis was willing to bet a month's pay that if he were inclined to research more deeply the Dearborn ranch house Spinney had bought but never lived in, he would find that she'd bought it from Sarnacki Construction or one of its subsidiaries.

Louis shut down his laptop, closed it carefully, and returned it to its leather carrying case. This afternoon, he would find Sarnacki's house, take a ride past, scope it out. What he saw there would determine his next move. Tonight, he'd have a nice dinner—on Brogan's dime, of course—then he'd sit down and formulate a carefully-thought-out plan. There were a number of viable options for getting his hands on Spinney's address, and Louis knew them all. He considered himself a Renaissance man, capable of any number of things. When the time came to act, he'd be ready, with all the necessary tools at hand.

But first things first. When he wasn't in a position to offer written reports, Louis always made a point of phoning his client whenever there was something to report. He considered staying in touch one more facet of the exemplary service he provided. And it was time to report in.

He picked up his cell phone and dialed a number in Mississippi. Luke Brogan was about to become a happy man.

Davy found Jeff Traynor working the breakfast shift at the McDonald's across the river. Traynor was somewhere in his early twenties, and the day manager had assigned him the highly skilled tasks of sweeping floors and taking out the garbage. He was clearly executive material. A tall, gaunt, hollow-chested kid, Traynor hunched over when he walked, reminding Davy of an old drawing of Ichabod Crane that he'd seen in one of Jessie's childhood storybooks. His pitted face was undoubtedly the legacy of a bad case of adolescent acne. He wore the standard fast-food uniform, covered over with an apron that had probably once been white, but which now bore the multicolored remnants of God only knew what. If Davy thought too hard about it, he'd probably never be able to choke down another Big Mac, so he focused instead on the kid's eyes, which held a glassiness that was just a shade beyond natural.

"Whatta you want with me?" Traynor asked.

Davy glanced around. Traynor's co-workers, while continuing to man their stations, evidenced clear interest in what the police had to say to him. "Is there some place we can talk in private?" he said.

"I ain't done nothing wrong."

"Then you don't have anything to worry about, do you?"

Traynor mumbled something under his breath that sounded suspiciously like *asshole,* but Davy decided not to call him on it. They sat on a picnic table out back of the parking lot in the bright morning sun. Traynor reached into his shirt pocket and pulled out a pack of Marlboros, lit one, and tossed the match onto the ground. "So?" he said.

Davy adjusted his sunglasses. Feet propped on the bench seat, hands braced against the table top, he leaned back and turned his face up to the sun. "I hear you had a run-in with the clerk at the Twilight Video a couple of weeks ago."

Traynor took a long drag on his cigarette and slowly exhaled the smoke. "So?"

Nearby, a pair of seagulls squabbled over the remains of an Egg McMuffin that had fallen from an overflowing trash can. "Want to tell me about it?"

"I didn't do nothing."

"Yeah," Davy said. "I seem to remember you already told me that. Now I want to hear about you and Estelle. What happened?"

Traynor flicked an ash. "Whatever that fucking bitch told you, it's a lie."

The squabble over the Egg McMuffin intensified, with much squawking and flapping. The victor flew off, prize dangling from its beak. "What makes you think she told me anything?" Davy said.

Traynor stared at him defiantly, then glanced away. "Fuck you, man."

"I'm pretty sure that would be an anatomical impossibility. Tell me, Jeffrey." Davy leaned forward, his elbows propped on his knees, and studied the kid's body language. "You know what I did before this? I worked for the DEA."

Traynor, still puffing on his Marlboro, stiffened perceptibly.

"I see you've heard of them," Davy said, "which means you know I'm familiar with pretty much every street drug out there. I know what they look like, I know their mortality rates, I know their short-term and long-term effects on behavior and general physiology. See, I may look stupid, but I'm really not." He took his time, let the kid think about it, let him squirm for a minute or two. "So," he continued, quiet and unhurried, "unless you want me to take a closer look at those dilated pupils of yours, maybe even make you empty your pockets, you're probably going to want to cooperate with me. Otherwise, we could end up taking a little trip together, to a place where I can demand samples of body fluids. You don't really want that."

A red Nissan pulled in and circled around to the drive-through. Traynor remained silent while the blonde behind the wheel gave her breakfast order to the anonymous voice coming from the speaker. "It's your call, champ."

"Look, man, I was drunk, okay? I wasn't in cóntrol of my faculties. I'd had a few too many beers. I wanted to rent *Wayne's World,* but they didn't have it. I got pissed and started mouthing off. That fucking Estelle, she can be a real pain in the ass when she wants to." The kid's eyes darted all around, looking everywhere but at Davy. "I never liked her anyway. She was a snotty bitch in high school, always thinking she was better than everyone else. That's why she's working in a video store now, right? Her superior intellect."

Traynor paused, finally met Davy's eyes, seeking affirmation. After a moment, when he didn't get it, he looked away again. Flicked an ash. "It wasn't that big a thing. I said some things to her, she said some things back to me, then she told me to get my ass out and not bother coming back. I didn't much like that, but my buddy grabbed me and dragged me out of there. He took me home, I went to bed, and I slept it off. End of story."

"Estelle suggested you might've gotten physical with her."

Traynor turned his head, his eyes widened in exaggerated innocence. "What? Oh, man, you gotta be kidding. I never touched a woman in my life. That bitch is lying."

"She claims you grabbed her arm."

Traynor took a quick puff on the cigarette. Shrugged. "I don't know."

"What do you mean, you don't know? Either you grabbed her arm or you didn't. The question's not that difficult, Traynor. Did you or didn't you?"

"I was drunk. I don't really remember." Traynor took a last drag on the cigarette and tossed it onto the ground. "I might've. It's all pretty hazy."

"So you might have grabbed Estelle's arm, but you're not sure. You don't like her much, do you?"

"I told you, she's a fucking bitch."

"Just how much do you dislike her, Jeffrey? Enough, maybe, to go back later and get even?"

"Hunh?" For the first time, Jeff Traynor seemed genuinely puzzled. "What're you talking about?"

"I don't know, Traynor. Why don't you tell me?"

"Dude, you're talking in riddles. I don't have time for this shit. If I don't get back in there pretty soon, they'll fire me."

"Where were you last night?"

Traynor blinked in confusion. "Last night? I was home in bed. What's this all about, anyway?"

"You got anybody who can verify that?"

"My mom was already in bed when I got home. I live with her. So she couldn't say what time I got in. I think it was around ten. But she knows I was there this morning. She got me up for work. I had to be here at five-thirty. What's going on? Did somebody do something to Estelle?" His already pale complexion grew appreciably more pallid. "Shit, man, you better not be trying to pin anything on me. I ain't done nothing wrong."

"Like I said, if you've done nothing wrong, you have nothing to be afraid of."

"Oh, yeah, that's the way it works, all right." His defiance seemed to give way to something else. "Is Estelle okay?"

"Estelle's fine."

"Look, man, I don't much like her, but I wouldn't do nothing to her. Christ, the woman's pregnant. I'm not that kind of guy."

As much as it pained him to admit it, he believed the kid. He would double-check, follow through just to be sure, but it looked as though he'd hit a brick wall. Jeff Traynor might not be the most admirable of men, but his story about being in bed by ten last night was probably the truth. Even the dumbest of criminals generally knew enough to set up some kind of an alibi before committing a crime. And Traynor's concern for Estelle's welfare seemed genuine. It was possible that somewhere beneath that belligerent exterior, skillfully hidden from sight, there beat the heart of a real human being.

"Go," he said. "Get back to work. I'm finished with you for now."

Without a word, Traynor slid down off the picnic table and headed for the back door of the restaurant. Halfway there, he turned. "You tell Estelle," he said. "You tell her I said I'd never do anything to hurt her."

Luke Brogan wasn't a happy man.

He had business to attend to, a sheriff's department to run. He didn't have time to waste cooling his heels for forty-five minutes in the district attorney's office while he waited for his brother to finish a conference call. Marcus had been the one to schedule this meeting. The least he could do was be on time for it. When Marcus's secretary, Sydney Ann, had called to tell Brogan that his brother wanted to see him, she hadn't said what it was about. But it was pretty obvious. After twenty years of ass-kissing and politicking, Marcus had finally gotten that bench appointment he'd been salivating over. The town was all abuzz with the news. And wasn't it a damn shame that he'd been forced to wait until poor old Abner Mellen kicked the bucket?

The cell phone in his pocket vibrated, and Brogan checked

the caller ID. Recognizing the number, he pushed a button, and said, "Yeah?"

"I have good news," Louis Farley said in greeting.

Brogan glanced up, caught Sydney eavesdropping from behind her work station. Scowling, he got up and walked to the far end of the room so he could talk in private. Tersely, he said, "You found her?"

"Not yet," Farley said. "But I've found out who's helping her. From there, it's only a matter of time until I locate her."

He ventured another glance at Sydney, who was busying herself shuffling papers and trying to pretend she had no interest in his private telephone conversation. Brogan turned away from her, toward the wall, and said, "Where are you?"

"Detroit."

"I thought you'd already been to Detroit and hit a dead end."

"I did. It just opened back up. Trust me, my friend. I'll have your information for you in no time."

Farley was a fool if he thought they were friends. Theirs was a business association and nothing more. "You damn well better," Brogan said. "And when you find her, you call me. Don't make a frigging move until I tell you to."

"You're the boss," Farley said. "I'll be in touch." And he hung up without saying good-bye.

"Sheriff?" It was Sydney Ann, smug smile in place. "The District Attorney will see you now."

"About time," he muttered, and shoved past her desk and into his brother's office.

Marcus Brogan was dressed, as usual, in an expensive three-piece suit and polished Italian loafers. He sat behind a burnished mahogany desk piled high with file folders and law tomes. On the wall behind him, he'd hung his ornately framed status symbols: an undergraduate degree in political science from Stanford and a law degree from Yale. Only the best for

Marcus Brogan, the Chosen One, the son who'd fulfilled every expectation their daddy had set forth for him.

Luke Brogan had often tried to tell himself it wasn't Marcus's fault that he'd been the favored son. Life just had a funny way of working out, that was all. It wasn't Marcus's fault that Darius Brogan had divorced his first wife when Luke was four years old, leaving his ex-wife and young son with barely enough money to survive. It wasn't Marcus's fault that Darius had moved on to establish a second, more socially acceptable family. It wasn't his fault that Luke had been raised by a single mother in a little shotgun house on the wrong side of the tracks while Marcus, child of Darius Brogan's second marriage to an Atlanta debutante whose daddy just happened to be a senator, got it all: the big house, the fancy cars, the expensive college education.

To his stepmother's credit, Luke had never been left out. On the surface, he was part of the family. He'd always been included in Brogan family outings and parties. He'd spent Christmases, Thanksgivings, and Easters with his father's new family, and Dorothy Brogan had never, until the day she died, forgotten her stepson's birthday. But in truth, he'd been little more to his father than an also-ran, and he'd spent his entire life resenting his younger half brother for being and having everything he'd been denied.

Still, as the old saying went, blood was thicker than water. The two half brothers might not have been close, but they'd always taken care of each other. It was what family did.

Right now, Marcus wasn't looking any too happy. "Shut the door," he said. "If Sydney Ann overhears what we're saying, it's apt to show up on the front page of the *Journal-Constitution* tomorrow morning. Why I haven't fired that woman before this is something I simply can't explain."

"Oh, I don't know," Luke said, settling comfortably into a plush visitor's chair. "She must be good at something."

His brother's poker face, perfected over a quarter of a century spent in the courtroom, first as a defense attorney, then as a prosecutor, was legendary. Luke must have touched a nerve with his comment, because Marcus wasn't bothering to hide the cool disdain with which he regarded his brother. Rumors about Marcus and his secretary had been circulating for years. Luke had never paid much attention to them. It was none of his business where his brother chose to get his wick dipped. The man's taste in women might be suspect—after all, he'd married that harpy Marilyn Evers—but that was Marcus's problem, wasn't it? Ignoring his brother's snotty expression, he said, "What's so all-fired important that you made me wait forty-five minutes in the outer office?"

In his best clipped Yale-lawyer voice, Marcus said, "I imagine you've heard about my judicial appointment."

"I heard. I also heard that Abner Mellen was barely cold in his grave before you hired a decorator to redo his chambers."

His barb hit its intended target. "Fuck you, Lucas," his brother said. "I've worked my ass off for twenty-seven years to get to this point. And I intend to let nothing—*nothing*—get in my way. Do you understand that?"

"Your point, Marcus?"

"Robin Spinney."

Oh, shit. Suddenly, his palms were clammy and his stomach began to churn. Luke closed his eyes, but the woman's face was still there, inside his head, taunting him. No matter how hard he tried, he couldn't make her go away. "I know you haven't found her yet," his brother continued. "That useless private investigator you hired couldn't find his own ass in the dark with a flashlight."

Luke opened his eyes. "Now, listen here, Marcus—"

"Fire him, Luke. The half-baked fool isn't doing us any good. I have somebody in mind who'll take care of the situation for us, once and for all. And he won't leave any loose ends."

Luke's hands, of their own free will, clenched into fists. "I have the situation under control."

"Like hell you do. You dragged me into this mess, Lucas. You got into trouble and I covered your worthless ass. Do you understand what that means? If you go down, I go down with you. You haven't forgotten that, have you?"

Jaw clenched, he muttered, "I haven't forgotten."

"Good. See that you don't." Marcus leaned forward over his desk. "Because I have no intention of going down, you hear me? Call off your bulldog. Let me send my man in."

He was tired of Marcus calling all the shots. From the time they were kids, he and his younger brother had been locked in a power struggle. "This is my deal," he said, "and I'll handle it. We don't even know what Spinney's got. She may have nothing on you."

"I'm not willing to take the chance. Since the day I graduated from law school, I've had one goal: that seat on the bench. And I'm not willing to sacrifice that just because I made the mistake of saving you from a lynching. We may be brothers, but blood only goes so far. And this brother's looking out for number one."

"Good to know where I stand."

"I'm just calling it the way I see it. You're an idiot, Luke. You do realize that, don't you? I can't put my entire future in the hands of an idiot."

Steaming, he said, "Farley just called me a few minutes ago from Detroit. Things are progressing nicely. He expects to pinpoint Spinney's whereabouts within a few days."

Marcus rapped his Mont Blanc pen against the desktop. The sound echoed like a gunshot in the room. "And how do you intend to resolve the situation once you find her?"

"I should think that would be pretty clear."

"If you fuck this up," Marcus warned, "we'll get the chance to spend the next twenty-five to life as cellmates over at Mississippi State Prison. I don't believe I like you well enough to spend the next three decades locked in a five-by-seven room with you."

His usually smooth manner had begun to deteriorate. Marcus Brogan, fearless district attorney, was scared. "I fully intend to be sitting on the bench," he continued, "not standing before it. Do you understand that, big brother?"

The way he said those words, *big brother,* made Luke want to draw back and let him have it. For an instant, he allowed himself to fantasize about the satisfaction he'd get from hearing the sharp crunch of his brother's nose breaking under his fist. "Louis Farley," he said in a voice as quiet as death, "knows what the hell he's doing. I'm not quite as stupid as you think I am, Marcus. If Farley tells me he'll find Robin Spinney, he'll find her. Stop expecting an overnight miracle and give the man time to do the job."

"Five days, Lucas. That's what I'm giving him. If Robin Spinney and her kid aren't dead and that envelope in my hands in five days, I'm sending in my man. And he'll leave no loose ends. That includes Louis Farley. Am I making myself clear?"

A trickle of sweat ran down Luke Brogan's spine. "Clear as crystal," he said.

"Good. Now get the hell out of here. I have work to do."

After he'd gone, Marcus Brogan sat there in the silence, thinking, for a very long time before he picked up the phone and dialed a number.

"Constantine?" he said. "This is Marcus Brogan. Farley's in Detroit." He paused. "Make sure you don't leave any loose ends."

Eight

Lengthening shadows cast slivers of darkness over bright green lawn as the sun worked its way westward. This was Davy's favorite time of day, and Jo's backyard tonight was an oasis of rich and varying shades of green, punctuated by splashes of crimson, pink and pale yellow. The roses she took such pride in were big as a man's fist and fragrant enough to override the mingled odors of charred beef and pool chemicals. In the pool, a half-dozen kids of various ages shrieked and splashed. While he watched, Jessie climbed out of the water and stood shivering on the concrete patio near the diving board. She looked up, saw him, and waved. He waved back. Jessie stepped onto the diving board and walked carefully to the end. She lined up her toes on the edge of the board and bounced a couple of times on the balls of her feet, setting the board in motion. Then, with a single, powerful bound, she plunged off the diving board and into the deep end of the pool.

The resulting splash had him wiping drops of chlorinated water from his face with his shirt sleeve. Jessie surfaced and started swimming toward the shallow end. Beside him, Dixie Lessard edged up to the redwood railing and set down her bottle of Budweiser. "Nice evening," she said. "I wasn't sure you'd show up here tonight."

"Neither was I." Elbows braced against the railing, he picked up his cup of coffee and took a sip. "But it seemed pointless to stay home. I knew if I didn't show up, Jo would come knocking on my door, pitchfork in hand, ready to prod me until I gave in."

"That's one scary picture."

Davy turned, one hip braced against the wooden railing, and said, "So you're here tonight with Keith Gagnon."

Across the deck, the tall, gaunt mortician stood engaged in earnest conversation with Jack Crowley, who was pretending to know how to cook. Smoke rose in a blue cloud from the grill as Jack flipped burgers. Keith Gagnon was a decade older than Dixie, and he looked it. He lowered his head to listen more closely to something Jack said, and the sun reflected off his shiny pate, clearly visible through the thin layer of hair he'd combed over in a useless attempt to camouflage his baldness. Davy didn't get it. Who the hell was Keith trying to impress? Everybody in Serenity already knew the man was bald. He wasn't fooling anyone but himself.

A breeze stirred Dixie's flowered cotton muumuu. She lifted the bottle of Bud to her lips and took a long, slow swallow. "Any port in a storm," she said.

"There's nothing wrong with Keith." Except for the hair thing. "He's a decent guy."

Dixie shrugged. "He'll never light the world on fire, but at least he has the decency to talk to my face instead of my chest. That has to be worth something. The last three losers I dated all had the same idea, that the word divorcée is synonymous with the initials DGL."

"DGL?"

"Dying to Get Laid. Cretins."

Another kid, one he didn't recognize, jumped off the diving board, sending plump drops of water his way. "I hate these get-togethers," he said. "People expect me to mingle and make small talk and act like—" He stopped abruptly.

Dixie turned and leaned her back against the railing. Smiling knowingly, she said, "Like a human being?"

"Ah, hell. Is the werewolf that visible?"

"Lurking right there in your eyes, my friend."

He gazed balefully into his coffee cup. "I wish to Christ this was something a little stronger."

"As you indubitably know," she said, "it doesn't help."

He gave her a cynical smile. "Indubitably."

From the kitchen window, a female voice called, "Davy Hunter! Can you come here for a minute? I need to talk to you."

"Busted," Dixie muttered under her breath.

"Yep. I've been summoned. And when Jo calls—" Coffee in hand, he straightened and stepped away from the railing. "Later, Dix."

"Later."

He found Jolene at the kitchen sink, struggling with a carving knife and the world's biggest watermelon. "Think you can slice this thing?" she said.

"Better than you can," he said, and set down the coffee. "You're a freaking accident waiting to happen." He took the knife from her and plunged it deep into the heart of the watermelon. "Don't I remember some old saying about not sending in a woman to do a man's job?"

"Bite me, Hunter."

"Do your students—" he hacked away at the hard rind "—know you talk that way?"

"They do not. And if you breathe a word of it to anybody under the age of twenty, I'll have to use that knife on you." She stood silent for a moment—a rare thing for Jo—and watched him carve the watermelon into neat slices. "How the hell do you do that?"

"Werewolf power."

"What?"

"Never mind. Private joke. You putting this on a platter, or what?"

She opened a cupboard door, took out a turkey platter, and set it on the counter. He began laying out slices of watermelon in a tidy circular pattern. "Presentation," he said dryly. "It's everything."

"So how are you?" she said. "Really."

Something about her solicitous manner sent up a red flag. He glanced up from his work. "I'm fine," he said evenly. "How're you?"

"Oh, I'm just peachy. How's the new job going?"

He studied her face. Her cheeks were flushed. Whenever Jo's cheeks were flushed, it meant she was up to something. "The new job's going fine," he said carefully. "Why do you ask?"

"I hear you've met my new neighbor. Annie Kendall."

He set down the knife. "All right," he said, "you're the third person who's brought that up to me in the past two days. I know this is a small town, but this goes beyond the norm for even Serenity's world-champion gossip-mongers. Am I missing something here?"

"I just wondered what you thought of her. She's a nice-looking woman. And easy to talk to. Very pleasant."

He stared at her, sighed, and returned to arranging watermelon. "No," he said.

"She's single, although I can't honestly say she's in dire need of a man—"

"No."

"—considering that she just got done fixing her own roof."

He paused, knife in hand, intrigued in spite of himself. "She did what?"

"Fixed her own roof." Jo dimpled prettily. "She had one

hell of a leak over one of the guest rooms. It pretty much ruined everything. The ceiling, the bed, the carpet. Jack told her how to repair it, and he loaned her his ladder and his pickup truck. She spent two days tearing it apart and putting it back together. Jack checked it out a couple of hours ago. He says he couldn't have done it better himself."

"Hunh. I saw the ladder, saw the old shingles all over the ground, but I never—I'll be damned."

Jo went to the refrigerator, took out a plastic container of lemonade, and busied herself shaking it. "She's smart, like Chelsea was."

Davy stiffened, but she didn't notice. Or, more likely, chose not to. "She has a sense of humor, too. I think the two of you—"

"Damn it, Jolene, what part of no don't you understand? N-O. Not interested. End of discussion. Got that?"

She raised her chin, ready to rumble. "Not interested?" she said. "Or scared?"

Stiffly, he said, "Stay out of it. My life is my own business."

"Oh." Her voice lowered to a dangerous level. "Is that it? Jack and I should just sit by and watch you slowly rotting out there in that horrible little trailer in the swamp? You don't talk to people, you don't socialize, you're just growing old and bitter!"

"What the hell business is it of yours, anyway? Who died and made you boss? Who are you to tell me how to live my life?"

"I'm your friend, that's who I am! I'm somebody who's known you since you rode a tricycle. I care about you, and I can't stand to see you give up on life. There's nothing wrong with mourning, Davy. It's healthy and necessary. But eventually, there comes a time when—"

Woodenly, he said, "She's only been dead for a year."

"It's been fourteen months. And the relationship was dead long before that."

Her words hurt more than they should have, probably because they were the truth. It didn't make them any easier to take. "Thank you for clarifying that," he said.

Any other woman would have flinched, but Jo just stood there, defiance painted all over her face. "Look," he said, "I appreciate your concern, but I don't need interference from my friends. I'm a big boy, and if I want to rot out there in my trailer in the swamp, I'll damn well do it. You can relay that message to all the rest of my well-meaning friends, too. When I'm ready to date, you'll be the first to hear. In the meantime, please don't try to set me up, because you're just going to piss me off worse than you already have. Do I need to repeat that, word for word, or have you got it?"

"Oh, to hell with you," she said irritably, dismissing him with a flippant wave of her hand. "You want to rot, you go ahead and rot. It's probably just as well that you're not interested anyway, because when we were talking about you the other day—"

He blinked. "We?" he said. "We, who?"

"Annie and I. She said—"

"Wait just a minute. Let me make sure I have this right. You and Annie Kendall were talking about me?"

"She made it sound as though she wasn't that impressed with you anyway."

Jesus Christ. Talk about kicking a man when he was down. "What do you mean, she wasn't that impressed?" he said. "I've met the woman twice, for Christ's sake. I wasn't trying to impress her. I was doing my job."

"I know, hon. You're an absolute knight in shining armor. But she said you seemed…let's see, how did she put it? Oh, I remember. Grim. That's it. She said you seemed rather grim."

Now there was a surprise. Maybe she'd like to tell him something he didn't already know about himself. Gruffly, he said, "Why the hell should I give a damn about what some woman thinks of me? Some woman I've met exactly twice? Hell, I don't even know her."

"Exactly!" She gave him one of those silky smiles that he knew meant trouble. "That's just what I told Jack. Which is why I'm sure you'll have no problem whatsoever with the fact that she's walking up the driveway, even as we speak."

"What? Christ, Jo, you didn't." He shoved her aside and stalked to the window. Sure enough, there she was, Annie Kendall, dressed in some kind of filmy white thing which, backlit by the sun, revealed every curve of her slender body. Her hair, a soft, muted shade of blond that was the antithesis of the brassy boldness that had been Chelsea, was pulled back from her face in a French braid. Cool and elegant. It suited her, this woman who thought he was grim. He closed his eyes. Let out a sigh. "Damn you, Jo," he said. "You fight dirty."

She patted his arm. "It's not me," she said cheerfully. "It's you."

He turned to look at her indignantly. "Me?"

Jo rolled her eyes. "Not you, singular. You, plural. Men. You're so easy. Like shooting fish in a barrel. Now stop scowling at me and get out there. And play nice, or this'll be the last invitation you get from me."

The driveway was lined with cars of various makes and vintages. This was Jack Crowley's idea of a few friends? Good Lord. She'd seriously considered staying home tonight. She really wasn't ready to face all these strangers, especially after the craziness of the last few days. She could have used some down time before being thrust into the limelight where, as the new kid in town, she would be examined like a bug

under a microscope. But when Jack had stopped by a couple
of hours ago to check on her roofing job, he'd made sure to
remind her that the get-together was tonight and she was expected to make an appearance. And Uncle Bobby's advice
about putting down roots kept echoing in her head. She supposed now was as good a time as any to start establishing
herself as that nice Annie Kendall, single mother and entrepreneur, who'd just moved in next door.

Sophie, on the other hand, was enthused about this little
party. Or as enthused as Sophie got these days. All it had taken
were the words *swimming pool* and Soph was ready to roll.
In honor of the occasion, she'd pulled her hair into a ponytail and dressed in athletic shorts and a white T-shirt with the
Budweiser lizards on the front. There wasn't so much as a
smear of black lipstick in sight. Had Sophie already learned
the lesson Annie was trying to teach herself about fitting in?
When in Rome, do as the Romans do. Or was she simply
dressing in the most practical manner for swimming? Annie
didn't dare to hope for too much, but any respite, however
brief, from living full-time with Morticia Addams was a good
thing, and Annie sent up a silent prayer of thanks.

They followed the party sounds to the backyard, where
people were gathered in clusters, drinking beer and talking
and generally having a good time. Annie scanned the crowd,
although she wasn't sure what or who she was looking for.
Strangers, every one of them, with the notable exception of
Jack Crowley, who manned the humongous grill that sat on
the redwood deck emitting heavenly smells.

In the swimming pool, kids splashed and squealed. One of
the twins—she couldn't be sure whether it was Sam or Jake,
since they were identical—waved and yelled, "Hey, Sophie,
come on in! We're playing volleyball! You can be on my
team!"

Her daughter turned to her with a hopeful face. "Mom?"

It was wonderful to have the old Sophie back, if only temporarily. "Go," she said. "Have fun. I'll just wander around, find a conversation to worm my way into."

She didn't have to say it twice. Sophie was off like a bullet. She reached the edge of the pool, left her towel and sneakers on a deck chair, peeled down to her bathing suit, and waded eagerly into the water. Kids. It was so easy for them. Once you reached adulthood, friendships didn't come so easy. People were wary of each other. With good reason, but still…these last six months, she'd been so intensely caught up in crisis mode, so involved in staying hidden from Brogan and creating a new life for Sophie and herself, that she hadn't taken the time to realize she was lonely.

But she realized it now. She'd never been a social butterfly, but she'd had a few close friends, and there'd been several couples she and Mac had socialized with on a regular basis. None of them had quite reached the level of close friends, but she would have called them friendly acquaintances. Somebody with whom to spend a few pleasant hours talking about mutual interests.

The last six months, her social life had revolved exclusively around her teenage daughter. Sophie was a great kid once you got past the belligerent adolescent act. Even so, their meeting of the minds was limited to a few obscure topics. They both thought the new retro-look Ford Mustang was destined to be a classic, and both of them adored steamer clams dripping with butter. But that was pretty much the extent of their overlapping interests. Annie's tastes ran to 19th-century antiques and Led Zeppelin. Soph was into black nail polish and Marilyn Manson. There wasn't a whole lot of common ground between those extremes.

She could really use somebody past the age of thirty to talk to.

Determined to put a good spin on the evening, whatever it

brought, Annie threw back her shoulders, plastered on a generic smile, and began scoping out the crowd in search of a mini-party to crash. She'd just about decided on hijacking two thirty-something women drinking wine coolers and talking animatedly while they lounged in deck chairs beside the pool when her attention was caught by a pair of blue eyes that were focused directly on her.

Davy Hunter stood on the deck next to the sliders, leaning against the cedar shingles, his gaze riveted on her face. His chambray shirt was the same shade of blue as his eyes, and his jeans hugged those lean hips like a lover's embrace. This was the first time she'd seen him out of uniform. He wasn't exactly hard on the eyes. Hunter wasn't a handsome man. His edges were too rough for handsomeness. But there was something compelling about him just the same, an attractiveness that couldn't be explained by something as superficial and transitory as perfect features or a nice smile. There was something primal and timeless about his appeal, something that grabbed at her heart and tugged for all it was worth. And right now, she was inordinately pleased to see him, a familiar face in a sea of strangers.

He raised his coffee cup in greeting, and soft feathers of pleasure tickled her insides. The wine cooler ladies totally forgotten, Annie moved straight toward him. "I didn't expect to see you here," she said.

"World's just full of surprises, isn't it?"

"It is," she said. "Some of them more pleasant than others." She tried to read those blue eyes, but found them impenetrable even when he wasn't wearing the sunglasses. Glancing around the yard, she said, "Who are all these people?"

"I could introduce you around."

Her attention swiftly returned to him. "Was that a threat, Hunter?"

He didn't answer. Instead, he said, "Are you hungry?"

"Not particularly, but I could go for a glass of iced tea, if you think you could scare one up for me."

"Wait here." He crossed the deck, knelt and rummaged around in a large cooler parked near the grill, pulling out a bottle of Snapple. "Success," he said, returning to her with his bounty.

"Thanks," she said, taking the ice-cold bottle from him. "Is this an example of my tax dollars at work?"

"I'm off duty."

And he obviously hadn't gotten the hang of light banter. "You're the police chief," she said, uncapping the bottle of iced tea and taking a sip. "I'd think that would mean you're never off duty."

"It's a temporary position. And in a manner of speaking, you're right."

By unspoken mutual accord, they left the deck to slowly circle Jo Crowley's backyard. Her roses were spectacular. Pausing before a particularly impressive specimen, Annie buried her face in a huge yellow blossom tinged with pink and inhaled its heavenly fragrance. "My mother used to grow roses," she said wistfully. "This brings back wonderful memories. I've always found it intriguing, the way memory is so closely intertwined with our sense of smell. Did you know that psychologists still haven't figured out why?" She glanced up, caught the indulgent look on his face, and grinned. "Sorry," she said. "I tend to get carried away about the most esoteric things."

"I don't mind."

"But I do. I'd rather talk about you anyway. So tell me, Davy Hunter, how you came to be the temporary police chief of Serenity."

"I did it as a favor to a friend," he said. "Except that I'm beginning to believe he's the one who did me the favor."

"Oh?"

"I'm also beginning to believe that was his intention all along. He was trying to save me from myself."

"I see. And do you need saving?"

"I don't know. What do you think?"

She took his question seriously because it felt serious. Pausing to study him more closely, she said, "I suspect you have trust issues. There's definitely a dark side to you. You're a little enigmatic, a little secretive, a little remote. You don't let people get too close. You're probably also a perfectionist who's far too hard on himself. But underneath it all, there's a good, solid core of decency. All in all, I'd say you're salvageable."

"Jesus Christ," he said. "What are you, a psychic?"

"Psychology major. I was a high school guidance counselor in a previous life." She hadn't meant to tell him anything about her past. It had simply slipped out, and it was too late now to take it back.

"And you left it behind," he said. "Just like that. For what?"

"To be an entrepreneur, of course. Now I own a run-down motel and a video store that somebody trashed the other night."

"Nice answer. You do elusive well. And you call me secretive?"

"There's nothing secretive about it. My marriage ended, things happened, and I left that life behind and came here to start a new one. So far, it's been interesting."

"I hear you shingled your own roof."

"I did. In case you decide to leave police work, I don't recommend roofing as a profession. Although by the time I finished, I did have quite a feeling of accomplishment."

"How'd it go with the insurance company?"

"It went. The adjuster came this morning, all the way from Portland, and he made sure I knew that his little trip out here to no-man's-land was more than just a hop and a skip."

"They planning to take care of it?"

"It looks that way. He asked about a zillion questions, and he took pictures. Both video and still. I have to inventory the damage and give him a list of lost items and estimated replacement costs, and then they'll write me a check. It was a little creepy. He kept staring at me through his Coke-bottle glasses as though he thought that if he stared hard enough, I'd admit to trashing the place myself for the insurance money. Hell, if I'd thought of it, I might have done that. Insurance fraud's bound to be more profitable than the Twilight Video store ever will be."

"Be careful what you say. You're talking to a cop. You don't want to incriminate yourself."

Maybe she'd been wrong before. Maybe he did have the hang of light banter. Maybe he was just a little rusty. "I plead the Fifth."

"Did you get any of the mess cleaned up?"

"Not really. By the time the insurance adjuster left, it was past noon. I still hadn't finished the work on the roof. As far as lifting and bending, Estelle's pretty much out of the picture. Sophie would've been willing to help out—which in itself is a miracle—but without guidance, I'm afraid she wouldn't have made much progress."

"I could probably give you a few hours tomorrow. It's my day off. I bet Jessie'd be willing to come along and help, too."

"Jessie?"

"My stepdaughter." He nodded in the direction of the swimming pool. "Over there, in the blue bathing suit. She's one of your part-time employees."

"Is she? Eventually I'll get to know everyone. And she's your stepdaughter? But I thought—" She paused awkwardly, not sure how to word the question, then decided to hell with it. She had a right to know the truth before she so much as sniffed another rose with this man. "Jo told me you're not married."

"Oh? And can I assume that information was shared during the same conversation in which you told her you thought I was grim?"

She felt a flush climb her face. "Damn the woman."

"Welcome to Serenity. One of the first lessons you'll learn is not to tell Jo Crowley anything you don't want to see on the front page of the *River City Gazette*. She's right. I'm not married. Chelsea and I were divorced a long time ago." Casually, pretending interest in something on the distant horizon, he continued, "She died last year. Jessie's spending the summer with me."

Maybe that accounted for some of the darkness inside him. If he was still this close to his stepdaughter, maybe he and his ex-wife hadn't yet put closure to their relationship. It would explain a lot. "If you and Jessie really would be willing to help out tomorrow," she said, "it would mean the world to me. I really need to get the place back up and running. You wouldn't believe how many customers I had to turn away today."

"We'd love to. What time do you want us to show up?"

She couldn't be sure, but she thought she saw relief on his face, relief because she hadn't pushed it. "Ten o'clock?" she said. "I'll spring for lunch. We can order a pizza or something."

Three hours later, Davy was sitting in semidarkness in his tiny kitchen, eating a bowl of chocolate ice cream, when Jessie came in, her hair still damp from the swimming pool, her wet bathing suit, wrapped in a plastic bag, tucked under one arm. "Ice cream," she said. "Excellent! Is there more where that came from?"

"Sure is. Want to join me?"

"You even have to ask? Let me hang up my bathing suit first."

She was back in a flash, bringing noise and movement to his kitchen, rattling bowls, clattering silverware, opening and closing the refrigerator door. While Davy watched, she spooned out an enormous serving of chocolate ice cream and topped it off with a river of Hershey's syrup. She sat down across from him, dug into her ice cream, and closed her eyes in sheer bliss. "I love this stuff," she said through a mouthful.

"Me, too."

She crinkled her nose in an elfin smile and took another spoonful of chocolate on chocolate. He'd missed this kind of easy father-daughter intimacy, had missed so much of her growing up. The years he'd spent in D.C., he'd hardly seen her. He and Chelsea had spent so much time apart. After the divorce, even when they were together, Chels had kept him at arm's length from her daughter when all he'd wanted was to be Jessie's father. He'd never understood her reasoning, had never understood her refusal to name the man who'd sired her daughter.

It was supposed to be me, he silently told Chelsea. *I was the one who changed her diapers and warmed her bottles. I was the one who took care of her when you were too hung over to get out of bed. I was the only father she ever knew, and you cheated me out of it, Chels. You cheated us both out of it, and I'm not sure I can ever forgive you for that.*

"Do you remember when we lived together?" he asked Jessie. "When your mom and I were still married?"

She paused, spoon in hand, and gave his question some thought. "Not a lot," she admitted. "Little bits and pieces. I remember that old dog we had."

"Cody."

"Right. Cody. He was my best friend. And I remember Disney World. You and I went on all the rides together."

"You were four years old," he said, "and fearless. I was in

absolute awe of you." And he'd loved her in a way he'd never known he could love anyone. Utterly, selflessly, unconditionally.

Three months after that family trip to Florida, he'd come home one night to find the house empty. While he was at work, Chelsea had packed everything she and Jessie owned, leaving him nothing but a Dear John letter and a heart that had been ripped out of his chest. When the divorce papers arrived a few weeks later, he didn't even bother to contest. He'd already lost everything that mattered. He just signed on the dotted line and moved on with his life.

It was two years before Chelsea called him out of the blue one day, two years before he climbed back on the merry-go-round. Two years before he saw Jessie again.

"When I was a kid," she said, "when Mom was drinking a lot and times were rough, sometimes I'd get so scared. I used to pretend you were my dad."

Me too, he thought. *Me, too.* "I was your dad," he said, his voice husky. "In every way that mattered."

"I used to pretend you'd come and find us. That you'd rescue me. Sometimes things just got so bad. Don't get me wrong, Mom was great. Really great. The best. But when the booze got the upper hand, things always fell apart."

"I'm so sorry," he said. "I would've rescued you if I could. Your mom just wouldn't—" He stopped, held out both hands, palms up, in a gesture of helplessness.

"I know." Aimlessly, she stirred ice cream and chocolate syrup with her spoon. "When I was eight or nine years old, I used to bug her all the time about my father. I kept begging her to tell me his name. That was all I wanted, just a name. But she wouldn't do it, wouldn't even talk about it. It wasn't until I got older that I understood."

"Understood what?"

She turned wide, solemn gray eyes on him. "I don't

think she knew. I don't think she had any idea who my father was."

His heart splintered. "Christ, Jessie," he said.

"It's okay now." Sounding older than her sixteen years, she said, "It doesn't matter so much anymore. I'll probably never know. Mom's gone now, so she can't even give me the names of the likely candidates."

"Ah, fuck." If Chelsea hadn't already been dead, he would have strangled her, right here, right now, for what she'd done to this beautiful child who should have been his.

"It's okay, Davy. Really. It's just that—" she set down her spoon and rested her chin in her hands "—I wish it could be you."

"So do I, sweetheart," he said brokenly. "So do I."

Bobby Sarnacki had dogs. Big ones, with sharp teeth.

If there was one thing Louis Farley hated, it was dogs. Like Indiana Jones and his snakes, Louis had an irrational fear of all things canine. When he was twelve years old, he'd been attacked by his neighbor's shepherd/collie mix, a big, hairy, ferocious brute that had nearly torn his arm off before the neighbor had subdued his evil monster. Louis still bore the scars, both physical and emotional. He'd received twenty stitches, and ever since that day, any dog bigger than ten pounds made him quiver in his boots. Sarnacki's guard dogs were a difficulty Louis hadn't prepared for. Generally, he loved a challenge. It was always so satisfying to beat the odds. But the pleasure he expected to receive from outsmarting Sarnacki was diluted by the knowledge that somewhere inside that ultramodern home, past the creeping phlox and the box hedge and the flowering crab trees, awaited The Enemy in the form of twin Dobermans trained to attack any and all uninvited visitors. After a great deal of thinking, Louis came to the conclusion that there was only one solution to his dilemma: He had to find a way to enter Sarnacki's home by invitation.

After more thoughtful deliberation, he decided on the most suitable approach, and then he went shopping. He was able to buy most of what he needed right at the Wal-Mart just down the street from his motel. A call to a local P.I. he found in the Yellow Pages netted him the name of an electronics supplier who gave him a good deal on a few inexpensive pieces of surveillance equipment. The rest he found at Home Depot. Thank God for chain stores. They made his life so much easier. He rented a white panel van and stuck his peel-off Verizon logos, carefully crafted by an associate in Cincinnati, on both front doors. The workman's uniform was generic, but he doubted anybody would question it. People looked right through workmen. He should know; he'd used the disguise often enough in the past. Put on a blue work shirt and a tool belt, and you became invisible.

Before he left his motel room, he checked himself in the mirror. The crisp blue Dickies shirt and pants, the tool belt with its screwdrivers and wire cutters and serious-looking electronic gadgets, were perfect. And the Detroit Pistons hat that he'd picked up at a Goodwill store was a nice touch. It branded him as a local. Just your basic blue-collar guy, drinking beer with his buddies after work, watching the Pistons on the TV over the bar. When the job was done, he'd keep the hat as a souvenir, add it to his extensive collection, along with the Florida Marlins jersey he'd bought at the airport in Miami. Everybody had a hobby. His was collecting sports memorabilia from the places he visited in his travels.

The dogs were out this morning, roaming a fenced-in section of side yard. Through the greenery that intertwined with the chain-link fence that kept them in, he caught a glimpse of them, all playful and innocent-looking, cavorting with a red Frisbee. Louis parked the van on the street a couple of houses away, got out and opened the rear doors, and began rummaging through the crap he'd loaded in the back. Whistling cheerfully, he kept an eye on the Sarnacki house, waiting for his chance. All he needed was five minutes, ten at most. Talk his way in, pretend to check out all the phone lines, install his listening devices, and leave. Easy in, easy out.

Except for those goddamn dogs.

While he waited, he took inventory of the property, surveying it with the eyes of a seasoned investigator. He'd driven by the place several times, but this was the first time he'd stopped, the first time he'd been able to get more than a brief glimpse as he passed. A man's home was his castle, or so pundits said, and Sarnacki's home was no exception. The house was large, even for this neighborhood, a modern architectural wonder of bricks and glass and jarring angles, surrounded by shade trees old enough to tell him that another house, some old and venerable antique, had once sat on the property where the Sarnacki residence had been built.

Adjacent to the house was a three-car garage, with a basketball hoop over one of the bays. The hoop, together with the gleaming red mountain bike parked inside the open bay, told him there was probably at least one teenager in the household. That could be a good or a bad thing, depending on circumstances. He'd never met a kid yet that he couldn't talk his way past. Louis was a good judge of character and a quick study. Ten seconds and he could size a person up, ferret out his most vulnerable point, and tailor his spiel accordingly. Still, kids were unpredictable, much more so than adults, so he'd have to be extra careful.

Parked near the garage, off to one side, was a hideous bile-green Ford Pinto. How many decades had it been since he'd seen one of those incinerators on wheels? Considering all those exploding gas tanks, he'd have thought by now they'd all be in Pinto Heaven. But there it sat, mute testimony to the bad judgment and worse taste of Ford Motor Company's designers. There was no way it belonged to Sarnacki, and he doubted it belonged to the kid, either. Not in this neighborhood. More likely the maid. Nobody else who lived in a house like this would be caught dead driving one of those things.

Louis closed the doors to the van and got back in the driver's seat. Pretending to read the owner's manual he'd found in the glove box, he kept an eye on the side-view mirror. While he watched, a heavyset woman in her fifties, dressed in jungle-print capris and a mustard-yellow knit top—Gulden's, not French's—came out of the house. Purse swinging, she walked to the garage, climbed into a silver Cadillac, and backed it out into the circular drive. Louis watched as she adjusted her mirrors, then slowly pulled to the end of the drive. She looked both ways and eased the Caddy out onto the street, passing the white van without so much as a sideways glance. Probably on her way to Marshall Field's to practice the great American pastime of consumerism. Judging by the looks of her, she probably had more than a passing acquaintance with the local Krispy Kreme franchise as well. Louis smiled, his theory confirmed. There had to be a kid. The mountain bike certainly didn't belong to the svelte Mrs. Sarnacki.

Ten minutes later, the man of the house himself came out the front door, walked to the gate that enclosed the side yard, opened it and whistled to his two slavering beasts. The dogs came running, leaping and bounding around their master. Sarnacki closed the gate back up, rubbed each of their heads in turn, and led the fearsome creatures indoors. He came back out a moment later, carrying a golf bag which he proceeded to toss into the back of a massive black four-wheel-drive SUV. Sarnacki backed the monstrosity out of the garage, shot to the end of the driveway, took a quick look right and then left, and barreled down the street in the opposite direction from where Louis was parked.

After a reasonable amount of time had passed, Louis pulled a packet of Juicy Fruit from his pocket, peeled open a couple of sticks, and popped them into his mouth. When they were chewed sufficiently so that he could open and close his mouth without difficulty, he got out of the van, clipboard in hand and tools dangling at his hip. Adjusting the Pistons cap, he strolled nonchalantly up the driveway of the nearest house, climbed the front steps, and rang the bell.

The woman who answered the door was in her midthirties and slender, with short, choppy blond hair and sharp features. She wore pink capris and a white tank top, the kind with the tiny little straps that hardly amounted to anything. Louis wondered what it was with the capris. Were they some kind of neighborhood uniform or something? At least she looked better in them than the Sarnacki woman had.

Sounding bored, she said, "Can I help you?"

Louis shifted the gum from one cheek to the other. "Yeah," he said, looking down at the fake work order attached to his clipboard. "I'm from Verizon. We got a complaint that your phone's out of order."

Looking puzzled, she said, "There's nothing wrong with my phone."

"It says right here, 22923 Mayflower Drive—"

"That's my address," she said, "but we haven't called the phone company."

"Sarnacki, right? 22923 Mayflower Drive."

"Oh," she said. "You're at the wrong house. You want 22927 Mayflower Drive. Two houses down."

"I don't get it," he said, lifting the bill of his cap and scratching his head. "It says right here, Robert Sarnacki, 22923 Mayflower Drive, phone not working. You're telling me you ain't Mrs. Sarnacki?" He looked her directly in the eye, snapped his gum, and waited.

Coolly, she said, "I've already told you, this isn't the Sarnacki residence. You have the wrong house." She started to close the door, but he stuck his foot in it.

"You sure?" he said. "Because I'm new at this, and I don't want to catch hell from my boss. You're absolutely certain that this is 22923 Mayflower, but nobody named Sarnacki lives here? Phone number 555-3281?"

"For the last time," she said, "you have the wrong house. This is the Miller residence. The Sarnackis live two houses down the street."

Louis managed to remove his foot an instant before she slammed the door shut in his face. Muttering loudly and irritably about the stupid broad in dispatch who couldn't even get the address right, he walked back down the driveway to the street. He opened and closed the back doors of the van again, just for show, then took his clipboard and sauntered off in the direction of the Sarnacki residence.

The door was answered by a red-haired beanpole of a kid wearing size-thirteen sneakers and an Ozzy Osbourne T-shirt. Three feet behind him, the twin Dobermans sat silently, their bright, watchful eyes trained directly on Louis. Probably wondering if he'd taste good with ketchup. "Yeah?" the kid said.

"I'm from the phone company. Mrs. Miller up the street's having a problem with her phone. Lots of static, calls not going through, that kind of thing. I've traced it to the pole outside your house, but I need to check all your phone lines, verify that it hasn't affected you, too, before I go up and replace the transmitter."

The kid just looked at him. "Hunh?" he said.

"You got DSL?" Louis said.

"Yeah. Why?"

"This issue we're having could screw it up pretty bad. You probably better let me check it out and be sure you're okay. If it goes bad, you could be without online service until Monday or Tuesday."

As if a light switch had been flipped, something sparked to life in the kid's eyes. "Yeah, dude," he said. "Come on in."

Louis glanced at the twin beasts who sat behind the kid, saliva dripping from their jaws, and felt his palms begin to sweat. "Can you do me one favor first?" he asked the kid.

"Sure. What's that?"

"Can you lock up those dogs somewhere?"

"Apollo and Troy? You scared of them? Dude, they wouldn't hurt a freaking flea."

"Humor me. I don't have a lot of time to waste. I got service calls up the ying-yang."

"Geez. Come on, boys." The kid opened a door off the hallway, shooed the Dobies through it, and closed it behind them.

Louis's stress level went down about twenty notches. "Thanks, kid," he said. "How many phone lines do you have in this place? Not including computers."

"Three. You gotta check 'em all?"

"Yep. Your mom or dad home?"

"Nah. Just me and Rosa." The kid led him into an opulent, state-of-the-art kitchen. Granite countertops, Sub-Zero fridge, glass-topped electric range, copper-bottomed pots hanging from a rack over a center work island. "Kitchen phone's on that wall over there," the kid said, pointing.

Louis moved toward it, picked up the receiver, and listened to the dial tone. From his tool belt, he took the little handheld voltage meter he'd picked up on eBay. Waving it around near the receiver, he snapped his gum and said casually, "Who's Rosa?"

"The maid. She's in the den, watching a Tony Robbins infomercial. She thinks that guy is, like, God or something."

"Hunh." Still waving the meter, Louis palmed the tiny transmitter he'd hidden up his sleeve and attached it in a spot where it would never be noticed. "This one looks good," he said. "See?" He pointed to the voltage meter, whose needle wasn't so much as quivering. "She's not showing anything."

The kid peered at the circular gauge with its still-as-death needle. "So what does this thing measure?" he said.

"Your telephone emits tiny radio waves," Louis said. "If something goes screwy with it, this little baby will pick it up in a heartbeat." He returned the phone receiver to its cradle. "Where's the next one?"

Six minutes later, he was back in his van, all three of Sarnacki's phones successfully bugged. In and out so quickly, so smoothly, that Rosa the maid, preoccupied by the mesmerizing Tony Robbins, never even noticed he was there. He'd succeeded in his mission. Better yet, he'd gotten out alive. The Dobies would have to look elsewhere for their midmorning snack. Louis was sure his blood pressure would be back to normal within an hour. Two at the most. Now all he had to do was find a parking spot nearby, sit there with his listening equipment, and wait.

He just loved it when a plan came together.

Nine

They assembled in the video store around ten, a motley group dressed in jeans and T-shirts, ready to tackle the wreckage and wrestle it into submission. Estelle showed up armed with a pen and clipboard for keeping track of what got tossed and what could be salvaged, and a bag of Tootsie Roll Pops to satisfy her sweet tooth. Perched on the neon-pink striped checkout counter, she waved the bag of pops in Annie's direction. "My addiction," she explained. "Ever since I got pregnant, I've been craving these things."

Davy Hunter arrived carrying a travel mug of coffee in one hand and a can of white paint in the other. Accompanied by his stepdaughter, he'd thought to bring trash bags, something Annie hadn't remembered. Although Jessie and Soph had met the night before at the Crowley house, now that they were expected to spend the day together at close range, the two girls eyed each other with all the distrust normally seen in a pair of tomcats circling a female in heat.

Annie set them to work sorting through the movies that littered the floor. "The salvageable ones you can put on the shelves," she told Sophie. "At this point, don't worry about organizing them. We can work on that later. The primary objective is to find the floor underneath the mess. Jessie, you can bring the destroyed videos to Estelle to put on her list, then start filling up trash bags."

Picking their way carefully through the rubble, both girls got to work. In the closet under the stairs, Annie found a broom and dustpan and an old upright stick vacuum. She took them out even though it was a little premature to be thinking about such things. They had to find the floor before they could sweep it. While Hunter returned to his car for paintbrushes and cleaning solvent, Annie waded into the mess.

The VCR that had provided Estelle with companionship on lonely workday afternoons was a total loss. It looked as though somebody had picked it up and heaved it with all their might at the wall. Stepping carefully, Annie carried its mortal remains over to Estelle, added it to her list of destroyed items, and placed it in a trash bag. The computer monitor suffered a similar fate. The vandals had put something—a baseball bat, a hammer, possibly somebody's work boot—right through the screen. By some minor miracle, they'd managed to miss the 19-inch Sony television that sat on a shelf behind the counter. When Estelle turned it on, it sprang to immediate, full-colored life.

The cash register hadn't been as fortunate. Annie's nocturnal visitors had tossed it on the floor with such force that it had gouged the hell out of the hardwood flooring. But the register was one of those old-fashioned, indestructible dinosaurs. It was dinged up a little, but as far as she could tell, it was still in working order. As bad as this was, she realized it could have been worse.

Once they'd cleared some space on the floor, she and Hunter heaved and tugged at the toppled wooden shelving unit, wrestling it back upright into a spot that was a fair approximation of its original location. It was scratched and dented, but usable. "I'll slap a coat of paint on it," Hunter said, "and you'll hardly know anything happened to it. These things are rugged. I built 'em that way on purpose."

Annie scraped back a fistful of hair from her face. Surprised, she said, "You built these?"

"Yep."

She waited for him to elaborate, but he didn't. "You're a carpenter?" she said.

"I build furniture, cabinets, that kind of thing. So, yeah, I guess some people might call me a carpenter."

"Don't let the humble act fool you," Estelle said around the lollipop in her mouth. "He's a damn good carpenter. He built my mom's kitchen cabinets. You don't have to worry about shoddy workmanship with this guy. Those cabinets will outlive us all."

"I'm impressed," Annie said. "You're a multifaceted man, Hunter."

"Well, golly gee. Keep up the compliments and you'll make me blush."

By twelve-thirty, they'd made a respectable dent in the disorder, and they broke for pizza and soft drinks. The girls dove in, ravenous, claiming half a pizza and carrying it outside, where they sat on the curb beneath the vacancy sign to eat. "Watch out for broken glass," Annie warned them. "We don't want to be carting you to the hospital to get stitches in your backside."

Sophie rolled her eyes, but Jessie giggled through a mouthful of pizza as though Annie'd said something incredibly funny. Nice to know that not everyone between the ages of ten and twenty found her inconceivably lame.

Estelle parked herself on the stool behind the counter so she could watch TV while she ate. Annie and Hunter took the last available seats, side by side on the front steps. "I think we've made progress," she said to him as she pulled a slice of pizza from the box he held on his lap.

"We'll get the worst of it cleaned up today." He helped

himself to a slice. "How soon will you get that check so you can start replacing things?"

"I think it should come pretty quickly. The adjuster saw the damage with his own eyes, so it's not as though they're questioning the validity of the claim." While she ate, she watched the two girls, who'd been so wary of each other just hours ago. Now they sat shoulder to shoulder, talking animatedly. "Look at those two," she said. "It didn't take them long to start bonding. How old is Jessie?"

Hunter swallowed before answering. "Sixteen going on thirty-five. In a good way. She's probably the most responsible teenager I've ever met." He picked up his bottle of Pepsi and took a sip. "I don't suppose she had a choice about that." His blue eyes, watching the girls, grew thoughtful, distant, and Annie wondered what his cryptic words meant. Wondered where he'd suddenly disappeared to.

A loaded pulp truck, headed for the paper mill in Rumford, roared past. Through the open doorway behind her, the television emitted the low murmur of conversation. "Did you talk to Jeffrey Traynor?" she said.

Hunter returned from wherever he'd been. "Yeah," he said, taking another slice of pizza. "But I didn't get anywhere."

"Thoughts, comments, impressions?"

"He's your typical small-town yahoo. Likes to drink too much and isn't averse to roughing up a woman if he's not happy with her, although he'll deny it if you press him. But I'd be surprised if he had anything to do with your break-in."

"Damn. Any other suspects?"

"None that spring to mind immediately. This kind of vandalism's usually teenagers. Except…"

"Except what?"

"I don't know. Something about it feels deliberate."

She raised an eyebrow. "It would be hard for something like this to be accidental."

He almost smiled. Almost, but not quite. "Bad word choice. What I meant was that it doesn't feel random."

"You mean it was aimed specifically at me."

"Or at somebody connected with the Twilight."

"Somebody female." When he looked at her, she said, "The word they painted on the wall. BITCH. It's not too likely they were aiming it at Kenny Moreau. Not unless he has a secret he's keeping from us."

There it was again, that almost-smile. "Which leaves you and Sophie, Estelle, and—" His gaze landed on Jessie. The near-smile disappeared, and deep furrows bracketed his mouth.

Following his gaze, she said, "Have you talked to Jessie? Questioned her?"

"Yeah. I didn't get any further with her than I did with any of you."

Three or four cars passed on the highway, all of them exceeding the 45 mph speed limit. "What about the fingerprints?" she said. "Any luck there?"

"Pete checked the samples you gave us and pulled out any matches from what we'd gathered. He sent the rest off to the state police to be run through the computer."

"The state police? Why involve them?"

"We're not involving them." He lifted the lid to the pizza box and took out the last slice. "You want half?" When she shook her head, he said, "Serenity's a small town with a small municipal budget. We can't afford the technology that no twenty-first-century police department should have to do without. The Maine State Police have access to a regional database. We have an agreement with them. If anything pops, they'll let us know."

"Is that typical? Small towns not having access to fingerprint databases?"

"Given budget restraints, unfortunately, yeah. There are a

lot of small towns in the same boat we're in. No modern technology, no money to train their officers to use it even if they had it. They have to turn to the Staties for help. Which means it could take a while."

"How long a while?"

"A few days at best. Could be longer."

"Shit."

"You have to understand how busy they are. Their priorities probably aren't the same as yours. This wasn't exactly the crime of the century."

"It is to me." She'd already invested so much in this place, in reinventing herself, in the concept of breathing new life into the Twilight. This act of vandalism had been a hard slap in the face, one she could have done without.

"Annie." He spoke her name softly, like a caress. It was the first time he'd called her by her first name, and the word hovered in the air between them, charging the atmosphere around them with a sudden, intense sexual awareness. Her insides tightened and tensed like catgut on a fiddle, and the tiny hairs on her forearms stood at attention. In that unforeseen instant of attraction, she became aware of the most minute of details. A tiny cut on his jaw where he'd nicked it while shaving. The scent of soap that clung to him, in spite of the fact that he'd been working for hours in the summer heat. A narrow scar at the corner of his lip. She hadn't felt this kind of pull towards a man since Mac. There were a million reasons why she shouldn't be feeling it now. At the top of the list, running neck and neck, were the two major truths that dangled like twin swords over her head: she wasn't who he thought she was, and somewhere out there was a madman who was determined to track her down and kill her. Those were pretty big reasons not to get involved with the man. A host of other, less urgent reasons followed, although at this precise moment she couldn't seem to remember what any of them were.

"We're done," Sophie announced from three feet away, dropping Annie abruptly back to earth. "What do you want us to work on now?"

The moment, fraught with possibility, vanished. But she could see it lingering in his eyes. The attraction wasn't one-sided. Davy Hunter felt it, too, and wasn't any too sure how he felt about the situation. *Multiply that times two,* she thought, and cleared her throat. "Why don't you girls start sweeping up?" she said. "Once that's done, we can start painting."

Parked a couple of blocks from the Sarnacki residence, Louis wasted an entire afternoon sitting in the white van, reading the latest issue of *Cosmo,* eating M&M's, and listening through a plastic earpiece to a dozen meaningless and inane telephone conversations. Occasionally during his career as a private investigator, he'd been approached at cocktail parties or backyard barbecues by civilians who, when they discovered what he did for a living, somehow found the idea of being privy to people's deepest, darkest secrets titillating. What they didn't know was a lot. You spent most of your time sitting on your ass until it turned numb. You drank endless cups of coffee until you had to pee like a racehorse—and in a neighborhood like this one, public bathrooms weren't exactly on every corner—usually without finding out anything worthwhile. The simple truth was that people just weren't that interesting. Their secrets weren't that interesting, and their telephone conversations were a real snooze fest.

Take, for example, the lady of the house, who'd spent a half-hour this afternoon relating to someone named Madge her adventures in the lingerie department at Lord & Taylor. The Sarnacki woman was built like a Sherman tank, and Louis tried not to picture her in the frothy and painfully revealing black lace teddy she gushed about buying. But it was like rubbernecking at a particularly horrific accident. The mental picture it created was so compellingly agonizing that he couldn't bring himself to look away from it.

He found out that the teenager, whose name was Josh, had his own little side business selling illegal goodie bags to the neighborhood kids. Like his dad, young Josh Sarnacki was quite the entrepreneur. At the rate he was going, he'd be a candidate for membership in the local Jaycees any day now. When Josh wasn't drumming up business, he was fending off calls from lovestruck teenage girls with lousy taste in men who kept calling him up so they could pretend they didn't like him. Ah, the mysterious workings of the adolescent mind!

And then there was Rosa, the maid, whose life rivaled a Mexican soap opera. Her husband was in jail for holding up a 7-Eleven. Her son had just been fired from his job at Burger King, and he was scrambling to find another job before his probation officer found out and sent him back to the slammer alongside his old man. Her sister was involved in a nasty custody battle with her soon-to-be-ex-husband for custody of their two *niñas*. Rosa spent nearly two hours on the phone with various friends and relatives, talking in rapid-fire Spanish and with dramatic flair, hoping to drum up some support in the form of good old U.S. greenbacks. The people she worked for were rich, greedy, tightwad pigs. They paid her slave wages, treated her like an idiot, and had repeatedly refused to give her a raise, in spite of the fact that she cleaned up after those disgusting dogs every day, put up with Josh's godless music, and scrubbed all three of their toilets at least twice a week.

Fortunately for Rosa, her employers didn't speak a word of Spanish.

Unfortunately for Louis, he did.

It seemed that everybody in the household had some kind of little drama going on, something they desperately needed to share with a phone buddy or two. Everyone, that was, except the one person he was hoping for. After five hours of sitting in the same spot, Louis was getting nowhere fast. Bobby Sarnacki had made a single routine business call that lasted approximately ninety-three seconds. Louis had read *Cosmo* from cover to cover twice, and he could no longer feel his own ass. It was time to pull the plug. Take a break. Come back later, and better luck next time.

He tossed *Cosmo* on the passenger seat, shut down his surveillance equipment, started the van and pulled away from the curb. He'd driven five or six blocks when his attention was caught by the blue Chevy sedan a couple of car lengths back. Nondescript and anonymous, something that might have been driven by a card-carrying member of the AARP, it blended right into city traffic, just like the cars he usually drove when he was on a job. It had been following him ever since he left the Sarnacki house, but he hadn't paid it much attention until suddenly his built-in radar went off.

Hunh. Interesting. Just as an experiment, he turned left at the next light. Behind him, the Chevy did the same. Coincidence? Yeah, right. He'd been in this business too long to believe in coincidence. Louis adjusted his sunglasses and tightened his hands on the wheel. Still just playing with the guy, he took a sharp right and watched his mirror. Sure enough, the Chevy followed suit.

Okay, then. Something very strange was going on here. Was it possible that Brogan had put a tail on him? For what purpose? Why would his own client have him followed? It didn't make sense. Unless it wasn't his client. Unless Brogan wasn't the only one who wanted to find Robin Spinney. Unless Spinney had something, or knew something, that would be of interest to more than one person.

He'd left Sarnacki's high-end residential neighborhood behind and was now traveling a commercial street lined with small shops. Payless Shoes. Dunkin' Donuts. A pet shop. In front of a styling salon called Hair There and Everywhere, he pulled into an empty parking space. The Chevy drove past him without so much as a moment's hesitation, the driver obeying the speed limit and seemingly unaware of his presence. But Louis Farley wasn't stupid. His instincts had never failed him, and right now, they were telling him that whoever was driving that blue Chevy was following him for a reason.

His mental wheels began spinning rapidly as he contemplated this unexpected turn of events. If not Brogan, who would have put a tail on him? What made finding Robin Spinney so important to not one, but two individuals? And just how long could Louis play cat and mouse with this guy before he figured out that Louis was on to him?

"Well, well, well," he said aloud. "This is getting interesting."

He wanted a drink.

Davy Hunter lay in the old hammock, his arms folded beneath his head, swaying gently as he gazed at the Milky Way spilling in a spectacular spread of stars across the sky. The night was warm, made tolerable by the light breeze that stirred the hair at his temple. He wanted a drink so bad he burned with it. This was the worst craving he'd felt since he quit drinking, worse even than the burning need he'd felt as he knelt by Chelsea's grave and faced the hard truth that when she died, he'd buried himself right alongside her.

He wasn't ready yet to be dragged, kicking and screaming, back to the land of the living. Living was too painful. What had happened this afternoon with Annie Kendall was meaningless. It had been nothing more than his subconscious responding to the power of suggestion. Jo had put the idea into his head, goddamn her, and now he couldn't seem to get it out. The dark monster had been unleashed, and he wasn't strong enough to corral it and lock it back up.

Inside the trailer, Jonny Lang was singing in that husky, rode-hard-and-put-away-wet voice. "Breakin' Me." Yeah, that was it. Like Kid Lang, he was broken, defective, irreparably damaged. Unfit for any woman, especially for one as classy as Annie Kendall. But that didn't stop him from thinking about her. Didn't stop him from wanting her.

She felt it, too. He could tell by the way she'd treated him after their little lunchtime incident. All afternoon she'd been cool and distant, stiff and businesslike. Sex had reared its ugly head, and Annie Kendall hadn't decided yet how she intended to deal with it. So she'd chosen to pretend it didn't exist, that hot and violent emotion that had sprung to life between them as they sat side by side on the front steps of her vandalized video store. Not that he blamed her. What she'd said about him to Jo was right on the money. He was grim. Grim and dark and brooding, a miserable excuse for a human being. Only a woman who was a masochist would willingly get mixed up with someone like him.

Above his head, a shooting star plummeted across the sky and burned out in a brilliant flash of light. Inside the trailer, Jonny Lang continued to wail. Davy took his cell phone from its clip at his hip, punched in a series of numbers he hadn't realized he'd memorized, and put the phone to his ear.

She answered on the second ring, sounding tentative. Wary. Well, hell, she should be wary. She should run as fast as she could in the opposite direction. He'd only fuck up her life. She didn't deserve to have her life fucked up by the likes of him.

"Hi," he said.

He heard her let out a hard breath. Of relief? Disgust? Exasperation? He couldn't tell. "Hi," she said.

"Are you still up?"

"It's past eleven, Hunter, in case you hadn't noticed."

Still gazing at the stars, he adjusted the phone so he

could hear her more clearly. "I know what time it is. Are you still up?"

"I am now."

"Got coffee?"

"Coffee?" she echoed blankly, as though she wasn't quite following his train of thought. "You want coffee at—"

"Eleven o'clock at night."

At her end of the line, there was a long silence. He breathed in. Breathed out. She still wasn't sure how she felt about him. Still wasn't sure what she wanted. *News flash:* Neither was he. "I have coffee," she said at last. "Or I could have it."

Some of the tension eased in his chest. She could have told him to take a flying fuck, but she hadn't. "Is that an invitation?"

"It seems to me," she said, "that you just issued your own invitation."

In the darkness, he smiled, a rare thing for him these days. Annie Kendall was the kind of woman who could hold her own. He liked that.

"My name is Davy," he said, "and I'm an alcoholic." He hadn't admitted those words to another living soul. Not until now. "I've been sober for twenty-three days, and I could really use a cup of coffee. And somebody to talk to."

Not just somebody, he thought. He needed to talk to her.

At her end, there was another brief, reflective silence before she made her decision. "I'll put the coffee on," she said.

When she heard his car out front, she was standing on a stepladder, paint roller in hand, attempting to cover the graffiti by painting the walls a soft shade of blue. It wasn't working very well, but then this was only the first coat, and it was still wet. Maybe subsequent coats would make a difference. If they didn't, she'd just cover it all with cheap paneling. It would be ugly, but then so was what she had now, fifties-chic knotty pine criss-crossed with neon-pink spray paint. This afternoon, Hunter had painted the shelves and the checkout counter. Those could stand a second coat, too. The white paint had camouflaged the worst of the damage, but in a few spots, the neon pink was starting to bleed through.

At his knock, she got down off the ladder to let him in. There wasn't a doubt in her mind that this was a blunder of monumental proportions. The man had a dark side that he didn't hide very well, and a plethora of secrets he seemed determined to keep hidden. She should have told him to look elsewhere, should have told him she wasn't interested in anything he had to offer. But on the phone, he'd sounded so, well—needy, for lack of a better word. Looking at him now, six feet of bone and muscle and sinew, that word sounded ridiculous. He didn't look needy, he looked dangerous. Dangerous and hungry and troubled, those blue eyes boring into her as if he could see clear through to her insides. Somehow, in spite of the barriers she'd erected in order to stay alive, he'd managed to get to her. Somehow, when she wasn't paying attention, he'd managed to burrow under her skin, starting an itch she didn't dare to scratch. But she wanted to. God help her, she wanted to shimmy up that long, lean body, wrap herself around him, and hold on tight for what was sure to be a tumultuous ride. If not for the thin veneer of civilization that tempered her baser instincts—and her sleeping fifteen-year-old daughter upstairs—she might have jumped him right here and now.

Instead, she held open the door, every nerve ending in her body going haywire as he moved past her. Without speaking, he followed his nose to the coffeepot she'd set up next to the cash register. He filled the oversized ceramic mug she'd brought downstairs for him, took a long swig of black coffee, and turned to look at her. "You didn't have the door locked," he pointed out. "You're working here all alone, and it's almost midnight."

She reached into her pocket and pulled out a small canister. "Pepper spray," she said, holding it up so he could see. "I'm fully capable of taking care of myself."

Instead of answering, he crossed the room to where her ladder stood. Sipping coffee, he studied her paint job. "Nice color," he said.

"Thank you."

"It'll need another coat. Maybe two." He took another sip of coffee. Still studying her paint job, he said, "The thing is, I want to touch you. I want to touch you so fucking bad I'm aching with it. But I'm not particularly happy about it. I haven't so much as looked at another woman since—" He stopped abruptly, raised his coffee mug, and emptied it as though it were a shot of whiskey.

Annie hadn't expected him to be so blunt. She realized now that she should have. Davy Hunter was a straight arrow, the kind of man who didn't believe in bullshit. With him, she would never wonder where she stood. And he'd expect her to be just as straight with him.

He finally turned to look at her. "If anything ever did happen between us—and I'm not saying it will, I'm just saying if it ever did—it wouldn't mean anything. It couldn't. And I don't think that's fair to you." His gaze ran over her face, studying. Contemplating. "A woman like you," he said, "you could do a hell of a lot better than someone like me. I'd just drag you down. You're not the kind to roll around in the mud. You understand what I'm saying?"

"Hunter," she said, "why did you come here tonight?"

"It was either this or Walt's Tavern. Considering the circumstances, you seemed the more prudent choice."

"Congratulations." She glanced at the clock. It was two minutes past midnight. "Looks like you just made it to twenty-four days of sobriety."

"Yeah," he said, looking a little startled. "It looks that way, doesn't it?"

"Just for the record," she said, "I'm not in a position right now to start anything with you, either. Or, for that matter, with any other man. There are things about me that you don't know." She licked her lips and shoved her hands into her pockets so he wouldn't see that they were trembling. "I'm not exactly free. That's all I can tell you." Irritated for some reason she couldn't explain, she said, "I don't know why the hell I'm attracted to you anyway. You're not that good-looking, you'll never win any personality contests—I've seen you smile maybe once since I met you—and you just admitted to me that you're an alcoholic. That's 0 for 3 in my book. Still—"

"A sober alcoholic," he corrected. "Twenty-four days sober. And thanks for that comprehensive list of my character flaws. I think you might've missed one or two, but I'd be glad to—"

"I'm not done talking."

"Oh. Well. Excuse me for interrupting."

"Still," she began again, more forcefully this time, "if the situation wasn't what it is—if I were free and you were willing…I wouldn't be averse to—" She stopped, not sure how to word what she wanted to say without sounding like she was issuing an invitation. Which she wasn't. She definitely wasn't.

"If you're trying to tell me you think I'm hot, you have a damn indirect way of giving a man a compliment."

She actually blushed. She could feel the heat climbing her face. Thirty-six years old, and this man had her blushing like a schoolgirl.

"Damn it, Annie." He took a step toward her, raised a hand as if to brush a lock of hair away from her face, and she stopped breathing. The world tilted crazily as she frantically wondered how the hell he'd managed to move from the opposite side of the room to six inches from her without her even noticing. He stood so close she could smell the coffee on his breath, so close she could feel the heat from his body, shimmering in the air between them. This was insane. She was old enough to know better. They both were. Davy Hunter would bring her nothing but trouble. He was the kind of man who would expect absolute honesty, and her entire life was a lie. She had no excuse to be standing here, the paint roller still in her hand, her heart racing and her knees knocking together as his callused fingertips moved steadily closer to her face.

When his cell phone rang, they both froze.

The emotion that flickered across his face could have been relief, could have been regret. He dropped his hand, and Annie sucked in a breath of oxygen as he reached for the offending object and flicked a button. "Yeah?" he said. He listened, and she saw his expression suddenly grow intent. "Shit," he said. "When? Yeah. Yeah, of course. Where'd they take her?" He drew a hand down over his face as if to wipe away his fatigue. "I'll be right there," he said. "Thanks for letting me know."

"What?" Annie said as he pushed the button to end the call. "What is it?"

Grimly, he said, "My grandmother."

Ten

"This is where you live?" Sophie asked, eyes wide as she gaped at the tiny, ancient trailer, caught in the Jeep's headlights. It was so ugly it reminded her of the abandoned sharecropper cabins that still existed here and there in rural Mississippi.

"For the summer," Jessie said, putting the Jeep into park and shutting off the ignition. "It's Davy's place."

There was something in her voice, Sophie thought, that reminded her of herself and the way she used to talk about her dad. Except that Davy Hunter wasn't Jessie's dad. He was some kind of stepdad, or something like that. But the way Jessie said his name, with an overtone of hero worship, you'd have thought he was her father.

The trailer looked a little better on the inside. It was spotless, and nothing was falling apart. Mr. Hunter obviously took good care of things. The kitchen had brand-new cabinets that looked handmade, and brightly-colored scatter rugs in the living room brought life to boring beige floor tiles. "You can take your things into my room," Jessie said. "Down the hall, first door on the right. I have to call Davy and let him know we're home."

Sophie found the room and flipped the light switch. It didn't look like much. A doorless closet, hung with Jessie's clothes. A three-quarter-size bed, shoved up against the wall and covered with a white chenille spread. A bunch of travel posters on the wall. London. Paris. Berlin. They brought a touch of class to an otherwise tiny and unremarkable room.

She wandered back into the living room. Jessie had the cordless phone up to her ear, and she was rummaging through the kitchen cabinets. "Everything's fine," she said. She rolled her eyes and winked at Sophie. "Yes, I locked the door behind me. Tell Mrs. Kendall that Sophie'll be just fine here with me." She sobered a bit. "How's Gram?"

Not knowing what else to do, Sophie sat down on the couch, next to a big, ugly, sleepy mutt who barely acknowledged her presence. Sophie patted his head. He twitched an ear, but didn't bother to lift his head. Soph wouldn't have admitted it to a soul, but she was secretly glad that her mother had woken her up and insisted that she pack her pajamas and come spend the night with Jessie. Not that she was a chicken, or needed a babysitter. But Mom had no idea how long she'd be at the hospital with Davy Hunter, and the idea of staying alone at the Twilight, at night, especially after the recent break-in, was a little too creepy for Sophie's taste. She might not know Jessie well, but they were only a year apart in age, and they seemed to get along okay. Staying here with her sure beat spending the night alone, listening to every creak of the old motel and waiting for the bogeyman to get her.

"Okay," Jessie said into the phone. "Call if there's any news. No, we won't stay up too late. Bye." She hung up the phone. To Sophie, she said, "That's Buddy you're sitting next to. He's our watchdog."

The dog opened an eye at the sound of his name, then closed it again. Sophie eyed him long and hard. "He doesn't look like much of a watchdog to me," she said.

"That's the beauty of it," Jessie said. "Nobody looking at him would ever believe he's a watchdog. He's like having a secret weapon. We have a cat, too, but he's probably hiding. He and Buddy don't play on the same team. Frosted Flakes or Froot Loops?"

"Hunh?"

Jessie took two boxes of cereal out of the cupboard and held them up, one in each hand. "Frosted Flakes or Froot Loops?"

"Frosted Flakes."

"Good choice."

Jessie put the Froot Loops back into the cupboard and took out bowls, spoons, a half-gallon of milk, and they sat at the kitchen table together and chowed down. Through a mouthful of Frosted Flakes, Sophie said, "So what do kids find to do in this heinous burg?"

Jessie shrugged. "I guess the same things kids do in other places."

"Serenity is the pits. There's absolutely nothing to do here."

"Maybe I can introduce you to some of my friends. They're pretty cool."

Sophie picked up the cereal box and poured more Frosted Flakes into her bowl. "So have you lived in this place all your life?" She tried to hide the contempt she felt, but it was there, in her voice, and she knew Jessie heard it.

But Jessie wasn't fazed. "I was born here," she said, "but my mom and I moved around a lot. New York, Boston, Montana, Florida. You name it, we probably lived there for a while. But we always kept coming back to Serenity. She grew up here, so it was home to her. And Davy was here. Now it's home for me."

"Sounds like you've moved around even more than I have."

"Where else have you lived?"

Because her mother had taught her that the easiest lie was the one that was closest to the truth, Sophie answered honestly. "Las Vegas. Before that it was Detroit. But we didn't stay there very long. Mostly we lived in Mississippi." She stirred her cereal with her spoon. "Why don't you live with your mom?"

"She died last year," Jessie said. "I've been living with her cousin, Faith, and her husband. But they had to go away for the summer, and I decided to stay here with Davy."

"That really bites," Sophie said. "My dad died two years ago. Sometimes—" she'd never admitted this to another soul "—I have a hard time remembering what he looked like. It's so awful."

"Want to see a picture of my mom?"

"Sure."

Jessie got up and walked the length of the trailer, to the master bedroom. She came back carrying a framed five-by-seven photo of a pretty, impish-looking blond woman. Sophie could see a little of Jessie in her, around the eyes. "She's pretty," Sophie said. "How'd she die?"

"She drowned."

Sophie shuddered, thinking of her dad, and how he'd gone off the road and died in his patrol car. She wanted to tell Jessie all about it, tell her about how it hadn't been an accident, but Mom had warned her that she never could tell anybody, so she kept quiet. Instead, she said, "What kind of music do you like to listen to?"

"I really like Celtic music," Jessie said.

Sophie went bug-eyed. "You mean, like that gay Riverdance stuff?"

Jessie laughed. "I like all kinds of traditional Irish and Scottish folk music. You should give it a try. Keep an open mind. You might be surprised."

"For sure. Why on earth do you listen to that stuff?"

"It gets me, right here." Jessie balled up a fist and pressed it to the center of her chest. "A lot of those ballads are just so sad, it chokes you up to listen to them."

"Hunh."

"So what chokes you up? What gets you right there in the heart?"

Sophie opened her mouth to respond, then realized she couldn't. There was nothing that grabbed her that way, nothing she could point to and say, "That speaks to me." It was a terrible revelation. Lamely, she said, "I listen to a lot of Marilyn Manson. Nine Inch Nails. Korn."

"Oh, my ears, my ears!" Jessie grabbed the sides of her head in mock anguish. "They're bleeding!"

"Those bands aren't that bad."

"They're not that good, either. Hey, I have an idea. Let's put this stuff away."

They cleared the table, Jessie wiped it clean, and Sophie rinsed out the bowls and spoons in the sink. She followed Jessie to her room, where the older girl picked up an instrument case that had been standing at the foot of the bed. "What's that?" Sophie said.

"My violin."

"You play the violin?"

"For years and years. Sit down. I want to play something for you."

Sophie watched as she cautiously and lovingly removed the violin from its case. "I used to play soccer," she said.

"That's cool." Jessie picked up the bow, tossed her dark hair back over her shoulder, and held the violin up to her chin. "How come you don't play any more?"

"We've moved around too much in the last year."

"Well, maybe you can play here. Serenity High has a great soccer team." She positioned the bow. "This is called a lament."

"Why do they call it that?"

"Listen, and you'll figure it out."

The music was sweet and somehow tragic, evoking images of past times and lost loves and windswept moors. Goose bumps popped out on Sophie's skin as Jessie played. The music made her feel all funny inside, as though her heart was breaking right along with the heart of whoever had written this poignant music. No wonder they called it a lament.

When the final note sounded, there was a moment of absolute, crystalline silence. Sophie tried to find her voice, but it took a minute to swallow the lump in her throat. "Not bad," she said. "It's no Marilyn Manson, but it's not bad."

Jessie smiled, an enigmatic, Mona Lisa smile, and tucked the violin back into its case. "Let's watch TV," she said. "Davy has a satellite dish. With three hundred channels to choose from, we should be able to find something on."

At this time of night, they were the only people in the hospital waiting room. Davy had spoken briefly with the E.R. doctor, but he hadn't seen Gram. By the time he got to the hospital, she was already in surgery. They'd promised to notify him once she got back to Recovery, but after two hours, he still hadn't heard a thing. He'd thought about calling Dee, decided there was no sense in waking the whole family in the middle of the night. There wasn't a thing Dee could have done if she'd been here. If she even bothered to show up. After their last conversation, he wasn't in the mood to talk to his sister anyway.

He didn't have to be reminded that at Gram's age, the complications of a broken hip could be life-altering. She'd be out of commission for weeks, maybe months. She'd almost certainly be spending time in rehab. He'd heard that elderly people in rehab had a tendency to get depressed. He'd have to visit her regularly to prevent that from happening. And somebody would have to keep an eye on the house, keep the plants watered and the cat fed. He knew who that somebody was. If Gram came home from rehab and found all her plants dead, she'd have his hide.

She'd been doing so well, living on her own. He'd seen it with his own eyes just a day or two ago. The old girl was as spry as a teenager. According to the E.R. doctor, she hadn't been able to adequately explain how she'd fallen. It had happened too quickly. She'd gotten out of bed and was headed to the kitchen for a drink of water, apparently tripped over something, and boom! She was on the floor. In excruciating pain, she'd still managed to crawl to the phone and call Elsa Donegan. It had been Elsa who'd called 911, Elsa who'd called him after the paramedics carted Gram off to the hospital. He instantly forgave the woman for the alien abduction thing. She might be a fruitcake, but in an emergency, Elsa maintained a level head.

From across the room, Annie said softly, "Why don't you sit down? You've been pacing ever since we got here."

He paused, hands in his pockets, to look at her. He'd actually forgotten she was here. *Good going, Hunter,* he thought. Aloud, he said, "I'm sorry. This can't be much fun for you."

"Don't be ridiculous. I'm sure it's even less fun for you. But you'll wear a path in the floor tiles if you don't stop pacing."

"Thanks for coming with me," he said. "I owe you one. I'll have to buy you dinner sometime."

"I'll take the dinner," she said, "but only because for some crazy reason, I enjoy the pleasure of your company. What that says about my sanity, I don't know. But you don't owe me a thing. I'm here because I didn't want you to be alone."

"You went out of your way to be decent to me. You dragged your kid out of bed—"

"You did the same with yours."

"Yeah, well, I figured they'd be safer together. Nobody'll bother them at my place. The bottom line is, you didn't have to do it, but you did. And I appreciate it more than you can imagine."

"Sit down," she said, patting the couch next to her hip. "Talk to me. Tell me about your grandmother. How old is she?"

"She's eighty-six," he said, sitting beside her on the rock-hard couch. "She hasn't had an easy life. My grandfather died before I was born, and she never remarried. Said he was her husband, dead or alive, and there wasn't room in her heart for any others. Her only son—my dad—died when I was a little kid. My mom had a drug and alcohol problem. She's spent most of her life in and out of jail. I don't even know where she is now. Don't even know if she's dead or alive. She pretty much wrote us off when we were little kids, so Gram raised the three of us. She was the only real mother I ever knew. Now she's legally blind and on insulin, and the tables have been turned. Now I'm taking care of her."

Softly, she said, "You love her, don't you?"

"She took care of me when nobody else gave a damn. She's a stubborn, irritating, manipulative old bat. And if anything happens to her—if she doesn't make it—" He shook his head, unable to imagine a world without Gram in it. "Hell," he said, "I know it's inevitable. I mean, the woman is in her eighties, for Christ's sake. I know she's not going to live forever. But I'm not ready for her to go just yet."

"I knew it."

"Knew what?"

"That underneath that grim and gruff exterior, you were a marshmallow."

"You must be psychic, then, because I didn't know it myself."

"You're a good man, Davy Hunter."

Why was it that coming from her, those words seemed to take on such significance? He barely knew the woman. But since she'd walked into his life, the emotions he'd kept on deep freeze were thawing at a terrifying rate. He was still trying to decide whether that was a good or a bad thing.

"Mr. Hunter?"

At the sound of his name, Davy was on his feet in an instant. He knew the doctor who stood in the doorway, still dressed in surgical scrubs. Everybody in town knew Ryan Gates. He was head of surgery at Androscoggin Valley Hospital. A big fish in a very small pond. His kid, Cooper, had been peripherally involved in the drug deal that had led to Chelsea's death. Cooper Gates hadn't been the one responsible for her death, but he'd known who was, and had kept that information to himself. The courts had gone easy on him because he was a juvenile, and because his family could afford a good lawyer. Dr. Ryan Gates would never be on Davy's list of favorite people, but he was a decent surgeon, the best that Androscoggin Valley had to offer, and at this point, Gram's best hope. Sometimes, you had to let bygones be bygones. No matter how much you didn't want to. "How is she?" he said.

"She made it through the surgery with flying colors. Your grandmother's a strong woman."

"Yes. She is." The relief that flooded him was almost overwhelming. "What now?"

"She's in Recovery right now, resting comfortably. We inserted a pin in her hip. That should take care of the immediate problem, but she'll be off her feet for a while. Assuming that there are no complications—"

"Complications?"

"She's in her eighties," Gates said, "and diabetic. After surgery, there's always a risk of complications. As a diabetic, she's at a slightly higher risk. But as I said, she's a strong woman. The surgery was routine. Once she's well enough to leave the hospital, I expect she'll need at least a month in rehab. Maybe longer, depending on how quickly she bounces back. Diabetics can take longer to heal. After that…well, she may or may not be capable of continuing to live on her own. At her age, and with her visual disability…well, it's something you'll want to take up with her family physician. Look at all the options. If you're thinking of placing her in a facility, you should probably start planning for it as soon as possible. Sometimes there are waiting lists."

He didn't like the way the man said the word *facility*. As if Gram were a piece of refuse that needed to be hauled off to the garbage dump and left there. He forced himself to remember that Gates was only doing his job. Forced himself to remember that, even though it would be a last resort, if things got bad enough, it might come to that. He might have to place her in some kind of nursing-care facility. But that wasn't something he was ready to think about. Not yet. "Can I see her?" Davy said.

"Once she's out of the Recovery room and on the post-surgical ward. But she'll be groggy, and she needs to rest. We'll be keeping her heavily sedated because of the pain. It might be better if you waited until tomorrow." Gates glanced at the clock on the wall and corrected himself. "Or, more accurately, later today."

"Thanks, Doc."

Gates disappeared down the corridor, and Davy was alone with Annie again. "Feel better?" she said.

"I'll feel better when I see her."

"Ah," she said. "You're the kind of man who has to see it to believe it."

She looked exhausted. Wiped out. As Gram would say, like something the cat dragged in. There was blue paint splattered all over her clothes, her hair was a rat's nest, and her eyes were red and puffy, probably from the effort she'd expended to stay awake all these hours in a place that was about as exciting as watching paint dry. Count on him to take the most gorgeous female to hit Serenity in a decade and turn her into something from a B-grade sci-fi flick. "You look tired," he said. "I should take you home."

"I can wait a little longer."

"You sure?"

"I'm sure. I'll leave when you leave."

They killed another half hour sitting silently on the ugly couch before a nurse finally came in and told him that his grandmother had been moved to a room on the second floor of the hospital. He could visit, the nurse said, but Gram needed her rest, so he should keep it brief.

He thanked her, and he and Annie took the elevator upstairs. The corridors were lit as bright as midday. Nurses bustled about, clanging carts, slamming doors, blood pressure cuffs and thermometers at the ready. He wondered how anybody ever managed to sleep, let alone get well, in this place with its lights and its noise and the constant interruptions from the nursing staff in their ongoing quest to measure the vital signs of every patient at least once an hour.

He stopped at the second-floor nurses' station and asked for Lorena Hunter's room, then followed the nurse's directions down a secondary corridor that veered off to the left. He located Room 215 and paused outside the door, which had been left slightly ajar. "You go in," Annie said. "I'll wait out here."

Davy cautiously pulled open the door and stepped inside the room. Gram lay beneath crisp white sheets, amid tubes and hoses and hanging bags of various fluids, both ingoing and outgoing. Someone had tucked a rolled-up bedspread against her side to keep her from moving around too much in the bed. Her face was ashen, the long white hair that was her pride and joy a tangled mess. Her dentures sat in a Dixie cup on the bed stand, beside one of those little plastic pans they give you in case you need to vomit. She would have a conniption about the teeth. Gram might be in her eighties, but she hadn't lost her vanity. She never let anybody see her without her dentures. Some things, she'd told him, were too private to share even with immediate family. All these strangers viewing her toothless gums would be the ultimate indignity.

He leaned over the hospital bed and touched her hand, the one that didn't have any tubes or needles stuck in it. Her eyes flickered, and she opened them. Her blindness wasn't total. She still could see light and shadow, could still recognize blurry colors if they were bright enough. But she couldn't recognize faces. "Hey," he said.

She might not be able to distinguish faces, but she had no trouble with voices. "Dabid," she said, her speech thickened by a combination of drugs, tubing, and missing dentures. "Brote—" Her mouth was dry, probably from the anesthesia. She ran her tongue over her lips and tried again. "Broke hip."

"That's right, Gram," he said gently, scooching down so that he was at eye level with her. "But you're okay now. The doctors fixed you up as good as new. They put in a pin to hold you together. Now you're just like the bionic woman." He took her thin, blue-veined hand in his and squeezed it. "You'll be out of here in no time."

"Cagh."

"What?"

"Cagh. Theed cagh."

He tried to figure out what she was saying, but it made no sense. "I'm sorry, Gram," he said, "but I don't understand."

She was starting to get agitated. He could tell by the way she squeezed his hand and raised her head off the pillow, working her mouth in frustration. "Theed cagh," she said. "Koko! Theed cagh."

A lightbulb went on over his head. "Feed the cat?" he said,

and she nodded, dropping her head back to the pillow as though she'd utilized her last reserve of strength. "Don't worry, Gram," he said. "I'll take care of Koko. And I'll water your plants, and take care of whatever else needs doing."

A tear spilled from the corner of her eye. "Home," she said.

An arrow of pain shot through his heart. "I know, hon," he said. "It won't be long. I promise."

"Dabid?"

"What, Gram?"

She wriggled her hand out of his grasp, reached up and pressed it against the side of his head. "Good boy," she said. "My boy."

He had to get out of here. If he didn't get out of here, he was going to lose it. He caught her hand in his and kissed it. "Gram," he said, "I have to go. I promised I'd only stay for a minute. You need to sleep. But I'll be back in a few hours. We'll both feel better then, and we can have a nice visit."

"Don' forget cagh."

"I won't, Gram. I'll stop over and feed her before I come back. You get some rest now."

She didn't want him to leave. She didn't say a word, didn't cling to his hand. But he could tell she didn't want him to go. He went anyway, found Annie leaning against the wall outside the door, her eyelids closed, a vertical frown line running between her eyes.

"Ready?" he said softly, and she opened her eyes.

"Are you okay?" she said.

"I'm fine."

"Liar." There was a tenderness to her voice that hadn't been there earlier. "I heard every word that was said in there."

"So I lied. Sue me. Can we just get out of here?"

The drive home from the hospital was silent, both of them thinking private thoughts as the police cruiser slipped through the darkness. The air was thick and humid, almost soupy, the town deserted at this hour, a monochromatic caricature of its real self. Even the bars that lined Androscoggin Street were closed. Only the Big Apple convenience store remained open, for any citizen who needed an emergency pack of Camels or a tank of gas. Business wasn't thriving. The lone clerk working the graveyard shift stood outside, leaning against the front of the building, smoking a cigarette, its crimson tip glowing in the dark. Hunter crossed the old iron bridge and headed out the state highway. They temporarily left civilization behind as they traveled the deserted stretch of road where she'd met him just a few days ago when her Volvo died. Then they came back into civilization, passing through the little settlement that surrounded the Twilight.

In the dark, the Twilight's dead neon sign loomed like an escapee from some modern-day Stonehenge. Hunter wheeled the cruiser into the parking lot and came to a stop at the foot of the outside stairway. "I'll walk you up," he said.

Annie, who'd been hoping for a quick escape, paused, her hand already on the door handle. "That won't be necessary."

He turned off the ignition and removed his keys. "Screw necessary. You're here all by yourself. Somebody broke into the place a few nights ago. I'm walking you up."

She didn't argue. It was three o'clock in the morning, she was beyond exhausted, and it didn't seem worth the effort. He followed her up the darkened staircase. She stumbled on the edge of a stair that needed fixing and he caught and steadied her, his hand pressed lightly against the small of her back. It was the first time he'd touched her, and her heart began a sudden, irrational thudding. It would have been nice, she thought with an irritation that was disproportionate to the situation, if Sophie could have bothered to leave the outside light on when Jessie picked her up. But that was a teenager for you.

They left the lights on when you wanted them off, then left you in the dark when you could have used the light.

She'd witnessed something extraordinary tonight, and she was still trying to process it. There was much more to Davy Hunter than she had thought. That hard outer shell of his had multiple layers that were gradually being peeled back to reveal the remarkable man beneath. The disclosure of his tender side had left her shaken, her breath coming in short, shallow inhalations. Or maybe it was just the climb up the steep staircase to the second floor with his hand pressed against her back that left her breathless.

She should have insisted that he let her walk up alone. Should have insisted that he stay in the car. Should have insisted that he go home, where she wouldn't be tempted to beg him to stay. This was a dangerous game she was playing, and the consequences could be deadly. She had no business getting involved with any man, not while Luke Brogan was out there gunning for her. If she let down her guard, she could jeopardize her safety, not to mention Sophie's.

Hunter would only complicate her life at a time when she could ill afford complications. He'd already made it clear that nothing could ever come of this heated attraction between them. The man had a dark side, and demons of his own to battle. His dead ex-wife, for one, and God only knew what else. She had no idea of the statistics regarding the percentage of sober alcoholics who fell off the wagon, but she suspected they were discouragingly high. It would be an idiotic move on her part to invite him in, at three o'clock in the morning, when she was so hungry for him she could taste it.

She'd been so careful. For six months, she hadn't made a single misstep. Hadn't let anybody get too close, for fear of revealing more than she intended. She'd already said too much to him, the other night at Jo's barbecue, which only served to prove that he was dangerous. Sexy and compelling and dangerous. Was she really willing to throw away all her caution and good sense for a roll in the hay with a man who would probably forget her the instant he climbed out of her bed?

They reached the landing outside her door. Annie took a deep breath and turned to tell him good-night. To send him packing, before she did the unthinkable. She opened her mouth to speak, but the scent of him, hot and dusky and male, invaded her senses. Powerless to resist, she drew that riveting scent of man into her lungs and held it captive. His fingers, splayed against her lower back, scorched her skin, even through the cotton work shirt she'd donned to paint in. The sultry night was a liquid presence that flowed around them, between them, heavy and sticky and sweet.

Oh, God. Once she touched him, she'd be lost.

She wasn't even aware of moving as she flowed into him, pelvis to pelvis, heat to heat, her aching breasts pressed hard against his chest. Relief because her indecision was ended mingled with anticipation over what was to come. Certain now, more certain than she'd ever been of anything, she reached up and found his face. Skimmed it with her fingers. He uttered a soft, unintelligible sound that might have been a word. Breathing hard, Annie tangled her fists in his hair and pulled his mouth down to hers.

Kissing Davy Hunter was like riding a nuclear missile. All that trapped energy, all that carefully restrained intensity, he let loose in an explosion of gargantuan proportions. The power he exuded was exhilarating. Terrifying. Determined to swallow him alive, she gripped his shirtfront in her hands, twisting and torturing it as she gave herself over to his steamy, liquid kisses.

He broke away from her with a gasp. Desperate for oxygen, she sucked in sweet, sticky air as his mouth worked its way down the slender column of her neck. Her head fell back, baring her throat to the prickle of whisker stubble, the warm feathery tickle of his breath, as with lips and teeth and tongue he plundered her. It was a ridiculous word, one that conjured up mental images of pirates and romance novel heroes. But it was the only word that fit. Davy Hunter, policeman, pirate and plunderer, tugged frantically at the buttons of her cotton shirt, peeling it back to reveal the sheer, lacy underwear she wore under her painting clothes.

"Christ Almighty," he said hoarsely. "Where the hell's your door key?"

It took her an instant to comprehend, took her an instant to remember that they were still outside her door, in plain view of not only every car that passed on the highway, but the prying eyes of her neighbors. With shaky hands, she fished the key out of her pocket. He took it from her and inserted it into the lock. The door opened, and they very nearly tumbled through it. He shoved it closed behind them and locked it, tossed the key on a table, and slipped the cotton shirt down over her arms.

It fell to the floor. She tugged at his T-shirt, and he helped her peel it off over his head. Annie skimmed her hands over his chest, his shoulders. God, he was perfect. Long and lean, sleek and silken smooth, his body as hard as that of a twenty-year-old. Only better. There was none of the callow youth about him. Davy Hunter was all man, solid and strong and exquisitely put together. They stood in the darkness, bodies locked together, swaying like reeds caught in a gentle breeze. Annie touched her mouth to his shoulder and tasted him. Drew in his scent, his flavor. Nipped and nibbled at skin as smooth as marble.

When he cupped her breasts, she nearly wept. Through lace as sheer as a spider's web, his searching fingers explored, circled, teased the sensitive tips to hardness, sending a stab of pure sensation like a lightning bolt directly to her pelvis.

She gasped at the pleasure of it, clung to his shoulders as his fingers continued the gentle pressure until she was so excited she couldn't stand still. He peeled off her bra and flung it aside, replaced his hands with his mouth, and she thought she might die. Right here, right now. She uttered a series of sharp gasps as he suckled her like an infant, alternating breasts, until she was panting like a dog on a hot August afternoon. It had been so long since a man had made love to her, too long, and she'd never before felt this frantic, almost frenzied need to couple.

His mouth found hers again. Like creatures of the night, they fed on each other, hot flesh pressed against hot flesh as they tore at each other's clothes. There was no hesitation, no false modesty. Only raw, aching need. Naked, he pulled her to the carpet. Limbs tangled, still kissing, they rolled and tumbled, skin to skin, hardness to softness.

He broke the kiss, lay on his back on the carpet, his chest rising and falling rapidly as with quick, teasing hands she explored his smooth, flat belly, combed her fingers through the thick nest of hair below, cupped his impressive erection between her hands.

"Jesus, Annie." His voice was barely recognizable as she stroked him, hard and fast, thrilled by his response, by the excited little noises he couldn't seem to hold back. "Stop," he said brokenly. "I want—" He caught her hands in his, halted them, and rolled her onto her back. Limbs splayed, she welcomed him, welcomed his heavy weight and his blistering heat, welcomed the quick fluid rush of rapture as he drove himself deep inside her.

"Oh, God." Her words came out as a moan, and she bit down hard on her lower lip to hold back the sob that wanted to follow. *Finally. Finally.* She'd spent years waiting for this moment, locked together in ecstasy with this man she'd met just days before. He whispered a shocking suggestion in her ear, and sweat popped out on her forehead, pooled beneath her arms and between her breasts. She arched her back, taking him in deeper, snugger, tighter. Lifting her legs, she wrapped them around him, locked herself around his waist, and rocked him mindlessly and ferociously, aware of nothing beyond the rock-hard flesh that impaled her and the harsh, disjointed words that he whispered in her ear. He was a relentless lover, driving her mercilessly, demanding that she follow him, that she keep up with him, that her pleasure reach heights she'd never before imagined.

They exploded together in a violent and noisy climax that shook the walls and threatened to bring the ceiling down in pieces on their heads. Falling into a tangled heap, they lay limp and gasping, hearts racing at an absurd velocity, bodies still twitching with aftershocks. "Holy mother of God," he said hoarsely. "What was that?"

"I'm…not sure." She struggled to draw in enough breath to fuel her burning lungs, but it was impossible. "I…can't…breathe."

He rolled onto his back beside her, and her breath slowly returned. Hunter reached down between them, found her hand, and took it in his. "You okay?" he said, threading fingers through hers.

There was something incredibly sweet about the gesture. "I'm okay," she said.

"I'm sorry," he said to the ceiling. "I didn't mean to be so—it's been a while."

He was apologizing for the hottest sex she'd ever experienced? Was this guy for real? "Trust me when I say this," she told him. "There's absolutely nothing to apologize for."

"Then it was good for you, too? I wasn't too rough?"

"The screaming didn't give me away? Good God, Hunter, just how long has it been for you?"

"I plead the Fifth."

"That long." She closed her eyes and floated on a soft cloud of satisfaction. "Me, too," she said dreamily. "I'm glad we didn't forget how."

"That makes two of us. That'd be a helluva thing, wouldn't it?"

Still floating, she said, "Maybe…just to be sure we got it right…we should try it again."

"You're an insatiable little witch, aren't you, Kendall? Give me a few minutes. I'm not as young as I used to be."

"Just…how old…are you?"

"I'm thirty-eight," he said. "Some days it feels more like eighty-eight."

"And is today one of those days?"

"It was, until about twenty minutes ago."

"Oh?" she said with exaggerated innocence. "What happened twenty minutes ago to change your mind?"

"Give me five more minutes, and I'll show you."

She smiled into the darkness. "You've got yourself a deal, hot stuff."

When he woke, it was daylight. Annie Kendall lay in the crook of his arm, her breathing slow and even, all that blond hair fanned out in a sexy tangle across his chest. Squinting, Davy raised his head to check his watch. It was past seven. He'd slept for three hours, sprawled out right here on the rock-hard floor, beneath the quilted comforter he'd pulled over them last night. *This morning,* he corrected himself.

Every muscle in his body ached. He was almost forty, too damn old to be sleeping on the floor. His back was stiff and his knees hurt. Old age was a bitch, especially when it hit you in your thirties. Twenty years ago, he could get away with pulling an all-nighter and then sacking out on the floor. He'd done it all the time when he was away at college. As young marrieds, he and Chelsea had partied until the wee hours and then crashed as the sun was coming up. They'd looked like zombies the next day, but they'd been too full of youthful energy to notice or care. But at thirty-eight, after the night he'd just been through, he felt like an old man. His head felt grainy and heavy, like a five-pound bag of sugar, and he had the world's worst hangover. Except that he hadn't had a drop to drink. He could blame this hangover exclusively on a lack of sleep and an overabundance of scorching, mind-blowing sex.

He hadn't intended to fall asleep. Hadn't intended to stay. He wasn't the kind of man who stayed. Except for Chelsea, he'd never stayed over with a woman. It complicated things too much, muddied the waters when it was time to move on. He'd never been a ladies' man, but he'd had his share of women over the years. He and Chels had spent more time apart than they had together, and he was a healthy, normal man for whom long-term celibacy was never an option. He always had a good time, always made sure the woman had a good time. But he never stayed. It was one of his cardinal rules. He never slept with the women he slept with.

Until now. He'd broken that cardinal rule and slept with Annie Kendall. He could deny the truth all he wanted, he could blame it on the emotional strain that Gram's accident had placed on him, could blame it on the fact that he hadn't slept in nearly twenty-four hours. But the truth was that he'd let down his guard with Annie. He'd wrapped himself around her as though they were longtime lovers and fallen into a deep, comfortable sleep without ever giving it a second thought. It terrified him. He was *not* going to have a romance with this woman. It just plain wasn't going to happen. The sex had been great—hell, better than great, it had been incredible, stunning, stupendous—but he wasn't about to fall in love with her. He wasn't interested in that kind of commitment, wasn't interested in that kind of gut-wrenching, brain-eating nightmare. He'd already been down that road with

Chelsea, and it had been an emotional mine field. He wasn't going through it again. Sex was one thing. Love was something totally different. That train had already left the station, and Davy Hunter wasn't on it.

He hoped to Christ Annie Kendall understood that.

Davy eased away from her hot little body and, careful not to wake her, pulled the comforter up over her and tucked it around her shoulders. He gathered up his clothes, flung haphazardly around the room, and went naked to the bathroom. Behind the locked bathroom door, he took care of business, then pulled on his clothes. Looked at himself in the mirror. His hair was a mess, and whisker stubble dotted his face. His eyes were bloodshot. Christ, he'd better escape while he could. If she ever got sight of him looking like this, he wouldn't have to worry about where to take her for their second date. There wouldn't be a second date.

Not, he reminded himself, that this had been a date.

Like the coward that he was, he tiptoed to the kitchen, searched until he found a piece of paper and a pencil, then hesitated, not sure what to say. *Hey, the sex was great. Can we do it again tonight?* Yeah, that would go over real good. Besides, it had been more than just sex. She'd gone with him to the hospital, had sat patiently for hours without complaining, had held his hand, figuratively speaking, through one of the darker nights of his life. She'd brought him back here and given him more than just the pleasure of that sweet, slick, heated place between her thighs. She'd given him tenderness when he sorely needed it, had offered strong, steady comfort at a time when he didn't know which way to turn.

In the end, he kept it simple. *Thanks,* he wrote. *For everything. I'll call you. D.*

He locked the door behind him, sat on the top stair to tug on his shoes, and laced them up. In the parking lot, the police cruiser stood out like a Ford pickup at a Corvette rally. That was just ducky. He should've left before daylight. Jo Crowley was an early riser. She'd undoubtedly already looked across the street and seen his car parked out front. By nightfall, word would be all over town that Davy Hunter was shacked up with the hot new blonde who'd just moved to town.

Serenity on a Sunday morning wasn't exactly partytown. The place was just as dead, just as deserted, as it had been at 3:00 a.m. A single car sat at the gas pumps in front of the Big Apple. Inside, Helen Goodwin made change for the driver. Even the churches hadn't come to life yet. Sunday morning services didn't start until nine o'clock, and even the holy rollers didn't start stirring much before eight.

When he pulled into his own driveway, there was no sign of life. He let himself in, silently stepped over a sleeping Buddy—some watchdog he was—and went immediately to the refrigerator. He still needed a couple hours of sleep or he'd fall over dead. If he drank coffee, there'd be no getting back to sleep. At thirty-eight, he couldn't slug caffeine the way he used to. One more goddamn concession to old age. Instead, he pulled out a gallon of milk and poured some in a mug. He replaced the carton of milk in the fridge and was just tipping up the mug to drink when he saw Jessie standing barefoot in the living room, dressed in a pair of flannel pajamas with rubber duckies all over them, bony arms crossed over her equally bony chest.

"How's Gram?" she said.

He was so damn tired he was swaying on his feet, like he used to do in the days after Chelsea died, when he'd come in at five in the morning so drunk he couldn't remember the drive home. It was a miracle he hadn't killed himself. Or somebody else. Maybe that's what he'd been hoping for. Suicide by automobile. A quick, conclusive end to the pain that was eating him up inside.

He took a slug of cold milk and gave Jessie the fifty-cent version of his night. He left out the part about Ryan Gates and his suggestion about putting Gram in a nursing-care facility, left out the part where he and Annie Kendall fucked each other's brains out. "Gram was worried about the cat," he concluded. "And she's already asking when she can go home."

Jessie tilted her head, and a ray of morning sun, filtering through the living room curtains, drew glossy highlights from her dark hair. "Can I visit her?" she said.

"I think that's a great idea. I'm going back later today. You can go with me if you want." He drained the mug of milk and set it in the sink. "Sophie asleep?"

"Yes."

"I'm going to bed for a couple of hours. It's been a long night."

"Davy? I just wanted you to know that it's okay."

He stood there looking at her, a slender, dark-haired, earnest young girl who looked younger than her age. "What's that, Skeets?" he said. "What's okay?"

"You and Mrs. Kendall."

"Me and—how the—" Flabbergasted, he realized he was spluttering and making a fool of himself, and he clamped his mouth shut.

"I'm not an idiot," she said. "I saw the way the two of you were looking at each other. And the way she avoided you all afternoon. And last night. You were with her when Elsa called you. At midnight, Davy. Now it's seven-thirty in the morning. You weren't with Gram all this time. Which tells me you went back to her place after you left the hospital."

Embarrassed, he said, "Christ, Skeets—"

"Davy, it's okay. Really. My mom wouldn't expect you to spend the rest of your life sitting around mourning her. If she was here, she'd tell you to get back out there and start living again or else she'd kick your butt." Jessie's gray eyes were solemn, but a flicker of humor crossed her face. She took a deep breath and went on. "I know how much it hurt you when she died. I thought it might kill you. For a while there, I was afraid you might kill yourself. But I've seen a change in you. You're starting to heal, and I'm so glad. You're the most solitary person I know, and it breaks my heart to see you that way. You need to be with someone. I want you to be happy. And if Mrs. Kendall makes you happy, then that's good enough for me."

He wondered how to explain to a starry-eyed sixteen-year-old girl that one night of hot sex didn't necessarily add up to happily-ever-after. He didn't want to shatter her adolescent illusions. Didn't want her to turn out like him, jaded by the age of eighteen. On the other hand, she needed to understand the difference between love and sex. It was a significant difference, one that could ruin the life of a young girl who failed to understand. And knowing Chelsea, he doubted that she'd adequately prepared her daughter for this crucial aspect of growing up. Chels might have lived her life bouncing from bed to bed, but when it came to talking about the birds and the bees, he suspected she'd abdicated that particular maternal responsibility.

"You need to understand," he said, then stopped when words failed him. He thought about it, tried again. "Sex is…it's like this…this incredible…uh…physically, you know…there's just nothing to compare it to. And when it's right—when the two people are right—it can be so much more than that. I mean, there's this spiritual element to it that—" Christ, this sounded lame, even to him. How must it sound to her? "I'm sorry," he said. "I'm not very good at this." He ran a hand through his hair, silently cursed her mother for leaving this crucial aspect of her upbringing to someone else. "I think you have to experience it to understand. I—" He stopped abruptly as the appalling thought struck him that at sixteen, Jessie might well have experienced it. In his day, at least kids waited until they were in high school. Nowadays, they were starting at twelve or thirteen. He cleared his throat. "I—you haven't—oh, shit."

"No!" she said, reddening. "I'm waiting for the right guy to come along. So far, I haven't seen him anywhere."

"Thank God. Look, Skeets, what I'm trying to say is that two people can like each other a lot, they can have great sex together, but it doesn't necessarily mean they love each other. Do you understand what I'm trying to say?"

"I'm trying to follow, but you're taking a really roundabout route to get to where you're going."

"All right. How about this? People confuse love and sex all the time. But they're two very different things. Don't let anybody convince you otherwise. Boys will tell you they love you. They'll tell you that if you really loved them, you'd do it. It's all bullshit. Teenage boys will say anything to get a girl to spread her legs. I know what I'm talking about. I used to be one."

"Are we going to reach the point soon?" Jessie said agreeably.

The point. Christ. What was his point? Somewhere along the way, he'd lost track of it. Not only was his body falling apart, but now he was having senior moments. "My point," he said, hoping he sounded as if he knew what he was talking about, "is that yeah, I slept with Annie. And I might sleep with her again. But please don't be thinking that means wedding bells are around the corner. Real life just doesn't work that way."

"Okay," she said, with just enough indulgence in her voice to make him wonder which of them was the kid and which one the adult.

"And…if any boy tries to talk you into doing something you're not a hundred percent sure you want to do…what are you going to tell him?"

Arms still crossed, she gave him a heart-stopping grin. "That I have a stepfather who carries a gun to work?"

It wasn't precisely the answer he'd been looking for. But it worked for him.

Eleven

Annie woke up alone. The sun was shining brightly, and her body ached in places she'd forgotten it could ache. She stretched and glanced at the clock, saw that it was nearly nine-thirty. *Eek!* Sophie could come home at any minute, and the last thing she needed was for her daughter to come in and find her sprawled out on the floor, naked as a jaybird, all sticky and smelling of sex. It wasn't exactly the kind of example she wanted to set for an impressionable adolescent daughter. Annie scrambled to her knees, gathered up the clothes that were flung haphazardly around the living room, and wrapped the comforter around her.

Hunter had left a note on the table. She scraped back her unruly hair, wadded up the comforter, and padded over to read it. *Thanks,* it said. *For everything. I'll call. D.*

Annie crumpled it up and buried it in the trash so Sophie wouldn't see it and ask questions she didn't have answers to. Wrapping the comforter more tightly around her, she trudged to the closet she and Sophie shared, gathered up clean clothes, carried them to the bathroom and set them on the john. Dropping the comforter, Annie studied herself critically in the mirror. Her body was in decent shape for a woman in her midthirties who got her exercise the natural way, by working hard instead of working out. She was still taut and toned. No paunch, no saddlebags, no sagging skin beneath her arms. Her stomach was still flat, and her breasts weren't yet showing signs of succumbing to gravity. Her eyes were still the same clear, bright blue, her hair still the sunny blond of her childhood, in spite of the fact that she was approaching forty. She wasn't a bad-looking woman, but the strain of the past six months had taken its toll on her. She could see it in her eyes, in the shadows beneath them, could see it in the tiny vertical lines that bracketed the corners of her mouth, lines that hadn't been there six months ago. The running, the lying, were making her old, and she was tired of it. Tired of hiding who she was. Tired of pretending to be somebody she wasn't.

Staring into her own eyes, she wondered if Annie Kendall and Robin Spinney were truly one and the same, or if they were distinct, separate people. Last night, with Davy Hunter, the sex had been so—*oh, God.* She closed her eyes, remembering it. Lush and wild and uninhibited, so hot that just thinking about it brought a heated flush to her face. She'd never had sex like that. If she'd been asked, she probably would have said that Robin Spinney didn't know how to have sex like that. Yet Annie Kendall hadn't seemed to have any problem following Hunter's lead last night. He'd brought out a side of her that she didn't know existed, one so startling that this morning, she'd almost expected to see a stranger looking back at her from the mirror. But all she saw was the same familiar face that had been looking back for thirty-six years.

That wasn't what worried her, though. Once they'd gotten the screaming out of their system, once that initial, frantic urgency to mate had been sated, their lovemaking had taken on a totally different aspect. It was that second time around that worried her. It had been the kind of slow, sweet, dreamy sex they wrote about in romance novels. The dangerous kind of sex, dangerous because it tricked unsuspecting women into believing it Meant Something. Knowing this was true should have rendered her immune, but it hadn't. She was as weak, as susceptible, as any other woman who believed in the fairy tale, and that was what scared the living shit out of her.

He was a needy man, dark and hungry and compelling, and she suspected he'd been denying that need for some time. Last night, he'd shown her a glimpse of his dark side, and she'd responded to his need. Somehow, she'd let him get to her. Somewhere between his twenty-three days of sobriety and the tenderness he'd displayed toward his grandmother, Davy Hunter had hooked her and reeled her in like a fish on a line.

What that said about her, she wasn't sure. That she was a sucker for needy, troubled, damaged men? She'd never shown any indication of it in the past. Mac had been a normal, average guy. So had the few boyfriends she'd had before Mac came along. Her teenage crushes had been equally innocuous; she'd been more into Rick Springfield than Ozzy Osbourne. Plain vanilla all the way. Until now. That meant the news wasn't good. It wasn't needy men, plural, for which she had a weakness. It was just one particular needy man.

She stepped into the shower, turned it on as hot as was humanly bearable, and washed Davy Hunter off her body. Ruthlessly, coldly, adamantly, without an ounce of compassion, she scrubbed away every trace of him, erased the night before as though it had never happened. It had been a mistake, one she couldn't afford to repeat, and the sooner she forgot about it, the better. If he called, she wouldn't answer the phone. What they'd started last night was an impossibility. It didn't matter how much she might yearn for him, didn't matter that last night had been about so much more than just sex. Didn't matter that the thought of not seeing him again brought scalding tears to her eyes, tears that she stubbornly squeezed into submission. Being with him was an impossibility, and that was that. She didn't love him, and he didn't love her, and it was a damn good thing, wasn't it? A damn good thing she could put a stop to this before it went any further, before one or both of them got hurt.

She was fully dressed, the bathroom door open wide to let out the steam, brushing her hair with hard, vicious yanks of the brush when she heard Sophie's voice. "Mom?" her daughter called out. "Are you home?"

"In here."

Sophie came in and sat on the edge of the tub, hands grasping the lip for balance. "You're just getting up?" she said with some surprise.

"I had a late night, Soph."

"Yeah. I heard."

Annie pulled her wet hair back and upward into a ponytail, gave it a neat twist, and folded the twist against the back of her head. "Hand me that barrette, kiddo."

Sophie got up, grabbed the oversized barrette, and handed it to her mother. "Have you eaten?" Annie said as she clipped the twisted hair to the back of her head.

"Jessie and I stopped at McDonald's on the way here."

Which meant that they'd actually driven past the Twilight, eaten breakfast, and then backtracked. "Is she a careful driver?" Annie said.

"She's a careful everything. Little Miss Goody-Two-Shoes."

"I see." Hazarding a final glance in the mirror, Annie turned to look at her daughter. Sometimes it still shocked her to see how tall Soph had gotten. Slender as a colt, with legs to match. Pretty soon she'd be taller than Annie. It was a discomfiting thought. "A little too boring for you, is she?"

Her feet tapping rhythmically against the floor, Sophie tucked a strand of hair behind her ear. "Actually, she's okay. For a nerd. She plays the violin."

"Oh?"

"She played it for me. It was okay."

Coming from Sophie, that was high praise indeed. "Well," Annie said, "maybe the two of you can be friends."

"We'll see." Sophie grew quiet for a moment, then said, "Do you have to work today?"

Surprised, Annie said, "I have to finish painting the shop. Why do you ask?"

Sophie shrugged and stared down at her shoes. "I just thought…maybe we could go to the mall."

"But, Soph, my car's not fixed yet."

Sophie looked back up at her, animated for the first time in a while. "So? You could take Mr. Crowley's truck. He wouldn't mind. Mrs. Crowley said we could keep it as long as we needed it."

"I know, but—that's asking a lot. And it would probably cost me forty dollars to drive it to Portland and back."

Sophie's face closed up, grew dark and sullen again. "We used to do mother-daughter things all the time," she said bitterly. "We don't any more."

A pang of guilt stabbed her directly in the heart. Sophie was right. They'd always been close, had always spent time together at the mall, at the movies or the beach, or sometimes just hanging out. She'd cherished those times with her daughter, and in the past six months, there had been far too few of them. The lapse hadn't been intentional; at first, she'd stayed indoors for fear that Brogan, or one of his emissaries, would spot them on the street somewhere. That was her own paranoia at work. She understood that now. But the distance between them hadn't been all her fault. Lately Sophie hadn't wanted to spend much time with her. It was uncool to hang out with your mother, and Soph was at that crucial age where the opinions of her peers mattered more than those of any parent.

But things were different now. They'd made a new start in Serenity, and part of that new start would be mending their torn relationship. She could paint the damn walls later. How long would it take to slap a paint roller on the wall and cover up what was there? "Get ready," she told Sophie. "I'll call Jack Crowley and make sure he doesn't mind."

It was the right decision. The look on Sophie's face told her that. Sleep deprivation be damned; what mattered was spending quality time with her little girl—who wouldn't be a little girl much longer—on this beautiful day when summer was in full bloom and the world was lush and green.

They took back roads from Serenity to Portland. Tall grasses waved gently in the breeze as they drove past, and wildflowers dotted the roadsides and the meadows. They drove with the windows down and the radio cranked, even managing to compromise on a radio station they could both tolerate.

Portland was an appealing city. Not too big, not too small, with a modern skyline, energy to burn, and an old-world charm characteristic of New England. They spent a couple of hours at the mall, where they splurged on Godiva chocolates and tried on every silly hat that Macy's carried. With money she'd saved from her allowance, Sophie bought a white T-shirt and jeans at Abercrombie & Fitch.

"Don't get any ideas," she told her mother. "Just because I bought white instead of black, it doesn't mean anything."

"Of course not," Annie said.

But she secretly wondered if Soph might be nearing the end of her Goth phase. Maybe Jessie Logan would be a good influence on her. After all, underneath the black clothing and the stringy hair and the spooky makeup, Sophie was a great kid. She just didn't want too many people figuring that out, because at fifteen, being a great kid wasn't exactly cool. Soph was just experimenting, trying to find herself. Trying on a different persona to see how it fit. And wasn't that what most of us were doing, most of the time? Figuring out just who we were and where we fit into the greater scheme of things? Which meant that the daughter Annie'd been so worried about was actually quite normal.

After they left the mall, they picked up deli sandwiches and drove through the Old Port, with its cobbled streets and boutiques and art galleries, eventually stopping to picnic at a waterfront park, amid dozens of other sun-worshippers who'd come out to play Frisbee, exercise their dogs, and just veg out to a cool sea breeze and the sight of bobbing boats on the water. Stomachs full, she and Soph lay on the grass, listening to the cry of gulls and watching the jets come and go overhead.

When it was time to leave, Annie was as reluctant as Sophie. The last six months had been fraught with fear and tension, and this was the first time she'd allowed herself to simply relax and forget her troubles. The first time she'd been able to laugh and joke and just be with Sophie, like a normal mother and daughter. Once they got back to Serenity, she knew reality would close in on them and they'd be back in the hypervigilant mode that had been forced on both of them.

As she clutched and shifted and steered Jack's pickup truck through the city traffic, she pondered their situation for the eleven-hundredth time. Was there something she could have done differently? She could have stayed and fought, the way her dad thought she should. She could have reported what she knew to the authorities. But who would that be? Brogan was county sheriff and his brother was district attorney. That pretty much took care of the authorities for Atchawalla County. Certainly, she could have gone further. To the state police, perhaps. Even to the governor, if it came to that.

But even she had to admit that the accusations she was leveling at Luke Brogan sounded far-fetched. And his brother was a powerful individual. Who knew how many equally powerful people he had in his pocket? It was said that politics made strange bedfellows. How far would Marcus Brogan go to protect his brother? If she'd turned to anybody else, she might have been signing her death warrant. Look at what had happened to Boyd.

Stop doubting yourself. You did the only thing you could do.

But still the doubts gnawed at her.

She stopped the truck at a red light. In the lane to their right sat a bright red Mini Cooper, trashy music pouring like solid waste from its open windows. The kid behind the wheel glanced up at Sophie and flashed her a grin. The light turned green, and he sped off.

"Did you see that guy?" Soph said. "I think he was flirting with me."

Annie wasn't ready for randy young men in foreign cars to be flirting with her daughter. "I don't want to know," she said. "He had to be at least twenty-one. You're only fifteen. I can't go there. I can't even think about going there."

But Sophie was immeasurably cheered by the incident. She hummed along with the radio all the way home. She was still in an expansive mood when they reached Serenity. To Annie's amazement, Sophie turned to her in the cab of the pickup, right there in plain sight of the world, and gave her a bone-squeezing hug. "Thanks for the day, Mom," she said. "It was great." And, grabbing a plastic bag with the Abercrombie logo, she hopped out of the truck and sprinted up the stairs to the apartment.

Annie watched her dig in her pocket for her door key, then insert it into the lock. When the door slammed shut behind her, Annie sat there, stupefied, for a full thirty seconds before she had the presence of mind to gather up her purse and her shopping bags and begin the trek up the stairs.

* * *

Louis picked up the tail a couple of blocks from his motel.

At least the guy was being consistent. But was he so arrogant, so sure of himself, that he thought Louis wouldn't notice him? Maybe the guy simply thought he was being clever. After all, he'd changed cars since last night. But then, so had Louis. He'd returned the rented van first thing this morning, then walked across the airport terminal to a different rental agency, hands in his pockets, whistling all the way, and picked up the champagne-colored Saturn he was now driving. There had to be a million of the things on the road, so many of them that people's eyes glazed over when they passed by. For sheer invisibility, you couldn't do better than a Saturn, not since Ford Motor Company stopped making the Tempo.

But the yahoo following him in the dung-colored Buick Century was starting to grate on his nerves. Either he'd been followed to and from the car rental agency, or the guy knew where he was staying, and had waited him out. Neither scenario impressed Louis very much. There was something eerily disquieting about being followed while he was on a job. It raised too many questions. Such as who he could and couldn't trust. Not to mention the burning question of just how many players were involved in this little scenario. He'd assumed it was two, himself and Luke Brogan. Three if you counted the absent Robin Spinney. But the presence of the guy in the Buick raised that number to four, and once you passed three—client, investigator, and investigatee—things could get messy very quickly.

Which was why he'd spent several hours last night on the computer and the telephone, doing a little information gathering on the people he knew were attached to this case, either directly or peripherally. It was amazing, the things you could find out if you did enough digging and asked the right questions. Amazing, the way people opened up when you told them you were a private investigator. Gossip was cheap, and it was plentiful, and if you hit the right source, information would gush like Jed Clampett's oil well.

First there was his client, Luke Brogan, county sheriff, a man who, judging by what Louis had been told, wasn't exactly loved by his constituents. Yet he kept being reelected. Possibly because the crime rate in Atchawalla County was at an all-time low, possibly because he came from a politically powerful family. Both his parents were dead. His brother had inherited all the money; Brogan had inherited the little shotgun house where he'd been raised and a life insurance policy that, after the expenses of burying his mother, might have paid for a weekend at one of the gambling casinos in Tunica. Brogan lived in the house alone now, with just his dog for company. He'd been married twice, had two grown daughters, at least one rancorous ex-wife (Wife Number One), and another who received hefty alimony payments (Wife Number Two).

It was the brother who was the more interesting of the two. Marcus Brogan, District Attorney, soon to become The Honorable Judge Brogan. Interesting family dynamics there. Marcus was the younger son, child of a second marriage, raised in the lap of power and wealth. He had the brains and the money and the drive to succeed. At a relatively young age, Marcus had already climbed higher on the success ladder than his older brother would ever reach. Louis wondered just how much control the younger Brogan had over his older half sibling. Could the Great and Powerful Marcus be the man behind the curtain, the man who pulled the strings that controlled the lives of a number of people, including Louis Farley? Or was Luke Brogan really what he pretended to be, the sole actor in this endeavor to locate Robin Spinney?

Then, there was Mac Spinney. By all accounts, a good cop, a decent guy, one who didn't take bribes, drink too much, or cheat on his wife. A squeaky clean, Dudley Do-Right kind of guy. He'd died two years ago in an auto accident on a lonely stretch of fog-drenched Mississippi highway. A single-car accident with no witnesses. Although his best friend since childhood, Deputy Boyd Northrup, had made a minor flap about it, there'd been no real investigation into Spinney's death. A car wreck was a car wreck, and in that part of rural Mississippi, accidents happened with surprising frequency. Atchawalla lost one of its finest, and everyone agreed it was a damn shame. Half the town turned out for his funeral before they went home to their safe little lives and forgot Mac Spinney ever existed. His widow had received a hefty life insurance settlement, and life in the quiet little Southern town had returned to normal.

So it was fascinating to learn that, eighteen months later, Boyd Northrup, Spinney's best friend and fellow deputy, had died in an apparent suicide. Coincidence? Louis didn't really buy it, but he supposed it was possible that Northrup had been despondent over something, even if nothing in his home life with the wife and the kids and the new baby on the way pointed in that direction. Boyd Northrup had simply climbed out of bed one winter morning, showered as he did every day before work. Then he'd poured himself a cup of coffee and sat down at his kitchen table, still dressed in a blue terrycloth bathrobe, and swallowed the muzzle of his police-issue handgun.

His death raised a red flag for Louis Farley, and left all kinds of unanswered questions. What could Northrup have been thinking, ending his life like that, in his own kitchen, where his wife or one of his kids was likely to come home and find pieces of him splattered all over the walls and ceiling? Why would he have bothered to shower first? Northrup was a cop. He knew what kind of damage a handgun would do to a man who put it in his mouth and pulled the trigger. The shower was at best a moot point. And why bother to pour himself a final, untouched cup of coffee before he sent himself off to the eternal fires of Hell? If you believed in the Christian fundamentalist perspective, as Boyd Northrup most likely had, that's where suicides went.

It didn't add up. Or maybe it did, only two and two didn't equal the four Louis had expected they would. Especially when he put this information together with the recollections of the high school guidance secretary, Emma Hickey, who'd been only too willing to spill everything she knew. Boyd Northrup had died the same day that Robin Spinney took an emergency leave of absence to care for an ailing great-aunt in Arkansas. The leave of absence was supposed to be temporary, but a month or so later, she'd phoned the school and resigned permanently, without apology or explanation. According to Hickey, nobody had seen or heard from Robin Spinney since, and her little two-story house, the one Mac Spinney had designed and built himself the summer before Sophie was born, was sitting there empty, the lawn unmowed and weeds growing up around the foundation.

Emma Hickey had sniffed and, with all the hauteur she could muster, added that it was a disgrace, the way Robin was disrespecting her husband's memory. If she wasn't coming home, she could at least pay for a gardening service to keep the lawn mowed.

Louis had wondered before, and he wondered again now, why a cop like Brogan, who possessed all the resources of a county police department, would turn to a private investigator to locate someone. It would be easier, not to mention cheaper, to use the resources at his disposal and locate her himself. Unless he was trying to keep his hands clean. Unless he didn't want anybody to know he was looking for her.

Unless his reason for finding her fell on the wrong side of the law.

Frowning, Louis pulled the Saturn over in front of an oversized ranch house a block from the Sarnacki residence. In his rearview mirror, he watched the Buick approach and then casually pass him. His impression of the driver was fleeting and frustratingly sketchy. Tall—at least six feet—with dark hair, or maybe he was wearing a dark cap. Most likely male, but even that he couldn't be certain of. At the end of the block, the car pulled up to the stop sign, sat there idling for a moment, then made a right turn and slowly disappeared from sight.

Louis snorted. Two could play at this game. If the tail wasn't even making an effort to stay hidden, then he wasn't about to hide either. If Buick Man had anything to say to him, let the guy make the first move. In the meantime, Louis had a job to do. He pulled the Pistons cap lower over his eyes, tucked his earpiece in his ear, and turned on his surveillance equipment. Picking up the Nora Roberts novel he'd bought at Target to replace the one he'd left in the hospital waiting room in Miami, he leaned back his seat, adjusted his sunglasses, and went to work.

Twelve

The moon must be full. It was the only explanation Davy could come up with that even came close to accounting for his morning. The nut cases were coming out of the woodwork. Irene MacMaster was off her medication again, and he'd gotten a frantic call that she was standing in the middle of Androscoggin Street, wearing a purple cape and directing traffic. According to Dixie, Irene's little episodes were a perpetual problem that kept cropping up at least once a month. Well, good. That meant he had the month of July down, and only had August left to deal with before Ty came back and rescued him from this fate that was worse than death. He should mark his calendar and plan a big welcome-home party.

Two of Serenity's more prominent citizens had gotten into a minor fender-bender in the Food City parking lot that had led to an all-out fistfight. Pete had hauled both their asses into the station. Looking as sheepish as they should have, considering their exalted positions and the fact that they were both stone cold sober and over the age of eighteen—way, way over the age of eighteen—they both posted bail and phoned their wives to come get them. Then there'd been the call from Stella Daggett, hysterical because Omar Abdallah's goats had gotten loose and were sampling her prize-winning Roma to-matoes. She'd turned the garden hose on them, but the stupid animals had just blinked a couple of times and continued munching.

"I am not rounding up goats," he told Dix when she passed the call on to him. "I am absolutely *not* rounding up goats."

Forty-five minutes later he was back at his desk, a little muddy, a little wrinkled, and plastered with wet goat hair. "What is that godawful smell?" Dixie said as she set a stack of papers on the corner of his desk.

"That's me. I decided to try a new aftershave. Think it'll catch on?"

"Hunh. *Eau de* goat. I doubt it'll make much of an impact in the U.S., but I bet you'd be a massive hit in the Swiss Alps."

He raised an eyebrow. "The Swiss Alps?"

"You know. *Heidi?*" At his blank look, she added, "Shirley Temple? With Grandfather and Peter the Goat Boy? And that poor little crippled girl who—oh, forget it." She rolled her eyes in utter contempt. "Your basic education is sorely lacking, Hunter."

"Interim Chief Hunter to you, Dix. How many times do I have to remind you?"

"So fire me."

"I don't think I have the power to fire you. I'm just a rent-a-cop."

"I don't know. Is that a real gun you have in that shoulder holster?"

"Well, yeah. Of course."

"I'd say that gives you the power to do pretty much anything you want. *Interim Chief* Hunter."

"Cheeky," he said. "You're really cheeky."

"And you should be glad of it," Dixie said. "At least there's somebody around here with a sense of humor."

Picturing his own grim visage, Pete's big sour puss, and René, who was so earnest it was painful to watch, he decided she was right. Somebody needed to keep them all from drowning in their own cheerlessness. "Maybe instead of firing you, I should promote you," he said.

"Yeah? To what?"

"I was thinking maybe court jester."

In between all the craziness, in between the phone calls and the constant stream of paperwork and the goat round-up, he spent a fair amount of time on the phone with Gram's doctor, Jeremy Colfer, and her attorney, Lou Cunningham. The news wasn't good. Doc Colfer had thought even before the fall that it was time Gram left her house and moved someplace where she'd have round-the-clock supervision. Lou explained the red tape of elderly care as best he could, although the terms he threw around—Medicare, Medicaid, Social Security, nursing homes, boarding homes, assisted living facilities, home health aides—had Davy's head spinning by the time he was done. He understood very little of what Lou told him, except the bottom line: the cost would be about equivalent to that of a five-star hotel, and she wouldn't get a penny of assistance from the government until she was destitute. At the prices they charged, it wouldn't take long.

And then there was Dee.

She swooped into his office like a hawk swooping down on fleeing prey, one kid at her hip and a second clinging to her leg. Her blue stretch pants had a hole in the knee, and there was something that looked suspiciously like grape jelly fingerprints on her shirt. The kid who'd been clinging to her leg launched himself at Davy. He caught his nephew and swung him in the air before plopping the kid down on his knee. "Hey, buddy," he said. "How's it going?"

"Grrrrrrreat!" Timmy said in his best Tony the Tiger imitation.

"Glad to hear it." Over Timmy's head, Davy hazarded a look at his sister. Her expression was thunderous. "Dee," he said mildly.

"I really appreciate you notifying me."

"You smell funny," Timmy said as he squirmed and twisted, digging his bony backside into Davy's thigh. "Uncle Davy, is that a real gun?"

"Get away from there," Dee said, "before you shoot someone!"

Davy let the kid slide down his leg to the floor. Timmy rushed to his mother's side. She caught him by a forearm and yanked him hard against her hip. "Stay," she said through gritted teeth, as though he were a dog. To Davy, she said bitterly, "Maybe you thought you'd just wait and let me read it in the paper when she dies."

"For Christ's sake, Dee, stop being a drama queen. She isn't dying. And frankly, I didn't think you'd give a damn if she did."

"Oh, that's precious. Yeah, I know you're embarrassed to admit you're related to the likes of me. But in case you forgot, I'm part of this family, too."

"I'm not the one who forgot, Dee."

"She's my grandmother, Davy. You could've told me she was in the hospital. I had to hear it from somebody else. Do you have any idea how much of an idiot I felt like? Looked like, too, I'm sure. What kind of moron doesn't even know when her own grandmother's been in the hospital for two days?"

"A day and a half," he corrected automatically. He should have known that she wasn't concerned about Gram's welfare. She was concerned about looking bad in front of the neighbors.

"Hunh?"

"I said it was a day and a half. Not two days." Wearily, he added, "Who'd you hear it from?"

"Etta Crowley. Jack's sister. She heard it from Jo, who heard it from Sally Springer. She's a nurse at the hospital."

Of course the news had come through Jo. The town gossip. She'd probably also told half the town that she'd seen him sneaking away from Annie Kendall's place around seven on Sunday morning. "I appreciate your concern," he said stiffly. "I'll pass it on to Gram when I see her."

"Fuck you, Davy. You know I care about what happens to Gram. I'm not so hardhearted that I don't give a shit."

"Good," he said, leaning back in his chair, "because we have some pretty serious decisions to make, and I'm not making them alone. I'm calling a family meeting, and the three of us are going to do this together. That way, later on down the road, nobody can point the finger of guilt at anybody else, because whatever decisions we make will be mutual."

"The three of us? You, me and Gram?"

"You, me and Brian. I already called him. He's flying home."

Astonishment flashed across her face, and he realized for the first time in his life just how unattractive his sister was. "Oh, that's just peachy," she said. "We really need him around. Tell me he's not bringing his boyfriend with him."

"Stop it," he said, his voice gone suddenly hard and cold. "He's your goddamn brother, Dee, and if I hear you say one bad word about him—a single negative comment—I swear to God I'll wrap my fingers around your neck and squeeze it until you turn blue."

"You're crazy," she said. "You're absolutely fucking apeshit crazy."

"Yeah? Well, take a look in the mirror, sis, because I'm pretty sure it's a genetic condition."

"Asshole." She stormed back out the same way she'd come in, like a battleship going full speed ahead, laying waste to whatever fell in her path. He heard the front door of the building open, heard his nephew's whiny complaint abruptly cut off when the door slammed shut again behind her.

In the hallway outside his door, soft footsteps approached. Dixie peeked around the door frame as if she wasn't quite sure she dared to step inside. "Is it safe to come in," she said, "or do you still have your boxing gloves on?"

He glared at her and snapped, "What do you want?"

"A lobster dinner and a pair of Chippendales dancers for starters. After that, we can negotiate. Right now, I have the prints from the break-in at the Twilight. They just came back from the state police."

He let out a hard breath, rubbed his temple with the palm of his hand. "Thanks."

"Can I say one thing?"

"Could I stop you even if I wanted to? Make it short."

"I just wanted to say bravo." She handed him the paperwork and gave him a round of silent applause. "About time somebody put her in her place. I went to school with Brian. He was one of my best friends. I don't give a damn if he sleeps with women or men or three-headed aliens. She's got no right to talk about him the way she does."

Suddenly exhausted, he said wearily, "She doesn't know any better."

"Maybe she didn't before. She sure as hell does now."

After Dixie left, he skimmed the information from the state police. They'd been able to match nearly all the fingerprints Pete had sent them, and had come up with a list of names. All the names but one were familiar. A couple of them had records; most didn't. Ziggy Llewellyn had a six-year-old OUI bust and one simple assault charge a couple of years later. Merle Atwood had been arrested for possession of marijuana eighteen years ago in Salem, Oregon. The rest were probably regular customers and solid citizens. Every damn one of them would have to be checked out.

He paused when he reached the lone unfamiliar name. Robin Spinney. It didn't ring any bells, wasn't even vaguely familiar. Who the hell was she?

Because he figured she had the entire Twilight Video customer database stored in that spiky little head of hers, he picked up the phone and called Estelle. "Does the name Robin Spinney ring any bells with you?"

"No. Should it?"

"I'm asking the questions here. She isn't one of your regular customers?"

"Nope. Not even a one-shot deal."

"You're sure?"

"I've been working there for four years, Davy. This town has fewer than five thousand residents. A small fraction of those people rent videos at the Twilight. I've never heard of anybody by that name."

"Okay. I guess you answered my question."

"I guess that means you're not going to answer mine."

"Police business," he said, and hung up the phone.

He sat back in his chair, frowning at the memo-laden bulletin board. There was too much going on in his life, in his head. He'd reached the point of information overload. He needed to clear his head, do some thinking. Preferably behind the steering wheel, with the window rolled down as he cruised the back roads of Serenity. He always did his best thinking while he drove. Maybe, while he was out there, he could kill two birds with one stone and try to track down Ziggy Llewellyn and Merle Atwood. He doubted either one had anything to do with the break-in at the Twilight, but they were the only two people on the list who had police records, so it was the logical place to start.

He tucked the list of names into the case file and walked out to the reception area. "I'm going out for a while," he told Dixie. "Think you can hold down the fort?"

"I handled it for years before you got here," she said smugly, swiveling in her secretarial chair. "It'll be hard, but I'll try to manage without you."

"Do you talk to Ty this way, too, or is it just me?"

"Hey, you just elevated me to the position of court jester. I'm simply trying to fulfill the requirements of the job."

"I'm surprised he hasn't fired you for insubordination."

Dixie grinned. "He's threatened to once or twice. But he knows I'm indispensable. He says I can read his mind. He even calls me Radar. As in O'Reilly. Get it?"

"That one I get. I'm not really as dumb as a box of rocks, I just look that way. So you read Ty's mind, and he likes it?"

"Apparently so. I'm still here, aren't I?"

"Absolutely amazing. Don't be reading my mind, Dix. You wouldn't like what you found there."

"Hey," she said to his retreating back, "if I need you—"

"Radio, cell phone, beeper," he tossed back over his shoulder without bothering to turn around. "Try not to need me for an hour or two."

Theodore Constantine was a sociopath.

It was a label he wore with great pride. He liked the word, liked its sibilant sound as it slithered off his tongue. He liked the fact that he shared a first name with that other, most infamous of sociopaths, Ted Bundy. Like Bundy, Teddy Constantine liked to kill. It excited him. Not in a sexual way. No, with Teddy it was all about power. There was nothing so thrilling as the possession of absolute control, nothing so gratifying as the look on the face of his victim at the precise instant when they realized there was no hope of escape. For Teddy Constantine, killing was the ultimate power trip.

And he was good at it. That was why Marcus Brogan had hired him. Teddy was an accomplished killer whose services could be bought—for the right price—and Brogan had been willing and able to pay his price. Half up front, the other half when the job was done. That was his standard fee structure. They were really quite a lot alike, he and Marcus. Both of them cold, calculating, and acquisitive. They both got off on power. Except that Brogan craved the kind of power that controlled people's lives, while Teddy craved the kind of power that ended them. But that was a minor difference, a surface discrepancy. On the inside, they could have been twins.

Tailing Louis Farley was about as challenging as playing dodgeball at recess. Farley wasn't exactly a master of deception, although he did a creditable job of changing his appearance to suit his needs. Farley could blend in anyplace, anytime. It was a useful skill for someone in his line of work. At least his frequent costume changes kept Teddy mildly entertained while he waited for something more exciting to happen.

But tailing Farley was critical if he wanted to locate his target and complete his mission. Teddy Constantine was a hired killer, not a detective. Generally he was given a name and an address, and he went over and did the job, tied it all up neatly in a big puffy bow, collected the balance of his fee, and that was that. This was the first time he could remember being paid to kill somebody who was invisible. Not that he wasn't up to the challenge. But he was more than willing to concede that Farley was the pro when it came to locating missing persons. Teddy would let him do the dirty work, then he'd swoop in and reap the rewards. As long as he kept Farley in his sights—and he was making sure not to lose the little chameleon—the guy would eventually lead him directly to Robin Spinney.

And that was the bottom line.

She'd been in a sour mood when she woke up this morning, and nothing that had happened so far today had done a thing to improve it. Sophie had left at the crack of dawn for her babysitting job, dressed in her new white T-shirt and jeans, and so nauseatingly cheerful that Annie wondered if she'd awakened in the Twilight Zone. At nine o'clock, she'd driven Jack Crowley's gas-guzzler into town to fax her list of destroyed items to the insurance company. It was a good thing she'd made a copy first, because the fax machine ate her original, and she ended up having to fax a copy of the copy instead. Then Estelle had called to ask if Annie really needed her today. Boomer, she said, had been complaining about the condition of their trailer, which bore a marked resemblance to Twilight Video after the vandals had hit. She could really use a day to muck the place out.

It was probably just as well. Annie's mood was so vile that she probably would've scared Estelle off permanently if the young woman had shown up to help her. So she'd given Estelle the day off, leaving herself alone to stew. And Annie Kendall stewing wasn't a pretty sight.

She'd finished painting last night around eleven-thirty. It wasn't the best paint job she'd ever seen, but it would have to do. She'd almost managed to cover the word BITCH. So what if it kept bleeding through? Maybe she could work it into some kind of artsy, ultramodern wall decoration. Stranger things had been called art; it was worth considering. In the meantime, today was devoted to sorting the movies they'd salvaged and trying to put them in at least semi-alphabetical order.

It was a killer job, tedious and crazy-making, not made any more pleasant by the news she got from Sonny Gaudette. He needed another day or two to finish the car. He'd located a radiator and was pretty sure it would fit, but he hadn't yet had time to run over to Rumford Point and pick it up. He'd heard she was using Jack Crowley's pickup truck, so he knew she wasn't without transportation. He'd get to it as soon as possible. If she didn't hear from him tomorrow, she should give him a ring on Wednesday morning. The Volvo would be ready by then for sure.

Wednesday, for God's sake. Another two days. Not a damn thing was going her way, and the frustration was so intense that she had a strong urge to sit down and bawl her eyes out. This wasn't the kind of thing that happened to her. She wasn't the kind of woman who had tantrums or wept when things went wrong. If she had been, she never would have made it this far; Brogan would have caught her and killed her months ago. In Annie Kendall's book, crying was a waste of time, time that was far better spent on solving problems instead of wallowing in them. She knew this intellectually, but for some inexplicable reason, she couldn't seem to get it on an emotional level. Not today, anyway. She couldn't even blame it on hormones, because it wasn't that time of the month. She simply felt as though the only possible solution to her problems at this particular point in time was a good, hard cry.

As long as she was making a laundry list of complaints, she might as well add Davy Hunter's name. God *damn* him. *I'll call you,* he'd written. Right. That was the line they all used when what they really meant was "Kiss off, sister." It didn't matter that barely more than a day ago, she'd vowed to have nothing further to do with him, had promised herself to not even answer the phone if it should ring, had scrubbed and soaped and showered every trace of him from her body. It didn't matter that it had only been thirty-one hours and change since he'd left her side and slunk away like a thief in the night. She'd expected him to call, had counted on him calling. She might have no intention of getting involved with the man, but damn it, she wanted that decision to be hers. By not calling, he'd taken the decision out of her hands, and she was furious about it.

She shouldn't be surprised that he'd wimped out. Davy

Hunter wasn't the kind of man to make a commitment. He'd been up-front with her right from the start. He hadn't painted her any rosy pictures of love ever after. It should have been clear to her that what had happened between them hadn't been about romance. It had been about hunger, about need. About two people who saw something in each other and reached out and grabbed it.

So why was she expecting more from him?

Maybe it had something to do with the age-old biological imperative that preprogrammed men to be warriors and women to be nest-builders. If so, it wasn't a side of herself that she found particularly admirable. This was the twenty-first century, and she didn't believe in that "Me Tarzan, You Jane" baloney. She'd seen too many women sucked into it, like lint into a dryer filter, trapped by their own hand because they believed it was better to live with a lousy man than with no man at all. Many of them, even if they figured out the truth, couldn't figure out how to extricate themselves once the trap closed behind them.

She'd always taught Sophie to be independent, to make her own way in the world. To depend on herself and nobody else, because when it came right down to it, who else could you depend on? Too much of life was the result of random circumstance. Unexpected events occurred even in the best of marriages. Look at her and Mac. How could she have predicted that she'd be a widow at the age of thirty-four? She'd had to be smart and resourceful to keep herself and Sophie afloat, even more so after she found out the truth about Mac's death. She'd tried to provide Sophie with a worthy role model, had tried to be the kind of mother, the kind of woman, that she would have admired as a young girl.

She thought she'd done a pretty good job of it. So why in God's name had she gone all girly and clingy the instant Davy Hunter gave her more than the time of day? She'd never been that way with Mac. They'd had a warm, rock-solid relationship based on mutual trust, mutual respect. With him, she'd never been tempted to act like a spoiled princess. At the age of thirty-six, she was a little old for that kind of adolescent behavior. She abhorred weakness in other women, yet here she was, obsessing over a man's failure to phone her a whopping thirty-one hours after he climbed out of her bed. It was totally adolescent, totally irrational, and it made her mad as hell.

She set an armload of videos on the floor and glared at the small shelving unit on the end wall. For some reason, it was irritating the hell out of her, probably because it seemed such a poor use of space. Whoever the bonehead was who'd nailed it up there, she could have done a far better job of designing it than he'd done. She walked over to it and examined the way it was put together. A little cut here, a couple of nails there, and she could convert the ugly thing into something that was both usable and aesthetically pleasing.

She shoved a clump of hair behind her ear and marched across the street. Sophie answered the door. In the background, Annie could hear shouts and laughter and loud music, some kind of nauseating, indecipherable noise, heavy on the drums and the power chords. Jolene would be ecstatic to know that Sophie was introducing her sons to Goth rock. "Mom," Sophie said, sounding surprised. "Are you here to check up on me?"

"While I think that's never a bad idea, I've actually come to talk to one of the boys. Can you grab one of them for me? Either one will do."

Sophie looked at her askance, undoubtedly wondering what her aged mother could possibly have to say to a nine-year-old boy. Shrugging, Soph disappeared into the depths of the house. After a minute or two, the ruckus quieted down. She returned with one of the twins, who ran into the living room, skidding the last twelve feet across the hardwood floor in socks that had probably been white a couple of hours ago. "Hi," he said.

"Hi. Are you Sam or Jake?"

"I'm Sam."

"Tell me, Sam, does your dad own a power saw?"

"You mean one of those electric things with the big round blade? Sure. You wanna borrow it?"

"Do you think he'd mind?"

"Nah. He thinks you're awesome. I heard him tell my mother that after you fixed the motel roof. He said he hadn't seen too many girls willing to tackle something like that."

She followed him to the garage, waited while he raised the door. "What did your mom say about that?"

Crossing the cement floor, still in his stocking feet, he said with the oblivious candor of a nine-year-old, "She told him to roll his tongue back into his head and stop drooling over that unattached blonde across the street."

Annie blanched. "Yikes."

Sam opened a cabinet beneath Jack Crowley's work bench, rummaged around, and pulled out his father's circular saw. "Here you go. You know how to run it? If you need any help figuring it out, Dad'll be home in a couple of hours."

"I'm fine." She'd already done enough damage in that area. "Tell him thanks, and I'll bring it back later tonight. Okay?"

"Okay. Oh, wait, you need safety glasses, too. Dad says you always have to wear safety glasses when you run a power saw. So you won't get sawdust in your eyes."

She took the saw from him, waited while he dug around some more. "Your dad's a smart man," she said.

"He's okay." Sam pulled out a pair of safety glasses and handed them to her. "So, are you gonna, like, take down a wall or something?"

"Something," she said. "But nothing quite that ambitious. Thanks, Sam."

He heard the screech of a circular saw the minute he pulled into the parking lot. Annie was inside the video shop, giving what-for to some poor, unfortunate slab of wood. Davy climbed out of the cruiser, closed the door behind him, and just listened, hoping to Christ she knew how to run the damn thing. Otherwise, she was apt to lose an arm or a leg. He crossed the broken asphalt, climbed the steps and, shading his eyes with his hands, peered through the window. God only knew what she was up to, but the place looked almost as bad as it had after the break-in. Hundreds of movies stacked in random piles all around the room, sawdust and wood chips flying, pine shelving cut into odd lengths lying around on the floor.

At least she'd had a new door installed, a sturdy steel door that would keep out the mildly motivated criminals, the ones who wouldn't try very hard. He rattled the doorknob, but the door was locked, so he rapped on the glass instead. Annie looked up and saw him standing there, and the circular saw in her hands whined its way to silence. She set it down and peeled off the safety goggles, tossing them onto the makeshift work bench she'd created using two kitchen chairs and an old door. Her blue eyes caught and held him. There was something faintly accusatory in them, although he couldn't quite pin it down. Crossing the room briskly, she undid the lock and flung the door open. "Hunter," she said, her intonation turning the single word into something halfway between a greeting and a question. "What are you doing here?"

It wasn't a particularly auspicious beginning. "Bad day," he said, and stepped inside. Examining the devastation she'd wrought at closer range, he added, "I guess I could ask you the same thing. What are you doing? Here?"

She shut the door and locked it. Looking around, she said, "I seemed to have a compelling urge to slice something to ribbons."

"I can see that. Was there anything Freudian about this compulsion?"

Scowling with a ferocity that would have been comical if she hadn't been so deadly earnest about it, she rubbed absently at her lower back. "Don't worry, Hunter. The urge didn't include castration fantasies."

"I'm so relieved."

"You should be."

She was mad at him. That much he understood. It was the why that eluded him. Had he committed some sexual faux pas? Besides the obvious one of sneaking out while she was still asleep? She'd enjoyed their little rendezvous the other night as much as he did. So what was wrong? Had they changed the rules while he wasn't looking? He'd left her a note, promised to call, only he'd done better than call. He'd shown up in person. It should have earned him a few brownie points. Instead, for some unknown reason, she was furious with him, and doing a damn poor job of hiding it.

She sniffed the air and wrinkled her nose. "What is that terrible smell?"

"Wet goat."

"Oh," she said, as though it were a perfectly rational explanation. "Well. Excuse me." Turning her back on him, she picked up a hammer and a length of pine, scooped up a couple of nails, and with hard, furious whacks of the hammer, she began nailing the board to the wall.

It was a good thing he was out of the line of fire. The way she was whaling at that nail, her hammer strokes could be lethal. She finished pounding a two-inch spike into the wall and started in on another. *Wham.* She hit the nail so hard the building shook. *Whack.* It shook again. "How's your grandmother?" she asked between wallops.

"About like you'd expect. Hurting, frustrated and home-sick."

She picked up a third nail and began driving it into the pine board. "What's the prognosis?"

"Her doctor thinks she'll heal pretty quickly." He crossed his arms and watched her work. "Assuming they can keep her still long enough to heal. It won't be easy. That woman has more energy than a tornado."

"How soon—" *whack, whack* "—will she be able to go home?"

He drew in a long, hard breath. "That's just the thing," he said, leaning his hips against the checkout counter. "She may not be able to. Doc Colfer thinks she's reached the point where she needs round-the-clock supervision."

"I'm sorry to hear that." She picked up a second piece of wood, examined it closely, and began nailing it to the first one.

"Annie? What the hell are you doing?"

"I'm rebuilding this ugly thing." She missed the nail, instead putting a neat, hammer-shaped hole in the drywall. "God *damn* it!"

"What's wrong?"

"Nothing's wrong. Can't a woman do a little redecorating without being dragged through the Spanish Inquisition?" She whacked again with the hammer, this time hitting the nail squarely and driving it deep into the soft pine.

He pulled away from the counter and made his way cautiously across the room. She raised the hammer high in the air above her head, and he ducked. In that instant of hesitation when it quivered in the air, poised for the imminent downstroke, he caught her forearm in an iron grip.

"Annie," he said softly, "put the goddamn hammer down."

For an instant, he thought she'd fight him. Then he felt her weaken. Her grip on the hammer loosened and he peeled it out of her hand, disarming her. He set the hammer on the work bench and rested his hands on her quaking shoulders. "Want to talk about it?" he said.

Silence. But her shoulders continued to quake. Could it be possible that she was crying? This woman who seemed as tough as the nails she was driving? "Annie?" he said.

"I am so…damn tired…of this."

He didn't know what she was talking about, but her tone, weary and defeated, cut him to the bone. "Tired of what?" he asked with a tenderness that nibbled with little sharp teeth at his comfort level.

"I can't have a relationship with you," she said to the wall. "Or with any other man, for that matter. I have…issues. Huge issues. Insurmountable issues. I can't live my life like a normal woman. It's so unfair."

Because he didn't understand what she meant, he didn't respond, just made circular stroking motions against her shoulders with his thumbs.

"I can drive a nail as well as any man." The words were defiant, but he could hear the tears building up behind them.

"Sure you can," he said. "I've been watching. You have a witness. I'll testify in court if you need me to."

A single sob broke through, and he turned her by the shoulders. "I don't even know my daughter anymore," she said. "She looks like something out of the *Rocky Horror Picture Show.* That idiot Gaudette can't even be bothered to pick up the damn radiator. Doesn't he have somebody he can send after it? And the fax machine ate my papers. You can't even trust a piece of office machinery to work right any more. And no matter how many layers of paint I put over it, that damn word just keeps coming back to haunt me." She squared her shoulders and sniffed. "Estelle didn't come to work today. Boomer made her stay home and clean house. What was I supposed to do, Hunter? Insist that she come in anyway? Damn it! Have you ever tried to alphabetize five thousand movies all at once? All by yourself?"

"Uh…no," he said carefully. "Bad day, hunh?"

"The worst." Those blue eyes, huge with unshed tears, ate a hole right through his heart. "Damn it, Hunter," she said. "Why didn't you call?"

He thought of all the possible responses he might come up with and rejected every one. "I'm sorry," he said instead, not really knowing what he was apologizing for, but understanding that at this particular instant, he was exclusively to blame for everything from global warming to the birth of hip-hop. Her tears spilled over, and Davy folded her into his arms and held her as she sobbed wildly and inexplicably against his shoulder. He stroked her hair with the palm of his hand, but didn't bother to offer soothing words, just the comfort of his warmth and solidity. It was safer this way. He probably wouldn't come up with the right words anyway.

He buried his face in her hair and drew in the sweet scent of woman. Perfume? Shampoo? Whatever it was, it smelled a hell of a lot better than *eau de* goat, and had a direct and immediate effect on his libido. That was great. Here she was, crying in his arms as though her heart were breaking, while he stood here sniffing her hair and getting horny. It was a nasty little trick that Mother Nature had perpetrated upon the male of the species because she was a woman and wanted revenge on men for their superior physical strength and difficulty in maintaining monogamy.

She finally stopped shaking, and her crying had subsided to an occasional hiccup. "I feel like an ass," she said, snuffling like a pig rooting for truffles. "I'm so sorry. I can't imagine what got into me."

"Stress," he said. "Believe me, I know all about it."

She turned her face up to his, and her poignant expression tugged at something inside him, something only peripherally connected to his libido. Gently, he kissed the wet track of a tear from her cheek. He intended to stop there, but she shuddered and exhaled a fluttery, warm breath, and he couldn't help nibbling at the corner of her bottom lip. She tasted so damn good. He pressed his tongue to her lip, traced its outline. Hesitantly, she opened her mouth and touched the tip of her tongue to his.

Instant hard-on. Was this the real reason he'd come here? Not sure he cared, Davy drew her tongue into his mouth and sucked on it. She moaned softly, and needles of anticipation danced in his belly. This wasn't good. It was two-thirty in the afternoon, and Dixie was probably starting to wonder where the hell he'd disappeared to. He needed to get back to work before she sent out a search party. Anybody who went looking for him wouldn't have much trouble finding him. His car was parked out front, big as life, with the Serenity Police logo on the door.

"Aren't you...supposed to be...on duty?"

"It's a temporary position." With his tongue, he traced a path down the long, silken column of her neck. "What are they gonna do, fire me?" He unbuttoned her shirt, his mouth following the path laid out by his fingers, and she shuddered as he neared her breasts. He wanted to get his hands on them again, wanted to take them in his mouth and suck on them until she wept with pleasure. She'd nearly gone ballistic when he did it before.

"This behavior," she said breathlessly, "is...unbecoming to a...police officer."

"Good thing I turn into a pumpkin in seven weeks. How long before your daughter comes home?"

"At least an hour. Maybe longer. I'm still mad at you, Hunter."

Through the sheer lace of her bra, her nipple, rock-hard and flushed, was clearly visible. "I can tell," he said, and closed his mouth over it.

"Oh, God," she moaned. "Stop. Please." But her hands at the back of his head urged him to continue.

He paused to slide the strap to her brassiere down her arm. Carefully, so he wouldn't tear the exquisitely delicate and undoubtedly expensive lingerie, he lifted her breast free. It was round and firm and high. Not too small, not too large. Perfect. Her skin was pale, revealing a road map of blue veins beneath. He touched his tongue to her bare skin, and the arms around his neck tightened. Pleased by her response, he lay his tongue flat against that sensitive peak. She gasped, and he circled it with his tongue, then drew it deeply into his mouth.

She went limp against him, her hands cradling his face against her. "Davy," she gasped. "We can't do this."

He gently scraped his teeth against her skin, and heard her sharp intake of breath. "You're giving me mixed signals," he said against her skin. "Make up your mind, for Christ's sake."

"We can't do it *here,* idiot. We're on display. Come on."

Oh, shit. He was thinking with his dick, instead of his brain. She took his hand and led him through the back door toward the stairs. But instead of going upstairs, she turned left into a small bathroom. He followed her in and closed the door. The place wasn't much bigger than a coat closet. "Lock it," she said, dropping her shirt to the floor. Reaching behind her, she unclasped the bra and dropped that, too, while he just stood there, mesmerized by the sight of all that soft, white skin. "I don't care if you leave your clothes on," she said, skimming her Tommy Hilfigers down over her hips, "but do you think you could at least take the gun off first?"

Reality caught up to him, and he quickly divested himself of the shoulder holster, the goat-scented shirt. He kicked off his shoes and socks, stepped out of his pants, and reached for her. She flowed into him, all that soft, naked skin warm and damp and sticky against his. He kissed her, a hot, wet, openmouthed kiss, their tongues tangling, driving him near the point of madness. Reaching down between them, he slipped his hand between her thighs and slid two fingers into all that moist heat.

She cried out, squirmed and wiggled and gasped as he stroked that most sensitive part of her with a liquid, feather-light touch. Christ Almighty, she was hot. Slick and hot and ready, almost as ready as he was. He took a quick glance around the room. There weren't many options. Backing toward the john, he sat on the seat cover and leaned back against the tank. It wasn't exactly a romantic position, but at this point, they were so far beyond romance that if they'd been in the middle of Times Square, they probably would have done it right there on the sidewalk. Annie braced herself against his shoulders and straddled his hips, and he pulled her down onto his lap, sinking deep inside hot, wet woman.

It was the wildest ride he'd ever taken, this daytime quickie with Ms. Annie Kendall at 2:45 on a Monday afternoon astride the john in the restroom out back of the Twilight Video. He'd never known a woman so combustible. She slithered and bucked and wriggled, gasped and moaned and uttered incredible sounds he couldn't even identify, threw her head back and rode him hard, all the while giving him a bird's-eye view of breasts like plump little apples, so luscious he could have eaten them. Come to think of it, he'd already given them a nibble or two, hadn't he? This little slice of afternoon delight was strictly her deal. All he could do was lean back against the toilet tank, let her take the lead, and hold on tight for the ride.

It was over too soon. Still shuddering from the aftershocks of a blistering climax, she rested her cheek against his bare shoulder and said weakly, "That wasn't supposed to happen."

Still deep inside her, still lost to the tiny thrills that came with each ongoing spasm of her body around him, he buried a hand in her hair. "I'm sorry," he said tenderly.

"Why is it that every time we make love, you apologize afterward? It doesn't do much for my ego."

He pressed his face to her hair. "Christ, Annie, you're a

hard woman to understand. But I can't seem to stay away from you." It was more of an admission than he was comfortable making, but it was the truth. And he suspected it meant he was in trouble.

"I know. Every time I swear to God I won't even look at you again, you walk into the room and the next thing I know, we're both naked. It's as though my brain stops functioning whenever you're around. What is it about you, Hunter?" She seemed honestly bewildered. "This just doesn't happen to me."

"Maybe it's fate."

He felt, rather than saw, her smile. "Maybe. More likely pheromones. What time is it?"

Davy glanced at the watch that was the only piece of clothing he still wore. "Ten after three."

"We still have a little longer. This is so nice."

"Yeah. It is." It wasn't the easiest thing in the world to admit, that he enjoyed just holding her in his arms, naked skin to naked skin, nearly as much as he enjoyed the blistering-hot sex. He wasn't ready for this. It was too soon. He hadn't worked through his grief over Chelsea. He needed closure before he traded one blond-haired obsession for another one. And he hadn't planned on making that trade. Not now, not ever. It reminded him of that old saying about the road to hell and good intentions. But somehow the decision had been taken out of his hands, steamrolled into a big, fat nothing by lust and something else, something more substantial and enduring. The lust he could handle. It was the something else that was tearing him apart. Like a mugger bent on destruction, it had jumped him while he was looking the other way.

He should have stayed at his desk, should have spent the afternoon shuffling mindless paperwork. He'd gone out to clear his head, and look where it had gotten him. Instead of clarifying things, he'd further muddied up the waters by getting in deeper, no pun intended. This was his life, damn it. He needed to take back control, before it began running him instead of the other way around.

"Annie?" he said softly. "I need to go. I've been gone too long already."

She raised her head and looked at him. It was back, the hint of accusation in those blue eyes. But she didn't argue. She was a grown woman, a rational adult, and she knew he had a job to get back to.

When they separated, he felt an overwhelming sense of loss. It scared him more than anything else he'd felt for this woman. While he'd been inside her, he'd been confused, pulled in a number of different directions, unsure which road to take. Now, all he wanted was to be back inside her, and to hell with the rest of the world. It was a scary, dangerous place to be.

Annie found a washcloth on the shelf beneath the sink, and they both took care of business, then rummaged around in the pile of clothing on the floor, locating and handing each other essential items of clothing as they were unearthed. They dressed quickly and silently in the tiny room. As he fumbled with his shoulder harness, she stepped forward and helped him with it, adjusting it to a comfortable position and making sure the strap was pulled snug around him.

"You seem pretty familiar with that thing," he said. "If I didn't know better, I'd think you'd done this before."

Her hands hesitated for the briefest of seconds before her eyes, cool and distant, met his. "It's not exactly rocket science," she said. "It's only a gun belt." She dropped her hands and stepped back, and he felt as though he'd been dismissed.

"You're still mad at me, aren't you?"

"No."

But he thought he saw the telltale hint of a tear forming at the corner of her eye. Reaching out a hand, he cupped her cheek, brushed his thumb over it. Drawing her face to his, he touched his mouth to hers with a tenderness he hadn't known he possessed. The kiss was featherlight, gentle and sweet, so sweet it shredded his insides into a bloody, unholy pulp. Which was pretty much how he'd been feeling ever since he'd seen her by the side of the road, standing over her dead Volvo.

God help him. He'd have been better off if he'd left her there.

He pulled away, adjusted the gun belt one last time. "I'll let myself out," he said.

She nodded and wrapped her arms around herself, rubbing at her upper arms as though she was cold, although it was a solid eighty degrees outside. He turned his back on her then, walked briskly and resolutely back to his cruiser without looking back. He started up the engine and raced it for a minute. Feeling as though he'd barely escaped with his life, he left in such a hurry to get away from her that he laid rubber pulling out onto the highway.

Coward. Lily-livered, chickenshit coward.

The joy of electronic eavesdropping was starting to wear thin.

Louis was so tired of the entire Sarnacki family that he wished they'd all hop on a slow boat to China—Rosa the maid included—and float away, never to be seen or heard from again. For days that seemed more like months, he'd been sitting here, parked in various spots around the neighborhood, slowly dying of boredom. He hadn't seen his buddy, the one in the Buick Century, since Saturday. Either the guy was lying low, or else he'd given up. Louis was hoping for the latter, but banking on the former. Whoever had paid this guy to tail him wasn't likely to give up after a single day. More likely, Buick Man was stretched out on a motel bed some-

where, probably directly across the street from the rat hole
where Louis was staying, watching *Seinfeld* reruns on cable
TV and checking Louis's door with a pair of Bushnell bin-
oculars during the commercials. All while Louis sat slumped
on his tailbone in this rental car, with its AM/FM radio and
no CD player, trying to find a Detroit-area radio station that
was even remotely listenable. No bed, no cable TV, no bathroom. Just Louis, the Sarnacki family, and Q95 FM.

At least he was getting caught up on his reading. He'd finally finished Nora, and had started in on Susan Elizabeth
Phillips. SEP, as she was known to romance fans around the
globe, might not be able to write a heavy-duty sex scene the
way Nora could, but she had other redeeming qualities, among
them a witty, slapstick kind of humor that made her Louis's
second-favorite author. Her series about the Chicago Stars
football team was side-splittingly funny, and disproved the
commonplace belief that a romance with an athlete hero
wouldn't sell. Hah! He pictured SEP laughing uproariously at
that one as she steered wheelbarrows full of money to the
bank.

He was so caught up in the story that he almost missed
what was coming from his earpiece. Sarnacki's calls were so
boring, so routine, that he'd started to tune them out. When
the woman asked for Bobby by his first name, it registered at
a subconscious level, but it wasn't until Sarnacki answered
and she called him Uncle Bobby that Louis scrambled upright
so suddenly that SEP went flying to the floor. He quickly
pressed the button of the recording device he hadn't used until
now, tightened the earpiece, and listened intently.

"What's wrong?" Uncle Bobby asked. "You sound down."

Annie sighed and rested her elbows on the kitchen table.
Running a hand through her hair, she said, "It's about a million different things. For starters, the video store was broken

into, and it's been such a hassle trying to put it all back to-gether that I'm ready to bite somebody. Then there's—"

"Hold it. Wait a minute. Your place was broken into?"

"Somebody vandalized it to within an inch of its life. I sus-pect it was teenagers, but of course we're not sure. The po-lice are investigating it, but you know how that goes. Especially in a small town."

"Are you sure it's not related to—" He left the sentence hanging between them.

"Not a hundred percent. But how could Brogan have found me that quickly? Besides, it's not his style. This looks more like the work of some local yahoos out for fun on a night when the bowling leagues have taken over the local alley and there isn't anywhere else to go if you're too young to drink legally."

"Annie, honey, you're starting to sound cynical. That's not like you. Are you sure there isn't something else?"

With her cell phone tucked between her ear and her shoul-der, she got up from the table and walked to the sink. Dou-ble-checked to make sure that Sophie's bedroom door was closed. The music—and she used that term loosely—coming from behind it was loud enough to kill a rhinoceros dead in its tracks, like an opera singer shattering glass. "I met a man," she said carefully.

"And?"

"What do you mean, and?" She took a glass from the cab-inet and filled it with water. "I can't do it, that's what. It's an absolute impossibility."

"Are you trying to convince me, or yourself?" When she failed to respond, he added, "Annie, you're only thirty-six years old. You can't spend the rest of your life alone. Sophie's going to grow up one of these days in the not-too-distant fu-ture. She'll be off to college, or getting married, and there you'll be, sitting in your rocking chair every evening, watch-ing the sun set all by yourself. Is that what you want?"

She took a sip of water and said, "Do I really have a choice?"

"Of course you have a choice. You're already forgetting what I told you."

"Right, put down roots. How am I supposed to do that? By lying to him? That's a really great foundation for a relationship. Base it on lies and then keep piling them on. Maybe at our fiftieth anniversary party I can say, 'Honey, there's something I've been meaning to tell you.'"

"It's not that big a lie—"

"Damn it, Bobby, he thinks my name is Annie Kendall! If you ask me, that's a pretty big lie."

"You *are* Annie Kendall. That's what it says on your driver's license and your birth certificate. It's what it says on the deed to that motel you bought. It's who you are now. Who you were before doesn't matter. You're still the same person."

"It doesn't say Annie Kendall inside my heart!" And that was the real issue, she realized, the one thing she couldn't live with. Not if she wanted to maintain any self-respect. She could lie to the world, but not to herself. "When you make love to a man," she said roughly, "and he calls out your name, you'd like it to be the right one."

"Oh, shit. You're right. Of course you're right. I'm so sorry, sweetheart."

"I'm so confused. I don't know who I am any more. Am I Annie Kendall, or am I Robin Spinney? I thought I'd put all those doubts aside, but meeting him has just set them back in motion."

"Maybe you should just tell him the truth."

"I've thought about that. But I can't. I don't dare. There's too much at stake. If it was just me, I might consider it. But there's Sophie to think of. I won't put her in further jeopardy, not for any man. I'll keep her safe, or die trying."

"It won't come to that."

"It did for Mac. I can't let that happen to Sophie."

"I wish I had an answer for you. But even if I did, it wouldn't be the right one. You have to find your own answers."

"That's why I love you," she said. "You understand me. You listen without being judgmental. You don't try to tell me how to live my life. You can't know how much that means to me. Just being able to talk to you helps so much. If I didn't have you, I'd have nobody to talk to. I can't tell Sophie these things. She's too young to understand. And God knows, I can't talk to Dad about it. He just doesn't get me at all. He never did."

"Have you talked to him lately?"

"I called him, the day after I got here. We had our usual go-round. The man is stubborn as granite, and about as warm. I just can't get through to him. I've pretty much given up trying."

"Sometimes these things take time."

"He's already had thirty-six years. How much more time does he need?"

Sophie's door opened, spilling noise into the room. She walked in her stocking feet to the refrigerator, opened it, and stood there staring at its contents. "I have to go," Annie said into the phone. "Sophie's looking for her supper."

"Give her my love. And keep me posted."

In the jeans and white T-shirt, Sophie looked sweet and innocent, almost happy. Until she opened her mouth and shattered the illusion. "There's nothing in the house to eat," she said plaintively.

"I have a better idea," Annie said. "Let's go out for supper."

"You mean there's someplace in this town to get a decent meal? Besides McDonald's?"

Annie scouted around for her purse, found it buried in the

couch cushions. "I've heard Lenny's Café serves a pretty good meal, if you like old-fashioned home cooking."

Sophie didn't look convinced. "You mean that divehole downtown? It looks to me like they'd specialize in roach-burger sandwiches."

Annie dug inside the purse and pulled out Jack's truck keys. Twirling them around her finger, she said, "Aw, come on, Soph. Live life on the edge for once."

"You're scaring me, Mom. Who the hel—I mean heck—are you?"

I'm a woman who had screaming sex with a man I barely know on a bathroom toilet seat in the middle of the afternoon, she thought. *And I loved every minute of it. What does that make me? I haven't a clue.*

But of course she couldn't say it to Sophie. "I'm the woman who's paying for your supper," she said dryly. "Now, dress your feet, and let's go sample the exotic cuisine of western Maine."

Among his peers, Louis Farley was known as a hacker extraordinaire. He understood computers, understood the way they operated, the way they thought, the way their little hearts beat to the tune of numeric code. What most people couldn't figure out how to do, he found so easy it was laughable. Sitting in his motel room with the television on for company, a Big Mac and a Coke on the desk beside his laptop, Louis went to work. Ten minutes later, he was in the phone company's database system. From there, it was an easy hop and skip to the information he needed, the origin of the call that had come into the Robert Sarnacki residence at 4:13 this afternoon. Louis jotted down the number from which the call had been placed, backed out of the system, and pulled up Google. The reverse phone directory identified the number as a Detroit-based cell phone, carried by Am-cell. Did that mean that Robin Spinney, aka Annie Kendall, was still in the area?

It was a good question. Picking up his cell phone, Louis dialed the number just to see what happened. It rang four times and switched over to voice mail. *I'm not available to take your call,* the female voice said. *Please leave a message.* She didn't identify herself as Annie Kendall, but he recognized the voice as belonging to the same woman who'd called Bobby Sarnacki.

Louis glanced at the clock. Five-fifteen. Two-fifteen in Los Angeles. Garcia should be in. He probably could have gotten what he needed by himself, but it was quicker and cleaner this way. He'd given Eduardo Garcia a freebie a couple of years back, when the LAPD detective's wife was running around on him. Louis had brought him photographic proof, Garcia had gotten the divorce he so badly wanted, and the bimbo had known better than to ask for alimony payments. Garcia's gratitude was all-encompassing. Since that time, they'd called on each other whenever the occasion arose to make use of each other's services. It was a great backup plan, like having money in the bank for a rainy day.

His rainy-day backup plan answered the phone, and Louis quickly explained what he needed. "It'll take a few minutes," Garcia said. "You gotta know how to work these people, bring 'em around to your way of thinking. Of course, I don't have to tell you that, do I?"

No, indeedy, he didn't. Louis was an old pro at working people. But some things were easier done with a police badge in hand, and this was one of them.

While he waited, he watched the local news. The city's coffers were running low, and the powers-that-be were thinking about raising property taxes. There'd been a bad accident on I-96, and a stabbing in the downtown area that had left one man dead and a second with serious injuries. The trial of a local pedophile was entering its third day, and the judge had ruled that the defendant's previous convictions weren't admissible in court. Louis shook his head. It was a terrible world out there, and Detroit didn't look like it would pick up any awards for City of the Year. Thank God his time here was nearly at an end. This job had been nothing but a pain from the beginning, and he'd be glad to be home in his tidy little house in a quiet neighborhood outside Tupelo.

A half-hour later, Garcia called back. "Told you I'd get it," he said. "I just turned on a little of that natural charm, and Louise, who sounded old enough to be my grandmother, practically fell at my feet. You were right. It's a Detroit-based cell phone, registered to a Robert Sarnacki."

"Really," Louis said.

"Yeah, but what's really interesting is that the call didn't come from Detroit. Louise told me they can't always pinpoint it with a hundred percent accuracy, but they can come pretty close by tracking which towers it bounced off of. As far as she can tell, the call originated from a little town in Maine called Serenity. Does that help at all?"

"It sure does. Thanks, buddy."

"Hey, next time you're in L.A., look me up. We'll play a couple rounds of golf. Or sit around the club and get shit-faced."

"You've got it," Louis said.

He hung up the phone, looked at the piece of paper in his hand. *Annie Kendall. Serenity, Maine.* "Gotcha," he whispered.

Thirteen

He must be going for some kind of record. Fourteen months without a single visit to the cemetery, then two trips in one week. At least there were no groundskeepers around. The place was deserted, which was just as well, considering the reason he was here. Half the town already thought he was nuts. If he was caught in a cemetery arguing with a dead woman, it would cinch the deal. He picked the dinner hour because he knew most people would be home, watching the Channel 13 news and getting ready to eat. Rush hour, such as it was in Serenity, was over, and it was too early for the evening dog walkers to be out. It was the ideal time to have it out with her once and for all.

In the distance, he heard a dog barking. Probably Andy Lester's black lab. Geronimo barked every night at this time, which didn't endear him to Ethel Crowe, who lived next door to the Lesters and had tried everything short of rat poison to make Geronimo shut up. She'd probably try that if she thought she could get away with it. He wouldn't put it past the old bat. But Serenity was a small town, and Ethel had never bothered to hide how she felt about Andy's dog. If anything ever happened to Geronimo, there'd be a dozen fingers pointing in her direction before nightfall.

The lowering sun threaded fingers of light through the trees. Chelsea's grave sat in a pool of brilliant sunshine. He squatted before it, studied the gravestone with a critical eye. "I imagine you were expecting me," he said. "No big surprise there. You knew every damn thought that went through my head when you were alive, so you probably have a pretty good idea of what I'm thinking now."

Chelsea didn't answer. She just lay there under six feet of dirt, slowly turning back to dirt herself. The thought didn't bother him as much as it used to, back in the early days, when he slept with a light on because the nightmares were so horrific and so vivid. That was what had eventually driven him to the bottle. He'd discovered that if he got shitfaced every night before he went to bed, he could keep the bogeyman in the closet. After a while, it just seemed easier to get through life if he deadened his senses a little. No wonder Chelsea had been hooked on the stuff for so long. When you were chemically impaired, you didn't have to feel, didn't have to worry, didn't have to give a shit about anything. Not even the fact that the woman you loved was slowly rotting in the cold ground.

"It didn't have to turn out this way," he told her now. "If you hadn't been so pig-ass stubborn, you wouldn't be dead now. Do you have any idea how pissed off I was when they pulled you out of the river? If you'd just listened to me for once in your damn life, if you'd just trusted me until I could tell you the truth about what was going on, I wouldn't be sitting here now. We'd be sitting together in one of the booths at Walt's instead, laughing and knocking back a couple of cold ones. I'm still pissed off at you, Chels. You see, you got out of it easy. You died, but I'm the one who spent the last fourteen months in hell."

He watched a blue Toyota pass slowly down the street, waited until it had gone out of sight before he continued.

And what about Jessie? Were you even thinking of her when ou went sailing off into the storm that night in search of jour-alistic glory? That's the thing with you, Chels. You never ought about other people. You always thought about your-elf first. And Jessie's the one who suffered. Christ…I wish ou could see her now. She's come so far, no thanks to you. was Ty and Faith who made the difference for her. If you id one thing right in your entire life, it was picking Faith to e her guardian. I have to give you credit for that. The rest of …"

He took a deep breath. A few feet away, a robin hopped cross the grass, searching industriously for its dinner. "The st of it's pretty much a total loss. Why the hell—" He had stop because his voice broke, and tears—tears, for Christ's ake—stung his eyelids. Davy cleared his throat. "Why the ell it took me twenty years to figure that out, I don't know. ut I finally did. I finally realized that I'm worth more than at. I deserve something better than a woman who sucked e dry and then ate the marrow out of my bones."

He stood up, took a last look at her final resting place. "I on't be back," he said. "This is it, Chels. The big goodbye. gave you twenty years of my life. I'm not giving you any ore. Maybe, if I'm damn lucky and do a few things right, I an make the second half of my life count for something."

He stalked back across the grass, yanked open his car door nd slid into the driver's seat. It wasn't until he started up the ar that he realized his hands were trembling so hard he ouldn't drive. Some police chief he was turning out to be. le couldn't even break up with a dead woman without going pieces. What would happen if he was ever faced with a real mergency?

It took him a few minutes to pull himself together. When finally accomplished the task, he drove home and went raight to his bedroom, bypassing the dog, who was snooz-

ing on the couch. He opened his closet and took down a box
from the shelf. It was loaded with pictures of Chelsea, years
of them, two decades of glossy memories he'd intended to pu
into an album someday. He lifted off the cover and looked dis
passionately at what was there. For a brief instant, he consid
ered disposing of them with kerosene and a flaming rag, bu
thought better of it. He might not want them, but Jessie would

Davy picked up the framed five-by-seven he kept on his
nightstand. Yes, she'd been beautiful, but that beauty had beer
only skin deep. Inside, she'd been cruel and selfish and
thoughtless. And yes, he'd loved her. But he wasn't blind any
longer. The scales had been lifted from his eyes. He under
stood the truth now, and didn't they say the truth would se
you free? She might still be Jessie's mother, thanks to an ac
cident of birth. But she was nothing to him, not any longer
Simply his ex-wife. Ex-lover. Ex-everything. Emphasis on the
ex.

He added the five-by-seven to the box, carefully placed the
lid back on top, and left the box in the center of Jessie's bed
There was no need for explanation. Jess was a smart kid
She'd understand. If she didn't now, she would someday. I
spite of Chelsea's neglect, they'd had a pretty good relation
ship, Jessie and her mom. She'd appreciate the pictures.

He felt a thousand pounds lighter when he pulled out o
the driveway and headed to the hospital for his daily visi
with Gram.

Louis couldn't get out of Detroit quickly enough. He
logged onto the Internet and Googled Serenity, Maine, to see
what he could find out. It was a little town out in the willi
wacks, population about five thousand, and nowhere nea
anything, as far as he could tell. The state of Maine only ha
two major airports. The nearest one big enough to fly into wa
in Portland, and it was still a bit of a haul from there to Seren

ity. He'd have to drive the rest of the way. That meant one more cheap, generic rental car with a smelly ashtray, a steering wheel that had been touched by a thousand germy hands, and a plethora of scratches and dents because nobody was the least bit careful about parking a rental car. The dents and dings were somebody else's problem, so people took advantage.

He called the airport and booked himself on the next flight to Portland. It departed from Detroit around eight-thirty, and landed in Portland around midnight. That was a crummy time to be arriving in a strange city, but it beat spending another night in Detroit. The place was starting to give him the willies, with Buick Man following him around everywhere.

Except that Buick Man had disappeared off the face of the earth. He'd seen no sign of the Buick, no sign of any kind of tail, for twenty-four hours. That bothered him more than being followed, because there was no logical explanation for it. The tail he could understand. Either Brogan didn't completely trust him, or somebody else was piggybacking on the work he'd done, trying to locate Robin Spinney by following him. Either way, it made perfect sense. But he couldn't find any rationale to sufficiently explain why the tail would suddenly be pulled.

It worried him all the way to the airport. Louis kept a watchful eye on the traffic around him, but there was no ugly brown Buick, nobody following too close or for too long. Cars, vans, and pickup trucks came and went at random, none of them alerting his radar, none of them overstaying their welcome. Unless Buick Man had superhuman powers, he wasn't being tailed any longer.

Either that, or Louis was losing his touch.

No, that was just paranoia speaking. If somebody had been following him, he would have known it. His radar was faultless. And Buick Man, whoever he was, was so incompetent that Louis could have been asleep at the wheel and he still would have picked up on the guy.

The thought gave him pause. That kind of incompetence seemed an awful lot like overkill. What if B-Man wasn't incompetent at all? What if Louis had been meant to see him all along? What if the guy had followed him openly and blatantly, then ducked back into the woodwork in order to lull him into a false sense of security?

It sounded crazy, like some movie script where the bad guy lured the detective down the primrose path in order to keep the audience in suspense. But this was real life. In his experience, most of the time things were pretty straightforward. If it walked like a duck and quacked like a duck and had downy white feathers, you could be pretty sure it was a duck.

But the niggling doubt remained: What if he were intended to think it was a duck, when really it was something else entirely?

Edgy for the first time since he'd begun this case, Louis turned in the rental car, stood in line to check his baggage, and went through the metal detector while they X-rayed his carry-on. While he jumped through each of these hoops, he studied the people around him, searching for anybody who might look nervous or secretive or out of place. Anybody who might be looking back at him in a manner that was slightly more than casual. But all he saw were weary travelers, headed to God only knew where at an hour when most of them would probably have preferred to be headed home to bed. Businessmen in wrinkled suits yakking on their cell phones. College kids in jeans and T-shirts, curled up on the floor, heads resting on their L.L. Bean backpacks. A couple of Indian women in saris, eyes downcast as they waited quietly for the boarding call. None of them paid him the least attention, and he decided he really was being paranoid.

It was other thoughts that occupied him during the three-hour flight. In flying to Maine without first calling Brogan, he was going directly against his client's wishes. He'd never done that before. The client's needs always came first with him, and Luke Brogan had clearly instructed him that he was to be notified as soon as Louis located Robin Spinney. There was just one problem with that. Until he knew the truth about what was going on—all of it—he didn't trust Luke Brogan. The man might be his client, but Brogan had lost a great deal of credibility the moment Louis first spied Buick Man tailing him. His instincts were telling him that there was more to this little endeavor than Brogan had let on. Now that he had the information Brogan so badly wanted, Louis was suddenly developing cold feet. Especially after hearing Spinney's conversation with Sarnacki.

"Maybe you should just tell him the truth."

"I've thought about that. But I can't. I don't dare. There's too much at stake. If it was just me, I might consider it. But there's Sophie to think of. I won't put her in further jeopardy, not for any man. I'll keep her safe, or die trying."

"It won't come to that."

"It did for Mac. I can't let that happen to Sophie."

Her words confused him. What kind of jeopardy was she putting Sophie in? And what did she mean about Mac Spinney? His death had been an accident, hadn't it? Or was there something else going on here, something dark and sinister, something Louis wanted no part of?

He pictured Luke Brogan in his mind. A slow-moving, slow-thinking good ole boy. Mean and stupid, not a good combination. A man who, no matter what the circumstances, would make an unpleasant adversary. But did he have it in him to be a killer? That seemed to be what Mrs. Spinney was implying, that Brogan had been involved somehow in her husband's death. It was hard to imagine, but Louis knew that killers came in all shapes and sizes. Why hadn't Brogan disclosed to him the reason he wanted to find Spinney? What was so important to him that he would go to such lengths, not to mention such expense, to locate the woman? A very ordinary woman, by all accounts, one who seemed unlikely to become involved in some kind of dangerous intrigue. Not unless she was dragged into it, kicking and screaming all the way.

No, he didn't trust the good sheriff of Atchawalla as far as he could throw the man's tubby, middle-aged body, and he wasn't spilling a word until he found out what was really going on here. Even if Brogan had a valid reason for hunting down Robin Spinney like an animal, her fifteen-year-old daughter was an innocent bystander. Louis didn't have any daughters, but he had two teenage nieces, and if any man ever dared to harm so much as a hair on either of their heads, God help him, because Louis's wrath would be boundless.

He would play it by ear. Keep his eyes open. Dig around a little, see what he could uncover. Try to figure out what Brogan was up to. If there was something funky going on, Sophie Spinney wasn't going to be caught in the middle of it. Not as long as Louis Farley had any say in the matter.

When Brian stepped off the plane, Davy barely recognized him. Even though it had been fifteen years, he was somehow still expecting the too-scrawny kid with straggly shoulder-length hair, a bad case of adolescent acne, and a boatload of insecurity. What he got instead was a man in his midthirties, a little pudgy around the middle, with a receding hairline he tried to disguise by trimming his remaining hair as close to the scalp as possible without actually shaving his head. Gone were the downcast eyes, the shuffling walk, the Texas-sized chip on his shoulder. This Brian walked with confidence, his head held high. Except for the twin hoops in his right ear—and nowadays a lot of straight guys had multiple piercings—he didn't give off any overt gay vibes. He was just an average-looking guy in his thirties who was doing his best to stave off as long as possible the approach of middle age.

Brian paused, his eyes scanning the crowd until they landed on Davy. He went still for an instant, then he moved forward with only a tad less confidence than he'd displayed a moment ago. "Davy," he said, and held out his hand.

"Bri." Davy took the hand, then thought *what the hell* and pulled his brother into a brief, awkward hug.

"Don't worry," Brian said. "It doesn't rub off." But there was no rancor behind his words, just a teasing glint in his eyes, so Davy didn't take offense.

"You're looking good, Bri," he said.

"Thank God. That means I'm successful at hiding the fact that inside, I'm quivering in my Ferragamos."

"Why, for God's sake?"

"Think about it. I wasn't exactly Serenity's favorite son when I left, and I suspect the entire welcoming committee is standing right here in front of me. I may look like I have it all together, but in reality, I'm scared shitless."

"I should've done more for you. When we were kids. I should've done a better job of protecting you."

"You were a kid, too, for Christ's sake. You had your own life to live. It wasn't up to you to coddle me. You need to stop blaming yourself for everything."

"But the way everybody treated you—like you were some kind of freak—"

"Welcome to my life. Look, Davy." Brian's eyes were intensely blue, filled with warmth and a self-acceptance that hadn't been there at eighteen. "Has it ever occurred to you that maybe things work out the way they're supposed to? A guy in my position has to develop a thick skin in order to survive. It was a good thing I got plenty of practice at home before I had to go out into the real world, because it's a lot tougher out there."

Brian's words might have been true, but Davy found them ineffably sad. Why did every conversation between them begin and end with Brian's gayness? Like a pink elephant parked squarely in the middle of the living room rug, it was impossible for them to tiptoe around the subject. They should have been able to talk about other things. There should have been innumerable topics they could choose from. After all, they had fifteen years to catch up on. So why did their conversation inevitably boil down to this one topic?

"Let's get your luggage," he said, "and go home."

Brian raised his carry-on. "This is all I brought." At Davy's surprised look, he said, "I'm not planning to stay long."

"Obviously."

"Hey, you called, I came. I could have told you to blow off. Does Gram know I'm coming?"

Taking out his car keys, Davy moved doggedly in the direction of the exit. "No," he said.

Brian, a good six inches shorter than him, scurried to keep up with his long legs. "What about Dee?"

"I don't want to talk about Dee. Right now, she's not on my list of favorite people."

"Of course. Well, it's nice to know that some things never change."

"Dee's a bitter, hardened woman. She's not happy with life, and she'd love to be able to blame it all on you or me. But the truth is, it's her own fault. She's made her choices. We're not responsible for the fact that they were the wrong ones."

"Amen. And what about you, big brother? Did you make the right choices?"

"God help me," he said, thinking of Chelsea and the years he'd spent caught in her toxic spell. "I'm really not sure."

"Are you and Chelsea still together?"

The question took him by surprise. He'd imagined that

Brian knew. But Bri was cut off from everybody here, and without some point of contact, there was no way the news would have filtered west to Taos.

"No," he said. "She died last year."

"Shit," Brian said. "Open mouth, insert foot. I'm sorry, man."

"It's all right. It was—" He paused, thought about it, recognized the truth he'd denied for so long. "It was over a long time before she died. I just hadn't figured it out yet." They crossed the crowded parking garage and he unlocked the door of his car. "What about you? Are you and Alec still together?"

"Yeah. The restaurant's been a big success, and so has our relationship. Six years now. It feels good to be with somebody you can trust. Somebody who understands where you're coming from. Somebody who's there when you come home at night, to hand you a glass of wine, rub your shoulders, and listen to you bitch about your day."

Davy imagined it probably did feel good. It sounded like heaven. Not that he was qualified to judge. He'd never had any of those things. Sliding into the driver's seat, he leaned across and unlocked the passenger door. "I'm happy for you," he said as Brian climbed in. "Really."

"Thanks." Brian glanced around the car's interior, taking note of all the gadgets and gizmos. "So what's with the cop car? You're a member of the esteemed blue brotherhood now?"

"Only temporarily. I worked DEA for a few years. Right now, I'm filling in as police chief for a couple of months. I can't wait for it to be over."

Brian fastened his seat belt. Grinning like a little kid, he said, "My brother, the cop. Man, does that sound funny. I knew you when. And in those days, I couldn't have imagined you ever wearing a uniform. But it must rock, driving around in this thing all the time. I've never seen one of these up close and personal. Not even from the back seat."

"It does have its moments," Davy admitted.

"Wait till I tell Alec I got to ride in a cop car. He'll be so jealous."

And because his love for his kid brother hadn't dimmed over the years, but still shone as bright as it had when Brian was five years old and he was ten, he said, "If you behave yourself, I might just let you play with the lights and the siren."

He got Brian settled in at Gram's place. There was no room to bring him to the trailer, not with Jessie staying there. It was just as well, because he was embarrassed for his brother to see where he lived. "We'll talk tomorrow before the meeting," he promised Bri. "I'll explain all this stuff to you as best I can, but the whole thing's complicated, and none of it sounds any too promising. I honestly don't know what to do with her. I know she wants her independence, and she'll probably scream bloody murder if we try to take it away from her. But there's the whole safety issue to consider. I guess at this point, the first thing we have to do is clarify in our own minds what our highest priority is. Gram's safety, or her independence."

"It's not an easy decision," Brian said. "It never is. We went through the same thing last year with Alec's grandfather. He'd lived in the same house for seventy-five years. How do you pack up seventy-five years of someone's life and move them into a three-hundred-square-foot room in a nursing home? How do you decide what to give away, what to throw and what to keep? Because stuff is never just stuff. It's memories. Generations of memories that you can't just toss on the front lawn and sell to strangers. It might all be part of the circle of life, but it's a damn cruel circle, complete with fangs and claws."

Davy said good-night to his brother and climbed back into the Crown Vic. The moon was a shiny silver orb that dogged him, like a homeless pup, from Gram's house to the state highway. At the stop sign, he hesitated. The chirp of a cricket floated through his open window, and the whine of a pulp truck ricocheted back and forth across the river valley. In the distance, he could see its headlights, could just make out the amber running lights down the side. The driver neared the 35 mph speed limit sign and began downshifting.

A car passed him on the main road, going a little too fast. The driver caught sight of the lights mounted on his roof and hit the brakes. Grinning, Davy pulled out behind him, just to give the guy something to worry about. He had no intention of pulling him over, not at this time of night, when he was off duty and the guy couldn't have been doing more than five miles over the limit. But sometimes it was fun to put the fear of God into them.

A mile down the road, he tired of playing head games with the motorist who was now traveling a sedate six miles per hour under the speed limit, and wheeled into the Twilight Motel parking lot. He turned off his headlights and sat there with his engine running and his parking lights on. The shop was dark, but upstairs, a lamp burned in the living room window. She was still up.

He should go home. It was eleven-thirty-six on a weeknight, and he had a long day tomorrow. He and Brian would need to talk before they met with Gram's entire team of doctors at one o'clock. They needed to make sure their heads were in the same place, make sure they presented a united front, before they faced all those medical people. He'd made sure that Dee knew about the meeting. If she chose to show up, fine. If she didn't, that was okay, too. He was beyond caring any more what his sister did or thought. But he really should get to bed. Morning came early, and at some point in between all the family meetings, he had to squeeze in a little work. Enough, at least, to keep him from being fired.

He pulled out his cell phone and dialed Annie's number.

"Hi," he said when she picked up on the second ring. "I'm calling to issue you an exclusive invitation to join Insomniacs R Us."

"What are you doing up so late? Don't you have to work tomorrow?"

"I could ask you the same thing. Your living room light's on. Don't you ever sleep?"

"How do you know it's on?"

"Look out the window."

A moment later, a curtain parted in the window above his head, and he caught a glimpse of her face, looking down at him. The curtain snapped shut. "Are you stalking me?" she said.

He leaned back and stretched out his long legs. "Only if you want me to, darlin' mine."

"It's almost midnight. Why aren't you home, tucked snug in your bed?"

He ran a finger back and forth along the steering wheel. "I had to pick up my brother at the airport. What's your excuse?"

"I'm being kept up by this delusional man who keeps calling me and showing up at my door at the most ridiculous hours."

"Sophie asleep?"

"Of course Sophie's asleep. She knows enough to go to bed at a reasonable hour when she has to work in the morning. Unlike certain people I know."

"So why don't you come out and play?"

"You're certifiable, Hunter."

"What if I said I wanted to tell you a bedtime story?"

"I'd say you'd better be able to tell it in twelve minutes, because at midnight, I turn into a pumpkin."

Suddenly serious, he said, "Come on down, Annie. Please? I just want to talk to you."

"Damn it, Davy." The humor had fled her voice, too, leaving it naked and vulnerable. "I'm afraid of you."

"Yeah," he said. "I know. I'm afraid of you, too. Are you coming down?"

"Eleven minutes. Eleven minutes, and not a minute longer."

She came down wearing flannel pajamas and a pair of oversized fuzzy slippers that looked like giant monster feet, complete with long, lethal-looking toenails. Pulling her white cardigan sweater tighter around her, she opened the car door and slipped into the passenger seat. "I'm here," she said. "Talk."

He turned off the parking lights and killed the engine, and the night, tender and sweet, draped them in its velvet cloak. "My brother's gay," he said into the darkness. "His name's Brian. Tonight was the first time I've seen him in fifteen years."

"Why?" she said.

"He left town twenty minutes after he graduated from high school. He wasn't treated very well here. It was easier for him not to come back."

"The road runs both ways. Why didn't you visit him?"

"I don't know," he said, surprised by her question. "I guess…it was easier for me if I didn't."

"Okay."

"My sister, Dee…we don't get along. The truth is, Dee doesn't get along with anyone. She's a miserable excuse for a human being. Life hasn't dealt her the hand she thought it should, and the only way she can compensate is to make everybody around her just as miserable as she is." He paused. "She always hated Brian. She was so damn embarrassed by him."

"NIMBY."

"Hunh?"

"Not In My Back Yard. Let the spread of evil happen some-where else, just please, God, don't let it hit close to home."

"Yeah. That's Dee in a nutshell." He went quiet, and she waited for him to continue, the silence between them so ab-solute that he could hear her slow, even breathing. "And then there's Chelsea. I was in love with Chelsea for twenty frig-ging years. Being in love with Chels was a little like having sandpaper rubbed all over your body and then being rolled in salt. She cheated on me for the first time while we were still in high school. I should've figured out right then and there that once she got started, she wouldn't stop. Maybe if I had, my life would've turned out differently. Or maybe not. Maybe I was just meant to be a masochist."

She made a small sound, as though she were about to speak. He waited, but she held her silence. "Chels got preg-nant with Jessie while I was away at college. I don't know who the man was. She never would tell me. After Jessie was born, I asked her to marry me. I loved her so damn much, loved that little girl as if she was my own. Chelsea thought about it for a while and then she said yes. Being married to her was—" he paused, searched his brain for a suitable word "—torturous. It was also the happiest time of my life."

Beside him, in the darkness, Annie's hand found his and held it loosely. "How long were you married?" she said softly.

"Three years, and then she couldn't take it any longer. The whole monogamy thing just wasn't working for her. She took Jessie away and divorced me. For a long time we didn't see each other. But eventually, we got back together again. Even-tually, we always got back together again. Over and over, for the better part of two decades, I let her lead me around by the nose. It didn't matter where I was or what I was doing. If Chelsea called, I was there." He laughed without humor. "And sooner or later, Chelsea always called."

He stopped, wet his lips. "The really damning thing is, I

knew better. I knew the relationship was destroying me. I just couldn't seem to end it. She was like—" He paused, shuddering as he remembered the effect she'd had on him. "She was like a drug. Being with Chelsea was like shooting up heroin. I was a junkie. I couldn't stop, I would've done anything to get a dose, and I always wanted more. How's that for self-destructive behavior?"

She squeezed his hand. "Two-and-a-half years ago," he said, "I was working in D.C. for the DEA. There was a big drug problem here in Serenity, and it was getting worse. This little nowhere town was becoming a major distribution center for heroin that was being sent all over the state. The agency sent me in undercover to try and plug the hole it was trickling through. It was a perfect setup. I'd grown up here, so people were used to me. And when I started hanging out with rejects from the local cesspool, nobody was surprised. Most of 'em figured I'd never amount to anything anyway.

"Then Chels came back from a couple years of wandering up and down the Eastern seaboard. Somehow, she managed to snag a job as a reporter for the *River City Gazette*. The damn newspaper's a joke, but you'd have thought it was the *Washington Post* and she was going for a Pulitzer, the way she acted. One way or another, she got a bug up her ass about the dope dealing, and she started digging around. Pretending she was some big-time reporter. I couldn't tell her the truth; if she found out I was DEA, it would've jeopardized my whole case. I guess I thought I was some hotshot cop or something. So I didn't tell her. I put the confidentiality of the case ahead of her safety. I tried to rein her in by throwing cold water all over her enthusiasm instead. But all it did was piss her off. I'd forgotten that the only thing worse than Chelsea Logan's stubbornness was her temper. I should've remembered, considering that she unleashed it on me with amazing regularity."

Quietly, Annie said, "What happened?"

"I pleaded with her to stay out of it, and she ignored me. It doesn't really matter how it happened. We were both at fault, both too stubborn to give even an inch. She got too close to the truth, and she ended up dead."

"I'm so sorry."

Darkly, he said, "I don't want your goddamn pity."

"How about compassion? What, then? Why'd you tell me all this, Hunter?"

"I wanted you to know. I wanted you to understand why I'd be bad for you. Why getting involved with me would be a mistake."

She removed her hand from his. Sounding peeved, she said, "Isn't that my decision? My mistake to make?"

"Don't you understand? I've never had a normal relationship with a woman. I was Chelsea's patsy for twenty years. It's all I know how to do. I don't even know what normal's supposed to look like. How the hell can I pull it off when I don't even know where to start? You want to know what really bites? Tonight, when my brother was talking about his live-in relationship, I was jealous. It sounds to me like Bri and Alec got it right, and I wonder if either one of them even has a clue just how lucky they are."

"So, basically, what you're telling me is that, out of the goodness of your heart, you've decided to save me from myself by scaring me away before I've even made up my mind about you. Thanks so much for the favor."

He rubbed a hand over his eyes. "It's not that bad," he said. "You make it sound absurd. I'm doing this for—"

"My own good. Yes, I get that. You know what, Hunter? You are one pathetic, fucked-up mess."

"That's what I've been trying to tell you."

"You're also an idiot." He thought he heard tears in her voice, but he couldn't be sure. Sounding suddenly weary, she said, "Your eleven minutes are up. I'm going to bed."

She opened the door, and the dome light came on. He snatched at her wrist, held on to it to prevent her from escaping. "You're pissed off at me again," he said. "Damn it, Annie, why are you always pissed off at me?"

She peeled his fingers away, one by one, and freed her wrist. Rubbing it, she slid away from him to stand in fuzzy slippers on broken pavement. Just before she shut the door in his face, she said, "You have all the answers, Hunter. Figure it out for yourself."

Luke Brogan was having a bad night.

This was his third trip to the bathroom since midnight. 3:00 a.m., and here he was on the hopper again, with the worst indigestion he'd had in years. His doctor had told him to stop eating all that fried food, and Luke had tried. He'd really tried. But this was the South, where everything was deep-fried and served with gravy. Around here, people didn't understand any of that low-fat, low-carb, artificially sweetened bullshit. That was yuppie food. If a dish wasn't loaded with sugar or swimming in fat, it was considered suspicious, and folks avoided it the way a rooster avoided a swinging axe.

Maybe his problem was just nerves. The last two years hadn't been easy on him, and he hadn't slept through an entire night in the six months since Robin Spinney found that envelope with its damning evidence. Now, because of the judicial appointment, Marcus was on his ass, poking and jabbing and tossing his weight around, and the stress was starting to get to him. He'd tried calling Louis Farley a couple of times yesterday, but Farley hadn't picked up. He'd left messages on Farley's voice mail, but the investigator had never called back. If he didn't know better, he'd think the little asshole was avoiding him.

Meanwhile, Marcus's deadline loomed ever nearer. He'd tried to keep his brother out of it, had tried to convince Marcus to let him handle it. He'd been the one to make this mess, and he damn well intended to be the one to clean it up. But their sibling rivalry hadn't faded with age. Their relationship was still all about which one of them had the bigger dick.

He thought he'd handled the situation pretty well. After all, he'd taken care of Mac Spinney and Boyd Northrup, hadn't he? Marcus had no reason to squawk about the way he'd dealt with those two. It was that damn Robin Spinney who was proving to be more of a challenge than he'd expected. He could tell that Marcus was starting to get antsy. Luke wasn't sure why. When Northrup had come whining to him about the contents of that envelope, he hadn't said a thing about Marcus. And Northrup had read every word that Mac Spinney'd written. If he'd seen anything that pointed in Marcus's direction, he would surely have said so. No, the evidence, putrid and utterly damning, pointed the finger of guilt directly and solely at Lucas Anthony Brogan.

Which probably accounted for the fact that he was sitting here at this time of night with his stomach tied up in knots.

He flushed the toilet, and was just pulling his pajamas back up when he heard a noise. It sounded like a footstep in the living room. A stealthy footstep. But who the hell would be stupid enough to break into his house in the middle of the night? Everybody in town knew he lived here, and everybody in town knew he kept an impressive gun collection. It would take a half-baked retard to think they could get away with robbing the county sheriff while he slept.

Except that he didn't have a weapon handy. His loaded service revolver was locked away in the gun safe he kept in a kitchen cupboard. Annabel spent a lot of time at his house, and kids and firearms were a bad combination. Luke didn't take any chances with his granddaughter. He kept his weapon locked up, safely away from curious fingers.

Outside the bathroom door, he heard a second noise. *God-*

damn young punks, he thought as he strode to the door. *Who the hell do they think they are?* Prepared to do battle, Brogan flung the door open, and came face to face with the man standing on the other side.

"Marcus?" he said in astonishment. "What in the name of all that's holy are you doing skulking around my living room at three in the morning?"

Dressed all in black, his brother wore a grim expression. "You were supposed to be in bed," Marcus said. "Why the hell aren't you in bed?"

"I had an upset stomach. What are you doing here? You almost gave me a heart attack. Isn't it a little late to be slumming?"

"I couldn't do it," his brother said evenly, as though they were discussing the weather. "I just couldn't take the chance."

Luke didn't understand. Even when the black-gloved hand raised the gun in slow motion, it took him a second or two to get it. And then Luke Brogan's bowels, already disturbed enough, turned to liquid. "Christ, Marcus," he whispered. "You're gonna kill me over this thing? You're gonna kill your own brother?"

"You were never any brother of mine," Marcus said. "As far as I'm concerned, Daddy should have snapped your neck like a toothpick the day your mother brought you home from the hospital. You've been nothing but an embarrassment to me since I first laid eyes on you. But this—getting me involved in this mess of yours—was the last straw. I'm tired of cleaning up after you, big brother. And I'm not about to let your idiot mistakes destroy my life."

"It was an accident," Luke said. "I didn't intend for it to happen. You know that. I was drunk. I didn't know what I was doing."

Marcus held the gun steady, without so much as a tremor of his hand. "You can whine all you want," he said, "but it won't help you."

"I have Farley on the case. He'll find her any day now, Marcus—"

"You're incompetent, Luke. You know what that word means, or should I explain it to you? You and that Farley person." Marcus snorted. "I bet you don't even know where he is tonight. When was the last time he reported in to you? Did he tell you he's in Portland, Maine?"

Luke tried to cover his surprise, but wasn't quite quick enough. "That's what I thought," Marcus said. "Farley's going to lead my man right to Spinney. In a matter of a day or two, it'll all be over for Spinney and her daughter. And for Louis Farley. It'll be worth the staggering fee I had to pay to make sure they're all neatly taken care of. As for you and me and our little friend here—" Wiggling the gun barrel, he smiled, slow and easy. It was a charming smile, a smile that effectively camouflaged the piranha beneath. "Remember that liquor store robbery over in Bentley last month? The one where they shot the clerk dead and ran off with all the money?"

"It'd be hard to forget," Luke said.

Smoothly, Marcus said, "This is the same gun that was used in that robbery. You never did find out who did it. That's what I mean by incompetence, Lucas. You're a black mark against the Brogan name, one that I can't afford, now that I'm going to be sitting on the bench. So while my man's taking care of Farley and the Spinneys, I'm taking care of you." He paused, his dark eyes glittering hard and cold in the dim light. "What a shame that sometime in the wee hours before dawn, those same unnamed robbery suspects broke into the house of Atchawalla's esteemed chief of police and shot him in cold blood with the same gun they used to shoot the liquor store clerk."

Luke was starting to sweat, in spite of the ice water that raced through his veins. "Christ, Marcus, don't do this. I'll back off. I'll call Farley and pull him off the case. I'll let you

take care of it. Just like you asked me to in the first place."
He heard the pleading in his own voice, heard the weakness
there, and hated it.

"Sorry. It's too late for that. Now that I know what a coward you are, and you know just how far I'd go to guarantee
my future, well…it just wouldn't work, that's all."

Nausea pushed hard at the back of his throat. "Marc, for
God's sake, we were kids together. Brothers. The same blood
runs in our veins. You wouldn't do this to your own brother,
would you?"

"Absolutely," Marcus said. And he pulled the trigger.

The rental car was about what he'd expected, but the hotel
in downtown Portland was a delightful surprise, a far cry
from the low-budget motel where he'd stayed in Detroit.
Louis slept hard, and woke feeling refreshed for the first time
in days. The place didn't come cheap, but he deserved a night
of luxury to celebrate his success before he took off for the
Maine woods. God only knew what he'd find there besides
Robin Spinney, but he'd heard the legendary stories of mosquitoes so large that the Maine State Legislature had considered replacing the chickadee with the mosquito as state bird.

But those were just stories, and he suspected the truth was
a little less daunting. So far, he'd found Maine more than welcoming. Breakfast in the hotel dining room was hearty and
delicious, and he lingered over his second cup of coffee while
he read the headlines in the local newspaper and pondered the
possibility of retiring to Maine. He still had years to go before he needed to make that kind of decision, but it was something to think about. Of course, he didn't have to wait for
retirement. As long as he had a telephone line and a modem
jack, he could do his job from anywhere in the world. He
could relocate at a moment's notice with hardly a blip on his
occupational radar screen.

The waitress, a sturdy, middle-aged woman who was both brisk and efficient, headed his way with a pot of coffee in her hand and a smile on her face. Louis waved her off, folded his paper, and took out his wallet. Pulling out a ten-dollar bill, he dropped it on the table, tucked the newspaper under his arm, and headed toward the hotel lobby.

The elevator whisked him silently to the seventh floor, where two hotel maids were busy changing linens. Their laundry carts parked in the corridor, they chatted back and forth through open doorways in a singsongy language that might have been Vietnamese. Louis strolled past and continued down the corridor, past somebody's room service tray, piled high with dirty dishes and left outside their door. These big hotels, no matter how elegant, were always a bland, confusing maze of adjoining hallways and doors that all looked alike. He reached the end of the corridor and, guided by the signs on the wall, turned left. If he remembered correctly—and it was difficult to remember with all these twists and turns and crazy angles—his door should be the third one on the right.

As he approached, he saw that it was slightly ajar, the hinged latch folded out to keep it from locking. Irritated because he'd clearly left the Do Not Disturb sign hanging on the knob, he double-checked the number on the door, then took a second glance at his key card. It was definitely his room, and he'd definitely left it locked. Damn those maids. He was going to have to complain to the hotel management. There was no excuse for this. If the hotel couldn't hire domestic help who could speak English, they had no business taking in guests at all.

Suddenly jittery, Louis hesitated for an instant before he placed a hand on the door and swung it inward. He took a quick glance at the bathroom, directly to his left, but it was empty, his dirty towels right where he'd left them, draped over the rim of the bathtub. The bed was still unmade, his used drinking glass still sitting on the night stand, his bags lined up neatly at the foot of the bed. Everything was just as he'd left it. That was odd. Why would the maid have left the door open if she hadn't started working on the room?

His mood as flat as an old helium balloon, Louis stuffed his newspaper into the trash can that was barely big enough for it. Why was it that hotel wastebaskets were always toy-sized? Once you threw a paper cup or two into them, there was never room for anything else.

Skirting the foot of the bed, Louis headed for the telephone to call a porter to come and pick up his luggage. He walked three steps past the bed and stopped, hesitated for half an instant, then whirled around to look at the two bags sitting on the standard-issue ugly hotel carpeting.

When he'd gone down to breakfast, there'd been three bags standing there.

Son of a bitch. Son of a goddamn bitch! His laptop was gone.

And Louis didn't have a single doubt about who'd taken it.

She'd stayed up too late last night, and after the interlude in the car with Davy Hunter, Annie hadn't been able to sleep. She'd spent hours thrashing around, flopping from one position to another, dozing and waking, finally going into a deep sleep just as the sun was creeping over the treetops. She'd awakened abruptly ninety minutes later when Sophie closed the door a little too hard before she hotfooted it down the outside staircase on her way to Jolene Crowley's.

And that had been that. Her night was over. She had too much work to do to justify spending half the morning lying in bed—or, more accurately, on the lumpy couch. It had taken a hot shower and three cups of coffee before she was able to elevate herself to a semicomatose state. She felt like a card-carrying member of the walking dead, but it was an improvement over comatose. At least she could see more than two feet in front of her, and her arms and legs appeared to be functioning properly.

She spent five minutes wolfing down a bowl of Sophie's sickeningly sweet sugared cereal before she went downstairs to the shop. Yesterday afternoon, after Davy had gone back to work and she'd pulled herself together, she'd finished the shelf she'd been remodeling. Last night, she'd thrown a touch-up coat of paint on it. This morning, the paint was dry and the shelf was ready for use. She might not be the most competent woodworker in the history of the craft, but at least tearing the thing apart and hammering it back together had been therapeutic.

Annie vacuumed up the sawdust that was pretty much everywhere, gathered up Jack Crowley's circular saw and his goggles, and scooted across the street to return them. When she got back, she began the endless task of shelving the thousands of movies she'd spent yesterday sorting. It was mindless work that gave her plenty of time to think. Too much time, if she wanted to be truthful about it, time to fret and stew over one particular topic she would have preferred to avoid. But it wouldn't leave her alone. *He* wouldn't leave her alone. Davy Hunter was such a strong presence that even when he wasn't around, she could still feel him. Could still smell him, still taste him.

Damn it. She swiped furiously at a tear and continued shelving videos. She should never have gone downstairs last night, should never have gotten in the car with him. Should never have allowed Davy Hunter to reveal to her his vulnerabilities. She should have run away screaming, instead of allowing him to let down his guard long enough to show her that little glimpse inside his head and his life.

But she had, and it was a little late now to undo what she'd done. She'd known full well that she couldn't involve herself with him on an emotional level, but she'd gone ahead and let it happen anyway. Now what? Now that she'd let the man weasel his way into her heart, how was she supposed to deal with the situation? Her initial response last night to the feelings he'd invoked in her had been anger. But was she really angry with Davy, or with herself? He'd only spoken the truth. Loving Davy Hunter wouldn't be easy, not for any woman. There was nothing easy about the guy. He carried on his back a heavy enough load of baggage to flatten a lesser man. His previous experience with women had made him understandably skittish, and hadn't exactly provided solid grounding in how to maintain a healthy relationship. He didn't know how to do relationships. Jumping into a romance with him, even if she were to allow herself to do something that crazy, would be a long shot. He was, to put it bluntly, a lousy risk.

Her logic was solid. There was just one problem with it. It came too late to do her any good. It was too late to debate the risks, too late to look at reason, too late to argue herself out of falling for Davy Hunter. She'd already taken that giant leap into uncharted territory. Regardless of how things stood between them after she'd walked away from him last night, regardless of what the future would bring, he'd already wrested control of her heart.

It wasn't possible. She'd known him for, what? A week? She'd dated Mac Spinney for a *year* before things even got serious between them. With Hunter there'd been no courtship, not a single normal, ordinary date where he picked her up in his car and took her to dinner or a movie. Just this—*thing,* for lack of a better word—between them, something that had started as pure animal attraction and had evolved into something else, something that involved tenderness and intimacy and notions about forever. She'd felt it in his touch yesterday, heard it in his voice last night. He was as bowled over by it as she was, and just as uncertain about where they were supposed to go from here. Like a pair of thoroughbreds racing frantically toward the finish line, they'd taken things far too quickly. But it hadn't been their fault. The little drama they were acting out had progressed at its own pace and in its own time, with little to no input from the principal players. They'd simply been carried along on a sea of emotions that were beyond their control.

Now she had decisions to make. Life-altering decisions about whether to maintain the status quo and hope for the best, or lay it all on him and pray she could trust him. A third, less feasible option hovered in the periphery of her mind: pack up everything she owned and keep on running. Away from here, away from him, away from herself.

But she couldn't bring herself to do it. Dad was right. Maybe he'd been right all along, and wasn't that a hoot? She'd have to call him when he got back from his cruise and tell him what she'd learned, which was that sooner or later, it always caught up to you. The lies, the deception, whatever you were running from. You could run as far and as long as you liked, but running eventually turned into a dead-end road, and when you reached that, there was nowhere left to go.

But Davy was a cop. Maybe there was a chance he could help her. Maybe he'd know what to do, where to turn, how to take down Brogan and reclaim her pilfered life.

Tonight. Tonight she'd sit him down and tell him everything. Maybe, once her conscience was cleared, they could start over again, try to build something that was based on truth instead of lies. She had to hold on to that hope. Had to make him understand that she was the victim in all of this. As a cop, he might not look too kindly on her actions. Some of what she'd done was simply unethical. Some of it was downright illegal. She might have done it in order to survive, but all of it weighed on her like a mountain of stone.

It was time to dislodge the mountain. Time to free herself and Sophie. Time to take back her life. With renewed determination and a sense of hope she hadn't felt since before Boyd Northrup died, Annie Kendall went back to shelving videos.

Fourteen

For the Serenity Police Department, it was yet another day from hell. The lunar cycle was wreaking havoc with the town's inhabitants, and the phone was ringing off the hook. Davy wondered how he could ever have thought he'd die of boredom in this job. His first couple of days might've been slow, but things had certainly picked up since then. First thing this morning, before he even got to work, he'd had to deal with a car/deer collision on Bald Mountain Road, just a couple of miles from his trailer. Nobody was injured, but the deer was killed, which meant he had to call in somebody from the Department of Inland Fisheries and Wildlife to dispose of it. By the time he got to work, his coffee had gone cold, and Dixie was practically tearing her hair out. "Thank God you're finally here," she said. "I was ready to commit hari-kiri with my letter opener."

"That bad?" he said, going to the pot to warm up his tepid coffee.

"Worse. René called in sick. He's caught some flu bug his kid brought home from day care. He spent the night yakking up everything he ever ate."

"Thanks for sharing. Love the visual."

"He said if we really needed him, he'd clean up and get dressed and come in."

"Christ," he said, alarmed. "I hope you told him not to."

"I told him if he dared to even come near this place before he was completely over it, I'd cast a voodoo spell on him that would make his testicles shrivel up and fall off."

Davy didn't bother to hide his grin. "Bet that did the trick."

"It did. He suddenly remembered that he needed to get back to bed real quick."

"Good call."

"Yeah, but that leaves us a man short when the place is—" The telephone rang, cutting her off. She spread out her arms as if to include all the woes of this world. "See what I mean?"

"Where's Pete?"

"Over at the Big Apple. Some customer drove off without paying for his gas."

"Well, calm down. Take a deep breath. Hold it in, then let it out slowly." She did as he said, held it in for so long he was starting to worry about her. The breath came bursting out of her in a sudden and violent rush, and the color returned to her face. "Jesus, Dix," he said. "I didn't mean you should suffocate yourself."

The phone continued to ring. "You should've given me better instructions, then."

Calmly, he said. "Repeat after me: *'One thing at a time.'* We can only do as much as we can do."

Giving him the evil eye, she said, "That was helpful." She picked up the phone and said smoothly, all trace of panic gone from her voice, "Good morning, Serenity Police Department. How may I direct your call?" She listened a moment, then raised an eyebrow. "Goats, you say? On the loose? Again?"

Davy nearly choked on his coffee. He shook his head and crossed his arms in a "no way" gesture, and Dixie smiled sweetly. "I'll send Officer Morin right on over, Mrs. Daggett. It'll just be a few minutes. Last time I checked, he was right around the corner from you. I'll call him on the radio right now."

By ten-thirty, he'd already had a full morning. He'd managed to separate a battling couple who'd both had a few too many beers after they got off the night shift at the paper mill in neighboring Rumford. Eddie Tiner was an easygoing sort until he started drinking, at which point he liked to slap the little lady around some. This morning's argument hadn't yet escalated beyond the shouting point, so Davy did his best to calm them both down. Once he'd convinced Eddie to shuffle off to bed, he loaded Eloise into his cruiser, with Eddie's car keys in her pocket just in case Eddie decided he needed to go somewhere before he'd sobered up, and dropped her off at her sister's house.

On his way back to the station, he pulled over a kid in a beat-up purple Javelin for having an expired inspection sticker. When he ran Ricky Cormier's license, he discovered the kid had an outstanding warrant from the Rumford PD. He cuffed the kid, read him his rights, called Sonny Gaudette to pick up the Javelin with his tow truck, and transported Cormier to the station until somebody from Rumford could pick him up.

A short time later, Angus McDonough called him out to the family farm to check on a possibly rabid raccoon who'd taken up residence inside one of the farm's crumbling outbuildings. It was a little beyond his area of expertise—but then again, so was most of this stuff—and he wasn't inclined to spend the next two months taking daily rabies shots, so he called in Doc Morgan, the local vet, who doubled as animal control officer. He was just leaving the McDonough farm when Dixie called him about a group of juveniles who'd been tossing Trojans filled with poster paint off the railroad trestle downtown. She'd had several calls from irate motorists who were innocently driving along, minding their own business, when the missiles struck. If the surprise plop as the condom landed wasn't enough to startle the living daylights out of motorists, the blood-red paint spreading across their windshields sent several of them into near-hysterics. The boys, all about ten or eleven, thought it was hilarious until he came driving up with his blue lights flashing. Then they'd just looked scared. He'd read them the riot act, confiscated their weapons of destruction, and sent them packing.

Relieved to have gotten out of it with just a warning, they didn't have to be told twice. The boys made themselves invisible with amazing speed, which was a good thing, because he wasn't sure how much longer he could maintain his gruff policeman face. When he thought of the things he and Ty had done at that age, what these kids were doing was tame. Potentially dangerous, yeah. If they didn't give some old lady a heart attack behind the wheel, they were apt to send her crashing into the puckerbrush beside the trestle. But it was small potatoes compared to some of the stuff he and Ty had done, stuff for which they should have received one hell of an ass-kicking. They never had, in spite of Ty's own father being the chief of police. He'd reamed them out pretty good a couple of times, but he'd never laid a hand on either of them. He hadn't tattled, either. Buck might have been a sour-tempered old coot, and they might have been the bane of his existence, but for whatever reason, he'd never told either Lorena Hunter or Glenda Savage what their precious baby boys were up to.

It was a good thing, Davy thought now, because Gram would have been more than happy to administer the ass-whipping that Buck had neglected to execute. He suspected Glenda Savage would have been equally obliging. Maybe that was why Buck kept his mouth shut, because he knew that if either of those fine and upright ladies ever found out, neither of the boys would have been sitting down for a week.

By the time he got back to the station, Pete had returned

from goat duty, looking relatively unscathed, and was at his desk in a back corner, typing up a report, fingers flying over the keys at lightning speed. Up front, sitting on the corner of Dixie's desk, was none other than Davy's own kid brother. "Bri," he said in surprise. "How'd you get here?"

"Taxi," his brother told him. "Next time I'll know better."

"Ah, geez. And you're still in one piece?"

"I told him it was a miracle he made it here alive," Dixie said.

"You should've called me if you wanted to come into town," Davy said. "I would've picked you up."

"I figured you were busy. I didn't want to bother you. Just thought I'd stop by and check the place out, see what you do all day. I had no idea Dixie worked here. We've been catching up on old times, in between the phone calls."

"I'd give you the grand tour, but you've pretty much already seen it all."

"That's what Dixie told me."

There was a commotion outside, and all four of them—including Pete, who'd stopped typing to hear better—glanced in the direction of the door Davy'd just come through. It blew open, and Estelle Cloutier stormed through it, leading with her pregnant belly. Judging by the look on her face, she was mad as hell and loaded for bear. Behind her, looking a little green around the gills and nowhere near as happy to be here, was Boomer Gunderson. Estelle marched up to Davy and said, "We have to talk to you."

Davy sized up the situation and gave Estelle a quick nod. "Right through that door," he told her. Estelle marched off, Boomer in tow. Davy met Pete's eyes across the room. Pete shrugged and went back to typing. "Hold my calls," he said to Dix, and followed them into his office.

The information Teddy Constantine had gleaned from Louis Farley's hard drive had been primo. He had to give Farley credit; the man was a bulldog when it came to digging for information. It hadn't taken him any time at all to track Spinney and her daughter to a little town called Serenity, Maine. It was a shame that Teddy was going to have to kill Farley. If Louis had been willing to come over to the dark side, they would have made a crackerjack team.

Serenity wasn't exactly a happening place. If he'd expected a fancy welcome sign at the edge of town, he'd have been sorely disappointed. There was just the plain black-and-white town line marker that was as common as pine trees in rural Maine. The town had long since lost its luster. If, indeed, it had ever had any. He crossed an old iron bridge, his tires singing on the grillwork. On the river bank, in the shadow of the bridge, sat an abandoned mill, its windows boarded up, its brickwork defaced by graffiti, its parking lot gradually giving way to dandelion and milkweed and soil erosion. No doubt the town's economy had once been based on that mill. Now, he suspected, it was based on nothing at all.

Downtown didn't look any better, with its empty storefronts, their windows dusty with neglect. This place looked just like a thousand other small towns across this great and prosperous nation. As a matter of fact, it looked just like the one he'd escaped from when he was sixteen and his stepfather had taken the belt to him one too many times. He'd left the son of a bitch lying in a pool of blood. Dead, for all Teddy knew, since he'd never bothered to go back and find out.

In the middle of a work day, people came and went: a mother in a ten-year-old minivan full of screaming, snot-nosed kids; a mail carrier in shorts and a blue shirt, his mailbag slung over his shoulder; the town barber, dressed in a white smock, standing outside his shop smoking a cigarette. Sheep, every last one of them, going about their daily lives because they weren't smart enough to leave a place that had died a long time ago. None of them was even remotely aware that a stone killer was driving through their midst. It was his secret alone. Teddy liked secrets. He liked being the only one who knew the real score. It was almost as much fun as killing.

In a town this small, he shouldn't have much trouble locating the Spinney woman. If she'd been here any time at all, people would know who she was. A discreet question or two should get him the information he needed. After she was dead, if anybody remembered the stranger who'd been asking about her, there was no way they'd ever track him down. Even if they copied down the license number of his rental car, they wouldn't find him. He'd paid for it with a stolen credit card that he'd used once and then thrown away. He had a wallet full of them, along with half a dozen fake driver's licenses. If there was one thing Teddy Constantine cared about, it was protecting his own ass. By the time they found the bodies, he'd be home, sitting in his hot tub, smoking a smuggled Cuban cigar and watching the fights on his fifty-inch plasma TV.

He didn't intend to dawdle here in Dogpatch, but there was no need to rush, either. He'd play it by ear, get the lay of the land. Maybe find some place where he could get a nice, juicy steak. While he ate, he'd watch the people interacting around him. He always found human behavior fascinating. The way people did the same things, made the same mistakes, lived the same lives day after day, again and again and again, like Bill Murray in *Groundhog Day,* until eventually they keeled over dead of old age. The worst thing was that most of the dumb schmucks weren't even aware of how meaningless their little lives were.

But not Teddy Constantine. He was too smart, too strong, to let that happen to him. Devoted to his work, yes, but not obsessed with it. If the day came when he started to get bored, he'd quit. Who knew where he might end up? Maybe he'd spend his old age digging in the dirt, raising orchids on some remote tropical island. But whatever he did, he'd do it because he wanted to. Not because he didn't have a choice.

These were heavy thoughts for such a beautiful, sunny day. He needed to lighten up. Enjoy himself a little. The job would take care of itself. He'd already planned his strategy. It would need a little fine-tuning, but the skeleton was already in place. First, the envelope. That was the single most crucial facet of his mission, getting his hands on the written proof that the Brogan brothers had been involved in the kid's death. Once he had the envelope tucked away for safekeeping, he'd take care of Farley. The man was little more than a minor inconvenience, but Teddy couldn't leave any loose ends. Farley was unpredictable; he might even run to the cops. And that wouldn't be pretty.

He would save the best for last. That was the way he always did it. The build-up of anticipation always felt so good. It was already beginning. Now that he was so close, he could almost smell the Spinney woman, the way a predator scents the nearness of its prey. Tonight, he would catch Robin Spinney and her daughter. He'd kill the kid first. Make the mother watch. When he got around to the woman, maybe he'd take a little extra time with her. She was a good-looking piece, and he wanted to make absolutely certain that Marcus Brogan got his money's worth.

But first, he needed a Dr Pepper and a bathroom. There had to be a public restroom somewhere in this pathetic excuse for a town. Spying a convenience store ahead, he signaled for a left turn and pulled into the parking lot. Maybe while he was here, he'd pick up a couple of steamed hot dogs. He'd skipped breakfast, having better spent the time breaking into Farley's hotel room, and his stomach was reminding him of that fact. Convenience stores always carried steamed hot dogs. If they were the red ones, the kind that snapped when you bit into them, all the better. The steak could wait until tonight. He'd eat it rare and bloody. By dinnertime, he'd need the red meat anyway, to bolster his strength for the job ahead of him.

For now, he'd turn on the charm. Put on his lady-killer smile and crank the wattage so blindingly high that the fat cow working behind the cash register at the Big Apple would swoon and fall over in a dead faint at his feet.

She was up to the letter N, and the place was really starting to shape up. Of course, it would probably all have to be rearranged again once she replaced the videos she'd lost, but that would be easy compared to this job. She hadn't heard from Estelle yet today, which meant that Boomer was probably going to allow her to work. With two people, the job would go much more quickly. This afternoon, she intended to sit Estelle down and have the young woman show her how and where to order those replacement videos. While they were at it, maybe it was time to step into the twenty-first century and consider replacing them with DVDs, as long as they were buying new ones anyway. Even in a town as small as this one, most people owned a DVD player. Nowadays, you could pick them up at Wal-Mart for a mere fifty bucks.

She should have her insurance check by the end of the week, and then she'd have to make a trip to the nearest Staples store—which she suspected was in Lewiston—to buy a new computer monitor. Maybe she'd even have her car back by then. If all went as planned, they could be back up and running by Saturday. And not a moment too soon. She'd been turning away customers like crazy. Not to mention that right now, she was paying Estelle's salary out of her own pocket. Some sort of income to offset the cost of paying the woman for doing nothing would be nice.

The phone rang, and she blew out a hard breath of air between pursed lips. That phone was one of the few things the vandals hadn't touched. Praying it wasn't Estelle calling to say she was taking another day off, Annie smoothed her tangled hair and went to answer it.

"Mrs. Kendall?"

It was a woman's voice at the other end, one she didn't recognize. "Yes?" she said cautiously.

"This is Dixie Lessard with the Serenity Police Department. Chief Hunter asked me to give you a call. He wants to know if you're available to stop by the station for a bit."

Like a fourteen-year-old with her first crush, Annie's heart began hammering. "Right now?" she said.

"If you can, ma'am. It'll only take a few minutes. He says there's something you'll want to hear."

Something she'd want to hear? "Does this have anything to do with the break-in at my video store?" she said.

"He didn't give me any details, but I suspect it might."

"All right," she said. "Tell him I'll be there in fifteen minutes."

She hung up the phone and sprinted up the stairs to her apartment, where she took the quickest shower on record. She arranged her hair in an easy upsweep and applied subtle makeup. Meeting her own eyes in the mirror, she chided herself for being ridiculous. He'd already seen her looking like the Bride of Frankenstein, when her hair was a mess and she was covered with paint and she hadn't slept all night. But it would be nice if just once Hunter could see her looking fresh and womanly and enticing. So instead of the usual jeans and T-shirt, she put on a lightweight summer dress of white cotton eyelet that left her arms and shoulders bare and emphasized her legs. Then she dug out the pair of white sandals she'd bought to go with the dress. They'd never even been out of the box. Studying herself in the full-length bathroom mirror, she knew she'd have blisters before lunch. But it was worth it. Damn, she looked hot. Hot enough to blow Interim

Police Chief Davy Hunter's most excellent ass right off his swivel chair and onto the floor.

Mindful of her destination, she carefully avoiding breaking any traffic laws. She was only three minutes late when she walked through the front door of the police station. The woman at the dispatch desk glanced up, gave her the once-over, and grinned. "The party's in there," she said, indicating with her shoulder. "They're waiting for you."

She knocked on the closed door, heard a grunted response, and let herself in. Behind the desk, Davy Hunter leaned back in his chair, tapping a ballpoint pen against his desk blotter. He took in her outfit, took in the hair and the makeup and the long, bare legs. His blue eyes, hot and intense, met hers and stayed there. "Good morning," she said.

"Morning. Have a seat."

Annie glanced around the room, a little surprised by the identities of its other occupants. She took the only empty chair, crossed her legs and adjusted her hemline so that it fell a couple inches above her knee. Just enough to give Hunter a teasing glimpse of her assets. She might have been born in Detroit, but she'd been raised in Mississippi, and like all southern belles, she understood what it took to drive a man to distraction. Discreetly, of course. "Estelle," she said, glancing to her left. "Boomer. And—" Smiling pleasantly, she glanced inquisitively at the mountainous man with bright red hair who was holding up one wall of Hunter's office.

"Officer Pete Morin," he said, giving her legs an appreciative glance. "Nice to meet you."

"All right," she said to Hunter, all business in spite of the tempting scrap of thigh she was flashing him. "I'm here. What's going on?"

Beneath the desk, he stretched out those long legs in her direction. "I believe Boomer has something he'd like to say to you."

Surprised, she turned to look at Boomer Gunderson. Beside him, Estelle's mouth was set in a grim line, her arms folded firmly above the mound of her belly. Boomer gazed steadily at his own clasped hands, hanging loosely between his outstretched knees. His face was beet-red. With difficulty, he said, "I'm the one that wrecked your video store."

· Annie sat up slowly, momentarily forgetting Davy Hunter, momentarily forgetting everything but what she'd just heard. "What?" she said.

Suddenly looking about twelve years old, Boomer took a long, shuddering breath. "I'm sorry," he said.

Estelle cuffed the side of his head. "Tell her the rest, putz."

"Estelle," Davy reprimanded softly, but nobody was listening to him.

"I did it for her," Boomer said, his voice barely audible in the room, although the silence was so heavy that Annie could hear the clock ticking. "Estelle loves the Twilight. She feels like it's hers. Mikey let her run it, you know? He didn't come around much, so she got to do whatever she wanted with the place. She's the one brought in all those new customers. The place was going under until Estelle took over. When Mikey put the business up for sale, she wanted to buy it. But before we could look into the financing, Mikey sold it right out from under her." He finally looked up at Annie. "She came home in tears! She was so afraid the new owner wouldn't want to keep her on. Or that they'd shut down the business. The place don't bring in much money. Mikey was keeping it open mostly for Estelle."

She was missing something here. This kid's logic seemed to be from the planet Mars. "I'm afraid I don't understand," she told Boomer. "How would your trashing the place benefit Estelle?"

He swiped a fist across his nose. "I thought if I scared you off, you'd leave town, and sell the place to her."

She looked to Estelle for confirmation, but the young woman had her face buried in her hands, apparently overwhelmed by all of this. Whether it was Boomer's grand gesture of love that had her overwhelmed, or merely his stupidity, Annie couldn't tell. "Well," she said, at a loss for words. Looking at Hunter, who was still focused on her legs, she said again, "Well."

The silence in the room was broken only by Boomer's sniffling. Annie tugged her skirt down over her knees, and Hunter finally looked at her face. "What now?" she said.

"We can proceed in any of several different directions," he said carefully, "depending on what you decide to do. Whether you want to press criminal charges, or settle this issue privately."

"So it's up to me?"

"Pretty much."

"I see." She thought about it for a while as Boomer sniffled in the background. "And if I should decide to press charges?"

He exchanged glances with Pete Morin. "Pete?" he said. "Care to jump in here? You're more familiar with the penal code than I am."

Pete cleared his throat. "Depending on who we get for a judge, Boomer here could be looking at a few months of jail time. We're talking B&E, criminal trespass, willful destruction of property, malicious mischief. We could probably think up one or two other charges if we had to, make us a nice round half-dozen. He's already confessed to the crime, so it would be pretty straightforward. Since he's expressed his…ah, remorse, a lenient judge might just give him probation and restitution. Maybe a little community service. If he ended up with Judge Bernier, on the other hand—" Pete shook his head and made a cutting motion across his throat.

"Judge Bernier?" she said.

"Also known," Davy said ominously, "as the hanging judge."

"He doesn't look at motivation or intent," Pete said, "or want to hear any sorry-ass excuses. Sob stories always piss him off. He doesn't care if your father was a drunk who beat you every other Sunday, or if you had to steal to finance your kid sister's chemotherapy, or if you burned down Joe Schmoe's house to get even with him for mugging your poor old granny and financing a trip to Monte Carlo with her credit cards. He doesn't give a damn how sorry you are, or how many mouths you have to feed. With him, none of that matters. If you did the crime, you do the time."

"Why do I get the feeling," she said, "that you're both trying to influence my decision? Aren't cops supposed to be unbiased?"

"On some alternate planet," Davy said. "Of course, the decision's entirely up to you."

"Of course." She shot a glance at Boomer, who had finally stopped sniffling. Now he was just looking scared. Estelle was leaning back in her chair, eyes closed, her hand resting protectively on her belly. Which, although Annie knew it was impossible, seemed bigger and rounder than it had when she'd arrived, approximately eight minutes ago. If Boomer went to jail, who would see Estelle through her last trimester? Who would run to the Big Apple to buy her pistachio ice cream at three in the morning? Who would buy Pampers and baby formula and share those midnight feedings?

"Shit," she said.

They all looked at her. "What?" she said. "Do you people all think I'm heartless?"

The tension in the room dissipated, whooshing away like helium let out of a balloon. "I'm sure Pete and I can work with you to come up with a suitable restitution plan," Davy said. "And I'm sure that Boomer, in his unending gratitude, will be more than willing to go along with whatever the three of us come up with. Am I right, Boomer?"

"Yeah. I mean, I know I did a stupid thing, but I learned my lesson. I swear, from this minute on, I walk the straight and narrow. Scout's honor."

Hunter looked at her. "You're sure about this?"

"I'm sure."

"Okay, then, Gunderson. Get the hell on out of here, and I don't want to see you back again. While you're at it, you should kiss this lady's feet. She just handed you a Get Out of Jail Free card. Act like you appreciate it."

"Thanks," Boomer mumbled, eyes downcast.

Pete Morin opened the office door, and Boomer scooted through it. While Pete held the door open, waiting, Estelle stood, arms crossed over her belly. Looking Annie straight in the eye, she said, "So am I fired?"

"I'll have to think about it. Boomer did a really stupid thing, Estelle."

"I know. I think his mother dropped him on his head when he was a baby. He's an idiot. But he's my idiot. Thanks for understanding." She glanced around at Davy and Pete. "That includes you guys."

She swept past Pete, who lumbered out the door and closed it firmly behind him. "You planning to fire her?" Davy said.

"Probably not. Do you think he's learned his lesson?"

"Probably not."

The air between them was thick with unspoken words, swirling and tumbling like the roiling emotions they represented. "About last night," she said.

"Forget last night. I was being an ass. It's what I do best."

"Really?" she said, rising from her chair. "I thought I was the ass."

He got up and ambled around the desk while her breath

tangled up inside her. Sliding a finger beneath the strap to her sundress, he said, "Did you wear this just to make me hot?"

"Yes."

"It worked. Then again, I've been hot ever since the first time I saw you." He touched his mouth to her bare shoulder, and a shudder ran through her.

"I thought you were a real hard-ass," she said.

"Yeah." His mouth, infinitely exciting, skimmed down her arm. "So did I."

"So what happened?"

He caught her hand in his, brought it up to his mouth. Kissed each of her fingers, one by one. "You cracked me wide open. Scared the hell out of me."

She coiled her free arm around his shoulder. With a single finger, she explored the back of his neck, the curve of his ear.

"This is what scares me the most," he whispered.

Her exploring finger drew a line through the hair just above the nape of his neck. "What?" she said, marveling at its silky texture.

"That you feel this good to me when we both still have our clothes on. Ah, shit, Annie." The vulgarity should have offended her, coming as it did in the midst of such an intimate moment. The fact that it didn't told her everything she needed to know about her feelings for this man. She lay her head against his chest and he tucked it beneath his chin. "You have to give me some time," he said. "This is all new to me, and I'm not very good at it."

Time? She had nothing but time. "I'm not going anywhere," she said.

"Me neither." It was probably as close as he was going to get to the *L* word, at least for now. "Last night," he said, "before I picked up Brian—I broke up with Chelsea."

"Um…Davy?"

"Yeah?"

"You do realize that Chelsea's dead?"

"I know. That's why you have to understand the significance of what I did."

And she did. The magnitude of his words, his actions, struck her full in the heart and left her reeling. She turned her face up to his. With his thumb, he tenderly wiped away a tear.

"Don't cry," he said. "For God's sake, Annie, don't cry. I never know what to do with a crying woman."

"I never cry," she said through tears. "Except that ever since I met you, it seems as though it's all I do."

"That's really great. It's gratifying to know I have the same effect on women as a peeled onion."

"I didn't mean it in a bad way."

"I make you cry all the time in a good way?"

"Damn you, Hunter, you're deliberately misconstruing my words."

"There's the Annie we all know and love. Feisty, fiery, sharp-tongued—"

"Shut up and kiss me. I have to get back to work, even if you don't. Those videos won't get shelved all by themselves. And it looks like Estelle won't be coming in to—"

The rest of her words were cut off abruptly as he kissed her so hard she saw stars. "That better?" he said when he was done.

"Maybe. I'll need a few minutes of recovery time before I know for sure. While we're on the subject, do the taxpayers of this town have any idea about the things you do while the meter's running?"

"I suspect you're the only one, sugarplum."

"Hmm. I never looked at it that way, but you're right. I'm a property owner here in Serenity. That means you work for me, doesn't it? I could demand that you be fired for dereliction of duty."

"You could, but you won't. If I had a real job, I wouldn't

be able to sneak away in the middle of the day to ravish your delectable body."

"You have a point." She glanced past his shoulder, at the clock on the wall. It was nearly eleven-thirty. "I'd love to stay and continue the verbal foreplay," she said with regret, "but I really do have to go."

"It's okay. I have an eleven-thirty lunch date anyway."

"Oh?" She drew her eyebrows together in a mock scowl. "Anybody I know?"

"My brother. We're having lunch so we can talk over Gram's situation before we meet with her doctors at one o'clock."

"Oh." She ran a hand up his cheek, left it resting near his brow. "Serious stuff."

"Yeah." He turned his head and kissed her wrist. "Serious stuff."

"As long as we're being serious…are you free tonight?"

"Do I look like I have a life? I'm pretty much free every night. Why?"

She took her hand away. "There are some things we need to talk about. Things I need to tell you. About me." She took a deep breath. "About my situation."

"Christ, Annie, you're not married, are you?"

"No! No, it's nothing like that. Just…will you come over? And bring an open mind with you?"

His eyebrows came together and the lines that bracketed his mouth deepened. "Are you in some kind of trouble? Is that why you're so secretive about your past?"

She fisted her hands in the front of his shirt. "Will you please stop being a cop for just two seconds? We don't have time to get into it right now. I'll tell you everything tonight."

Stretching on tiptoe, she kissed him on the lips. He let out a hard breath and responded with enthusiasm. The kiss lasted for a while before they both had to come up for air or risk asphyxiation.

"All right?" she said softly.

He let out a sigh. Sounding a little miffed, he said, "I guess it'll have to be."

Louis Farley's day had started out like crap, and so far, it hadn't gotten much better. The idiot who'd stolen his Gateway had slowed him down considerably. Even though he knew it was a waste of time, he'd spoken to the hotel manager, who'd been solicitous and courteous and sincerely apologetic. The police had been called, and he'd filed a theft report. But of course they weren't going to recover the computer. Buick Man would take all the information he wanted from it and then either pawn it or toss it in a river somewhere. The computer wasn't the real issue here, not for Louis or for the bozo who'd taken it. If the hotel didn't cover its cost, he had insurance that probably would. No, it wasn't the loss of the hardware that was so devastating. It was the information the computer held that was irreplaceable. And if Buick Man knew anything at all about computers, it would take him about thirty seconds of rooting around in the IE history file to figure out where Louis was headed. Which meant that Buick Man not only knew where Robin Spinney was, but he was probably two hours ahead of Louis in getting there.

The idea made him antsy. Something was going on here, something he didn't like. He'd tried three times today to reach Luke Brogan. The first time, he'd been told that the sheriff wasn't in yet. The second and third times, he'd been given the runaround. What, exactly, was the deal here? Brogan had seemed distracted the last couple of times they'd talked. Nervous, almost. Now, he couldn't reach the man. And that made Louis nervous.

He passed a sign that read SERENITY 15 MILES. The countryside reminded him a lot of home. Corn that was tall and already starting to tassel; black and white Holsteins graz-

ing contentedly in rocky pastures by the roadside. Everything green as far as the eye could see, and a fresh scent of
pine drifting through his open window. He'd grown up on a
farm in rural Vermont, not so very far from here. His parents
were gone now, the farm sold, the old farmhouse torn down
and the land subdivided and turned into a housing develop-
ment. It had been years since he'd visited. You couldn't go
home again, especially when they'd razed home in favor of
a bland row of generic two-bedroom, one-and-a-half-bath
ranch houses. But this part of Maine felt enough like Vermont
to make him homesick for the first time in ten or twelve
years.

A few miles outside Serenity, he pulled off the road into a
small sandpit used by winter road crews, and tried again to
reach Brogan. The woman who answered the phone was a real
hard-ass. He should know. He'd been dealing with her all day.
"Sheriff's Department," she said through her nose. "Can I
help you?"

"Sheriff Brogan, please."

"I'm sorry, the sheriff isn't available. Is there somebody
else who can help you?"

"I really need to speak to him personally. This is the fourth
time I've called today, and all anybody can tell me is that he's
not available. I need to know when he will be."

For the first time, Miss High-and-Mighty hesitated.
"Who's calling?" she demanded.

"This is his cousin Raymond. We were supposed to meet
for lunch today in Tupelo, but we must've got our wires
crossed, because Luke didn't show up. I'm just a little bit worried, Miss. It's not like my cousin to miss an appointment."

"Just a minute," she snapped, and put him on hold. While
the Backstreet Boys sang in his ear, Louis waited. He wasn't
sure what he'd say to Brogan when he got him on the phone,
but this job was turning out to be more trouble than it was

worth. He'd figured out where she was; maybe it was time to turn the information over to Brogan and get out of here. Turn the rental car around and head on back. Maybe spend a couple days tooling around Vermont. It had been a while since he'd taken a real vacation. Maybe it was time to revisit the hills and valleys of his childhood. Rent himself a little fishing cabin, kick back, and relax.

"Sergeant Vincent. Can I help you?"

It wasn't Brogan, but at least he'd moved up from the surly dispatcher. "I hope so," he said in his most ingratiating Southern drawl. "My name's Raymond Cardwell, and I've been tryin' all day to reach my cousin, Luke Brogan. He stood me up for a lunch date, and that's just not like him. But nobody can seem to tell me where he is or when he'll be back. I don't suppose you could help me, could you?"

"You're his cousin, you say?"

"That's right. His momma and mine were sisters. Esther and Muriel. You never saw two sisters so close. Why, I can remember when—"

"Mr. Cardwell," Sergeant Vincent interrupted. "I'm afraid I have bad news for you."

Louis's hand tightened on the cell phone. "Bad news?" he said.

"I regret to inform you, sir, that your cousin passed away early this morning. He was shot and killed by an intruder who broke into his house."

Louis could feel the color draining from his face. Funny how he'd always thought that was just an expression. At the other end of the phone, Vincent said, "Mr. Cardwell? Are you all right? Mr. Cardwell?"

With the flick of a button, Louis broke the connection. He looked at his hand. It was shaking. For a minute, he thought he might lose his breakfast. Now what? Not for an instant did he believe the intruder story. It was all just too neat. Whoever killed Brogan had done it for a reason. Just as they'd had him followed for a reason.

And now they knew where Robin Spinney was.

If there was one thing Louis Farley wasn't, it was a hero. He didn't have any particular beliefs about what came after death, and he wasn't in any hurry to find out. But whatever was going on here, he was in it up to his contact lenses. He knew too much. He wasn't even sure what it was that he knew, but whatever it was, it made him a marked man. So even though his natural inclination would have been to turn tail and save his own hide, there was little sense in it. Sooner or later, they'd catch up to him anyway. As long as he had to stick around and see it through, he might as well track down Spinney and warn her. Maybe if they pooled their information, maybe if they used two heads instead of one, they could find a way out of this mess without getting killed.

Otherwise, he had a sinking feeling they were both toast.

They arrived at the hospital a little early, and he sat in the waiting room to allow Brian and Gram a little privacy for their long-overdue reunion. He was riffling through a magazine when his cell phone rang. He checked the caller ID, but didn't recognize the number. Flipping the phone open, he said, "Hunter."

"Davy, it's Dee."

He dropped the magazine on the couch beside him. "Dee," he said stiffly.

"I'm not coming to the meeting."

Dryly, he said, "There's a surprise."

"I was planning to come. Somebody called in sick, and I had to work early. I've spent the last hour trying to find somebody to cover for me, but nobody's home. Or if they are, they're not answering their phones."

"Fine, Dee. Thanks for letting me know."

"Wait a minute. I'm not done." She paused, and he could hear her breathing, a little too hard, a little too fast. "Look," she said, "I'm trying. I really am."

"I can tell."

"Shut up, asshole, and listen to me. I know you don't always agree with me. Hell, I figure if we hit ten percent agreement, we're doing good. I know I have old-fashioned ideas, Davy, but I can't help it. It's the way I am. I'm too old to change. And being old-fashioned doesn't make me wrong. It just makes me different from you. Understand?"

He felt a twinge of guilt. It was a small twinge, but a twinge nevertheless.

"I love Gram," she went on. "I know I don't always act like it, but I do. I'm doing the best I can. Hell, Davy." She laughed, but there wasn't any humor in it. "Maybe I shouldn't go around judging people, but you're just as bad as I am. You judge me without knowing anything about my life. I guess it's okay when the shoe's on the other foot."

Again, that twinge of guilt prodded at him. "What's your point, Dee?"

"My point is that whatever you and Brian decide to do, I'll go along with it. I want to be part of this thing. I can't be there right now, but I want to be part of it." Again, she paused. "I went to see Gram last night. She tell you that?"

"No," he said, surprised. "I haven't seen her yet today. Bri's with her right now."

"I would've brought the kids with me, but they have that under-twelve rule. You know?"

"Yeah," he said. "I know."

"Will you let me know what you and Brian decide?"

"Yeah." He sighed. "I'll let you know."

Silence at her end. He waited it out. "So…how is he?"

"Bri's doing great, Dee. You could see for yourself if you were here."

"Damn it, Davy, I told you, it's not my fault. I could've refused to come to work, but guess what? I need this job. I have to support my family, in case you forgot. Look, I don't want to fight. It seems like that's all we ever do. Can we just this once try to be civil?"

"I thought I was being civil."

"Good, because there's something else."

"What do you mean, something else?"

"Something happened this morning, and I thought you should know about it. Some guy came into the Big Apple. I've never seen him before. Nice-looking guy, real friendly. He flashed a picture of Annie Kendall and started asking questions about her."

He sat up straighter on the couch. "What kind of questions?"

"Where she lived, if I knew her, that kind of stuff. Claimed he was an old college buddy who was passing through town, and thought he'd look her up."

"Was he a cop?"

"Hmm…I suppose he could've been, but I don't think so. He didn't look like one. Cops, they all have something. I can't explain what it is, but there's just something about 'em. I could go into a room full of people and probably pick out every cop in the room."

Surprised, he said, "What about me? Do I have this indefinable something?"

"Are you kidding? You have it in spades."

He mentally filed the surprising information to pull out at a future time and examine. Right now, he had more pressing things to worry about. "Did you tell him anything? About Annie…ah, Ms. Kendall?"

"You can drop the act, Davy. I know you're sleeping with her."

"Jesus Christ."

"If you're going to be sneaking out of a woman's house at

seven-fifteen on a Sunday morning, you probably shouldn't pick one who lives across the street from Jo Crowley. Anyway, yeah, I told him where she lived. Like I said, he was all nice and good-looking and he seemed sincere as hell. It wasn't until after he left that I started thinking about it and realized maybe I should've kept my mouth shut."

"Yeah," he said. "Maybe you should have."

"I just thought, with you and her being…you know… maybe I ought to tell you. Listen, I have to go. I have a customer. You'll call me later?"

"I'll call you. Thanks, Dee."

He didn't like this. Didn't like the idea of some stranger running around town asking questions about Annie. If she was in trouble—and he suspected she was—he needed to know.

He dialed the station on his cell phone. "Dix," he said when she picked up, "I need you to do something for me, and I need you to keep it quiet. Can you do that?"

"I'm the soul of discretion. You can trust me completely."

"I want you to run a background check on Annie Kendall."

"On Annie—"

"Shh! Jesus, Dix. Discretion. Should I spell out the word for you?"

"Sorry. Uh…may I ask why?"

"No, you may not. I want every piece of information you can find on her in the next hour or so. Put it in an envelope, seal it up, and leave it on my desk. And don't let anybody know what you're up to." With his thumb and forefinger, he pinched the bridge of his nose. "It's not exactly, uh, kosher."

"Gotcha."

"Thanks, Dix. I owe you one. I'll buy you lunch at Lenny's some day next week."

"Be still, my beating heart. But don't go blowing your entire paycheck on little old me, Hunter."

"Oh, shut up," he said, and cut off the call.

Fifteen

"The thing is, Lorena," Dr. Jeremy Colfer said from his perch at the foot of Gram's hospital bed, "once you get out of rehab, we really don't feel it would be in your best interests to continue to live alone."

"I see." But it was clear to Davy that she didn't see, not at all. "Why don't you just put me on an iceberg and set me adrift? I'll just float away, out to sea, like the Eskimos do."

Across the hospital bed, Davy exchanged a glance with Brian. This wasn't going well. He'd known it wouldn't go well. Gram was too independent, too stubborn, to give up that independence without a struggle. "Gram," he said, "we're concerned about your safety."

"No, you're not. I'm just a disposable old woman. Somebody you can crumple up like a used piece of tinfoil and toss out with the rest of the garbage."

"Damn it, Gram," he said. "You know better than that."

Trudy Barrows, the hospital social worker, spoke up. "There are options, Lorena," she said. "There are some very nice nursing care facilities nearby. They're all clean and modern. You could have your own room. Maybe even be able to bring along some of your own furniture. I can give your family a list of facilities. They can drop in any time to check them out—"

"I'd rather be dead."

"You don't mean that, Lorena," the young woman said solicitously.

"Who the hell are you to tell me what I mean? You try walking in my shoes for a while, young lady, and then you come back and we'll talk. And stop calling me by my first name. I'm sixty years older than you, and we don't even know each other. Didn't your parents ever teach you any manners?"

Trudy blanched, but she shut up. "Listen," Brian said out of the blue. "What if you came to live with me?"

All heads turned toward him. "With you?" Davy said.

"I've given it a lot of thought." Glancing around the room, Brian said, "I called Alec last night and we talked about it. He said that whatever I wanted to do was fine with him."

Score one for Alec. "In New Mexico?" Gram said weakly.

"We have a wonderful house," he said, "with a brick patio surrounded by yucca and saguaro, and the desert just a few yards away. We eat breakfast out there every morning. You could have your own room, and the house is all on one level, so you'd never have to climb stairs again. We have a housekeeper who comes in five days a week, so you wouldn't be alone. There's so much to do there. Music and arts festivals and wonderful restaurants. Including mine. Gram, you'd love it there."

"It sounds wonderful," Gram said wistfully. "But I've lived here for eighty-six years. I don't even know what saguaro is. I'd love to visit some time, but—I don't want to leave here. This is home."

"The offer's on the table, Gram. At least think it over."

Davy saw the glint of a tear in her eye. "I'm tired," she said. "I need to sleep now. Get out, all of you. Just go away and leave me alone."

Ah, shit. He knew he was going to regret this, but he couldn't seem to stop himself. Rising to his feet, he said, "She can live with me."

"But—" Trudy Barrows shot a nervous glance at Gram, probably afraid of being verbally decapitated. "You work during the day, Mr. Hunter. She needs somebody to be with her."

"I'm not completely helpless," Gram said, her exhaustion suddenly and miraculously cured. "I may be a cripple right now, but I don't intend to be for long."

"I'll figure something out," he told the social worker. "I'm already paying Elsa Donegan to come in part-time. Maybe I can convince her she needs full-time hours."

"Your place is too small," Brian pointed out. "You told me that just this morning."

"Screw it. I'll buy a house if I have to."

"You could move in with me," Gram said.

"I'm not moving in with you. Your house is falling down around your ears. I don't intend to wake up some morning and find the roof lying in pieces around me. I'll buy something livable."

Now that he'd had time to get past the shock of what he'd just done, the idea didn't sound quite so horrifying. As a matter of fact, he was starting to warm up to it. "You'll have to leave your house behind, Gram, but you can bring along as much of your stuff as you want, and you won't have to move away from Serenity. What do you say?"

Primly, she said, "I don't want to interfere with your life."

"Face it, Gram, you've been interfering with my life since the day I grew up and moved out of your house. Why should you stop now? If you're living with me, at least I won't have to drive across town every time you drag me out of bed at three in the morning."

"And I can bring Koko?"

"Yeah," he said, suddenly weary. "You can bring Koko."

"Fine, then. Start house hunting."

Outside, in the parking lot, Brian shut the car door behind him and said, "Congratulations, big brother. You always were her favorite."

Davy stuck his keys in the ignition and fired up the engine. "Before this is over," he said, "I'm going to want to kill myself. I can just tell."

Brian chuckled. "You'll do fine. And if you need help, I'm just a phone call away."

"A phone call and the better part of a continent."

"You could visit me, you know. The road runs both ways. Hell, bring Gram along with you. I meant what I said. I think she'd love it there. You both would."

"Maybe. You never know." He watched as Brian pulled out his wallet, removed a slender piece of paper, and held it out to him. "What's that?"

"What's it look like? It's a check for six thousand dollars. Made out to you."

"But what's it for?"

"Payback, Davy. Five thousand plus interest. I know it's a little overdue, but better late than never."

"I didn't expect you to do this," he said, taking the check from his brother and admiring the bold, looping script of Alec Turturro's signature.

"I know you didn't. That's why we did it. You helped give us a start, and somehow, we managed to make something of it. Alec and I owe you a hell of a lot more than just money, but I guess for now this check will have to do."

"I don't know what to say."

"Don't say anything. Just take the money. With a new house to buy and Gram coming on board, I'm sure you can use it. You know, Davy—" Brian refolded his wallet and tucked it back into his hip pocket "—I'm not that messed-up kid any longer, desperate to get away from everything he's ever known. I didn't even know where I wanted to get away to. Just knew what I was running from."

Davy rested his wrists on the top of the steering wheel. "I know, Bri."

"I'm almost thirty-four years old. Where the hell has the time gone?" Brian paused, studied Davy's face as though he wanted to remember every detail of it. "I think it's time we started being a family again. What do you think?"

Davy put the car into gear and backed out of the parking space. "I'd like that," he said.

Jessie had bought the bleach. It was all her idea. Sophie still wasn't sure how she felt about it. But Jessie was a year older and totally awesome, and Sophie had great faith in her. The Goth look, Jess had said, wasn't going to fly in Serenity. Especially if she wanted to play soccer. And Sophie wanted to play soccer, wanted it so bad she ached with it. She missed the physical activity, missed spending time with kids her age. She was tired of lying around doing nothing. The babysitting gig was okay, but Sophie couldn't wait for school to start. She'd always liked school, or at least she had until Daddy died and the other kids treated her like she had the plague.

But Jessie said that was normal. She'd been treated the same way after her mom died. People didn't know how to act, so they made damn fools of themselves. But eventually it faded away. Besides, Sophie was starting over in a new school, in a new town, where nobody cared about her past. Best of all, Jessie had promised to watch out for her. Sort of like a big sister. Introduce Sophie to all her friends, show her the ropes, make sure she had somebody to sit with during lunch period.

So she let Jessie buy the Lady Clairol, then she knelt in a

kitchen chair, head bowed over Mrs. Crowley's kitchen sink while Jess applied the foul-smelling stuff to her head. The twins stood by, goggle-eyed, watching the whole process even though Jessie had told them to go play on the computer or something.

First, they'd had to bleach out all that black hair dye. Because the color was so dark, it had taken two applications of bleach to remove it. Sophie'd looked in the mirror and giggled. Her hair was this icky platinum blond that Jessie said made her look like a cheap cocktail waitress. "Now what?" Sophie said.

"Now we apply the new color. Sit still while I read the directions."

Jessie had picked that out, too. Sophie had told her what her hair had looked like before. "Sort of like soft butter," she'd said, and Jess had searched the aisles at Rite Aid until she found something she considered a soft buttery color. The picture on the box came pretty close, Sophie had to admit. Jessie was probably the smartest person she knew. Still, this was scary, a lot more scary than it had been dyeing her hair black in the first place. There wasn't much you could do to make black turn out wrong. But blond was more risky. If something went wrong, she could end up with green hair. Green hair when you wanted it green was okay. Accidental green hair was a different thing. She just hoped Jessie followed the directions carefully, because if they screwed it up, her mom would probably kill her.

"Okay," Jessie said. "Let's do this thing."

"Can we help?" Sam asked.

"No!" Jessie said firmly, shaking the bottle of hair color. "I told you guys to go do something else."

"There's nothing else to do," Jake whined. "Besides, this is more interesting."

Jessie began squirting gooey, cool liquid onto Sophie's

head and working it in with her fingers. "More interesting than nothing? I imagine it is."

"Let me do that," Sam said, reaching.

Sophie edged away from him, but she couldn't go far. "Get out of here, you little weasel!" she said.

"You have to wear gloves," Jessie said.

"Then how come her head doesn't have to wear gloves, huh? Answer that one." Both boys chortled as if Sam had said something hilarious.

"Jesus," Sophie said. "Kids."

"Stay still," Jessie said, "or I'll miss some of it and you'll come out looking like a calico cat."

Sophie stayed still. Calico-cat-colored hair might quite possibly be even worse than green. She wasn't quite sure what a calico cat looked like, but she was pretty sure she didn't want her hair to look like one. "How much longer?" she said.

"I'm almost done. We let it set for twenty minutes, and then we rinse it out."

"I hope this comes out okay. My mom won't be happy if I come out looking like a freak."

"Don't worry." Jessie applied the last of the color to Sophie's head and tossed the empty tube into the sink. "Your mom will be blown away." She smoothed all Sophie's hair up flat on top of her head. The goop held it in place. "Sam," she instructed, "get me a bath towel. An old one, if you can find it. Soph, you can lift your head now."

"How's it look?" Sophie glanced around for the hand mirror Jessie had brought with her.

"You can't tell yet. Give it time."

Sophie found the mirror, held it up, chewed her lower lip as she studied her reflection. It was impossible to tell anything. She looked as though somebody had glued her hair to the top of her head with half a vat of Hershey's syrup. "You're sure about this?" she said.

"I'm sure." Jessie rinsed her plastic gloves under the tap. Then, with the spray nozzle, she rinsed out the sink. Sam came running with the towel she'd requested, and she dried her hands with it, then wiped down Mrs. Crowley's brand-new Corian countertop. "There," she said. "Now, if you can manage to sit still for twenty minutes, we'll wash it out and I'll comb it and blow dry it for you. You're going to look so great, Soph."

"I hope so." She still wasn't a hundred percent with this thing, although it was a little late now to back out.

"You will. I guarantee it. And when we're done, I'll watch the boys while you run across the street and show your mom the new Sophie Kendall."

The Twilight Motel was a crumbling heap that should have been put out of its misery with a few well-placed charges of dynamite. Louis parked out front, next to a disreputable old pickup truck that looked to be from roughly the same era as the building. It was hard to believe that his journey would end in a place like this. What could the woman be thinking? If he'd been given a choice between this and Luke Brogan, he'd probably have chosen Brogan. Then again, considering what he'd just heard about Brogan, there was something to be said for distance.

Downstairs, beneath what was probably the owner's quarters, it appeared as though somebody had put a video rental store in what had once been the motel office. Louis climbed the steps and tried the door, but it was locked. Inside, Robin Spinney was arranging videos on the shelves. He rattled the knob, and she turned and saw him. Swiping at a strand of hair that was playing peekaboo with her forehead, she set down an armload of videos and came to the door.

"Sorry," she said, "we're not open. We were vandalized a few of nights ago, but we should be open again by Saturday."

"I'm not a customer," he said, holding up his P.I. license. "My name is Louis Farley, and I was hired by Luke Brogan to find you."

He saw the emotions flitter across her face. Surprise, fear, a sudden heated anger. "Get out of here," she said. "Get the hell out!"

She tried to slam the door in his face, but he was too quick for her. The door closed hard on his foot. Through gritted teeth, he said, "I'm not here to hurt you, Mrs. Spinney. I'm on your side—"

"Take your foot out of my door, little man, or you'll lose it. My boyfriend's a cop, and he's about twice your size—"

"Brogan's dead."

"What?"

He took advantage of her surprise to force the door open and squeeze through it. "Last night," he said. "An intruder broke into his house and shot him."

"You lie."

"I only wish. There goes the rest of my commission. It gets better. Somebody's been following me. This morning, he stole my laptop. Which means he knows where you are. Pretty coincidental, wouldn't you say? First somebody starts tailing the investigator Brogan hired, then Brogan gets bumped off? Too bad I don't believe in coincidence."

"Oh, God," she said, "you're telling the truth, aren't you?"

"You have a computer? Check it out if you don't believe me. I imagine by now the *Journal-Constitution*'s picked up the story."

"But why—who—"

"I can't be sure, but my money's on Marcus."

"Oh, shit," she said.

"I don't know what it is you have on the Brogan brothers, but it must be good."

Something changed in her eyes, some subtle change of

color, and he knew he was right. "Look," he said, "I know a small portion of this puzzle. You know the rest of it. Somebody's out there killing people, and I suspect that unless we get together and do a little information sharing, you and I will be the next victims."

It lay on his desk, neatly lined up with his desk blotter, the plain manila envelope that Dixie had left there for him. Davy picked it up and held it for a while in his hands. What he was about to do was unethical, and a clear violation of Annie Kendall's civil rights. He had no business digging into her personal life. She wasn't a crime suspect, and he could probably be fired for using police resources for what would be looked at by most people as a personal matter.

But something wasn't right here. Something was a little off. Annie's words, earlier today, had really bothered him: *We don't have time to get into it right now. I'll tell you everything tonight.* She hadn't answered his question when he'd asked if she was in some kind of trouble. Instead, she'd danced her way around it. Even more worrying was the stranger who was flashing her picture around town, asking questions about her, trying to track her down. Claiming to be an old college buddy. Even Dee hadn't bought that one, not once she'd had time to think about it.

No, Davy thought, he wasn't invading Annie's privacy. He was trying to protect her. With renewed confidence, he peeled open the flap of the envelope and removed its contents.

There wasn't much. Driver's license record, a brief work history, an equally brief credit record. To his immense relief, no criminal record. Annie Kendall was squeaky clean. A little too clean, he thought as he perused the documents. The woman had to be in her midthirties. Yet the only work history connected to her social security number went back only four months. Before she moved here, she'd worked at some kind of diner in Vegas. Davy frowned. Hadn't she told him she used to be a high school guidance counselor?

Her credit record was equally scanty. She had a single VISA card she'd taken out five months ago. Her spending was moderate, and she paid off her balance every month. Other than that, she had no credit at all. The only previous address on record was an apartment in Vegas, where she'd lived for close to five months. Her driver's license had been issued by the state of Nevada approximately four months ago. Beyond that, there was nothing. No previous address, no previous license. No nothing. It was though she'd sprung to life, fully formed, less than six months ago.

Before that, Annie Kendall hadn't existed.

His insides knotted up as he studied her far-too-scanty background. As a federal agent, he'd regularly dealt with unsavory people who possessed a list of aliases and fake identities as long as the Great Wall of China. Generally, it was done to cover up a criminal background. Sure, there could be other reasons, but ninety-nine times out of a hundred, people hid behind an alias to conceal their misdeeds. You do something you shouldn't, you don't want to be found, so you become somebody else.

The reason Annie Kendall's background went back only a few months was because Annie Kendall was a total fabrication. The woman he was trying to protect, the woman he was in love with—Christ, he knew how to pick 'em, didn't he—didn't really exist.

He wondered dully how many other lies she'd told him. Not that she'd told him much of anything. They'd been too busy responding to the animal attraction between them to do much talking. But it explained a lot of things. Why she drove an old beater of a car. People without credit didn't buy new cars. Why she was tight-lipped about her background. Why, as rumor had it, she'd paid cash for the Twilight. Where had that cash come from? Was it drug money? Had she stolen it? Had the stranger showing her photo around Serenity come here to recover what was rightfully his? If so, he wasn't going to be impressed to find that she'd invested it in a crumbling, fly-by-night motel whose roof was caving in while weeds overtook the parking lot.

"Fuck," he said to the empty room.

If she wasn't Annie Kendall, then who the hell was she? Davy thought about it some more, while the clock ticked in the silence. Then he picked up his phone and buzzed Dix. "Bring me the file on the break-in at the Twilight."

Ignoring the typed notes, the statements, the photos, he went directly to the fingerprint records. He found the info he'd gotten back from the state police and quickly skimmed it. There, near the bottom, was the name he'd been looking for. Robin Spinney, DOB 9/19/69, last known address 43 Preston Drive, Atchawalla, Mississippi. No criminal record. Pete had said he'd separated the prints of the employees from the others, but maybe he'd missed one. Maybe he'd accidentally sent Annie's on through with the others. The age was right. She didn't have a southern accent, but she might not have lived in Mississippi all her life. It was a long shot, but nobody seemed to know who this Robin Spinney was. And how many thirty-six-year-old women from Mississippi could be renting videos at the Twilight?

So he did a little more digging, this time without Dixie's help. It didn't take long. Within minutes, he had it, staring up at him from his computer screen. Robin Spinney's DMV record, complete with photo. Like most driver's license photos, it looked like a mug shot. Not at all flattering. She was much better looking in person, this Robin Spinney. Or, as he knew her, Annie Kendall.

Damn it, Annie. Why didn't you tell me you were in trouble? Why didn't you trust me enough to tell me?

Of course, she did intend to tell him. At least that was what she'd said. Who knew how much of what she planned to tell him was truth, and how much was fabricated? Just as her entire existence was fabricated. He was surprised by how much it hurt. He might not know much about relationships, but he was smart enough to know you didn't build one on lies. Not if you wanted it to last, anyway.

He put his hand on the phone, intending to call her, then left it resting there. What was he supposed to say to her? *You lied to me, shame on you.* What good would that do? He didn't know who she was or what she was running from. Until he knew that, he couldn't begin to determine his next move. He might only be a rent-a-cop, but he was still a sworn officer of the law. If she was mixed up in something illegal, he was duty-bound to arrest her. He tried to imagine slapping a set of hard metal handcuffs on those lovely, slender wrists. Tried to picture her in a holding cell, with a rock-hard bunk and a seatless toilet that smelled of urine and God only knew what else. The mental image made him sick to his stomach.

He picked up the phone and buzzed Dixie again. "I need you to find the number of the police department in Atchawalla, Mississippi—"

"Hang on," Dixie said. "Spell that, will you?"

He spelled it for her, waited until she'd written it down and given him the go-ahead. "Call them," he said, "and see if you can get the chief on the phone for me. If the chief's not available, then get me somebody who's been on the force for a while."

He hung up, drummed his fingers on the desk, pondering what kind of mess he'd stepped into and just how he was going to extricate himself. Or if he was going to extricate himself. Sex put crazy ideas into a man's head. Love put even crazier ones there. Visions flitted through his head, visions of Mexico, Canada. Someplace where they could hide, he and Annie and her daughter, and nobody would ever find them.

Dix rang back through, effectively shredding his outlaw fantasies. "Deputy Wade Pickett of the Atchawalla County Sheriff's Department on the line for you."

He thanked her, waited for the click that told him she'd transferred the call. "Deputy Pickett?" he said. "Thanks for talking to me."

Pickett seemed a jovial type. "So you're calling from Maine," he said expansively. "What's the weather like up there?"

"Sunny and warm. Nice and dry. We had a few days of high humidity, but it's passed."

"Shoot, it's hotter down here than summer loving. Damn air conditioner's broke again. It breaks down at least a couple times every summer. County's too cheap to invest in a new one. I got a fan in the window to keep me from suffocating, but it ain't doing much. Anyway, you don't want to know about that, I'm sure. What can I do you for?"

"A name came up in an investigation I'm working on. One of your local citizens. I'm just taking a shot in the dark, hoping you might have some information you could pass on."

"I'll do what I can do. Shoot."

"Robin Spinney. Female, DOB 9/19/69, blond and blue—"

"Hell, yeah, I know Robin. Mac's wife. We went to grammar school together."

"Mac?"

"Mac Spinney. Deputy Mac Spinney. Great guy. He died a couple years ago in a car wreck. It was a damn shame. But you don't want to talk about Mac. It's Robin you're interested in."

So she was a cop's wife. A cop's widow, to be precise. It explained her familiarity with his gun belt. She'd probably helped her husband with an identical one a hundred times over the years. "That's right," he said. "What can you tell me about her?"

"Nice lady. She and Mac had a little girl. Cute little thing. She used to play soccer with my daughter. Uh...what the hell was her name? Sophie? Yeah, that's it. Sophie. That kid's one hell of a soccer player. Robin used to be at all the games, cheering her on." He finally took a breath. "You say her name came up in an investigation? She's not in any kind of trouble, is she?"

"Why do you ask? She get in trouble a lot?"

"Robin Spinney?" He chuckled. "Hell, no. Just the opposite. She was active in just about every community endeavor that took place in Atchawalla, at least she was before Mac died. She also worked full-time at the high school. Guidance counselor or something like that. The kids liked her. Everybody liked her."

So at least something she'd told him was true. "You know her well?" he asked.

"Well enough. When Mac was alive, the four of us—her and Mac, me and my wife—used to get together once a month for dinner and a movie. After he died, well...you know how it is. You don't know what to say to somebody in that kind of situation. You sort of drift apart. The numbers don't add up any more. Four's a nice even number. Three's just plain awkward. Know what I mean?"

"Yeah. I know."

"The last couple of years were rough on her. Losing Mac like that. And then Boyd. She left town right after he died. Kinda sudden. Said something about a sick aunt. Just pulled Sophie out of school and took off. Her house is still sitting there with the grass growing up around the windows."

"Boyd," he said. "Who's Boyd?"

"Mac's best friend. Matter of fact, now that I think about it, she left the same day he died. People were talking about it, saying she could at least have stuck around for the funeral. Hell, I don't know. Maybe she was just being paranoid. I been

a little bit that way myself. But you know that saying, abou
things happening in threes? I figure now we got our third hit
my ass is probably safe for a while."

"Your third hit?"

"We've had three members of the Atchawalla County Sheriff's Department die in the last two years. Sudden deaths
every one of 'em. First there was Mac. Died in a car wreck
while he was on patrol. Six months ago, Boyd Northrup blew
his brains out with his service revolver at the breakfast table
one morning. Nobody could believe it. He hadn't been acting depressed or anything. Not a single warning sign. His poor
wife came home and found him. She was eight and a half
months pregnant at the time. It was an awful thing."

Davy's stomach knotted itself into a hard little ball. There
was something here, something dark and scary that Robin
Spinney had stumbled into the middle of. He just hadn't figured out yet what it was. He drummed his fingers on the
desktop. He did his best thinking when he was in motion.
"You said there were three?"

"Last night," Pickett said, "somebody broke into Sheriff
Brogan's house. A burglar's the best we can figure, although
he didn't own much worth taking. The noise must've woke
him up. When he confronted the fella, the intruder shot the
sheriff dead right where he stood."

The fat broad at the Big Apple had been more than
helpful.

He'd learned a long time ago that most people generally
were, if you knew how to handle them. And Teddy Constantine knew how to handle people. You just flattered them a little, asked your questions, and stood back and waited. Most
people would fall all over themselves in an effort to fill the
silence. This broad—Dee, according to her name tag—had
been no exception. She'd responded to his smile, to his charm.

Responded like a giggly teenage girl to his compliment about how nicely her blue shirt brought out the blue in her eyes. Then she'd spilled like a geyser about Annie Kendall, who'd just moved to town with her daughter Sophie and had bought the Twilight Motel, which should have been flattened by a wrecking ball years ago. But the former owner had turned it into a video rental store, except that somebody had trashed the place a few days ago and put it out of commission, at least temporarily, so she wasn't sure what the Kendall woman would do now. Especially with Estelle needing a job because she was pregnant, big as a house at only six months, and she needed to save as much money as possible to tide her over while she was out of work when the baby came.

He'd almost shot the bitch, just to shut her up. She'd given him way more information than he needed. He didn't know who the hell Estelle was, and he didn't care. An address for the Twilight would have been sufficient. Her directions were easy to follow, though. Just cross the old bridge and follow the state highway along the river. It was a couple of miles on the right. He couldn't miss it.

She was right. Decrepit and wretched, the Twilight Motel was impossible to miss. Teddy drove by slowly so he could scope the place out. Six rental units that hadn't been rented in at least a decade. The motel office, which had been converted into the aforementioned video store with its pathetic hand-stenciled sign. Overhead, an apartment, probably where Spinney and her daughter were staying. There were outside stairs leading to the apartment. He suspected there were probably interior ones as well. Two ways in, two ways out. He mentally filed the information for future reference.

Out front, a white Camry was parked next to a faded red pickup truck. Did this mean that Spinney wasn't alone? Had Farley already caught up to her? Teddy had deliberately taken his time to allow Louis to catch up. He'd eaten his hot dogs and slugged back his Dr Pepper and then spent a couple of hours driving around town, familiarizing himself with the place, just in case. He liked to be prepared for any and all eventualities. As he drove past the motel, he took a closer look at the Camry. There, on the rear bumper, was the sticker that identified it as a rental. Teddy smiled. Excellent. All the players were assembling, just as he'd planned it. Now that he knew what kind of rental car Farley was driving, he could follow Louis when he left the Twilight. Maybe drive him off the road, just for the fun of it. Put the fear of Ted into him before he pulled the trigger and put an end to the man's pointless existence.

He continued on by, drove another half mile, and turned around in the driveway of a TV repair shop that didn't look to be in much better condition than the Twilight. This time around, he took a closer look at the neighborhood. It was rural—surrounded by woods and fields—but the houses strung out along the highway like starlings on a telephone wire hugged each other shoulder to shoulder in a little settlement of sorts that seemed to have grown apart from the rest of Serenity. Spinney had neighbors directly across the street, another neighbor to one side, a thick stand of pines on the other side. In back, the river flowed peacefully past, just a couple dozen yards from the back wall of the motel.

It was a peaceful, bucolic setting, quiet at this time of day. Driveways were empty. Most of Spinney's neighbors were probably at work. Window shades were drawn to keep out the July heat, and window air conditioners hummed quietly. Across the street and up three houses, an elderly woman climbed the steps to her front door with an armful of long-stemmed flowers she'd cut from her garden. Gladiolas, he thought. Red, the color of blood. Teddy smiled. At the top of the steps, the woman paused, screen door held open, and watched him drive past. Teddy gave her a neighborly wave, and she waved back, looking vaguely puzzled, as if trying to figure out whether or not she knew him. With a shrug, she continued into the house, and the screen door slapped shut behind her.

Three houses down from the flower lady, directly across from the Twilight, he saw a basketball hoop over the garage. A trampoline on the front lawn. In the back, an in-ground pool. These people might not be affluent, but judging by what he'd seen during his little drive-around, in this neck of the woods they were practically royalty. He wondered how many kids they had. Even one kid was too many as far as Teddy was concerned. Kids asked too many questions and had a tendency to get in the way. Not that he'd hesitate to kill one of them if the little brat interfered in his work. But at this point, he was sticking to the plan. There were three names on his hit list. Spinney, her daughter, and Louis Farley. Those were the people he'd been hired to kill. As long as the local civilians stayed out of his way, they didn't have a thing to worry about. But now that he knew there were kids in the neighborhood, he decided he'd be better off waiting until after dark, until the kids were in bed for the night and the adults were settled down in front of their televisions, watching *Law and Order* or the nightly news on CNN.

He was on his third pass-by when he saw her. The girl was a year or two older than she'd been in the picture Marcus Brogan had given him. Taller, and her hair was different. But he recognized her immediately. Sophie Spinney. She'd just come out of the neighbor's house across the street, the one with the trampoline. A bath towel clutched in her hand, she was walking barefoot across the lawn.

Adrenaline shot through his veins as he realized that the opening gambit in this exercise had just been handed to him. This wasn't how he'd planned it; he'd intended to take them together. But opportunity had just presented itself, and Teddy

Laurie Breton

Constantine wasn't one to hesitate in the face of opportunity. He needed leverage to convince Spinney to give him that envelope. What better leverage than her own daughter?

The girl stopped at the end of the driveway and looked both ways. She started to cross the road, then changed her mind and turned back. As Teddy approached, already braking, she went to the cluster of mailboxes at the end of the driveway and opened one of them. With the towel draped over her arm, the kid pulled out the mail and shuffled through it. Teddy eased the car to a halt on the shoulder beside her, blocking an easy getaway. She turned around, looking surprised. Teddy quickly glanced around him. No traffic in either direction. No nosy flower lady gawking at him from her front doorstep. No faces glued to the windows of the motel or any of the neighboring houses. Not a single witness. This was good fortune beyond belief.

He pushed a button, and the passenger-side window rolled down. Sophie Spinney, who at fifteen—and considering her circumstances—should have known better, leaned down to peer in at him.

"Hi, there!" he said, and flashed her a smile he'd spent years perfecting. "I'm not sure what happened, but I seem to be lost. Think you could help me out?"

Sixteen

They sat at the scratched wooden table, Annie and the man Brogan had hired to track her down, and stared grimly at the screen of her laptop. SHERIFF SLAIN, the headline read. Beneath that, in smaller letters, it said, *Sheriff Luke Brogan Killed by Intruder in Own Home.*

"Now do you believe me?" Louis Farley said.

"If I hadn't believed you, you'd be in police custody right now."

"Then you must understand that the intruder story is a bunch of hogwash. Whoever killed him made it look like the work of an intruder. But Brogan was killed deliberately. Why did he hire me, Mrs. Spinney? What is it you have in your possession that was so valuable to him?"

His eyes were a nice shade of brown, and there wasn't an ounce of deceit in them. Still, he was a stranger, and she hesitated while he continued to regard her with that steady brown gaze.

"Evidence," she said. "Evidence my husband gathered."

"Evidence that could get Luke Brogan into a lot of trouble?"

"Evidence," she said, "that could destroy his life."

"Who else? Who else besides Brogan does this evidence condemn? Brogan's dead, and it looks like somebody else is very determined to get that envelope out of your hands and into his."

She wet her lips. "Marcus Brogan," she said.

"You're sure?"

"I can't believe I was so stupid, but it didn't occur to me until now. Mac never used his name. He only alluded to a powerful and influential person who'd helped Luke Brogan out. But if you read between the lines, it has to be Marcus." Anxiety began to nibble at her stomach. "What are we going to do?"

"First you're going to tell me the whole story. Then we're going to figure out what to do about it."

She still wasn't a hundred percent sure she trusted him. "If I tell you the story," she said, "what do I get out of it?"

"Maybe, if we're lucky," he said, "we'll both get the chance to continue breathing for another day."

This was quite possibly the most bizarre conversation she'd ever taken part in. But then, the entire last six months of her life had been bizarre, so why should this be any different? "Tell me something," she said. "What were you supposed to do when you found me?"

"I was supposed to call Luke Brogan and tell him where you were, then wait for further instructions."

"And why didn't you do that?"

He considered her question somberly. "I'm not really sure," he said. "You could call it bad vibes. Or intuition. Something just didn't feel right, especially after Buick Man started following me. It occurred to me that Brogan's motives for finding you might be—shall we say, unsavory? I didn't intend to be a part of something like that. I'm not a violent man, Mrs. Spinney, and I had no intention of handing you over to him, like a lamb to the slaughter. Not without a damn good reason."

She studied his face, gauging his sincerity. Her instincts told her he was the real deal. She prayed to God they were right.

"Two and a half years ago," she said, "a fourteen-year-old kid named Timmy Rivers was killed in a hit-and-run accident on a highway outside Atchawalla. It was late at night, and there were no lights on his bike, no reflectors. The driver who hit him probably never saw him until it was too late. There weren't even any skid marks. But he was hit with enough force to send both him and the bicycle into a stand of trees a good fifty feet away from the point of impact.

"It was clearly an accident, but nobody ever came forward to claim responsibility. Timmy's parents were devastated. The whole town was devastated. He was a nice kid, the kind of kid you can imagine will grow up and make a difference in the world. I know they always say that when anybody that young dies, but in Timmy's case, it was the truth.

"There wasn't much of an investigation. It ended up in the cold case file and sat there gathering dust. Mac—my husband—couldn't seem to get over it. Maybe because he knew Timmy; maybe because his own instincts told him something wasn't right. For whatever reason, the case wouldn't leave him alone. He brought home the case file and started working on it, on his own time. He was obsessed. Night after night, he'd toss and turn, stewing over it. I'd wake up at three in the morning and the other side of the bed would be empty, and I'd find Mac pacing around the kitchen. He devoted all his spare time to digging. Poking and prodding and asking questions. Apparently he asked too many questions, of the wrong people."

She combed the fingers of both hands through her hair, tugged it away from her face. "When he died, I honestly believed it was an accident. How could I have suspected anything else? I was thirty-four years old and I'd just been made a widow. I had a thirteen-year-old daughter who'd just lost her daddy. I didn't have time to cook up murder theories. I was too busy trying to hold things together."

The kitchen clock ticked in the silence. "Six months ago," she said, elbows resting on the tabletop, "I was cleaning out Mac's desk so I could donate it to a charity auction. When I pulled out a drawer so I could vacuum away the cobwebs, I found a manila envelope taped to the back. Inside was the Rivers case file, with all Mac's notes. Observations, interviews, evidence he'd gathered. All of which—" she paused and took a deep breath "—all of which pointed to Luke Brogan as the driver of the car that killed Timmy. I finally understood why Mac paced the floors at night instead of sleeping. He had a real ethical dilemma on his hands. There was nothing to indicate that Timmy's death had been anything but a tragic accident. Still, Brogan was the sheriff of Atchawalla County, not to mention Mac's boss, and he hadn't come forward to admit his part in the boy's death. Witnesses told him Brogan had been drinking that night—a lot—just before he got behind the wheel. And somebody with the power to sweep the dirt under the rug did just that. It's all there. Names, dates, telephone numbers. Enough to put Brogan away for three lifetimes. Along with whoever helped him cover his tracks."

"And your husband was killed because of this information."

"Of course he was. You see, there was one more thing in that envelope. Mac was keeping a journal. He was afraid of them, you see. Brave and foolish and afraid. He was a good man. The best, and he died because he tried to get justice for a young boy. His last journal entry was on May tenth. Something must have happened, something he didn't tell me because he didn't want to frighten me. But the entry spoke for itself. *I fear for my life.* That was all. Just five words." She paused, lost in a time and place far away from the here and now. "He was killed the next day."

Louis let out a hard breath. "Jesus."

"When I found the envelope, when I read through his notes, I spent a few days thinking it over before I decided what to do. I was devastated to think that Mac had been murdered. I'd loved him so much." Her voice broke a little, and she struggled to maintain control. "I called Boyd Northrup and asked him to come over. He and Mac had been best friends since childhood. They'd started working for the sheriff's department the same year. Our kids were growing up together. He was the only person I trusted in that entire town. Boyd came over and I showed him what I'd found. He read it all through, and I could see him getting angrier and angrier with each page. When he was done, he told me to put it in a safe place where nobody could find it, and keep my mouth shut. Boyd said he'd take care of it." She looked at Louis dolefully. "Twelve hours later, he was dead."

"And that's when you and your daughter pulled your disappearing act."

"I didn't know what else to do. Boyd was the only person I trusted, and because of me, he was dead. I had no idea who else knew about the envelope. I didn't know who the Brogans had in their pockets. Especially Marcus. We're talking old boys club here. Marcus Brogan was the county district attorney. He could have been drinking buddies with everybody from the local state police lieutenant to the governor. There was nobody I dared to turn to. So I ran."

"Whew. So here we are."

"So here we are."

"I suppose you've heard about Marcus Brogan's judicial appointment."

"I heard. And I'd hoped that with Rachel Feldman sitting in the district attorney's office, there might be one person in Atchawalla County government who isn't corrupt."

"It's possible. But if you turn over that evidence to Rachel Feldman and upset Marcus Brogan's tidy little apple cart, I can guarantee there'll be consequences."

"Not if he's sitting in jail."

"There is that to hope for. Unfortunately, there's one other thing you can bank on. If Brogan gets his hands on that envelope, you and I, and your daughter, will be history."

Her heart lurched. "Jesus Christ," she said. "Sophie."

"Where is she?"

"Across the street. Babysitting. Oh, my God. *Oh my god oh my god oh my god.*"

"Mrs. Spinney." Louis took hold of her wrist and held it in his hand. "If you fall apart now, you won't do any of us any good."

He was right. She knew he was right. But this was her baby they were talking about. "I need to call her," she said.

"I think that's a good idea. But you don't want to panic her. How many kids is she babysitting?"

"Twin boys. Nine years old."

"We'll take all three of them in my car and get out of here. By now, this man knows where you live. It isn't safe to stay. I think it's time we went to the police."

Police, she thought. *Davy.* "Yes," she said. "Yes, we'll go to the police."

With trembling hands, she picked up her cell phone and dialed Jo Crowley's number. The voice that answered was young and female, but definitely not her daughter. "I need to speak to Sophie," she said, trying to calm her racing heart. "This is her mother."

"Hi, Mrs. Kendall. This is Jessie. She's not back yet. So what did you think?"

Blankly, she said, "What did I think about what?"

"Sophie's hair. The bleach job."

Fear began to gnaw, like tiny razor-toothed rodents, at the

edges of her belly. "Jessie," she said, "I have no idea what you're talking about."

"We dyed her hair back to blond. She came over to show it to you twenty minutes ago. I figured she was still over there with—"

"Sweet Jesus." She cut Jessie off midsentence. Phone still in her hand, she raced for the stairs that led down to the shop. "Sophie!" she called, thundering down to the first floor. "Soph?"

The shop was deserted. There was no answer, no sound at all except her own labored breathing and the clatter of Louis Farley's footsteps descending the stairs behind her. She burst through the front door of the video store, looked right, then left.

Across the street, Jessie and the boys came out of the house. Annie started toward them, stumbled on a piece of broken pavement and nearly fell. Louis Farley caught her. She yanked her arm away from him, skirted the vacancy sign, and began running across the road. Halfway across, she stopped dead when she saw the mail scattered in the dry dust on the roadside. "No," she whispered, not ready to admit what her eyes were telling her. *"No!"*

Louis took her by the elbow and dragged her the rest of the way across before they could both be mowed down by a pulp truck. Terror roiled around inside her as Louis bent and picked up the scattered mail. Wordlessly, he handed her the towel. Raising it to her face, she closed her eyes and inhaled the telltale odor of hair dye.

And began to shake uncontrollably.

"He's got Sophie," she said. "Jesus Christ, Louis, you have to help me. The son of a bitch has my daughter!"

Davy replaced the telephone receiver with a feeling of dread. Whatever Annie was mixed up in, it was serious. Three men dead, including her husband. All of them cops, one within the last twenty-four hours. And now some stranger was prowling the streets of Serenity, looking for her. Damn the woman. He wanted to shake some sense into her. Wanted to take her over his knee and administer some good, old-fashioned common sense. Wanted to wrap her in his arms and insulate her from whatever evil was stalking her.

He'd picked up the phone to dial her number when Dixie rushed in, her cheeks bright red and her eyes filled with excitement. "That damn Eddie Tiner," she said. "He's been drinking all day, and he's causing one hell of a commotion."

"Christ Almighty, Dix. I already calmed him down once today and sent him off to bed to sleep it off."

"Well, he didn't sleep for long. He drove over to Eloise's sister's house and now he's pacing back and forth on the front lawn with a bottle of Jim Beam in one hand and a BB gun in the other. He already shot out the sister's kitchen window, and he's demanding that Eloise come home with him or he'll start pointing it at her. Half the town's out there watching the show."

"Where's Pete, for Chrissake? Can't he take care of it?"

"You sent him to Rumford to transfer the Cormier kid into their custody."

He slowly replaced the telephone receiver. "Ah, shit. The kid I picked up on the arrest warrant this morning."

"Shit indeed. I'm afraid you're it for the time being."

"A BB gun's not lethal," he said darkly. "Maybe I should just let him have at it. Eventually he'll get either too tired or too drunk, and he'll pass out."

"Maybe so, but I wouldn't want to get shot in the ass with one."

He thought about it for a while. Sighed. "I suppose not. I would probably hurt like a son of a bitch. Besides, if he somehow got lucky, he could put somebody's eye out with the thing. Have I mentioned that I'm thinking about turning in my resignation?"

"Six weeks," she said, grinning. "Just six more weeks. You can handle it."

"Euthanasia," he said as he rose from his chair. "That's the answer. Why'd they have to put Kevorkian in prison?"

Dixie dimpled. "Who you planning to euthanize, Hunter? Yourself, or Eddie?"

"To tell you the truth, Dix, right now I don't much care."

After he took the girl out of his trunk, Teddy tied her up, hands and feet, with a piece of old rope he cut into two pieces, and he carried her into the house. She was so scared, she didn't even put up a protest. He'd noticed the abandoned house earlier, while he was driving around, and after he snatched her and threw her in the trunk of his rental car, he thought of the place immediately. It was perfect for what he had in mind. Abandoned for years, it sat at the end of a long driveway that gave it a sweeping view of the surrounding area. What had once been a half acre of lawn had now turned to hay, and lilacs gone wild nearly obscured the windows. There were no near neighbors, and the orange-and-black NO TRESPASS-ING sign at the end of the driveway should discourage most people from coming near. That and the old barn, its roof half caved in and the rest of it ready to go any minute. Nobody would bother him here, and when he was gone, nobody would think to look here for the bodies. Not for a long, long time.

Teddy strode across warped pine floorboards to the window and lifted the tattered green shade. From here, he could see the length of the driveway and a quarter mile of roadfront property. Perfect. He dropped the shade and glanced at the kid. She sat on the floor, hunched up in a corner, watching his every move with huge, accusing blue eyes. "Why are you doing this?" she said.

"Because it's what I do."

"What's that supposed to mean?"

Taking his cell phone from its belt clip, he said, "It's nothing personal, kid. It's my job. I'm a hired killer."

"People actually pay you to kill other people?"

He grinned, that same disarming grin he'd used to win her over at the mailbox. "Fucking amazing, isn't it?"

Her eyes narrowed. "You're crazy."

"Nope. Heartless, maybe. Ruthless, for sure. But not crazy." He came near her, squatted down in front of her, and she flinched. Holding his cell phone up in front of her, he said, "Get your mother on the phone."

"No."

"Did you see the knife I used to cut the rope? Did you get a good look at the blade?"

She glared at him without answering.

"I know you saw it, kid. You watched me slice that rope in two. You saw how sharp the knife is. If you don't do what I say, I'll start chopping off fingers. Amputation without anesthesia. Ugh." He mock-shuddered. "Messy and painful."

"You'd do it, wouldn't you?"

"If you do what I say, Sophie, you'll never have to find out."

She looked at him without speaking, then she lifted her joined hands and with one finger, punched a series of digits into the phone.

"Wise choice," Teddy said. "You're not only pretty, you're smart." He lifted the phone to Sophie's ear, heard the muffled response at the other end.

"Mom?" the girl said. "Mom, I'm here with this awful man. I don't even know where we are! He grabbed me while I was getting the mail and he put me in his trunk, and now he's threatening to cut off my fing—"

He took away the phone, pushed the end button, and began silently counting.

"Why'd you do that?" she said.

When he reached five, the phone rang. "Psychology 101," he said, and pushed the send button. "Good afternoon, Mrs. Spinney."

"Don't hurt her! For God's sake, don't hurt her. Please. She's only fifteen years old. She had nothing to do with any of this. If you want to kill me, fine. But you have to let her go."

"I believe you have something I want, Mrs. Spinney. I'll make an even trade. The envelope for your daughter."

"I'll bring it to you. Just, please, don't hurt her."

Teddy studied his cuticles. He really was due for a manicure. "You know," he said casually, "I'd thought that before this was all over, you and I might have a little fun together. But now that I've seen your daughter—" he smiled over at the kid "—I think I like her better."

"You lay a finger on her, you son of a bitch, and I'll tear out your heart with my bare hands!"

"The envelope, Robin. Bring me the envelope."

"Where are you?"

"About two miles out of town, on Route 113, there's an old abandoned farmhouse on the left. Pull into the driveway and wait. When I see you sitting there, I'll call you. Bring Louis with you."

"How do you know about Louis?"

"I know about everything. And I have a bird's-eye view of everything that comes and goes around here. If I see any cops—if I see anybody besides you and Farley—I'll kill her first and ask questions later. Got that?"

"I've got it. Listen, you have to give me a few minutes. I have the envelope, but it's not here. I have to get it."

"You do that. I'm a patient man. Just remember, at the first sign of trouble, your daughter gets a bullet between her eyes."

He broke the connection, reattached his cell phone to its

belt clip. Pulled out a pack of cigarettes, shook one free, and took it in his mouth. He flicked his lighter, watched the flame for a while before he brought it to the tip of his cigarette.

"Now what?" the kid said.

He sat down on the floor across from her, crossed-legged. Took a long drag on the cigarette, exhaled, and flicked an ash on the floor. "Now we wait," he said.

You'd have thought the circus was in town, the way people were acting. The only thing missing was the cotton candy concession. How this many supposedly rational people could be entertained by a drunken fool with a BB gun courting catastrophe and humiliation, he couldn't imagine. But this was Serenity, where this kind of entertainment didn't come along all that often. People took what they could get. Once Eddie sobered up, he'd probably die of embarrassment. Men made such fools of themselves over women. Especially when they had a bottle in their hands.

He spied Randy Moreau at the fringes of the crowd. Moreau was a good kid who tended bar over at the River City Pub while he worked his way through the local community college. Randy had dreams of becoming a cop. He might as well start getting in a little practice now. "Hey, Moreau," Davy shouted, and waved his arm in a come-here gesture.

Randy trotted over with the enthusiasm of a golden retriever pup, a wide grin on his face. "Well, if it ain't the Lone Ranger," he said.

Davy tossed him the keys to his cruiser. "Here you go, Tonto."

"What's this?"

"I just deputized you. There's a roll of crime scene tape in my trunk. Start herding these yahoos across the street, string up the tape, and tell 'em to stay behind it. If that doesn't work, you have my permission to start shooting 'em."

"Yes sir!" Snapping him a sharp salute that would have done Gomer Pyle proud, Randy wheeled around and marched off toward the cruiser.

The cell phone at his hip vibrated. Ignoring it, he waded into the crowd. There were probably only about forty people gathered in a cluster on the sidewalk, but it felt more like four hundred. He wasn't sure if it was his uniform or the grim expression on his face that did the trick, but they parted before him like the Red Sea parting for Moses. It might have been his imagination, but he almost thought he heard a collective intake of breath, as though they were all waiting to see how he was going to handle the situation. A new, grudging admiration for Ty Savage overtook him. Any man who'd choose to spend his days this way had to be a lunatic. But nobody would ever mistake him for a chickenshit.

Eloise Tiner's sister Debbie lived in a tidy white house behind a lush front lawn. Right now, Eddie was standing in the middle of that lawn, his balance a little off kilter as he gazed up at the house. His bottle of Jim Beam sat in the grass beside him, yawing at about the same angle as Eddie. "You listen to me, Eloise!" he shouted. "You come out here now, you hear?"

At one of the downstairs windows, a curtain lifted and somebody peeked out before quickly retreating. "I mean it!" Eddie shouted, swaying and nearly losing his balance. "We are gonna have this out right here, right now!"

When he got no response, Eddie raised the BB gun and aimed it at one of the bedroom windows. He pulled the trigger, missed the window, and a BB pinged off the rain gutter. Somebody hooted, and a smattering of applause rippled through the assembled multitude.

"Hey, Eddie," Davy said amiably, "haven't we already been through this once today?"

Eddie swung around, still pointing the BB gun, and Davy

sensed a collective shift in the crowd behind him, away from its business end. "You go on home now, Hunter," Eddie said. "This is between me and my wife. It ain't none of your business."

"That's where you're wrong," he said. "What you're doing here is against the law, and I happen to be the law in this town. Way I see it, that makes it my business."

"You're fulla shit. There ain't no law against a man talking to his wife."

"There's a law against threatening with a loaded firearm—"

"Shit, Davy, it ain't no real gun."

"Public drunkenness, vandalism, terrorizing. Should I go on?"

Eddie blinked a couple of times. "Cripe, Davy," he whined, "you ain't no fun at all since you quit drinking."

At Davy's hip, his cell phone vibrated again. "Even when I was a drunk," he said, "I had better sense than to pull a stunt like this. Why don't you put down the BB gun and I'll give you a ride over to the station? We can sit down and drink some coffee and talk about it."

"Ain't nothing to talk about. Either she comes home with me right now, or I'm having the locks changed tomorrow morning, and that's it." Eddie wheeled around in the direction of the house. "You hear that, Eloise?" he shouted. "I mean it. This is it. The! End!"

From somewhere in the crowd, somebody yelled, "Maybe that's what she's hoping for." The anonymous jokester's words brought a few chuckles.

Eddie reached down, picked up his bottle of Jim Beam, and took a slug. Clutching the bottle to his chest, he said, "I just want to know one thing, Eloise. Why? Why'd you go with him? Didn't I give you everything you ever wanted?"

From behind Davy, that same anonymous voice yelled, "And probably a few she didn't want."

Somebody snickered, and Davy wheeled around, giving the entire group the full force of his coldest stare. "Shut the fuck up!" he snapped.

Stunned silence greeted his words. Most of the faces staring back at him were familiar. People he'd known all his life. Randy Moreau, standing by his makeshift police line, started to cough, but cut it off abruptly.

"Bloodsuckers," Davy muttered, and turned his attention back to Tiner. Diplomacy was getting him nowhere. He should have remembered you couldn't reason with a drunk. He ought to know. He'd spent enough years living with one. Had even been one himself for a while. But not anymore. For the first time in a long time, Davy Hunter didn't see the future stretching out ahead of him as one long, bleak subway ride to hell. "Eddie," he said, "it's time to end this little charade. I'm coming over there and I'm taking the BB gun."

"Stand back!" Eddie squeaked, pointing the gun directly at him. "Don't come no closer or I'll shoot ya!"

Trying not to think about the conversation he'd had with Dixie about how it would feel to be shot by one of those hard little pellets, he began walking slowly and evenly in Eddie's direction.

"You shoot me with that thing," he said, steadily bearing down on Eddie, "you'll be paying whatever it costs to have those BB's scraped out of my hide."

"I mean it, Davy!"

"Not to mention reimbursing the town of Serenity for the cost of a replacement uniform. One without holes in it."

"I'm warning ya. I'll shoot you, and then I'll shoot myself."

Death by BB gun. He supposed it was possible, but he doubted that Eddie Tiner, in his current state of inebriation, possessed the coordination to pull it off. Staring Tiner straight in the eye, Davy walked up to him and removed the gun from his hands. Eddie didn't even try to stop him. Tears filled the man's red-rimmed, rheumy eyes. "Damn it, Davy," he said, "she cheated on me. What'm I supposed to do now?"

Been there, done that. Bought a whole closet full of the fucking T-shirts.

Davy handed the BB gun to Randy Moreau, who'd jogged up to stand beside him. Pulling Eddie's arms behind his back, he cuffed him, then patted him on the shoulder. "You move on," he said, turning Eddie and giving him a gentle shove in the direction of the police cruiser. "That's what you're supposed to do. You just put one foot in front of the other and keep on moving."

This was her worst nightmare, come to vivid and terrifying life. This was all her biggest fears and all the bad things that had ever happened to her all rolled into one. This was fourteen-year-old Timmy Rivers, hit by a drunk driver and left to die; this was her mother, slowly and agonizingly dying of cancer less than a year after she retired from a job she'd spent twenty-five years hating; this was Mac, perishing in the flames of his wrecked cruiser in a ravine beside a deserted Mississippi highway. This was nuclear war and school shootings and airplanes crashing into skyscrapers. This was the bogeyman under the bed. This was, for God's sake, *Sophie.*

"Drive faster," Annie ordered as Louis took a corner so quickly the dust flew.

"I'm driving as fast as I can," he said. "If I get us both killed, it'll defeat our whole purpose."

"Tell me, Louis, do you have any kids?"

"No."

"Then shut up, because you don't have a fucking clue where I'm coming from. Turn here."

Louis turned. Trees and houses passed in a blur. The car made a slow slide into the correct lane, and she let out the breath she'd been holding.

"What's the story with your boyfriend, the cop?" he said. The one who's twice my size?"

"I can't reach him." She'd tried four times to reach Hunter, but she kept getting his voice mail. "And he's not really my boyfriend. I've only known him for a week."

"A lot can happen in a week."

"Yeah." The word came out on a brittle laugh that was half sob. Hard to believe it had been just a few hours since she'd last seen him. It felt like a lifetime ago. Then again, it had been. This morning, her daughter had been safe. Now she was in the hands of a madman.

"Right here," she shouted. "Right here!"

Louis applied the brakes and turned the wheel, and the Camry came to a screeching, shuddering halt in the dusty parking lot beside an ugly chain-link fence. A man in greasy blue coveralls stood next to the front door, keys in his hand, gaping, openmouthed, at their arrival.

Annie was out of the car before the dust settled. "Mr. Gaudette?" she said.

"Ayuh."

"I'm Annie Kendall. The blue Volvo?"

"Yup. Your car's not ready yet."

"It doesn't matter. I need to get something out of it. Where it?"

"In the shop. But I was just locking up for the day. My wife expects me home every day at 4:30 for supper." He lifted his watch and jiggled it for emphasis.

"Well, today, she'll just have to wait. If you don't let us in so I can get an envelope out of my car, my daughter's going to die!"

Looking faintly shocked, Gaudette unlocked the door, and the three of them crowded into his tiny office. "Now, let's see," he said. "Where did I put those Volvo keys?"

"Oh, for Christ's sake. Think!"

Louis squeezed past her, through the door that led to the service bay, while Gaudette opened and closed drawers and Annie squeezed her hands into fists to keep herself from strangling him.

"Robin?" Louis's voice floated in from the service area. "Found them."

Gaudette already forgotten, she rushed to where Louis was opening the rear door of her station wagon.

"Hunh," Gaudette said from behind her. "Musta left 'em in the ignition." He watched as Louis removed the carpet that covered the spare tire and spun the wing nut that held it in place.

"Hey, wait a minute. I thought your name was Annie."

"Long story," she said as Louis lifted the spare tire. She reached into the tire well and pulled out the manila envelope she'd hidden in there months ago. At the time, it had guaranteed her safety. Now it might just possibly save her daughter's life.

"Let's go," she said, and Louis slammed the door shut and tossed the keys at Gaudette as they raced past.

Over his shoulder, he said breathlessly, "Thanks for your trouble."

"No trouble a-tall." Gaudette stood and watched them go. "You have yourselves a nice day, now."

He got Eddie Tiner booked and into lockup, where this time there was no danger of him disturbing the peace before he slept off his drunk. It had been one hell of a day, and Davy was looking forward to sleeping the sleep of the dead tonight himself.

While he was out dealing with Eddie, the evening shift had come on duty. Dixie had left for the day, and the evening dispatcher, a grandmotherly lady named Iris Slocum, was sitting at her desk, drinking something tall and cool in a takeout cup

nd reading a paperback mystery. "Evening," she said dis-
ractedly, without bothering to look up from her book.

"Evening, Iris."

Both of the night shift officers were already out on patrol.
Late-afternoon sun angled in through the long window at the
back of the room. In the corner, his red hair turned a flaming
copper by the sun, Pete Morin swept a pile of paperwork off
his desk and locked it in a drawer. He leaned back in his chair
and stretched, arms held high above his head. "You're here
late," he said to Davy.

"I could say the same about you."

"Been a long day. If that damn René isn't back tomorrow, I
might have to go over to his house and shoot him." Beefy fingers clasped together atop his head, Pete studied Davy like a
bug under a microscope. "I'm stopping by the River City Pub
for a beer before I head home," he said finally. "You interested?"

Davy weighed the relative merits of bonding with his
prickly right-hand man versus the dangers of entering a place
that existed for the express purpose of serving alcohol. Pete
was offering the proverbial olive branch here. A smart man
would latch onto it and hold on for all he was worth. But was
he ready for the bar scene? He'd only been sober for a month.

"They do serve nonalcoholic beer," Pete said, "if that's
what you're worried about."

He hadn't set foot in a bar since he quit drinking. But he
couldn't run away from it forever. Alcohol was always going
to be around to tempt him and test his resolve. He was just
going to have to learn to cope with it.

"I'll go with you," he said. "Just let me check my voice
mail first. I missed a couple of calls while I was dealing with
Tiner."

He perched on the corner of Pete's desk to check his messages. The digital readout on his cell phone showed four

missed calls. The first two were hang-ups. The third was from Annie Kendall. "Damn it, Hunter," she said, her voice rising to a scale he'd never before heard it reach, not even during her recent meltdown. "Where the hell are you? I need you."

Christ Almighty. In the commotion surrounding the Eloise and Eddie show, he'd totally forgotten Annie. Totally forgotten his concerns about her. He sat up straighter, his innards suddenly strangled by the tone of her voice. He punched the button for the next message and Annie's voice, in a stunning demonstration of controlled hysteria, floated into his ear.

"I'm in trouble," she said, and he could hear the sound of an automobile engine in the background. "Serious trouble. I can't explain it all now, but I need your help. There's a man in town who's come here to kill me, and—he has Sophie." Her voice broke for an instant before it regained its steely core. "I have something he wants. An envelope. We've arranged a trade. The envelope for my daughter. Louis and I are meeting him at an old abandoned farmhouse a couple miles out on Route 113."

Louis? he thought. *Who the hell is Louis?*

"I know I'm crazy to go there, but this is my baby we're talking about, Hunter. I don't have a choice."

The fear that was eating away at his insides grew exponentially as she continued talking. "He told me he'd kill her if he saw any cops, so I don't know why I'm calling you. I just thought—Christ, Hunter, I don't know what I thought." She paused, then with renewed determination, she said, "I'm going after her."

No! he thought frantically, his heart thudding so hard he could hear its steady *lop-lop* inside his head. *Don't go. For Christ's sake, don't go.*

But of course she would. Just as he would. Love made people do crazy things. "So if there's anything at all you can do, Hunter...I'd really appreciate it." She paused again, took a deep breath. "I just wanted to say one more thing. In case I don't see you again." Davy's stomach muscles contracting and expanding like crazy, he held his breath in anticipation. "I think I'm sort of in love with you." Her voice broke again, and the breath he'd been holding came gushing out of him. "Pretty crazy, isn't it? I've only known you for a few days. But when it's right, you just…oh, hell. I'm making a damn fool of myself."

Her message ended there. Barely able to breathe, he pushed the end button. "Jesus Christ," he said thickly. "She'll get herself killed."

"Who?" Pete said. "What?"

"The old Letourneau place," he said, thinking quickly. "Isn't there a back way in?"

"Sure. There's that old tote road. It branches off about a quarter mile into the woods. One branch leads to Kinley Pond. The other one comes out on Route 113, just up the road from the house. Kenny Letourneau and I used to sneak in and out that way when we were kids and we didn't want his mother catching us."

He grabbed Pete roughly by the arm. "Then you know how to get in that way? You can get us in there without being seen by anybody inside the house?"

Pete stared at Davy's hand, tightly gripping his forearm. "Sure I can, but nobody lives there any more, Hunter. The place is deserted." His gaze returned to Davy's face. "What the hell is going on?"

"Come on." He released Pete's arm and sprinted toward the door. Over his shoulder, he said, "I'll tell you in the car."

They sat in the car at the foot of the driveway, staring up at the old house. Watching. Waiting. On either side of them, waist-high grass nodded gently in the breeze. "Why the hell hasn't he called us yet?" she said.

"He wants to torture us before he kills us?"

She threw Louis a withering glance. "I could live without the gallows humor, Farley. My daughter is in there." In spite of the sunny July afternoon, a shiver ran through her, and she clasped her arms around herself for warmth. "With him."

"You're right. I'm sorry."

"As long as he lets her go——" she scrutinized the facade of the old farmhouse for any sign of human habitation "——it doesn't matter if he kills us."

"I understand what you're saying, and it's an admirable sentiment, your willingness to die for your kid. But if you don't mind, I'd just as soon you left me out of the equation."

Rubbing her shoulders absently in an attempt to get her sluggish blood circulating, she glanced shrewdly at him. "I don't see you going anywhere," she said. "You could've left me to deal with this alone, but you're still here. Right beside me."

"Yes," he said, with some surprise. "I am, aren't I?"

"You're not half the tough guy you think you are, Louis Farley. You're a good man, even if you don't want to admit it."

"As long as we're on the topic of admissions…and since I'm probably about to die anyway…I might as well tell you. You might want to check on your father."

"My father?" she said, not understanding the connection. "My father's on a Caribbean cruise with his girlfriend."

"Um…no. Actually, the last time I saw him, he was flat on his back in a Miami hospital bed, out cold, with an egg the size of Rhode Island on his head."

She gaped at him in astonishment. "You know my father? And how the hell did he get an egg the size of Rhode Island on his head?"

"Taking your questions in order: no, not personally. And I sort of gave it to him."

"How sort of?"

"Sort of as in I cold-cocked him with a rolling pin."

"Good Christ. Not that marble monstrosity he keeps on his kitchen counter?"

Looking slightly abashed, he said, "That would be the one."

"And he's still alive? Oh, my God, is he going to be all right? Oh, shit, I don't need this right now!"

"I know. I'm sorry. Really. But I thought you should know. Lottie would have called, but she didn't know how to get in touch with you." His hands shifted restlessly on the steering wheel. "If it's any consolation, his girlfriend seems very nice."

"If we get out of this alive, Farley, I'm going to kill you."

Her cell phone rang, startling them both. Meeting his eyes, she pressed the button to answer it. "Yes?" she said.

"Did you bring the envelope?"

"Yes. I have it right here."

"Good. Now get out of the car. Both of you. Hands out in the open. I want to see you plainly."

They each opened a door and stepped out. "Good," he said. "Now, you didn't do anything stupid, did you? Like go to the cops?"

Did the rambling message she'd left on Hunter's voice mail count, with its embarrassing deathbed confession of undying devotion? What the hell was she thinking?

"Do you think I place so little value on my daughter's life?" she said coldly. "Or do you just think I'm stupid?"

"Shut up and get back in the car. Drive up the driveway and around the back of the house. Don't get out of the car until I tell you to."

The Camry bumped its way up the rutted driveway. As directed, Louis parked behind the house, out of sight of the road. "Excellent," the voice at the other end of the phone said. "You're very good at following directions. You can get out of the car now. Just be forewarned, I'm frisking you both at the door, so if anybody's carrying, now's the time to come clean."

"First," she said, "I want to talk to my daughter."

"You're a cautious woman, Mrs. Spinney." There was dead air between them, and then her daughter came on the line.

"Mom? Don't come in here. He's crazy. He's going to—"

The phone was muffled, and she couldn't hear the rest of what Soph was saying. "That's enough, sunshine," the guy said, the echo of his voice in the empty room magnified by the phone connection. Into the phone, he said, "Come to the back door now. Both of you."

And he hung up.

They got out of the Camry. Clutching the manila envelope to her chest, Annie stood there for a moment, side by side with Louis, and looked at the house. It was in bad shape. Half the windows were broken out, and the back door didn't even latch, just hung there on a single hinge. The fear that was gnawing a hole in her innards pumped fiery stomach acid up into the back of her throat. This wasn't going to be good. She knew that if she set foot inside the place, her chances of coming out alive were almost zero. But if she didn't go in, Sophie's chances were less than zero.

Louis Farley slipped his hand into hers and squeezed it. "We'll get your daughter out of this," he said softly, "or die trying."

She looked at him dispassionately. The back door of the house, hanging at its crazy angle, scraped open. It only went halfway before it stopped, wedged solidly against a warped floorboard. The man who stood in the narrow opening was tall and slender, with dark hair and dark eyes. Youngish and good-looking, she thought with surprise. He wore jeans and a black T-shirt. He didn't look like a killer. Except for the gun in his hand, he could have been just one more suburban dad, dressed for a Saturday outing with the kids.

He smiled and said, "We meet at last."

She wanted to spit in his face. Instead, she said, "Do you have a name, or should I just call you Spawn of Satan?"

His grin broadened, but his eyes, those glittering dark eyes, remained cold and dead. "I like you," he said.

"Believe me, the feeling's not mutual."

"I'm Teddy," he said. "Welcome to my party."

It was still sunny out in the real world, but the woods out back of the Letourneau place were darker than the inside of a dog. Twenty years had passed since the last time Pete had trekked down this tote road with Kenny Letourneau in an effort to prevent Kenny's mother from learning about their extracurricular nocturnal activities. In the intervening years, the forest had taken over, to the point where the road was barely discernible. They got lost a couple of times and had to backtrack to pick up the trail again. Branches slapped at their faces as they slogged their way through thick ferns and scrub alders. "I hope to Christ none of this is sumac," Pete said, brushing a spray of green leaves away from his face. "I'm ungodly allergic to it."

"That so?" Davy said, breathing hard. He'd thought he was in fairly good shape, but fighting his way through these woods was like trying to run through quicksand. It must be hell on Pete, who had a good sixty pounds on him and was red as a boiled lobster.

"I caught it once when I was a kid." Panting, Pete shoved aside a rubbery branch that snapped back and would have caught Davy across the face if he hadn't seen it coming. "My face swelled all up and I couldn't open my eyes for a week."

"Good to know." Something drilled a hole into the side of his neck and he slapped at it. Goddamn bloodthirsty mosquitoes were like vampires. "Are you sure you know where we're going?"

"I'm sure. We're almost there."

Except for the occasional chatter of a chipmunk and the buzzing of the mosquitoes that hovered, waiting to dive like heat-seeking missiles, the woods were eerily silent. If he hadn't known that Route 113 was just a quarter mile away, he might have thought he was lost deep inside some enchanted forest straight out of the Brothers Grimm. He half expected to stumble across a gingerbread cottage owned by a witch who liked to dine on innocent children. Or maybe on a pair of middle-aged cops whose firearms were useless against her evil magic.

Without warning, they staggered into daylight so bright he had to shade his eyes until they adjusted. "See?" Pete said. "I told you."

Dropping back into the edge of the woods, they took stock of the situation. They were about a hundred yards out back of the Letourneau homestead, which made Gram's crumbling house look like Donald Trump's summer place. Two cars were parked near the back steps, a white Camry and a beige Oldsmobile. The back door of the house hung partway open. Twittering birds flitted from branch to branch in the lilacs bordering an old stone wall that probably marked the property line, but there was no sound from the house.

"What do you think?" Pete said. "Do we dare to just walk up, brazen and bold, and hope to God he doesn't see us? Or do we wait and see what comes down?"

Neither scenario was ideal. Both scenarios were risky. Inside the house with a hired killer were three civilians, including the woman he loved and her fifteen-year-old daughter. If he made the wrong decision, it could lead to a bloodbath. Tossing the ball back into Pete's court, he asked, "What do you think?"

Studying the house and those three hundred feet of waving grass between their hiding place and the back door, Pete hought on it for a minute. "I say we go for it. If he has three 1ostages in there, he's probably too busy right now to be vatching his back."

"Good call." His respect for Pete Morin, as an officer and 1 human being, took a sharp upturn. "I'll go first. You stay 1ere and cover me. If we walk up to the house together, he :ould pick us both off with a couple of shots."

"You're the chief," Pete said. "I'm more expendable. You hould be the one that waits here."

"I thought you didn't trust me to watch your back?"

"I've had time to reconsider."

"At some point in time, I imagine I'll appreciate that. Right 1ow, I don't have time. Don't make a move until I tell you o." Pete started to protest, but Davy held up a hand to stop 1im. "My woman," he said. "My job."

"Well, don't go getting your ass shot, then, because I don't vant to have to be the one to break the news to her."

"The envelope?" Teddy said, holding out his hand.

Breathing hard, her entire body trembling, she told him, "We had a deal. The envelope for my daughter. Where the hell s Sophie?"

"In the living room."

Still clutching the envelope, Annie shoved past him, heed-ess of the fact that he could easily put a bullet between her houlder blades. The crooked wooden floors creaked when he walked over them. They were littered with the detritus of 1 dozen teenage social gatherings: empty pizza boxes, beer 1ottles, a used condom or two. Apparently the NO TRES-PASSING sign at the end of the driveway had done nothing o discourage the local kids from turning the place into party :entral. Sophie sat in a darkened corner of the living room, 1ale as new-fallen snow, her formerly stringy black hair rimmed into a short blond cut that made her look about twelve years old. Her hands and feet were tied with an old rope, and even from twelve feet away, Annie could see the blood-speckled, angry red marks where the rope had chafed her.

"Mom," Sophie said, and started to cry. "I'm so sorry. Mom."

"Oh, God, Soph." Annie flew across the room, knelt and gathered her daughter close. "It's not your fault, baby. None of this is because of you. This is all my fault."

"I thought I'd never—" Sophie hiccupped "—see you again."

Fiercely, Annie said, "Did you really think I wouldn't come after you?"

Her blue eyes awash with tears, Sophie said, "He's going to kill us, Mom. Somebody paid him to kill us. Why would they do that? All because of what Daddy put in that envelope?"

Edging her body gradually between Sophie and the man with the gun, Annie said bitterly, "Marcus Brogan paid him. And yes, it's all because of this damnable envelope." For the first time since this nightmare began, she was furious with Mac. His obsession had led to this. He was dead, Boyd was dead, Luke Brogan was dead, all because he hadn't been able to let it go. Pretty soon they'd all be dead, all because of her husband, the Great Crusader.

"The envelope, Mrs. Spinney."

"Take it, you bastard!"

She flung it at him with all her might. It landed on the floor by his feet. Pointing with the gun, he told Louis, "Pick it up."

Louis briefly met her eyes before he bent and picked up the envelope and handed it to Teddy. "Go sit over there with them," Teddy told him. Holding the envelope between his elbow and the side of his body, he peeled it open with the fingers of his free hand and removed the contents. His eyes quickly skimmed the first page. Looking thoughtful, he dropped the envelope, took the raft of papers in his hand, and flipped through a few pages.

He looked back at Annie, a single dark brow raised in question. "This isn't the original," he said. "This is a photocopy."

"That's right," she said, her face set in a mask of defiance. "It is."

He looked pained. "I'm a patient man, Mrs. Spinney," he said, "but this is getting to be too much for even me. Where's the original?"

"That's for me to know and you to find out."

He blinked as if in surprise before that smooth mask slipped back over his face and he smiled. "Fucking amazing," he said. "Defiant to the end, aren't you? It's really a shame that I have to shoot you."

"I'm the only person who knows where the original is. If you kill me, you'll never find it. I doubt that Marcus Brogan will be impressed."

"How about if I shoot your daughter? Maybe that will loosen your lips."

"You'll have to go through me to get to her," Annie said, trying to will herself to be bigger, so she could more easily shield her child. "That would defeat your purpose."

Beside her, Louis edged closer. "You'll have to go through both of us," he said.

God bless you, she thought. *God bless you, Louis Farley.*

"Hmm. We do have a dilemma, then, don't we?"

"I'll make you a deal," she said. "The envelope for my daughter. You let her go, I'll tell you where the original is."

Teddy dropped the stack of papers. They skimmed and skittered their way to the floor.

"Bravo," he said. "I'm impressed. But…no. I don't think so. Really, Mrs. Spinney, I'm not that gullible. And just how far do you think she'd get before I catch up to her? I'm a hired killer. It's what I do for a living, and I'm pretty good at it. I don't let people get away. Maybe you'd like a little demonstration." Smoothly, without a moment's hesitation, he turned the gun on Louis Farley.

And pulled the trigger.

He couldn't remember the last time he'd felt this naked, but it had probably been while he was asleep. One of those recurring dreams where you had to go back to high school, and there you were sitting in class with a bunch of sixteen-year-olds, and suddenly you realized you'd forgot your clothes and were sitting there buck-ass naked. Wading through unmowed grass up to his ass, waiting for the lunatic inside the house to take a potshot at him, felt an awful lot like that dream. And crossing those three hundred feet of empty space, like a lone gazelle crossing the savanna, gave him plenty of time to think about his life and what he might have done differently. He hadn't been any saint, that was for sure. He wondered if this was what they meant when they said your whole life flashed in front of your eyes just before you died.

With his stomach somewhere in the vicinity of his tonsils, he moved steadily toward the house, that old chestnut playing over and over in his head: *There's a thin line between a brave man and a fool.* Today, he'd crossed the line for sure. How the hell he'd gotten to this place was a mystery. A week ago, he'd simply been living his pathetic little life, struggling each day to get through those empty hours between sunup and sunset. Then he'd seen Annie Kendall standing by the side of the road, and his world had gone upside down. She'd taken him on a hell of a ride, and somehow he'd ended up here, an empty shell of a man crossing an open field, waiting to get his ass shot off, empty because his heart and all the rest of his insides were in there, with her, the woman who'd brought the light back into his life.

He'd never been so scared. Scared of dying on this beautiful summer day when the lowering sun painted deepening shadows beneath the trees and around the foundation of the old house. Scared of losing her, the one good thing he'd found in thirty-eight years of living. Scared that what they'd found would be cut off before it even got a chance to start. Scared that they'd both live through this nightmare, and they'd get their chance after all, and he'd somehow manage to fuck it up the way he'd fucked up every other chance life had thrown his way. Damned if you do, and damned if you don't. It was the way he'd lived his entire life.

He was three-quarters of the way to the house when he heard the gunshot. In an instant, it all dissipated, all the fear, all the insecurity, all the uncertainty. The cop in him took over, and somehow his gun was in his hand, and he didn't remember drawing it. With a furious hand signal that he hoped to Christ Pete saw, he took off running.

He took the back steps in a single leap and slithered through the narrow opening into an old country kitchen with an ancient slate sink and checkered oilcloth tacked up on the walls. From somewhere at the front of the house, he could hear sobbing. He thought it was Sophie, but he couldn't be sure. That meant that at least one of them was still alive. Davy kicked off his shoes and tiptoed across the kitchen. Hugging the wall, he inched forward, trying not to breathe, trying not to make a sound that would give him away.

Then he heard Annie's voice, strong and frightened and furious, and for an instant, his knees went weak. "You bastard," she said as Davy leaned against the wall, closed his eyes, and sucked in a ragged breath. "You monster! He never did anything to you!"

An unfamiliar male voice said, "He was expendable."

"Human beings are never expendable!"

"I told you, Mrs. Spinney. This is what I do. I'm not the

least bit squeamish. You and your daughter are nothing more to me than names inside a file folder."

"How the hell do you sleep at night, Teddy?"

"It's just a job," the man said as Davy began inching forward again. "I don't take my work home with me at night. I sleep like a baby."

He reached the living room doorway. The man named Teddy stood in the middle of the room, facing away from him, but he could see Annie clearly, huddled with Sophie on the floor beneath the window, could see the blood all over her clothes. Davy's heart lurched until he realized that it wasn't her blood. It had come from the man lying silently on the floor beside her. *Louis,* he thought. Whoever the hell Louis was.

"If you don't tell me where it is," Teddy said, "your kid will be next."

His heartbeat thundering in his ears, Davy inched forward. She hadn't seen him yet, didn't know he'd come for her. Sitting there bold as noon, trying to shield her daughter with her slender body, Annie Kendall raised her chin. "You're going to kill us anyway, aren't you?" The tremor in her voice gave away her fear, but that didn't stop her. *Annie,* he thought. *Oh, Christ, Annie.* "If you do," she said, "I'll take the secret with me to my grave."

In his stocking feet, he slid a half inch closer. Another half inch, and then Sophie saw him. Recognition widened her eyes. He lifted a finger to his lips as Annie said, "Just know that I have a friend in Detroit who has a key to my safe-deposit box and instructions to look there if anything should happen to me. Inside the box, there's a letter telling everything, including where to find Mac's original envelope."

Davy inched closer, so close he had to hold his breath so his breathing would give him away.

"Let her go," Annie said. "She's just a little girl. This is between me and Brogan. It's not her battle."

"Sorry," Teddy said. "No can do. But it looks like you've covered all the bases and I'm wasting my time here." He raised his shooting arm. "*Adieu*, Mrs. Spinney. Sorry we couldn't come to an agreem—"

Davy pressed the muzzle of his gun to the back of Teddy's head. "You pull that trigger," he said in a deadly quiet voice, "and I'll blow your fucking head off."

Annie gasped. She breathed his name, half greeting, half prayer.

"Well, well," Teddy said. "If it isn't a member of the local constabulary."

"Drop the gun, Teddy."

"You shoot me, I shoot her." His words were brash, but nowhere near as confident as they'd been just fifteen seconds ago. "Looks like we're at an impasse."

There was a horrific splintering sound as Pete Morin kicked in the rotted front door. He came through it like a charging bull—and about the same size—his gun drawn and aimed directly at Teddy's heart. "Wrong," he said. "Now be a good boy and drop the fucking gun."

"And if I don't?"

"If you don't," Pete said, "I'll kill you with one shot."

"Is it really worth it?" Davy said. "I heard you tell her that it's just a job. You really want to go down over somebody else's beef?"

"I have a reputation to protect."

"I'll make sure they etch that on your gravestone." With deceptive casualness, he said, "If I were you, I'd cooperate. I used to be a federal agent, Teddy, and I can tell you right now, there's nothing the feds like better than making deals. Of course, that's up to you. If it was up to me, I'd shoot you right here."

Teddy considered his words, considered the relative merits of ten years in prison versus certain death, and shrugged.

Slowly lowering his arm, he loosened his fingers, and the gun dropped to the floor.

With his foot, Davy shoved it out of reach. Together, he and Pete got Teddy cuffed. "Read him his rights," he told Pete. "and call for backup. If he gives you any trouble, drop him I doubt there's anybody in this room who wouldn't testify that you did it in self-defense."

Across the room, Annie was already untying the ropes that bound her daughter. Suddenly exhausted, Davy holstered his gun and knelt beside Louis. He was in shock, and his pulse was thin and thready, but he was alive.

"Get an ambulance out here while you're at it," he told Pete. "This guy's lost a lot of blood, but if we can get him to the hospital quick enough, he might make it."

Annie released the last of the ropes and freed her daughter. "You okay, sweetheart?" Davy asked her.

"I'm okay," Sophie said, stretching to bring back the circulation. "He didn't hurt me. But I've never been so scared in my life."

"I think that makes it unanimous," he said.

"Look at those rope burns," Annie said to him. "How could he do this to her?"

"Mom, it's okay. We're both alive. That's what matters."

In the distance, a siren began to wail. "That's right," Davy said, reaching out and touching the top of Sophie's head. I had been close. A little too close. Past the lump in his throat he said, "Hey, great hair."

She gave him a bashful smile and then sat there, rubbing at her sore ankles as her mother slowly rose to her feet. Annie looked like she'd been hit by a Mack truck that had then backed up and run over her a second time. Her hair was a mess, her face smeared with dirt and her clothes saturated with blood. For once, there didn't seem to be much fight left in her. She just stood there, looking at him, those big blue eyes elegraphing all the things she wanted to say to him but couldn't.

"I'm buying a house," he said. It wasn't what he'd intended to say; it was just what came out when he opened his mouth.

"Really?" she said, a hint of a smile playing about her mouth. "That's nice, Hunter."

He was an idiot. She'd nearly died, and here he was, talking real estate. He tried again. "I got your message."

"I noticed. Thank you. I know that words are inadequate, but—"

"Annie," he said hoarsely, the word wrenched from somewhere deep inside him, "do you really think you have to thank me?"

"It's not my real name," she said. "I'm sorry I lied. It's not how I wanted things to be between us."

"I don't care. You'll always be Annie to me. Is that okay with you?"

"You just saved my life. A little accommodation wouldn't be out of order."

"Listen, what you said in your message. About—" He glanced at Sophie, who was watching them with avid curiosity, and swallowed. "You know."

"Forget it, Hunter. I was under a lot of stress. People say stupid things when they're under stress."

"That's the thing," he said. "I can't forget it."

Those blue eyes seemed to grow bigger and rounder. "No?" she said.

He took a step closer. He needed to touch her. Had to touch her. Would die if he didn't touch her. Reaching down, he took her hand in his. She was trembling, or maybe that was him. Maybe it was both of them. He couldn't tell for sure just yet. "Come with me," he said.

"Come with you?" she said, as the wailing siren drew closer. "Come with you where?"

He brought her hand to his lips and kissed it. "House hunting," he said.

Those blue eyes widened. The corner of her mouth trembled a little, and then it turned up in a smile. "I'd like that," she said, and stepped into his arms.

Epilogue

Six months later
Portland, Maine

When she stepped off the plane, he was waiting for her, a tall, rangy man with dark blond hair and anxious blue eyes that warmed when he picked her out of the crowd. Hands tucked into the pockets of his navy-blue ski parka, he stood there and watched her moving toward him. Her heart stumbled just a bit, as it always did when she first saw him. Her carry-on bag slung over her shoulder, she fought her way through the crowd, laughed and skipped the last few steps and threw her arms around him. They stood there, warmth pressed to warmth, mouth pressed to mouth, swaying slowly as people streamed like a river around them. "I missed you so much," she said against his lips.

"I missed you, too, baby. So it's over."

"It's over." She took a step back, but still stayed within the circle of his arms. "Teddy Constantine sang like a little canary. Between that and my testimony, and the written evidence from Mac's notes, Rachel Feldman had enough to put

Marcus Brogan away for five or six lifetimes. I think she's
going to be the best thing that ever happened to Atchawalla
County. They already have a nickname for her."

"Oh? What's that?"

She grinned. "The Terminator."

"Good for her. How's Louis?"

"He's recovering nicely. He sends his regards." Sobering,
she said, "How's Soph?" As much as she trusted Davy, leaving Sophie with him for a week had been difficult. They'd gotten her into counseling almost immediately after she'd been
kidnapped and nearly killed by Teddy Constantine, and Sophie was doing well. Even so, she still had occasional nightmares, and she suffered from mild bouts of anxiety when she
had to deal with strangers. In the past six months, she hadn't
strayed far from her mother's side.

"She's doing great," he said. "No nightmares since you left.
I think it's been good for us, having you gone for a few days.
It's given us a chance to do some bonding. She needs that.
We both need that. I would've let her play hooky today and
come with me, but she had a big math test and she didn't want
to miss it."

"Thank you."

"For what?"

"For being you. For caring about my daughter. For being
a father to her when she needs one so badly."

"Sophie's a great kid. She makes it easy. Speaking of
which, you saw your dad while you were there?"

"I did." They turned and began walking, arm in arm, toward the baggage claim area. "It went a lot better than I
thought it would. Maybe we were both softened up by the fact
that he almost died." Her pause was thoughtful. "We're not
ready for any cozy father-daughter stuff just yet, but we
talked, and I think he's starting to come around. His recovery has been amazing, especially for a man his age. Lottie

ays she always told him he had the hardest head she'd ever een. I guess she was right."

"Sounds like Lottie's been good for him."

"She has. She stayed right by his side while he was in the ospital, and when he came home, she moved in and took care f him. If it weren't for her, I suspect his recuperation would ave taken a lot longer. I wish he'd found her years ago." She uieted. "I also talked to Peggy Northrup. Boyd's wife. I eeded to tell her how sorry I am. I still feel as though I'm sponsible for getting him killed."

"You damn near got yourself killed, too. Don't forget that. ow'd it go with her?"

"Amazingly enough, she doesn't blame me. She says that oyd was a grown man who knew that confronting Luke Bro-an was risky. He did it anyway, because that's the kind of man e was. He cared about other people. It's why he became a op. And she hasn't forgotten that I lost a husband, too." Annie esitated, took a breath. "The two of us did a little hugging, little crying. It was cathartic. I felt so much better afterward."

"I'm glad. You needed to put it behind you."

"I can't forget. I don't want to forget."

"Forgetting's not the same as putting it behind you."

"I know." She briefly gnawed on her bottom lip, then said, ore brightly, "So did I miss anything earth-shattering while was gone?"

"I think Koko and Lance are in a family way."

"Oh, that's terrific. Just what we need. As if we don't al-ady have a big enough household, now we can add seven-en kittens to the mix."

"And I had to call the plumber yesterday. The pipes in the ownstairs bathroom froze. You can imagine how that went ver with Gram."

Picturing his feisty and opinionated grandmother, she held ack a grin. "How much did that cost?"

"You don't even want to know. Let's just say it's a good thing you put your house in Atchawalla up for sale."

"How's work going?" Another surprise. When Ty and Faith had returned from New York in September with newborn twin boys, they'd announced their intentions to divide their time between the new house he'd built in Serenity and her townhouse in Manhattan. Ty had resigned his position as police chief to play househusband and nanny while Faith wrote her next blockbuster. The Board of Selectmen had offered the chief's position to Davy, and to Annie's surprise, her new husband, who'd spent the last eight weeks waiting for his final day with the Serenity PD, had accepted the job. It just proved her theory that if you scratched a cop, underneath the surface you'd find…a cop.

"It's been crazy," he said. "I think we're coming up on another full moon."

"Poor baby." They walked a little farther, and she said, "Has Jessie heard anything back on her college apps yet?"

"I was saving that for later, but since you ask…she got into Stanford."

The former high school guidance counselor in her leaped to the forefront, and she stopped walking so abruptly that he nearly tripped. "Davy Hunter," she scolded, "how could you not tell me that first thing? Stanford! That's incredible! When did she hear?"

"Yesterday. She called me last night. We must've talked for almost an hour. I'm so damn proud of her, Annie. A kid like that, coming from nothing, getting into a prestigious college like Stanford."

"Can she afford Stanford?"

"Her mother left her a big life insurance policy. It should be enough to cover all four years. If she needs help, Faith and Ty will kick in."

"So will we."

"If the damn house doesn't bleed us dry. And we still have Sophie to think about. She'll be heading off to college soon."

"Don't remind me. I'm not ready to think about it yet."

They reached the baggage claim, and he rummaged through luggage of various shapes and sizes until he located hers. "Better zip up that coat," he told her. "The weather out there's a far cry from Mississippi."

Annie rolled her eyes and put on a pained expression. "Yes, dear," she said contritely.

"You're a real pain in the ass," he said. "Have I ever told you that?"

"More times than I can count."

He set down the luggage and zipped her coat himself, all the way to her chin, then raised the fur-trimmed hood. His hands framing her face, he paused for an instant to place a gentle kiss on her lips. "I love you, Annie Hunter," he said.

She folded her hands around his bigger ones and kissed him back. "I love you, too," she said. Then murmured against his lips, "Come on, Hunter. If we get home before Sophie does, you can show me just how much you missed me."

NEW YORK TIMES BESTSELLING AUTHOR

STELLA CAMERON

Emma Lachance is taken by surprise when she runs into her old friend and high school crush Finn Duhon on a construction site in Pointe Judah, Louisiana. But the last thing she expects to find is the corpse of her friend, a local journalist whose relentlessly scathing articles have enraged every lawmaker and opportunist in town, including the mayor—Emma's husband.

When more bodies are found, Emma and Finn wonder if the link is an eclectic support group for women in which all the murder victims were members. But in their search for the truth, Emma may become the next body of evidence....

Body of Evidence

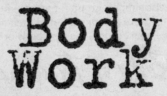

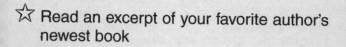

LAURIE BRETON

32151 LETHAL LIES	___ $6.99 U.S.	___ $8.50 CAN.
66660 FINAL EXIT	___ $6.50 U.S.	___ $7.99 CAN.

(limited quantities available)

TOTAL AMOUNT	$ _____
POSTAGE & HANDLING	$ _____
($1.00 FOR 1 BOOK, 50¢ for each additional)	
APPLICABLE TAXES*	$ _____
TOTAL PAYABLE	$ _____

(check or money order—please do not send cash)

To order, complete this form and send it, along with a check or money order for the total above, payable to MIRA Books, to: **In the U.S.:** 3010 Walden Avenue, P.O. Box 9077, Buffalo, NY 14269-9077; **In Canada:** P.O. Box 636, Fort Erie, Ontario, L2A 5X3.

Name: _____
Address: _____ City: _____
State/Prov.: _____ Zip/Postal Code: _____
Account Number (if applicable): _____

075 CSAS

*New York residents remit applicable sales taxes.
*Canadian residents remit applicable GST and provincial taxes.

MIRA®

www.MIRABooks.com

MLB0306BL